LAW #2: DON'T PLAY WITH A PLAYER

LAWS OF LOVE SERIES

AGNES CANESTRI

GIFT TO MY READERS

JOIN MY READER CLUB AND GET THE BONUS MATERIAL OF THIS BOOK AND ANOTHER SWEET READ FOR FREE!

www.agnescanestri.com/lol2-bonus

Please note: if you're already receive my newsletter, no need to sign-up again, you can retrieve your bonus on your VIP Reader Vault (access at the bottom of my emails)

OTHER BOOKS BY THE AUTHOR

LAWS OF LOVE SERIES

Law #1: Never Bet on Love

A billionaire. A salsa dancer. And a bet that might mean losing their hearts..

Go to: mybook.to/lol1-bm

Law #3: Don't Fall for the Athlete

A football star. His friend's little sister.

He broke her heart years ago. Now, they need to work together to save their respective jobs. Will their collaboration lead to a second chance at love?

Go to: mybook.to/lol3-bm

GEMS OF LOVE SERIES

Loving the Boss (BOOK ONE)

It could be her fresh start. If only she can avoid falling for her boss…

Go to: mybook.to/gol1-bm

Gambling with the Billionaire (BOOK TWO)

Love was never on the menu…

Go to: mybook.to/gol2-bm

Fake-Dating the Single Dad (BOOK THREE)

It was the perfect plan. Until their feelings turned all too real….

Go to: mybook.to/gol3-bm

Saving the Brother's Best Friend (BOOK FOUR)

It was only a simple favor between friends. Until it wasn't…

Go to: mybook.to/gol4-bm

Falling for the Undercover Agent (BOOK FIVE)

She was just a job. Until she wasn't …

Go to: mybook.to/gol5-bm

Gems of Love BOXSET

All five books in one collection. The BEST DEAL on the series.

Go to: mybook.to/gol-boxset-bm

OTHER BOOKS

Saving His Heart (Jackson & Hole Firefighters)

Rule #1: Don't date a fireman.

Rule #2: Don't fall for your best friend.

Rule #3: Never forget rules one and two

Go to: mybook.to/saving-his-heart-bm

A Lesson in Love (Standalone forbidden love story)

Sometimes what's forbidden can't be ignored…

Go to: mybook.to/alessoninlove

CHAPTER 1

(Laia)

"I've found the perfect solution to *all* our problems, Laia!" Chelsea's signature, over-the-top squeak reaches my ear before my bedroom door slams open, making the countless movie posters fastened to the wall with scotch tape flutter.

I peek up from the document that, despite my struggles of the past two hours, only contains two miserable lines.

She grins triumphantly with a copy of the local tabloid, *Fancy & Stylish*, clutched under her arm.

Ah, just as I thought.

My bestie can make the discovery of a trendy eyeshadow sound like she's unveiled the secret to ending world famine. Her enthusiasm is part of her charm, really.

But, at this moment, I'm not ready to listen to whatever juicy celebrity gossip may go viral on her FabGal YouTube channel. I've barricaded myself in my room for an excellent reason. To avoid *any* distractions.

And that includes Chelsea's news.

"Are you doing your applications?" she asks.

"Uhm, yeah," I mumble, turning my laptop screen away so Chelsea can't peer at the content.

I feel guilty for saying that I'm busy with my job search, when, in reality, I didn't send out any resumes today.

Chelsea gives me a suspicious glare.

Her green eyes have a slight dropping on the outer corners, which might be considered a flaw by some, but my roomie knows exactly how to turn this feature into an advantage. She enhances her eyes with a black pencil so masterfully that she builds a glance that's powerful and intriguing at the same time.

"You started that crazy bucket list thing you mentioned at dinner yesterday, didn't you?" she says.

Busted!

"Maybe." I keep my eyes on my screen.

If I don't make eye contact, Chelsea might just leave.

My roomie refuses to take notice of my not-so-subtle hint and totters toward my bed. She zigzags between the stacks of books and heaps of papers scattered on the floor.

"I don't get it, Laia," she grumbles, almost tripping over a collection of hardcover Jane Austen classics. "You're neat with our kitchen, but your room looks like the national library after a bomb explosion."

"My books have outgrown the bookshelf. I'll buy a larger one, right after I reimburse Alicia." I shrug.

Chelsea comes as close as the romances I've stacked in front of my bed will allow. Still a few feet away, she launches over them onto my pink bedcover.

The sudden weight shakes the bed and jiggles my laptop.

"Why don't we sell some of your books on eBay and use the money to upgrade your wardrobe instead?" She picks up the copy of *Success lies Within Us* from my bed and wiggles it at me.

"We could start with this." She blinks at the cover and reads the blurb aloud. "Acclaimed motivational guide the *New York Times* describes as the book that will unshackle anyone's hidden potential…"

I snatch the book from her hand and hide it behind my pillow. "You can't sell this. I'm using it right now."

Chelsea rolls her eyes. "You don't need a book to tell you that when the poop hits the fan, people get drab…I could have told you that. And for less than sixteen bucks, which is what you spent on this guide."

I shake my head. "It's a bit more sophisticated than that. The author speaks about the 'curse of the depleted heart chakra.'"

Which is *definitely* what I've got after the countless refusal letters.

Chelsea grimaces. "Just as I said, only in guru-ish mumbo jumbo. I don't understand how this is supposed to help you find a job."

I huff. "I explained to you yesterday. If I direct my energy on something I desire and can directly influence, hence nourishing my heart chakra, I'll start to attract positive external events. Maybe even find employment…?"

I know the promise is too simplistic. And I didn't miss out on the strong new-age flavor of the whole.

But I'm at my wit's end, and thus I'm game to try out anything that might turn my stagnating life around.

"So, that's why you're writing a kissing book?" Chelsea asks.

"Yep. Starting a novel is a desire that I can actually act upon. After examining the list of things I hope to accomplish before I die, I found out that many of my aspirations are entirely out of my control. And, what's worse, some have already passed their expiration date. Like number one, which would be, 'Finding my soulmate before I'm twenty-four.'"

Chelsea gives me a dramatic eye-roll, but I ignore her and continue, "Anyway, writing a romance is still within my reach."

It's #3 on my list and a wish I've been harboring ever since I read "The Beauty and the Beast" as a child. And, best of all, I won't need anything to pull it off except my laptop, some courage, and time. Thus, it might just be the right choice to start my heart energy flowing—or whatever it is that, according to the book, will happen.

Chelsea leans toward my screen and scans what I've written so far.

"That's not a lot. Maybe instead of playing the aspiring novelist, you should put *me* in charge of your future. If you haven't paid attention, I've got a *terrific* idea."

I bite my tongue to stop myself from asking about her enigmatic statement. She'll reveal her grandiose plan even if I don't ask. Her chin is already quivering from a desire to blurt it out.

By ignoring her, I'm repaying her for her dismissive comment about my efforts to jumpstart my future.

Chelsea knows very well that if I can't score a suitable job soon, or *any* paid employment, I'll need to ask Alicia for money again.

And I'd rather not do that.

I've been borrowing from my sister for the past four months. Alicia doesn't purposely make me feel bad about helping me out. She's a good sport about it, considering I can't even give her a ballpark idea for when I'll be able to pay her back. But she never misses out on reminding me that if I'd only followed her advice—and in her footsteps—I'd be building my dental practice right now, instead of trying to repackage my Master's in Comparative Literature as a palatable option for companies that couldn't care less about who I am.

Chelsea gives me a calculating gaze and smooths down blonde hair that she must have freshly hot-ironed, because her locks are frizz-free. I don't comprehend why her tresses never dry out. She washes them each day, treats them with all the tools that are claimed to ruin hair structure, but her mane is still soft and shiny.

If I tried straightening my black waves even once, I'd end up with a bunch of hay.

"You know what?" Chelsea scoffs. "I'm just going to tell you about my plan."

I knew she wouldn't last long.

I hit save on my document, so that the fifty precious words I've squeezed out of my brain won't get lost, and then shut my laptop.

"So, what's this big announcement?"

Chelsea takes a deep, theatrical inhale. "I figured out how you can pay the rent without needing a dime from your sis."

I straighten from my stooping, cross-legged pose and pivot my chest to her. "How?"

"Huh!" A gloating smirk appears on her lips. "I see I've got your attention."

I bet she did. "Chels, don't beat around the bush! Did your father agree to help us out?"

Chelsea scrunches her nose and a small wrinkle forms above her upper lip. It makes her look like a scornful seven-year-old, which is her default facial expression when she talks about her dad. "No, unfortunately. He's still unimpressed by my social media followers and wants me to get a job. Until I do, I'm on a tight leash and can't make any requests."

Chelsea's father, Mr. Anderson, financed his daughter's business degree and paid our rent as long as Chelsea was still studying. But when he saw that Chelsea was unwilling to enter the "real world," as he calls it, he decided to withdraw his support.

"It's okay." Chelsea pats my thigh and puts the tabloid on my lap, opening it to the central page. "We'll let my dad have what he wants, while doing something good for you and me."

I stare at the photo of a handsome dark-haired man, who appears to be coming out of a nightclub with a gorgeous blonde. The man is holding a hand against the camera lens as if he doesn't want his picture taken.

I throw a questioning glance at my friend. "Why are we looking at this?"

"This…" Chelsea taps her French-manicured nail on the man's face. "Is Devon Griffin. He's the owner and CEO of Hudson Communications."

The guy doesn't look like a businessman in his button-down red shirt and casual black blazer. He looks more like a movie star…or a carefree playboy, especially with that all-legged bombshell clinging to his arm.

But the name Hudson Communications rings a bell. It's a middle-size advertising agency that's been on the rise since it was founded.

And no wonder. They make super fresh and bold campaigns.

"I adored their commercial for rainbow candies that you used for your marketing case study in your thesis," I say.

"Duh, as if I didn't know." Chelsea gives me a knowing

look. "Ever since, you sort those sweets by color before munching on them."

Chelsea's right. I do.

But the little girl in their video was too cute, and her gestures stuck in my mind.

"I wasn't aware that Hudson Communications has such a young director," I mutter.

"And *hot!*" Chelsea moans and brushes her thumb over Devon Griffin's contours.

I scan the article.

My only superpower is to read fast, so in less than thirty seconds, I finish the double-page spread discussing the CEO's take-no-prisoners, life philosophy and countless affairs.

"*Is the creative genius having a new fling?*" I read the headline out loud and make a bemused snort. "What a question. I say, who cares?"

"I do. And you should too, because this article is my inspiration to solve our money issues." Chelsea gives me a crooked smirk.

I knit my eyebrows. "What does this guy, and his assumedly busy but shallow love life, have to do with us?"

Chelsea snaps her fingers. "I'm glad you asked. After reading this article, I went on the company's home page to check out the hunky director better. I discovered that his firm has recently opened three well-paying internships across their various departments. I sent our resumes and—"

"You did what?" I exclaim. "How do you even *have* my resume?"

"I picked up a printed copy lying around on your floor while you showered and scanned it. I didn't want to tell you about this opportunity, in case we didn't get invited to the interviews. I know how badly you take refusals, sweetie."

I kneel up so my body is positioned toward my friend. "Are you saying we've got an interview? *Both* of us?"

"*Yesssss!*" Chelsea stretches the last sound while wiggling her brows at me.

"But, Chels, how is this possible? I don't have a business or marketing degree."

"No, you don't." Chelsea grins. "But you're great with words. You make the drollest metaphors. I sent them two articles you did for the student newspaper, and they must have liked them."

"That was sneaky." Admiration tints my voice, because the idea of including writing samples in my unsolicited applications never occurred to me.

Chelsea thrusts out her chest and pats herself on the shoulder. "It was, right? The interviews take place on Monday morning at nine. What do you say, do you love me or what?"

My heart leaps. This nourishing heart chakra really does work. I only just started my romance novel this morning, and the stars are already aligning in my favor.

"This is awesome. No, you're awesome. Thanks for thinking of me, too."

Chelsea winks. "Sure thing. One of the internships is for the creative department as a copywriting assistant. You could totally nail that."

"Copywriting?" I taste the name on my tongue. Though I'm not sure how an ad is created, words are surely involved. And that, at least, is a universe I'm familiar with. "Was I called in for that position?"

"Nope. They had a generalized application for the overall internship program. I imagine they'll sort out who gets which position during the selection process. You'll become their copywriter intern, and I"—she caresses Devon Griffin once more—"I'll take the PA position for this cute boss."

"What?" I gape at my friend in confusion. "Don't tell me you're only doing this to spend time with Devon Griffin?"

Chelsea giggles. "I hope I'll score a date with him after taking notes for him for a few weeks. It'd be cool to narrate my adventure to my fans." She slides her fingers through the air designating a stripe. "The FabGal reveals a notorious player's secrets."

"Ah, Chels, you can't be serious. You want to work for this man so you can air his dirty laundry for your viewers?"

"Maybe. Or maybe I also need some of his exquisite muscles in my life." She indicates the large poster of *The Notebook* hanging above my bed. "Tell me Devon Griffin doesn't look like a guy from one of your romance binges."

"Well…" I start to protest but break off.

I can't negate that the man, at least according to this one picture, is pretty much how I would flesh out the physical attributes of any desirable male lead.

Athletic, toned, wide-shouldered.

But so much more goes into being a true, swoon-worthy hero than just a sculpted exterior.

And, based on this tabloid article, Devon Griffin lacks most of those qualities.

"The man seems like a womanizer to me." I distill my thoughts into one short phrase.

Chelsea nods. "Exactly. It means that he has loads of experience and probably utterly smooth seduction skills. Just what will make him fun."

I roll my eyes.

A notorious gigolo isn't my type of man. At all.

Chelsea pokes my arm. "Stop being judgmental, Laia.

Maybe less chastity would do you some good. Who knows, perhaps it'd help with your romance novel."

I stick out my tongue, but she only laughs.

Though I feign annoyance, I don't mind her teasing. Chelsea and I are friends, but we sit on the opposite ends of the spectrum when it comes to how we choose to—or, in my case, choose not to—live out our sexuality.

I redirect the conversation to a topic that interests me more. "So, your choice of applying to Hudson Communications has nothing to do with doing right by your dad?"

Chelsea shrugs. "Let's just say I can kill two birds with one stone. Dad only said I needed a job at a reputable company. He didn't say what my role should be, nor how long I have to hold on to it. So…"

"Right," I murmur.

It's pointless to dig deeper into Chelsea's reasons. Whatever motivated her to send out our resumes, it has landed me an incredible opportunity, and I'm thankful for that.

"Since it's Friday, we have two days to prepare and ensure that we both get picked," I add.

Chelsea claps her hands a few times, like it's a fun game we're about to play and not a nerve-racking process, for which we'll need to absorb as much information as possible about Hudson Communications.

"Where do we start?" she chirps.

"Let's begin by checking the company's homepage. We should study their client portfolio, history, last PR gigs—"

"And choose our outfits." Chelsea flashes me a grin.

"That won't be hard for me." I wave my hand in dismissal. "I only have the one professional outfit that I used for my graduation."

Chelsea sniffs. "I'll lend you something else."

"Thanks for the offer, Chels, but I'm not size-two like you."

"But that pantsuit looks hideous on you." She masks her horrified expression behind a smile. "Why don't we go and buy you a new one?"

My roomie would never be caught wearing anything less than a meticulously composed ensemble. Even at home, she wears skinny jeans and tight tops, while I hang out in sweatpants and oversized T-shirts that may or may not have holes.

This time she has a point, though.

The pantsuit isn't the most flattering piece I own. It's a hand-me-down gift from my mother's second cousin's daughter, Juanita, so it doesn't fit me perfectly and it's a tick old-fashioned.

But if we go out shopping now, I'll lose precious time.

I can't have that. I *absolutely* need this job. There's just too much I must learn about this ad agency before I'll feel confident to show up for the interview.

Being well-prepared trumps looking pretty.

Besides, no dress I could buy would make me look as gorgeous as my roomie. For that, I'd need to lose at least another ten pounds (not impossible but tough with my sweet tooth) and grow a foot (which is unachievable anyway).

I give Chelsea a reassuring look. "I'm not aiming to become Devon Griffin's personal assistant. To get *that* position"—I tap his photo—"you'll need to look fabulous, but Juanita's suit should be enough to land me the copywriting internship…*if* I come across as knowledgeable about their business."

"Fine, but once we're hired, we're going on a shopping spree, okay?" Chelsea asks.

"Okay, I give in."

Chelsea picks at her nails, and when she notices that the polish on one is slightly chipped, she jumps up.

"Laia, do you mind starting with the background search alone? I have a nail emergency."

Without waiting for my answer, she dashes out of my room.

I sigh and open my computer. I fire up a browser window and type "Hudson Communications".

As the page loads, a hopeful voice hums in my chest. Maybe Chelsea didn't exaggerate when she boasted that all our problems would be solved thanks to her idea.

CHAPTER 2

(Devon)

I shift the phone further from my ear before the high-pitched female voice I've been listening to for ten minutes risks bursting my eardrum and lean back on my executive chair.

"Are you ready to throw away all the magic we shared, Devon?"

The magic? What is this girl even talking about?

Before I can react to her question, my office door opens and my secretary Katja enters, carrying a dubious murky liquid in a tall glass.

"Not again," I murmur under my breath as I observe the curious juice.

I hired Katja five years ago. In her mid-fifties, she's practically old enough to be my mother, and this fact makes her disregard several rules that normally apply to a boss-employee relationship. I cut her some slack on that because her robust build, wide jaw, and always impeccably woven milkmaid braids discourage visitors from ignoring my closed-door policy. Also, if I'm honest, I quite like her bossy matron style.

But her new hobby of fixing up health concoctions instead of serving me my usual cup of joe—a double Arabica—is starting to get on my nerves.

There is a vexed sniff from the phone. "Devon, are you talking to me?"

"Ah, no, I wasn't. Sorry, Clarissa, I—"

"My name is *Claudia*!"

"Right. Claudia," I correct, shooting a nasty glance at Katja's gloating face.

My secretary must've given me the wrong name on purpose when she announced the call. Her little retaliation for leaving her in charge of my personal cell phone, I suppose.

"That's what I meant," I hurry to cover up my slip. "Listen, Claudia, I'm sorry if you misunderstood how things stood between us. We had a fun weekend together. Three days, nothing more. I was quite clear that I'm not looking for anything else beyond that, so…"

"I thought you would realize what a special connection we had. But you only used me!" Claudia exclaims.

"I didn't use you. You said you wanted pleasure with no strings attached. You made me assume we were on the same page."

Katja reaches my double pedestal desk and places the glass in front of me. She gives me a condemning look to show she isn't buying my excuse to Claudia.

Well, too bad.

I'm not the bad person here.

My only fault is that I believed Claudia's fib. She obviously assumed that I don't know myself and my own wishes well enough. A conclusion at which too many women arrive, unfortunately, despite my best efforts at being transparent with them.

My buddy Pete is much better at sensing this kind of female neediness from the get-go. That's why these calls rarely happen to him.

Katja's chiding gaze is getting unnerving, and I shift my glance to the glass once more. With the table's oak shade as a backdrop, the drink isn't mud-grey as it looked from a distance, but plays in a green undertone.

This new color doesn't make it more inviting.

"You know what, Devon? I think I'm done with you," Claudia whimpers in my ear. "You don't deserve me."

I see a chance to close this utterly pointless discussion with a positive note, so I quickly agree. "No, I definitely don't. I'm so sorry."

My admission must puzzle Claudia, because her timbre becomes softer. "Oh, I thought you did. I wanted you to be the *one*."

My eyes flick to the clock on my screen.

Jeez, I need to get back to this briefing report if I want the photographers to start with the shooting tomorrow.

I try for a voice that's understanding but not too tender. "You deserve someone much better than me, Claudia. And don't worry, you'll find him." Then, desperate to cut the call short, I add, "I think it's best to leave it at this, no?"

Claudia gives out an indignant snort. "Fine, you're a man with an empty heart, and I don't have anything more to tell you. Live well, Devon. Or don't!"

After her theatrical good-bye, Claudia hangs up, and I lower my phone.

Katja pushes the glass closer to me, risking the eerie content spilling onto a re-branding plan I've just approved.

"Drink up, please," she barks in her familiarly harsh voice.

"What is this?"

"Sauerkraut juice with cucumber and ginger." Katja's mild Slavic accent gets accentuated as she rolls the 'r' in her words. "Don't be a baby, drink it!"

"You shouldn't have bothered," I say, but she answers my words with a small shrug and points at the juice.

The ingredients in her creation don't sound appetizing, but I did skip breakfast to get to my first conference call on time.

Maybe it tastes better than it looks… or smells?

I take a sip, and Katja nods encouragingly.

Ughh….no.

The drink burns sourly on my tongue and has a nasty tinge to it. I force myself to swallow, while my natural instinct is to spray the disgusting stuff on Katja's cotton shirt. After ensuring that my stomach obeys and accepts the unwelcome treat, I shove the glass away. "Mhmm, interesting. Remind me again why I should be drinking it?"

Katja points at my face, and her lips purse into an isn't-it-obvious frown. "It helps with hangovers. Lord knows you need it."

Last night I attended a client's corporate event instead of going out with Pete. But I only had tonic water, so Katja's insinuations are entirely off.

I adjust my reclined posture into a straight-backed, I'm-still-the-boss-here pose. "I don't have a hangover, Katja. I don't spend every night clubbing and having fun, you know."

Katja lifts a brow but doesn't add a word.

It shouldn't surprise me that she doubts my statement. I do have a bit of a reputation, after all. And the call from Claudia must have increased Katja's assumption about my private life.

I decide to set the record straight. I need her to know that her joke wasn't appreciated.

"Katja," I pronounce her name with a hint of emphasis, "the next time you pass on a call to me, I'd like the name of the caller spelled out correctly. Agreed?"

"Agreed." Katja brushes a speck of non-existent dust from her high-waist plaid pants. "Even better if you stop entrusting me with your shady affairs."

"There's nothing *shady* in what I ask of you. Any woman who calls me at that phone number, including Claudia, is phone stalking me. Your task is only to reiterate the message I've already personally given them, which is that I'm unavailable for their calls."

Katja pulls her nose into a grimace of disgust. "Yes, but your flings don't get that I'm only an innocent go-between. Last week, one of your women told me to go squat on a cactus."

"That must have been Jennifer," I chuckle.

Jennifer and I went on a few dates before I decided to call it off. She has a penchant for picturesque expressions to voice her discontent. I had my taste of it when I told her we should stop seeing each other.

"Jennifer, Claudia, Cynthia…whatever their names, the end result is the same. These poor, silly girls—"

I hold up my hand.

My secretary is approaching my level of tolerance for her well-meaning but gratuitous comments.

"The women I date know what they are getting into. I always tell them in crystal clear terms what they can expect from me, right out of the gates."

I never lie—not at work and not in my private life.

Still, women always hope I'm joking when I say I'm not a relationship guy.

Katja shakes her head disapprovingly. "This attitude will make you lonely, Devon. It's not worth it."

Katja has no idea about the benefits of my lifestyle. Living as I do has way more advantages and definitely fewer disadvantages than being a boyfriend. Boyfriends can be betrayed. Casual companions cannot.

Besides, I've had my share of serious feelings for a woman already and that relationship almost ate me alive. As the memory of my ex threatens to reach the threshold of my consciousness, I shove it back where it belongs.

I don't need to dwell on the past. I'm finally in a good place. One that's filled with fun, pleasure, and lightness.

And the occasional phone call I have to dismiss.

"Katja, approving my choices doesn't belong to your job description. What does, is answering my calls the way I ask you to."

My secretary has the patience of an elephant and the verbal delicacy of a bulldozer. If she comes at me long enough with her arguments, she might succeed at making me feel guilty about how I live my life.

Instead of her usual narrowed glare, Katja wiggles her eyebrows at me. "Only for today. Soon your new PA can handle your personal calls."

My eyes snap to the calendar that stands on my desk.

Crud! I forgot that the interns are being interviewed today.

"Are the candidates here already?"

Katja nods. "I believe they're downstairs with Sarah as we speak. All seven of them."

"Seven? That will take my whole morning," I grumble.

"Aren't you delegating to Sarah? She's doing the selection for the other intern positions. She's good at identifying suitable people and has more time to spare than you do."

I need the extra-workload from these interviews like a

deaf person needs a new stereo, but I don't have a choice. "No, I can't let anyone else pick my assistant this time. I don't want another Hayley fiasco."

Katja's eyes widen. She clicks her tongue in two rapid shots that sound like a gun being cocked, then bobs her head. "Ah, of course."

I lock my screen and stand. "I'll go and greet the candidates."

Katja points at my drink. "Won't you finish that first?"

"No, I'll save it for later. I might get thirsty after the interviews…" Or perhaps I'll pour it on the giant rubber plant in front of my window. It seems to like my secretary's culinary creations way more than I do. It's been sprouting new leaves since I started to water it with my smoothies.

We walk out of my office, and I head straight for the elevator.

While I wait, I calculate how much time I'll have left to do some actual work before Pete and I have to go and get my sister. Ellie wanted to join us for dinner, but we have to pick her up from her health center, adding an extra fifteen minutes to our drive downtown.

The elevator arrives, and I enter.

I lean back against one of the large mirrors and close my eyes. I massage the tender spot between my eyebrows.

I hope at least one of the seven applicants will fulfill my expectations and prove to be serious. I don't want another embarrassing situation in the office.

I might be viewed as a womanizer outside work, but in my company, I *never* mix business with pleasure.

CHAPTER 3

(Laia)

Chelsea maneuvers her Pontiac into the last remaining parking spot in front of Hudson Communications, and we both jump out.

A hot and exceptionally dry waft of air slams me in the face, making me adjust my thick blazer. A long-forgotten quote from J.R. Lowell surfaces in my mind.

"*May is a pious fraud of the almanac.*"

Though the poet probably didn't have Phoenix in mind when writing these words, they are only too right for our weather here. While in some areas of our country, May brings balmy spring, here it only leads into the start of an arid and torrid summer. At least until the monsoons come, but I'll have to wait for another two months before they hit.

Unlike Chelsea, who always tries to escape to her father's estate in San Diego when July starts, I love to stay in the Valley of the Sun when monsoon season arrives. Not only because the tempests bring life-sustaining water to the desert, but also because of the distinctive smell of the creosote bush that lingers everywhere after the rain. Its musky and earthy scent makes me want to drench small towels in the rain and soak up the fragrance to carry it with me anywhere.

Chelsea pulls on my elbow. "Come now and stop daydreaming, or we'll be late."

We hurry to the entrance. Hudson Communications is housed in a former department store building in Phoenix's trendiest neighborhoods and extends over multiple floors.

Saluting the two security officers, we step into the spacious entry hall. I can't suppress a bewildered gasp. Chelsea googled pictures of the office this morning and raved about its gizmos, but I didn't have time to look at the photos. I was too busy memorizing the company's mission statement.

Every inch of the space is covered in bright, inviting colors, from the boldly patterned floors to the vibrant hanging light fixtures. It might even appear gaudy, if it weren't for plenty of neutral elements artfully added into the mix, like polished wooden panels and walls covered with plants.

One thing is sure—whoever envisioned this interior design was aiming to avoiding boredom and monotony.

"I guess we should register at the reception," I tell Chelsea in a low voice as we approach a large desk that stands in the middle of the hall.

"But there is nobody," Chelsea protests.

The yellow-painted counter is indeed empty. So is the rest of the reception area. Where are all the other candidates?

"Maybe the receptionist is having a coffee break." I shrug.

"Or maybe we're late, and the other applicants were

taken to the designated interview location. All because you couldn't stop yourself from taking a peek at my engine. I told you the noise was fine."

A slight annoyance curls through me. "That pinging could have been something terrible, like your EGR valve malfunctioning. Anyway, we're still ten minutes early."

Instead of thanking me for keeping close tabs on her car, Chelsea is trying to lecture me on being punctual. *I* was ready and dressed when *she* was still applying her second coat of mascara.

My friend must sense my irritation, because she gives me a soothing nudge between my ribs. "Sorry, Laia. I know you spare me loads of trips to the mechanic. Come, let's walk closer and wait over there."

We sidle to the reception.

To the left of the desk, there's an enormous sculpture of a bulldog. Its shiny, white surface reflects natural light flowing in from the large windows.

Chelsea pats the statue's head, giggling. "This is the only kind of pet I could keep at home. It doesn't need much and always looks clean."

"Chels, I'm not sure we're allowed to touch it," I whisper.

"No, no, that's quite okay."

We whip around and find ourselves face to face with a smiling black woman. Her curly hair is pulled back in a low chignon, which accentuates her dimples.

I didn't hear her approach, and as my eyes wander to her shoes, the reason she managed to sneak up on us becomes clear.

She's wearing flats just like I do.

Of course, her tall figure doesn't need any heels, while my short frame could use the advantageous lengthening of a pair of stilettos. But I can't walk straight in pumps, and I didn't have time to practice during the weekend.

"I'm Sarah, the HR manager. I'll be doing your interviews today. You're here for the intern positions, am I right?" she asks.

"Yes, exactly." Chelsea gathers her wits first.

After we introduce ourselves, Sarah waves to us to follow. "Let's join the other five candidates."

I ignore Chelsea's didn't-I-tell-you-the-others-were-here smirk and strut behind Sarah.

She leads us to a corridor with black and white tiles that remind me of the chessboard my father brought home from an overseas deployment.

Chelsea shows me a seven, then a three, and finally gives me a thumbs up. She obviously thinks that both of us have a great chance to snatch our desired spots.

I wish I shared her self-assurance, but I don't. Despite thorough studying, I still feel unprepared. Looking at Sarah's fitted dress and Chelsea's elegant pencil skirt, I'm suddenly feeling bad about my own clothes. I didn't remember my blazer being so askew. True, the last time I wore it, I had my graduation regalia covering it, but still.

I'd tried to pull out the shoulder pads at home—without those, I'd look slightly less like a lost soul from the eighties—but those danged things were sewn on so tightly that if I'd kept tearing at them, I would have made a hole in the fabric.

We arrive at the casual sitting area where the other candidates are gathered, and my embarrassment grows.

Four women and a man rise as they see us approach. All the females are impeccably dressed, as if they've stepped out of a magazine. Not from the working gals' section, but rather from the dress-to-impress-your-date one. Their stilettos are so high I'd break an ankle if I tried to stand on them, and their necklines are generously low-cut —with the accent on *generously*.

Compared to them, Chelsea's silk blouse is rather sober.

My friend must make the same realization because she fiddles at her collarbone and pops another button open.

"So," Sarah says when we are all standing in a circle, "let's start with breaking you up into three groups. How many of you would like to interview for the accounting intern position?"

No hands shoot in the air.

Sarah nods twice. "And who is interested in the job in our creative department?" I raise my arm, and so does the man, an Asian guy with slicked-back hair and a grey suit. His clothes are similar in shade to mine, only his outfit is well-tailored, shiny, and topped with a thin red tie.

We exchange a quick glance filled with a mixture of mutual respect, since we both chose the most interesting of the three internships, and the realization that we are each other's only competition.

Sarah sighs. She eyes Chelsea and the other women with furrowed brows. "So, I guess that leaves you five for the PA position?"

"Indeed," replies a redhead. "That's the most interesting one. Right, gals?" She bends forward and ends with a giggle that couldn't sound more obnoxious, even if she practiced it for weeks.

I turn my eyes away from her because I don't want to peer at her belly button, a real possibility considering how plunging her dress is.

The other women nod, but they throw daggers at each other.

I'm tempted to interject that making coffee and

answering phones can hardly qualify as exciting, but I swallow back my comment.

Sarah scratches her chin. "Well, that depends on your ambitions. Though I can't deny that working for Devon Griffin isn't like working for any other CEO."

"Oh, I think we all know that," a brunette agrees promptly. "Or, at least *almost* all of us."

She runs a hand through her asymmetrical bob and gives me a belittling smirk as if to make it clear for those who didn't get her subtle hint.

Chelsea shakes her head imperceptibly. But I don't need my roomie to remind me that it's better to let the snarky remark slide. After all, I'm not here to compete in a beauty pageant.

Sarah claps her hands. "Since most of you came for the PA position, we'll start with that, okay?"

Her question is directed at the man and me, and we both nod.

"Excuse me, Sarah," a melodious male baritone interrupts. "I'd like to propose a small change to the plans, if I may."

Sarah's eyes widen, and her shoulders pull back. "Oh, hello, Devon. I didn't know you'd be joining us for the interviews. You're most welcome to suggest anything you like. Everyone, this is Devon Griffin, our CEO. Devon, these are our candidates."

I turn around, and all the others do the same.

"Good morning, Mr. Griffin," the women call out in a seductive chorus.

"Good morning." I sound like a middle school student, my voice trailing a half-second behind the others.

Sarah chuckles. "Just call him Devon. We all do."

Devon saunters closer to us.

He's wearing slim-cut navy chinos, a white button-down shirt, and a striped jacket. While his clothes are business smart, he could walk into a club and spend the evening there without anyone thinking that he doesn't belong. Especially if he tousled up that French crop haircut the way it was done up in that tabloid picture.

Almost everyone adjusts their postures, and even I find myself standing a little straighter as Devon draws closer.

Why is he here? Does he want to inspect if we're to his liking before we even get a chance to prove our worth?

"Hi, everyone," Devon says. "As you know, I'm looking for a new assistant. This position is listed as an internship, but if the person who gets it performs well, the contract could transform into a permanent one. The right candidate will have a secure job at her," he nods to the male candidate, "or his, hand."

"Oh no, Devon." Sarah points at the guy. "Fu is here for the copywriting position only."

I raise my hand to signal that I'm also here for the same internship, but Sarah doesn't notice me.

The old me would undoubtedly stay quiet and avoid drawing further attention to herself. But won't it be better for my rebooted-heart-chakra self if I speak up? I open my mouth to intervene.

"So you don't wish to become my PA. Why is that?" Devon asks Fu.

I close my mouth again.

It's wiser to listen to my opponent's answer. I might be confronted with a similar question.

Fu fingers his shirt collar as if it's suddenly too tight. "Uhm, I'm not sure. I think I might be a better fit in your creative team," he mutters.

Devon nods. "Very well, Fu. You don't mind if I call you by your first name, do you? In this company, we like to keep things casual and friendly. If I'm honest, I'd also be happier with one of these ladies here. In my experience, male PAs make the worst coffee ever."

He flashes a smile to show that his comment is a joke.

"I can make a *wicked* espresso," the redhead moans.

"I learned how to stir up a good cuppa from my Italian grandmother," the brunette purrs.

"Me, too," Chelsea adds, not wanting to be outdone.

While I give an are-you-nuts glance to my bestie for her fib, the remaining two candidates also voice how interested they would be in preparing the perfect coffee for Devon.

Devon chuckles. "Wow, wow. I'm happy to see your professional enthusiasm."

Professional enthusiasm? Ah, please. I roll my eyes at his comment.

Unexpectedly, his glance travels to me, and he gives me a once-over.

His brows round as he studies me. I can't help but think that he's wondering what I'm doing among these supermodels, dressed like an ABBA fan.

Devon steps over to me. He's almost a head taller than I am, and he has to dip his chin to his chest to intercept my gaze.

He has a symmetrical bone structure, with sharp cheekbones and a stubborn cleft chin. This gives his face a bit of a voracious feel, as if he's not only eager to take a bite from what the world has to offer, but also ready to eat it all up.

"What's your name?" he says.

"Laia, Laia Flores. I belong to the rare species of non-coffee drinkers," I jabber. It's pure nervousness that made me add that last silly bit.

Though I'm not affected by Devon Griffin's devilishly good looks, I'm uncomfortable about being singled out by him.

Despite my quivering stomach, I stand his observing glance with a straight face. After all, I'm here to demonstrate my aptitude for writing and not my barista skills.

His lips twitch. The tiny movement makes his eyes flicker, adding a certain softness to his features.

"A non-coffee drinker. Interesting. And so is your name. It's not very common. Do you write it with a simple 'i'?" he inquires.

I can literally feel the other candidates' gazes, including Chelsea's, dig a hole into my chest. They must be pondering the exact same thing I am.

Why is Devon wasting so many words on *my* name?

"Yes, with an 'i'." I nod. "It's a shortened version of the Catalan name Eulàlia. It means sweet-speaking."

"Ah, really? And are you sweet-speaking?" Devon arches his brows.

He has a very peculiar shade of blue irises. It gives me a sense of déjà vu. I know I've seen his color somewhere, but I can't recall where. Probably because I'm distracted by the accelerated pulse slamming in my neck.

"Uhm, not always. No," I mutter.

Especially not now, dang it.

This could be my occasion to outshine Fu and his fancy suit. While I have the CEO's attention, I could show him that I'd be a valuable addition to his creative team, thanks to my wit.

But what do I do instead? I bore him with an idiotic detail about my name.

I inhale and set on to correct my mistake. "Mr. Griffin, just like Fu, I—"

Devon is already moving on to Sarah. "Let's do it like this, Sarah. You start with Fu, and I'll start with…" He smiles at Chelsea.

"Chelsea," my friend says, batting her long lashes.

"My name is Helena," the redhead adds.

"Good to know," Devon answers. "But I'd like to start with…" His eyes flick to me. "Laia."

I freeze. Why does Devon want to begin the rounds with *me*?

"I'm not interviewing for the…" My eyes dart to Sarah. This time she notices my pleading glance and takes the relay from me with a confident smile.

"Devon, Laia would like to apply to our creative department, just like Fu."

"Is that so? Well, then…" Devon's eyes narrow at me, then he turns to Sarah. "Then just send Laia up to my office once she's done with you. In the meantime, I'll speak to the other candidates."

"But—" I squeak.

"But what, Laia?" Devon's penetrating glance is on my face once more. "Is there a problem?"

There couldn't be a worse moment for my mind to draw a blank, but my brain hasn't received the memo. Instead of coming up with a polite way to refuse his invitation, I find myself musing about how it would be to work for Devon.

What's happening to me?

Sarah comes to my aid. "What I meant is that Laia came to do *only* the copywriting interview. Like Fu."

"Ah." Devon taps on his forehead. "I see. That's no problem. I imagine that Laia won't mind doing two interviews, instead of one?"

I want to tell him that I very much would mind it. I'm not here to compete with his groupies, especially not with my roomie, so there's no need for me to endure a second round of questions once I survive my first meeting with Sarah. But I'm afraid if I blurt this out bluntly, he'll take offense and won't let me do any internship.

Why does he even want to speak to me? Could it be just his attempt to annoy me? He can't be that peevish about the fact that I didn't want to prepare his morning cup, can he?

I inhale and raise my eyes to meet his. "No, it won't be a problem, Mr. Griffin."

"Devon." He smiles.

"No, it won't be a problem, Devon," I repeat while I stare at him.

As his cheeks lift and press his eyes into tiny crinkles, I suddenly know where I saw his eye color. It's the exact shade of those cornflowers my mother used to plant in our backyard when I was little.

Almost as if the puzzling hue of Devon's eyes have occupied a hidden corner of my brain since he appeared.

"Everything okay, Laia? Ready to start the interview with me?" Sarah's voice snaps me out of my reverie.

"Yes, ready. Very," I declare cheerfully.

"Then let's go into the orange room over there," Sarah says.

I exchange a look with Chelsea and mouth "good luck" at her.

She gawks at me with her what's-going-on gaze. Her brows furrow and she purses her lips, but I can't stop to explain my take on events, because Sarah's already moving toward the meeting room.

I stride behind the HR manager, trying to instill some pep into my timid step when I hear Devon's baritone.

"Until later, Laia."

CHAPTER 4

(Devon)

I bury my face into my palms and let out a long, exhausted sigh.

My fifth interviewee, a sassy and overly flirty brunette, has just finished sashaying her way out of my office. To think, only one-tenth of the applicants were invited to an actual interview. The remaining candidates should be the crème de la crème, but they clearly are not.

Katja warned me that this would happen when I asked her to add the PA position to the other internships on our website. She predicted that my reputation would attract a vast number—but the wrong kind—of applicants. According to Sarah's report, even those who didn't make the cut were predominantly female. Which, together with the interviews I've just conducted, makes me suspect that my secretary might have been right.

None of the women I spoke to is the right fit for my company. Not when they all act like they're auditioning for *The Bachelor.*

To be honest, I'd have gladly offered a drink to any of them, had I met them in a club, but I can't, with a clear conscience, take them on board as my assistant. Not when I'm set on avoiding the same situation as happened with Hayley.

I don't want to hire someone who is more interested in chatting with me about my private life than learning about the job she will need to perform. So, although these women technically have the proper credentials, they don't possesses the mindset, diligence, and wit I'm looking for.

All the better that I forced that drably dressed girl to accept an interview with me. Laia didn't dress up to impress me, which shows that she's interested in my company and not in going on a date with me.

I snort as I remember her unflattering grey pants. As if those trousers aren't ugly enough, Laia paired them with a matching blazer one size too large. The cut has distorted her otherwise likely well-proportioned figure into that of a wide-shouldered swimming champion, especially with those shoulder pads sticking out on either side.

My lips move into a smile.

I also like that Laia didn't turn into a crazy cheerleader when I spoke about my love for caffeine. Maybe my interview with her will be more uplifting and exciting than the others. The fact that she didn't come here to become my assistant could, paradoxically, make her the best contestant after all.

A soft knock and the screeching of the door cut through the silence. "Mr. Griffin?"

Laia's voice was soft like a lullaby. It surprised me, even the first time I heard it.

"Devon, not Mr. Griffin. But please come on in, Laia."

Laia pushes the door ajar and enters. Her brown eyes

quickly meet mine before she drops her gaze to the floor. She keeps it there as she bustles to my desk.

Is Laia shy or just interested in the abstract patterns of my colorful rug? Perhaps she needs to watch her step in those oversized pants of hers.

Laia makes it to the chair positioned on the other side of my desk and sits down.

Her blazer opens as she leans to the backrest, and I see that I've judged her figure correctly. She has a perfectly normal waist beneath all that fabric.

Laia crosses her ankles instead of her knees like the other candidates did and arranges her hands into a neatly folded position.

Once settled, she raises her chin.

I might have sized up her body accurately, but I certainly made a mistake, thinking she had brown eyes. Laia's eyes resemble something between a toffee and cinnamon hue. Like a well-brewed Earl Grey tea with a hint of lemon. There are also tiny yellow dots in her irises that somehow remind me of Cat, my cat.

"May I ask why you wished to interview me?"

Her dulcet tone snaps me out of my thoughts.

Even if her straightforward question takes me by surprise, I don't mind it. I prefer to come to the point. "I wanted to discuss why you didn't apply for my PA position?"

Laia licks her lips. "I…I just…"

"Please, give it to me straight," I say. "I've heard enough flattery for one day from the other candidates. It would be refreshing if you tell me things as they are."

"Very well…Devon," Laia nods. "I think your company is amazing. All your campaigns have a fresh twist, a small wink to the consumer. But I only learned on Friday that you were looking for interns."

My brows drift high. “Didn’t you apply to our internship earlier than that?”

I checked Laia’s application, and it said that we received her resume ten days ago.

Laia shifts on her chair. “I didn’t apply myself. Chelsea Anderson, the blonde candidate you spoke to, is my friend. She sent in my documents without my knowledge.”

Okay, so Laia does understand what honesty is. “I see. Interesting. Why is that?”

Laia swallows.

I give her an encouraging smile. “Don’t worry, it’s not a crime if you didn’t file your own application. The important thing is that what’s on your paper is true. I assume your degree isn’t a farce, is it?”

Laia’s eyes widen. It makes the yellow speckles drift into a new pattern, almost as if I were watching a kaleidoscope.

“No, of course it isn’t a farce.” Her face moves into a grimace of horror. “I would never lie about my education. I graduated *summa cum laude* last year.”

“Great.” I nod. “So can you share with me why your friend sent your documents instead of you?”

“To be honest, your company simply wasn’t on my radar when I started my job search. I mostly contacted publishing firms. I didn’t think my profile would be considered at a company like yours. Chelsea had more faith in me.”

“You don’t think a master’s in literature would be useful in an ad agency? Do you know how I founded Hudson Communications?”

“Yes.” Laia bobs her head and begins to recite almost word for word the information published in the history section of our webpage.

She knows how I single-handedly built the company, and even mentions that I worked from my favorite wooden armchair when I scored my first successful project with a significant sports brand.

"I see you did your homework. You're missing only the small detail about my dog."

"A dog?" Laia's cheeks tint a delicate pink that suits her creamy complexion.

Her eyes move to the ceiling as if she's checking some internal database, then she blinks back at me. "There wasn't anything about a dog on your website or in any of the newspaper articles I googled."

"You even googled articles on us? Didn't you say you learned about your interview on Friday?"

Laia squares her shoulders, which makes her shoulder pads stand out even more. "I might not have applied to your company myself, but I'm very motivated to work for you. So I gathered and digested all the information I could find. What is this info about the dog that I missed?"

"You saw the statue at the reception?"

"You mean the giant, white porcelain bulldog?" She smiles. "It's hard to miss."

This is the first smile she's given me, and it makes her look a tiny bit like Salma Hayek in that old movie she did with Antonio Banderas. "Yeah, well, that's Hudson. The name of the company comes from him. He was my dog. He died four years ago."

"I'm so sorry for your loss. Losing him must have been hard."

Laia's reaction surprises me. I mentioned Hudson during all the other interviews, and none of the women reacted empathically like this.

"Well, it wasn't easy at first. But having Hudson at the

entrance and petting his head each day before heading up to my office keeps his memory alive."

Laia's mouth moves into a circle. "You caress that statue every morning? That's…"

"Weird? Childish?"

Why did I reveal this personal detail to her? It must have been the compassionate glint in her eyes that made it slip.

"I wanted to say sweet and unexpected." Laia smiles.

I'd like to inquire what she means by unexpected, but I realize we've deteriorated from our original topic, so I steer the conversation back. "You prepared well for your interview, for which you didn't apply. Does that mean you would like to work for us?"

My hunch that Laia could be the perfect assistant is cementing with each minute.

She has a good degree and an excellent memory, which she demonstrated when she chanted, *ipsissimis verbis*, my company's mission statement. She's honest, seems modest and kind, and is definitely not here to tempt me. What more could I wish for?

"Yes, I'd love to be your copywriting intern."

"And *not* my assistant?"

Before Laia can answer, my cell phone buzzes.

"Excuse me for a second." I stand up and walk to the corner of my office, then press reply. "Hi, Sarah."

"Hi, Devon. I'm calling to give you my impressions of the two candidates for the creative department. I'd come up in person, but there is an emergency with one of the training schedules, so I'm a little short on time."

"No problem, just tell me on the phone. How did Laia and Fu do? What's your verdict?"

A slight creak behind me tells me that Laia must've

heard her name, and she may have shifted her chair in an attempt to eavesdrop.

Sarah clears her throat. "I think the woman is the better option. But the man isn't bad, either. If we had two intern positions, I'd take them both."

I exhale. "I see. Well, we might find a way to get around that. What about the accounting internship? Do we need to repost that position?"

"Not necessarily. I know Chelsea Anderson applied for the PA position, but I think she would be a great fit for the accounting internship with her business degree. Plus, she knows a lot about how our company is run, given that we featured in her thesis work. So, unless you really want her for your assistant, we could make her an offer."

I scratch my head as the image of the attractive blonde flashes through my mind. Her manners were too coy for me to consider her as my PA, but her resume was valid, and she might spice up the accounting department with her tight pencil skirt. That wouldn't be the worst thing in the world.

"I think I have a better candidate in mind for the PA job, and I trust your judgment, Sarah. Go ahead and propose Chelsea the accounting position. I'll get back to my interview now. Thanks for checking in."

"Of course, Devon. Thanks for your time."

Sarah hangs up, and I turn to Laia.

She peers up at me while frenetically chewing on her lower lip. "That was your HR manager, right? What did she say about my interview?"

I slowly amble back, but instead of sitting, I circle around to stand in front of Laia. I lean my hips on the desk and cross my arms in front of my chest.

I could easily lie. If I tell her that she wasn't accepted to our creative department, she might be happy with the

PA position. After all, she did say she would like to work for my company.

The thing is, I don't want to dupe her.

If she decides to work for me it must be because the job sounds interesting, not because it's her only option. Otherwise, she might not put the dedication and zeal she showed me a glimpse of into her new duties.

"Sarah said you're her preferred candidate. However, were you to choose another option, like working for me, Fu would get the internship. He was good too, but you're Sarah's first choice."

Laia's face illuminates. "That's amazing. Does it mean I get the job?"

"Yes, unless..."

"Unless what?"

"Unless you decide that you'd prefer to be my assistant."

A confused frown settles on Laia's face. "You have five women practically dying to work for you. My friend, Chelsea, for example..."

"Your friend will be offered an internship in our accounting department, and I assume she'll take it because I already told her that she isn't suitable to be my PA."

"Wait, you ruled out Chelsea?" Laia sounds like she can't believe what I'm saying. "But...she would have been perfect."

I smack my lips. "I think I'm in the position to decide who would be the perfect candidate. And I don't think it's your friend. By the way, I ruled out all the other candidates too. *Except you.*"

"Why me? I'm not more capable than the others. I might not even have the skills you're looking for." Laia shakes her head. The hairpin keeping her dark locks in an up-do gives way, and her hair comes cascading down.

Wow, does she have long hair.

Her mane reaches below her elbows and with it down her similarity to a young Salma Hayek is no longer an opinion—it's a fact.

"Can you read?" I ask.

"Of course I can read," she snaps at me with an almost offended tone. She starts twirling her hair and fastens it back up into a low ponytail. "How do you think I got through my degree without reading?"

I let out an amused snort. Laia tilts her head, and her lips curl up as she realizes I'm teasing. "But I make terrible coffee."

I wave. "To be honest, my secretary takes care of that. It was only a jest I made to cover up my preference for female assistants in front of Fu."

"Why female assistants?" Laia inquires.

I shrug. "I find that I work better with the opposite gender when under pressure. My assistant will see me sweating over deadlines. Women tend to deal with my grumpy self better than men do."

"So, you're saying you're a grumpy boss? It's not exactly the most attractive argument in favor of this position." Laia tries to hide her smile.

I chuckle. "You're right, it isn't. Let me tell you what you'll be doing if you decide to work for me. You won't be handling my administrative tasks, that's done by my secretary. As my assistant, you'll do extensive research to build new client portfolios. There will be a good chunk of writing involved, because you'll need to prepare client briefs, write proposals, and support current projects. You'll also help control my public image, so preparing my speeches and press communication will be your rcsponsibility. Finally, you'll act as a filter for anything that reaches me, so all internal reports will be first read by you, and you'll provide me with your key takes on them."

Laia's eyes widen as she listens.

I can tell that she didn't even read the PA job description. She'd merely assumed it was boring phone-answering, calendar-tidying work.

For someone who studied my company's entire website by heart, it seems an incongruent behavior.

Why wasn't she as thorough with this part of her application as with the rest? Was it because she didn't want to compete with her blonde friend? That's the type of thing my sister would do for her besties.

I raise a finger to drive home the final two arguments. "All in all, I'd say there will be *more* creativity and writing involved in what you would do than what Fu, assuming he gets the internship, would get to see during his five months in my company. Don't forget the assistant position has long-term potential, and it's better paid than the other two internships."

"I'm sorry. I haven't done many job interviews. I might not know the rules but…" Laia furrows her brows. "Are you supposed to be *selling* me this position? Isn't it usually the other way around?"

"Not all interviews unfold identically. I'm a pretty peculiar CEO." I shrug. "Let this encounter be your first taste of that. What do you say? Would you like to become my assistant?"

"If I say no, will I still be able to do the internship in your creative department?"

It's not the answer I was hoping for, but if that's what she wants… "If you say no, it won't influence the outcome of your interview with Sarah."

Laia's thumbs roll in rapid sequence around each other, but she doesn't say a word.

I watch her tensed posture patiently, but I can deduce her answer already. It seems I'll need to take Katja's suggestion after all and hire a headhunter to find the right assistant for me. It's a pity, though. My gut tells me Laia would have been a darned good option.

CHAPTER 5

(Laia)

I stare at Devon, my thoughts scrambling faster than the Thrust SSC race car in the Black Rock Desert.

What he tells me about the duties I'd need to perform as his PA exceed any expectations I had about the copywriting position. Not at all the tedious job I'd envisioned.

If I work for him, I'd be able to write all sorts of exciting things, not just ad copies. I would acquire much-needed business skills that would improve my hireability for the future. Plus, the position comes with long-term potential and a better salary.

I'll be able to pay back Alicia and refurbish my entire bedroom in no time.

So why am I hesitant to accept? The decision should be a cakewalk.

Except, for my risk-averse nature, it isn't. My palms are sweating, and my ears are buzzing like an untuned radio.

Although I'm determined to get out of the rut I've

been dwelling in since graduation, Devon's proposal scares me.

With more exposure comes more possibility of failing. If I screw up as his assistant, I'll be doing it right under the watchful eyes of the CEO.

Am I ready for that?

"Leap and the net will appear," Devon murmurs.

I jerk back at his unexpected comment. "Excuse me, what did you just say?"

Devon smiles. "It's something my sister loves to say. Your torn expression made me remember it."

His phrase strikes a particular chord in me. It reminds me of the Chinese proverb the author of *Success Lies Within Us* quotes repeatedly in the book.

"Pearls don't lie on the seashore. If you want them, you must dive for them."

A determination settles in me.

I'm not going to let my past insecurities corrupt my future. I can perform with flying colors as Devon's PA. Anything that I don't know, I can learn.

I clear my throat. "You know, I think my answer is…a yes. I'd like to become your assistant."

His jaw drops and his eyes bulge, but he recovers fast, clapping his hands. "Excellent. Then, Laia, there is only one thing to say. Welcome on board."

His enthusiasm makes me realize what I've just done.

I came into this building doubting whether I'd be good enough for a five-month internship, and I'm leaving as the CEO's PA, the most coveted job among all the candidates.

I should be pleased with myself, but my stomach harbors mixed feelings.

I accepted the job Chelsea originally wanted. What will my friend think of me? Will she be upset?

Devon said he told her she wasn't the right choice for

him, and that Chelsea will be offered the accounting internship. Will she accept it?

Before I dwell on my culpability any further, Devon tears me from it by moving closer and stretching his hand to me.

I jump up to shake it and, in my haste, step on the hem of my pants, losing my equilibrium. My blazer billows out as I trip.

Before I can officially land on my bum, Devon's hands close around my waist. His palms are firm, and an agreeable warmth seeps from his touch into my ribs, despite the relatively thick cotton of my blouse.

"I've got you." He straightens me back to my feet.

"Uhm, thanks," I mumble. I don't dare to blink at him.

My face must look like I sunbathed on the Grand Canyon's highest peak without protection. *At midday.*

"No problem. Do you want me to assist you out, or can you manage?" There is a teasing edge to his voice, but his expression is serious.

"No, Mr.—" His eyes narrow, and I correct myself. "No, Devon. Thanks. I'll be fine on my own."

His blue irises illuminate when he hears me switch to his first name. He flashes me a smile that would be heart-melting if I were into the all-teeth, plump lips, and dimples kind of look.

Which I am not.

Not *one* bit.

"I'm glad we're starting out on a friendly basis," he says. "I hope our relationship will only improve from here."

"Sure. I hope so too." I smile. "I might not have much experience, but I always aim to please."

My last word comes out with an unintended hitch. I try

to stop it from rolling off my tongue, but it's too late. Even as I pronounced it, I realize my innocent expression could sound ambiguous to a man of Devon's reputation.

I don't want Devon to interpret my accent as an out-of-place, provocative remark, so I hurriedly add, "Sorry, I didn't mean please like, *please*…I meant… "

My eyes meet Devon's.

From the way his jaw goes slack, I deduce he wasn't thinking of any potential double-meaning before I so ineptly put my foot into my mouth.

Devon struggles to keep a straight face. "That's….uhm, that's good to know."

Wanting to end our meeting with a positive and professional note, I stick out my hand to him to try again. "Thank you, Devon. I'm looking forward to working with you."

He takes my hand and shakes it again. "Me, too. You can come in around nine tomorrow. That's when I usually arrive. Katja, my secretary, will sort out your contract and arrange everything else."

I ignore how the way his palm closed around my fingers felt right. Not too strong, but not too soft. Confident, but not pushy.

But of course, he is a CEO, so he should be an expert in shaking hands.

"Sounds good. See you tomorrow," I reply, then turn to the door and shuffle out.

I keep my head high but peer down at my shoes so I don't trip again. I've had enough clumsiness for one day.

Outside his office, I bump into Katja.

She's close to the door, as if she retreated from it the minute she heard me coming.

"How did it go?" she asks eagerly, her intimidatingly square jaw widening.

With her Russian braids, she looks like the main female lead in one of my favorite plays from Chekhov. A hint of accent in her raspy voice strengthens the similarity.

"I'm hired," I mumble, still dumbfounded from the events of the past half an hour.

One of Katja's thin eyebrows lifts, and from the asymmetrical line it makes, I realize she must have drawn it with a pencil. "Interesting. You're not his typical choice. It's for the better, though. Your predecessor—" She stops and shakes her head. "You know what? It doesn't matter."

Before I can inquire what she meant by her enigmatic words, Katja taps on a desk that stands across from her own.

It's empty except for a white notepad, a pen, and a pencil holder bearing the company logo. The objects shimmy from the weight of her palm.

"This here," she tips her head downward, "will be your territory. You can decorate it with your own objects, but please avoid any plants that have flowers, for Devon's sake."

Why should Devon be contrary to flowers?

Before I can voice my question, Katja turns and walks back to her table.

"I need to send out a couple of urgent emails," she says while lowering to her chair. "You'll wait for me, and then we'll sort out your contract and the rest." With that, she ducks her head and begins to type frenetically.

I'd love some sugary treat to boost my brain, because it's swimming in a foggy state ever since I left Devon's office, but Katja's voice is so categorical that I don't dare ask whether I can go get a snack.

I take a seat at the desk, which is now officially mine and rest my chin on my palms.

As I stare into nothing and listen to the rhythmic clicks of Katja's keyboard, my mind wanders off.

An electrifying plot idea pops into my head for the romance novel I was trying to outline on Friday. A smile spreads on my lips.

Wouldn't it be the perfect makeover for my life if I managed to be employed and write my romance at the same time?

I tear off a piece of paper from the notepad Katja left me, and checking that she's still engrossed in her work, I pick up the pen and scribble down a few lines.

After two dense paragraphs are done, I read what I've produced. The storyline is still a bit vague, like a dream after waking, but it thrills me all the same. I can see how the conflict could be fleshed out, and the protagonists I envisioned are characters I feel ready to spend considerable time with together.

There is only one aspect that startles me.

I've never swooned over actors with penetrating blue gazes. Bobby, my biggest crush ever, had brown irises.

So why did I suddenly describe my hero's eyes as the shade of freshly picked cornflowers?

"I'm ready. Shall we go to the IT department and get your laptop?" Katja's voice jars me out of my musing. I jump up and quickly fold the paper, hiding it in my blazer pocket. "Yes, let's go."

CHAPTER 6

(Laia)

Our living room fills with the enticing aroma of chicken quesadilla.

The plate I'm heating up in the microwave is only a frozen dish I bought in a supermarket on my way home from the interview. However, it still triggers countless memories about our house in San Sebastian where my nose regularly feasted on the most mouthwatering fragrances, thanks to my mother's culinary skills.

As I change into my comfy leggings, my eyes wander to my hips, and I wince.

Unfortunately, it wasn't just my sense of smell basking in the glory of homemade lunches, dinners, and snacks. In the past six years, I've been abandoned to my own cooking —or my severe lack thereof—but even my lack of talent didn't erase the disastrous consequences of spending my childhood with a mother who cooked like a real chef.

I pull the long T-shirt down over my trousers with a hasty gesture.

Today of all days, I'm not going to obsess about my body. I don't need another concern to add to my list of worries.

The performance anxiety that plagues me whenever I think of tomorrow—my first official workday—coupled with the apprehension that Chelsea still doesn't know what I've done is more than enough to fret about.

The clock in our living room chirps like a sparrow. Even without glancing up, I know it's four pm.

The clock was a gift from my mother and each hour it imitates the voice of a different bird. Thankfully not at night, though, because it has a light sensor. My roomie loves to take advantage of this built-in trick and often covers the clock with a rag when she plans to sleep in.

The thought about Chelsea makes me wonder where she could be. By the time I finished in the IT department, Chelsea was gone. She'd left me a note at the reception saying that she went to buy new outfits—an activity she'd initially proposed for us to do together after our interviews.

I'm not sorry she didn't force me to join her—I hate trying on clothes in tiny dressing rooms where every extra-pound or wrinkle becomes more evident—but I'm concerned she might have dashed off because she was upset that I agreed to interview for the assistant position. If this is the case, she might be furious when she learns I got the job.

The microwave beeps loudly, pulling me out of my guilt trip.

I dash into our open kitchen.

I haven't eaten lunch, and as the spicy fragrance wafts around me, my stomach protests loudly. The sudden cramps make me forget to use oven mitts when I grab the plate.

Ouch! The ceramic burns my skin like glowing embers.

I drop the dish on the counter and race over to the sink. While I let the cold rinse soothe my fingertips, I curse under my breath.

The last thing I need is to lose my ability to type. I have a job now, one that comes with a salary and a possible future. I can't screw it up because I skipped the basic safety rules that even a six-year-old should be aware of.

Despite the pain that throbs on my fingertips, excitement buzzes through my belly.

A little voice in my head suggests that my excitement is partly due to the anticipation that I'll be working with Devon, but I immediately discard the deranged argument. I didn't accept the position to be in daily contact with him. I don't even know why I'm still going back and forth about this. My decision was entirely logic-driven and not related to Devon's undeniable charisma.

First, there is the likely promise of a permanent contract. I mean, who can ignore that in today's uncertain economy?

Then that excellent salary. I couldn't refuse that since money is a thing I obviously need.

Finally, and most importantly, I'll soon contribute to TV commercials, write press communications for famous newspapers, and—

The entry door lock clicks, stopping my thoughts in their tracks.

I switch off the sink and turn in time to see Chelsea strut in with a bunch of shopping bags in her hands.

"Hey, Laia," she greets me, kicking off her heels and plopping down on our sofa.

There's no trace of frustration or hidden annoyance in her voice. My shoulders relax.

She settles herself on a large pillow with a sigh, dropping her purchases to the floor. "Ah, this feels good. My whole body is sore."

"Have you been shopping the whole afternoon?" I ask.

"Indeed. And I bought a lot of great things."

I fetch my plate, now cool enough to hold, and amble to our living room table.

"I heard you were offered the accounting internship. What's up with that? Did you accept?"

I half-expect Chelsea to either say no or give me a grimace to indicate that, yes, she agreed to work in accounting, but only to satisfy her father's condition. To my surprise, however, she gives me a bright grin.

"Yes, I did. When I came out of my chat with Devon, I was somewhat demotivated. But in the elevator, I bumped into a blond demi-god. He chatted me up, and guess what? He turned out to be a senior accounting manager. He's called Howard, his suit bulges at all the right places, and his bangs are to die for."

Chelsea waggles her brows at me suggestively.

"So, after meeting him," she continues, "I bumped into Sarah who asked if I was interested in interviewing for the accounting internship. I agreed, and our conversation went great. It seems that I retained more from Mr. Johnson's boring lectures than I thought. Long story short, I landed the job."

"You're happy about it?" I ask.

Even if Chelsea always got good grades on her finance exams, she used to grumble that she preferred licking toilettes to crunching numbers.

"*Claro, claro,*" she says, imitating my brother's deep baritone and favorite way to confirm something. "The best part of the whole thing is I'll be sitting next to Howard, as he volunteered to be my mentor."

A bemused snort escapes my throat.

It's just so much like Chelsea to abandon something she seemed utterly determined to achieve and then set out to chase an entirely different objective on a whim, without feeling conflicted about her own behavior.

Some might label her go-with-the-wind attitude as inconsistent, but I'm convinced that her readiness to embrace whatever life brings and disregard the past is a quality.

I always worry and overthink my decisions.

This is probably why I still haven't blurted out that I'll be Devon's assistant, a position I said I'd never want.

I shove some quesadilla into my mouth, hoping the creamy cheese will fill me with the courage to come clean. "So," I say after swallowing, "I also have some news."

Chelsea gives me an exaggerated wink. "I know, sweetie. You got the PA job."

My brows fly to my hairline. "How'd you know?"

"It was obvious he would choose you. You must have charmed him as soon as he laid eyes on you. I think Devon is kinkier than the tabloids suggest and has a strong fetish for shoulder pads." She wiggles her brows at me then breaks into a giggle.

I make an air-circle beside my ear with a finger. "You've gone nuts. It must be the effect of too much shopping."

But then I join in her laugh because my embarrassment over my odd blazer has already dissipated.

"Anyway," Chelsea says after she catches her breath, "I'm just kidding. I knew he would pick you when he explained his PA's daily tasks. I expected it to be a more straightforward assistant job, like filing papers and keeping his schedule. I probably should have read the job description with more care. I couldn't pull off all the writing and out-of-the-box thinking the position requires, and I doubt any of those other girls could either. But for you, Laia, it will be smooth cruising."

My cheeks flush. "I'm not sure."

Chelsea gives me a *don't you dare go modest on me* glance. "Sweetie, you're an incredibly creative person. You'll nail this. Also, let's not forget that you have one ace up your sleeve that no other candidate, including me, had."

"And what's that?"

"Your good taste in men." Chelsea leans forward and meets my gaze with a reassuring smile. "You're waiting for your Prince Charming, and thus you won't be fooled by Devon Griffin's charm. You won't become his lapdog when he smiles at you. And since his manly allure can't affect you, you'll focus solely on your job and do it well."

"Thanks, Chels," I mumble.

It's not rare for Chelsea to compliment me, but she usually praises the way I look. And I know those kudos are strongly biased by her love for me, so I automatically deflect them.

Now, however, I let her kind words sink in and they warm my chest. Perhaps because deep inside I also believe I can do a good job as Devon's assistant.

Moreover, Chelsea is right. I would never worship a playboy like Devon, and it will be indeed a strength when working with him.

His exceptional eyes flash in my mind, and for a second, my self-assurance wavers, then I shake my head and cast the silly doubt aside.

Chelsea bends to the floor and holds up two shopping bags. "Thank me once you've opened these."

She pushes the bags toward me.

I inspect them with a raised brow. "What are these?"

"Your new work clothes. At least for the beginning. After your first paycheck, we'll hit the road again and buy some more stuff. These, however, are *my* gift to you."

My jaw drops as I peek into the first bag.

It's full of blouses, at least five or six of them. I lift the first one. It's light pink and has tiny pearl buttons. It's very pretty—not too alluring but elegant and chic. The size should fit, also.

I press it to my chest just to try. "How does it look? I don't usually wear fancy tops like this."

Chelsea claps. "It looks perfect on your olive skin, sweetie."

"It's beautiful," I say, lowering the blouse into my lap. I shove the quesadilla far away with a hand, afraid that even the greasy sauce's vague closeness could stain the delicate fabric. "But I can't accept it. Nor the others. You'll need to take them back to the shop."

Chelsea shakes her head. "No can do. After my interviews, I called Daddy to announce that I'm officially an employed citizen. He was so pleased with me that he offered to load serious money on my card so I could buy a whole new working wardrobe, which I graciously accepted."

"But…you got clothes for me!"

Chelsea waves. "Oh, there's plenty of stuff for me as well. Though they aren't for work. I already have way too many pencil skirts, elegant tops, and smart pants. But you, sweetie, you don't."

"I have trousers…" I protest.

Chelsea snorts. "Right. I didn't mean jeans, but sleek office pants. Don't forget you're the CEO's assistant now. You'll be going to all kinds of meetings. You can't dress like a grad student or a character from some old Madonna song." She tilts her head to my interview blazer resting on the back of a chair.

Okay, she has a point.

As if Chelsea realizes that I'm softening up to her overly generous gifts, she adds, "The other bag has a few high-waist pants. They'll lengthen your legs if you wear them with the tops and blouses tucked in. You can even complete your new-sophisticated look with your beloved flats or…" She jumps up, hurries to my side, and holds out a box to me. "With these."

I open it, and a pair of block-heeled pumps peek at me. They are cute and don't look uncomfortable at all.

Chelsea taps my shoulder. "Want to play dress-up? I'm dying to see how the outfits look on you."

Her excited voice lures a smile from me.

I reach up and pull her into a hug. "You're so awesome, Chels. Thank you. I'll pay you back for all these clothes, I promise."

Chelsea rolls her eyes. "I told you, I paid with Dad's money. We both know he has plenty of cash to waste. Besides, it's far better if you and I make good use of his generosity and not his teenage wife."

Mr. Anderson's fourth wife is indeed young, though definitely not an adolescent. Still, I stop myself from correcting Chelsea because I don't want to spoil her mood by defending her father's relationship choices.

Chelsea points at the pink blouse still on my lap. "Start with that and pair it with the black tweed pants, please. I bet they'll look amazing on you. So good that Mr. CEO will need to keep his fantasy in check when he works with you."

Though her last comment is an obvious joke, it still makes me wonder whether Devon will like my new, prettier wardrobe.

I know I shouldn't even contemplate such absurdity.

No amount of gorgeous clothes can turn an average girl into a beauty like my roomie. And since Devon wasn't impressed by Chelsea, he might not even notice my change of style at all.

Also, I've already established that Devon isn't a man who should interest me on any level other than on a professional one.

But I can't help it.

As I hurry into my room to change, an itsy-bitsy part of me hopes that when I walk into Hudson Communications tomorrow, Devon will be impressed by what he sees.

CHAPTER 7

(Devon)

After an excellent Chinese dinner, Pete and I drop Ellie off.

Since there's no parking close to my sister's apartment, my friend stops his Toyota Tacoma a block away from her entrance. He switches off the engine and turns to the backseat to say goodbye to Ellie.

His styled pompadour cut bounces gently with his movement. With his shiny black shirt, he reminds me of Elvis.

Ellie leans her freckled cheek toward Pete so they can exchange a kiss. "Thanks for taking me home," she chirps. "I know it was a detour on the way to your club."

"No problem. It was good to see you, kiddo," Pete replies.

Pete is only two years my senior, but he insists on calling my sister "kiddo" for some weird reason. Ellie's bet is that Pete does it as a way to deflect her criticism about our womanizing lifestyle. Some kind of mental protective barrier.

Since Ellie works for a behavioral clinic, I don't feel like arguing with her hypothesis about this particular topic.

Ellie turns to me, but I shake my head. "I'll walk you," I say instead.

"That's not necessary, Dev, but if you insist…" Ellie feign-protests, but her relieved tone tells me she's happy I offered.

Ever since my sister's neighbor got mugged in a nearby alley, I've been worrying more about Ellie. I want to make sure I see her safely to the door first, even if Pete wants to get to Red Heaven before happy hour ends.

Ellie has been more wary too. She even picked up a new quirk, and she started carrying a lipstick knife in her purse.

It's a ridiculous gadget that, quite frankly, is more likely to cause her an accidental mouth stabbing if she mixes it up with her lip balm rather than wound an even mildly skillful thief. But my sister insists it makes her feel more protected.

I hop out of the car and take a deep, conscious inhale. I hold it in for a few counts before releasing it. Though the times when I needed to practice breathing techniques to enhance my thoracic capacity are long gone, I still have the habit of doing this exercise each time I set foot outside.

The late-spring air is still too hot and dry for my taste, as the concrete walls continue to release the heat they've accumulated throughout the day.

My eyes fall on the thirsty shrub on the sidewalk, and I wish I had a bottle to water the poor fern.

I'm looking forward to July when finally the rainy season starts, which is much more to my liking.

Ellie jumps out too and slams the car door with a

mighty bang that sends her light-brown locks dancing around her shoulders.

My buddy's head pops out of the passenger window as his windscreens quiver. "Watch out, kiddo," he complains. "My ride is my treasure. Don't you break it."

Ellie rolls her eyes, but before she can shoot back one of her fiery comments, I grab her arm and drag her toward her house.

"Don't criticize Pete's adoration of his toy, please," I whisper as we walk away from the Toyota.

Ellie throws me an annoyed glance. "I wasn't gonna. I can recognize a pathologically strong bond between a human and an object, and far be it from me to shatter it. Though I suspect that the only reason Pete likes his ride is because he thinks it's a chick magnet. He isn't obsessed with the nitty-gritty of cars like you are."

I answer the remark with a short nod.

My friend would switch in a minute if he found another model of vehicle that would make his gigolo act more successful.

Ellie leans on me and suppresses a yawn. "Oh gosh, Dev, you can't imagine how tired I am. I'm looking forward to a shower and then jumping into bed. I can't fathom how you still have the energy for a club. It's almost ten."

I shrug. "I'll just stay for a drink. Or maybe two." Even if Pete definitely has other plans for us.

But tonight I can't be his sidekick for too long. The interviews drained all my need for social interaction. I could easily call it a night right now. I'm going out because I promised Pete I'd keep him company, and I hate to back out on my word.

We arrive at thc tall brick building with a rusty fire escape where Ellie and her two besties live.

My sister fetches her keys and hugs me. “Thanks for the delivery.” She winks and gives a peck on my cheek. “Have fun with Pete, but please behave. I don’t want to be pestered at work with gossip about my hunky brother’s newest conquest.”

“Ah, Ellie,” I smack my lips, “you exaggerate. It’s not like paparazzi lurk behind every corner, ready to write a juicy piece on me. I’m not that famous.”

“What about that double spread in *Fancy & Stylish*?”

I open my arms. “The reporter just happened to celebrate his birthday in the same bar Pete and I went to. I didn’t expect that he would trade his celebration to snap a few compromising pictures of me. In any case, I only accompanied that blonde to her car, much like I’m doing it with you now.”

“That’s not what the article said…” Ellie gives me an accusing glance.

“I never even drink Long Island Ice tea, so that should be an indication of how much the journalist made up. I was only being Pete’s wingman that night.”

“Maybe that night, yes. But you’re too frequently in the tabloid headlines.” Ellie scrunches her nose. “I don’t like to see people bet on how long your next fling will last. You’re not getting any younger. Being an irresponsible tomcat is okay in your twenties, but when you’re in your thirties, it becomes hideous. It’s time you tune your social life down a notch, don’t you think?”

My jaw tightens. I hate it when my sister lectures me. While I can brush off my secretary’s remarks with ease, Ellie’s disapproval bothers me far more.

Also, her comments don’t fall on entirely deaf ears.

Lately, I’ve noticed that my carefree lifestyle doesn’t provide much satisfaction anymore. The girls I meet seem somehow identical, as if made by a stamp.

It would be simpler to admit to Ellie that I can relate to her worries, but that would start a long chat. Pete must be impatient for me to return.

Ellie notices that she's stepped on my toes, because she pats my arm. "Sorry, I don't mean to be a nudnik. I'd just love to see you dial back on your after-work agenda. The steamy, airless clubs are not good for your lungs."

That's her ultimate weapon—my health.

She knows that I'd do almost anything to avoid the hospital. I spent too much time there as a child. Now, whenever I merely pass in front of one, my stomach roils.

"My lungs are perfectly okay now, and you know it." I give her a don't-even-try-with-this-angle glance. "And, for the record, you sound like Mom when you fuss like this."

My sister doesn't like to be compared to our mother. Mom is a lovely woman and we both love her to death, but she can be a real pain in the neck when she picks on you for something.

As expected, Ellie's face contorts into a shocked grimace. "Take that back," she squeaks, waving at me.

Her keyring flies out of her fingers and whacks me on the chest.

I catch it and I'm about to hand it back, when I realize she's still holding onto it with the help of a pink keychain.

I lift the string with two fingers. It's made out of rubber and feels oddly slimy. "What on earth is this thing?"

"It's a self-defense swing keyring," Ellie states in a matter-of-fact voice.

She snatches the keys from my hand by pulling on the thread. She dangles the device in front of me so I can see how the keyring is fastened on a long elastic cord that ties into a tiny elliptic-shaped handle of sorts.

I have a hard time keeping my face straight. "Sis, whipping a keyring at an attacker is the kind of weapon a seven-year-old might come up with after first learning about ninjas. You won't scare anyone with this. It's even worse than your lipstick dagger."

Ellie's lips curl down. "The guy in the shop told me the concept is based on an ancient jiu-jitsu technique and that it could take out a much larger man than you. You think he lied to me?"

Likely yes.

"Lucky you didn't mean to hurt me just now. If you did, I'm sure I would have blacked out immediately."

I withhold the fact that she would need muscles like Dwayne "the Rock" Johnson to accomplish what the vendor promised. And if she were that tough, she could probably incapacitate anyone without some special gadget anyway.

But I don't want to burst Ellie's bubble.

She must be genuinely scared if she decided to purchase such a thing. I'll have to sit down with her sometime and brainstorm better options to increase her sense of safety.

Ellie smiles. "Indeed. I knew it was a useful purchase. So, see you, Dev. Be a good boy, like you promised. Goodnight!"

She opens the door and disappears inside her building.

As I saunter back to Pete's car, my eyes travel to his large fender bulges. Were they part of the original design, or a special request of Pete's? Just as I make a mental note to ask my buddy about it at some point, I notice from the corner of my eye the silhouette of a woman on the other side of the road.

There's something familiar about her. She has long, sweeping dark hair and a petite build. What would Laia be doing in my sister's neighborhood?

"Laia! Laia!" I yell without deciding consciously to shout.

The woman doesn't stir.

She probably didn't hear me. Should I go after her and say hi? It'd be a polite thing to do as her new boss.

My gaze flicks to Pete's arm hanging out of the car window. He's drumming his fingers on the door, anxious to get going. I take a quick peek at my watch.

We still have a little time before the two-for-one offer is over at the club.

I'll be *very* quick. Before I can overthink it, I cross the road. Pete calls out, but I wave to him without turning to signal that I'll be back shortly.

I jog leisurely behind the woman. In my head, I'm assessing what I'll say to her. I don't want to come across as some creeper who's following her. I just want ask how she's doing.

When I'm two feet away, I reach out to tap her shoulder.

"Hi, Laia—"

My voice breaks off as a throaty contralto squeaks at me. "What do you want?"

I know I've made a mistake even before my eyes reach the woman's face. If the missing mellifluous timbre hadn't been enough of confirmation that I acted like a fool, the woman's narrowed blue eyes ram my error home.

"I'm sorry, I thought you were someone else," I blather and then bolt back to Pete.

My buddy is laughing his head off as I hop into the passenger seat.

"Done with your chasing act, mate? Why did you even harass that girl? We'll have enough nice company in Red Heaven."

"I didn't harass anyone." I stick up my chin indignantly. "I thought she was someone I know. My new assistant, actually."

"Is your new assistant hot? That chick looked quite cute from a distance. I find long hair so sensual. I love how the soft curls caress you in all the right places when—"

"Stop," I bark before Pete's words can instill any inappropriate image about Laia in my head. "Laia, because that's her name, isn't hot. She's pretty, but in a chaste kind of way. Her face looks a lot like Salma Hayek's, only younger."

"Not bad." Pete wiggles his brows. "By chaste, you mean…?"

"No! Ah, buddy, what's wrong with you?" I bump a fist into Pete's shoulder. "She is my *employee*. I wasn't insinuating anything about her sexual experiences. I just meant that she appears innocent and genuine."

"In an enticingly curvy, Salma Hayek-y way, huh?"

"That's your dirty mind talking. Anyway, we're dropping the subject of my new assistant now." I reach for the ignition and turn it. "Just drive, Pete. If we sit around talking, we'll miss happy hour."

My last argument motivates Pete enough to stop bugging me about Laia. He steps on the gas and steers the car to the road.

I glare out of the window and watch the quiet residential area turn into the busy streets of Downtown Phoenix, while a sullen mood brews in my stomach.

Pete's remark is still bothering me.

Why?

I've a soft spot for tall, blonde women. Laia wouldn't be the type of girl I'd hit on, even if we met outside of work. I can dismiss Pete's innuendo with a clear conscience. I don't harbor any attraction toward my new assistant.

"Devon, you coming? The pretty ladies are waiting for us," Pete says. "Look, your welcome party's outside."

We've arrived? Did I spend the entire car idling about Laia?

My eyes flick to the window, and I spot the two reporters Pete mentioned, lingering outside Red Heaven's entrance with their cameras, eager to get a shot at some minor celebrity—which, unfortunately, is what they consider me to be.

Lucky that I don't plan on socializing tonight, otherwise the juicy tabloid article Ellie feared might just turn into reality.

Pete's enthusiastic grin shows how ready he is to jump into action, but I'm wondering whether Ellie is right.

Maybe I am indeed getting too old to be a playboy.

CHAPTER 8

(Devon)

The next morning, as I enter my company's lobby, Chuck salutes me by knocking his heels and pulling his back into a straight line.

"Good morning, Mr. Devon," he calls out in the same disciplined tone he must have used with his captain back in his army days.

I pat Chuck on his back. "Thank you, and good morning to you too. I hope good old Steve isn't giving you a hard time."

Chuck shakes his head, then gives a slanted glance at the elderly man beside him. "Steve and I are getting along superbly, Mr. Devon."

Steve twists his mustache between his index and thumb and nods. "Indeed. Chuck is learning quickly."

"I'm glad to hear that." I smile and continue on my way.

I wave to Michael at the reception desk, then stop to caress Hudson's head. It's like summoning my mojo for the day. Hudson has been my partner in crime since I was still working out of my bedroom, chasing down my first paying clients. Without his constant presence, I might have given up before I made a breakthrough.

As I amble to the elevator, Chuck's jovial face dances in front of my eyes, and my lips curl up.

I'm happy that he's doing well. I hired the young security officer a couple of months ago, straight from a soldier reintegration program. Chuck was struggling with severe PTSD and couldn't continue his previous career. His new work in my company seems to be doing him tremendous good. He doesn't have the haunted frown and empty glare that he used to wear. If he'd only quit addressing me with that formal Mr., he'd blend in perfectly with the rest of my staff.

Katja called me an altruist for taking Chuck on board, but hiring a young veteran was a no-brainer to me.

When I dropped out of college after Morgan's betrayal, I went through my own private hell. But I came out of it stronger, thanks to my family and friends who stood by me when I launched into my grandiose plan of building Hudson Communications. I'd like to give others the same chance of rebuilding their life.

I press the call button on the elevator and let my eyes flutter shut.

Though I'd respected my own rule and left the club early, I still didn't get enough rest last night.

My sleep was plagued by the weirdest nightmare. I dreamed I was closed in a room filled with cigar smoke and heavy female perfume. The air was so saturated with the nauseatingly artificial fragrances that I began to choke. In the end, I woke up sweaty and gasping for air.

The elevator bell chimes, and I quickly open my eyes.

As my vision refocuses, I blink at a curious pair of eyes observing me.

At first, I don't recognize to whom they belong. They remind me of Laia with their peculiar pattern and color, but the woman in front of me, in her well-fitted black pants and a light-pink silk blouse, can't be her.

No, the girl I'd hired had a questionable—not to say awful—taste in clothes.

Plus, with how she stumbled in her flats, there's no way she'd suddenly start using pumps, even low heels.

Just as I assemble these rational arguments in my head, the familiar sweet soprano that had me questioning whether Laia sang in a choir as a kid, greets me. "Good morning Mr.…*uhm*…Devon. Are you going up too?"

My facial muscles give up, and my jaw slides an inch.

Oh, goodness. This is indeed my assistant.

Was she snatched by a fashion makeover team as she headed for work?

The doors of the elevator begin to close, and Laia holds out her arm to stop them. "Do you prefer to come in or stay and wait for an empty ride?" A hint of teasing tugs her lower lip into a smirk, as if she's amused by my bafflement.

I haven't seen Laia acting coy yet, and I must admit her breezy playfulness moves something in me.

Or maybe it's the realization that the shiny pearls on her blouse resemble her teeth.

"No, I'll come," I reply.

She steps backward, leaving me space to enter.

The floor we're traveling to is already selected, but I push the button again to cancel out my previously indecisive behavior.

The doors shut, and I turn around to face Laia.

I give her a once-over, a slower and more deliberate

one than I'd typically allow myself at work. On some unconscious level, I want her to feel as fazed as I was by her unexpected transformation. A slight suspicion forms, and I'd like to see if I'm right or not.

My plan seems to work because Laia shifts uncomfortably and brushes her palms against her pants. Her cheeks deepen into a darker hue.

I allow myself to enjoy her embarrassment until she starts to chew on her lower lip, then I redirect my glance to her face.

"So, I guess you were playing me yesterday, right?" I ask.

Her eyes, hovering over her shoes, dart to my face. They're so wide her irises seem to overtake the entire space. Having them reflected at me by the mirrors of the elevator from every angles magnifies the effect.

"What do you mean 'playing you'? I wasn't…I didn't…"

I meant my comment as a provocation and hoped I could make her confess her trick, but Laia's genuinely flustered expression tells me my hunch might have been off.

"So, you didn't dress differently for the interview because you wanted to ensure that I'd focus on your resume and not be blinded by your….you know…"

Her brows round. "My what?"

I point at her figure and move my finger up and down. "Your womanly charms."

I wouldn't have thought her eyes could become larger, but they do.

"Are you easily blinded by such aspects?"

I shrug. "It depends. In my private life, sometimes. At work, no. Though if you trust the rumors about me, you may assume something different."

Laia cocks her head to the side. “You know what they say…a rumor always contains a grain of truth.”

In my case, probably more than just a grain. But never when it comes to my employees.

That’s why Laia’s phrase makes me cringe. I don’t want her to feel uneasy with me.

“Laia, I need to make something clear to you.” I lean a bit closer to her to make sure she pays attention to my words, and her scent wafts over me. My nostrils flare, allowing her perfume to sink right into my lungs.

“Devon? You were saying?”

Laia’s voice jars me out of my sensual distraction.

“Oh, yes. You may hear gossip about me being a…”

I squirm with my shirt collar while Laia’s curious gaze makes an unusual heat flow to my neck.

What word should I use to sound professional but still truthful?

Womanizer? Nah. I’m not really that.

Playboy? Maybe, but calling myself that in front of an employee would sound wrong.

“Player?” Laia chimes in.

I could probably go with that. “Yes, some may call me a player, even if I’m not one. Players often lie, and I don’t. But since you came up with this word, can I ask whether you’ve read any tabloid articles about me?”

“Yes, one.” She nods, and by her slightly disapproving tone, I deduce that the publication she saw might have been on the racier side.

“That’s okay,” I say as casually as I can. “Is that the reason you dressed in a shapeless suit for the interview, instead of the clothes you’re wearing today?”

She stares at me, then her mouth moves into a smile that’s an exquisite mixture of shy and amused. “No, of course not. I used that suit for my graduation, too. I know it's kind of ugly." She bobs her head back and forth, then smacks her lips. "Or maybe even a lot, but I didn't have time to find a better alternative on such short notice. I'm not really a fashionista."

When she sees my doubtful frown as I eye her chic blouse, she pinches the fabric on her shoulders and adds, "This top, together with these pants, are gifts from my roomie. She wanted me to look the part of a CEO's assistant."

"Well, you certainly do." I smile.

Not only that. Laia looks pretty. Very. Her new style suits her way more than that oversized pantsuit.

It's not just her new clothes, though. She's chosen to wear her impressive dark mane loose, which plays up her eyes and emphasizes her enticing skin color.

"Believe it or not," I chuckle, relieved that my suspicion about her was without foundation, "your weird blazer was the first reason you stood out to me among the other applicants."

"How so?"

I didn't plan on mentioning anything to Laia about Hayley, but maybe I should. I don't want Laia to fret that she might get entangled in something scandalous while working for me. She'll undoubtedly hear soon enough all the whacky theories circulating about my former assistant's departure.

I clear my throat. "I didn't want to hire anyone who would use her looks on me. I had some issues, *personal issues*, with my ex-assistant. That's why I explicitly wanted someone who will be focused solely on her job. In my company, private life and work don't mix—not for me and not for my employees. As my PA, you'll be privy to a lot of sensitive information about me, which increases the importance of keeping personal boundaries clear between us."

Laia's mouth opens slightly, then her features smooth out. "I don't have any problem with this. It sounds just right."

"Good, because—"

The elevator door opens. Katja rushes over to us with a pile of documents in her arms. "Robert Leonic just called and confirmed your tea together for Thursday. The invitation to the CCF gala arrived. It'll be held in a luxury resort outside Tucson this year. Shall I book your spot now?"

"Yes, please," I answer.

Katja blinks at Laia. "You may peek over my shoulders as I make the reservation. I handle the admin work for Devon's trips, but when I'm on vacation, it will fall onto your plate."

Laia nods. "Of course."

Katja turns to me. "And these reports? Shall I give them to you or to Laia?"

I flash a questioning glance at Laia.

I'd promised myself I'd make her first days as easy as possible so she can adapt to her new responsibilities without feeling pressured, but Laia is already reaching for the stack. "I can take them. It'll be a great way to jump into my role." She peers up at me. "Do you like highlighters? I could signal the crucial insights with blue, the good-to-know bits with pink, and perhaps green for the superfluous can-be-skimmed-overs?"

Is she a mind reader? How did she guess the exact color scheme I like?

I can't suppress an appreciative smile as I nod. "If you'll prepare them that way, it would be perfect."

Katja observes me with furrowed brows as if wondering why I'm grinning at Laia, then she snorts. "I didn't have time to prepare your health cocktail yet, but I will soon."

I cringe as the rancid stench of sauerkraut comes back to me. "This morning, I'd prefer a double espresso with one spoonful of sugar, if it's not too much trouble."

I say my polite words in a firm tone, so Katja will have no choice but to accept them.

Katja purses her lips. "Whatever you wish, Devon. I'll bring it after I file the contract I've been working on." Her vexed tone contradicts her agreement.

I suspect that my secretary secretly considers caffeine to be a legalized poison, because every time she brings me a cup, she does it with a grimace of dislike.

Laia gives a smile to Katja. "I wanted to check where the kitchen is. If you like, I can make the coffee while I'm at it." As she sees Katja's aghast expression, she quickly adds, "Just this once, so you can take your time with filing."

I'm surprised by Laia's kind offer and interested in my secretary's response.

Katja used to defend her duties from Hayley with tooth and nail and would never allow my ex-assistant to replace her in any task, however small it might be.

Katja's jaw relaxes, and she nods. "Great, that would be nice of you, Laia. We have a Breville One-Touch machine in the kitchen. Just press the button, and it will take care of the rest."

"Easy-peasy, even for the rare species of non-coffee drinkers like you." I wink at Laia.

A smile tugs at the corner of her mouth as I borrow her exact words from the interview. "I'll do my best to make a decent cup, I promise."

"Thank you," I answer.

Laia steps over to her desk and puts down the documents that Katja handed to her. "I'll be right back with it."

When Laia is gone, Katja scratches her scalp, which

makes her thick braids shimmy above her ears, and murmurs something under her breath.

"What's the matter, Katja?"

She cocks her head to the direction where Laia went.

"Her. She's…odd."

Odd? Not the first word I'd associate with Laia's swaying curves.

"Isn't it just a bit weird?" Katja grumbles. "Yesterday she looked like she was dressed by her blind great-grandfather and today she's the winner of *Pimp Your Look*. What's her deal? Aren't you concerned you'll soon have another tricky situation on your hands?"

I shake my head, because I finally understand what she's getting at. "No, no, don't worry. Laia won't be another Hayley. By the way…*Pimp Your Look*? I didn't take you for a reality show junkie, my dear Katja. You just gave me ammunition for a good joke later."

Katja wags her finger at me. "Don't, Devon, or else I'll fix you another sauerkraut juice. Don't think I didn't notice what you did with the one yesterday! Your rubber plant smelled like Shchi soup this morning."

Luckily Katja's phone rings and saves me from answering her (justified) accusation.

I walk to my office. I settle at my desk and fire up my computer. While I wait for my calendar and messages to sync, I keep peeking at the door to check whether Laia is coming with my coffee.

Only because I need caffeine before my brain can function properly.

Exactly. For no other reason than that.

CHAPTER 9

(Laia)

The kitchen on our floor is in a spacious corner room. It's airy and absolutely streamlined.

After my small tour in the building yesterday, I shouldn't be surprised that even this space is jammed with trendy fine points like the lacquered blue faucet and the warm-orange back splash behind the counter.

Despite these accents of color, what attracts my eyes immediately is the large, glazed window overlooking the city.

It's not the grey skyline view that fascinates me, but the surrounding mountain preserve I'm able to peek at, thanks to our building's height. I walk over to the window and stick my nose to the glass.

The saguaro-studded hillsides untie my mind from the looping thoughts about Devon and our strange chat in the elevator. I'm surprised that my colleagues don't spend half of their days glued to the window, gazing at the desert.

Of course, if they did that, they would probably be fired. Like I'm about to be if I don't get on with the coffee I promised Devon.

I trot over to the coffee machine that takes up a good portion of the steel counter.

It's one of those fancy models. My fingers hover above the buttons.

Grrrr, easy peasy, my eye…

Is the double espresso the larger cup with one wavy line or the smaller one with two? Maybe it's the simple cup with two dots but without any lines? And what about that weird form that looks like a ball? Could that be sugar?

I blow out the air from my cheeks and close my eyes.

As soon as my eyelids shut, Devon's sweeping glance flashes through my mind, and my cheeks warm a couple of degrees.

I should have told him that if he genuinely wants to live by his rule of separating private life and work, he'd better stop giving his female employees dashing smiles and lingering looks.

They're infuriatingly confusing.

I wish I could tell what he thought of my new clothes. While he was observing me, his brows were set in a confused frown and his lips in a small circle, but he'd arched his shoulders unconsciously as if to enhance his pectoral muscles.

Not that he needs it. Devon has the perfect build—athletic without looking like a weightlifting champion.

No. His looks are beside the point. I shouldn't even contemplate them—especially not after the uncomfortable heat his proximity unleashed in me.

And that's why I'm going to stop revisiting his textured haircut and broad shoulders. *Right now.*

I open my eyes and tap my cheeks twice to rid my head from any idle reverie.

I examine the coffee machine once more. It can't be more challenging than writing a dissertation about the Sturm und Drang literary movement, and I've done that. I can surely figure out how to make this device work. Even if I need to toss away a few failed attempts in the process.

I grab a cup from a shelf and position it in the cupholder. I'll try the simple cup with two lines. Two must stand for double. I push the button, and the machine wheezes loudly, but no liquid comes out.

"*¡Venga!*" I murmur under my breath. "What's your problem?"

"Hello!"

A high-pitched soprano makes me jump. I whip around and find a woman only a couple of feet away from me.

Her hair is blond. Not the impeccably sun-bleached shade of Chelsea's, but rather a vibrant platinum that forces me to squint.

I should have heard her approach on her chopstick stilettos, but the machine's angry grunts stifled her clicking noise.

"What are you're trying to do?" The woman tilts her foxlike head to the side as she studies me.

I was so caught up by her unnaturally bright hair that I forgot to answer her first question. Desperate to cancel out this lousy first impression—whoever this woman is, she's my new colleague—I stick out my hand to her.

"Hi, I'm Laia. I'm Devon's new PA. I'm trying to make this coffee machine work. Without success, as you can see." I top my words with a friendly smile.

After a second of hesitation, she takes my hand, but only my fingertips.

Her skin is cold and oozy as if she put on lotion, and it hasn't finished absorbing into her palms.

"Right, Laia. I knew who you were, just not your name. I'm Fanta."

Fanta?

Who names their kid after a sparkling orange beverage? Are her parents huge soft drink fans?

I bite back my gasp and say, "Nice to meet you. Which department are you in?"

"I work for Sarah at HR. I came up here to see for myself what all the fuss is about."

"Fuss?" I arch my brows. "What do you mean?"

Fanta waves. "Don't pretend you don't know that the entire team is talking about you."

Even if her accusing tone takes me by surprise, it's the meaning of her words that truly startles me.

"About me? Why?"

She makes a one-shouldered shrug. "People are curious why Devon picked you. Whether you'll be Hayley 2.0."

"Who is Hayley?"

"Devon's former assistant," she announces in a slightly nasal tone, constricting her nostrils as if she smelled an unexpected stench. "Aaaand…his ex-lover."

My jaw goes slack. "Ex-*lover*?"

Devon had an affair with the woman who worked for him before me?

Katja's brief mention of my predecessor and her dubious, "*not his usual choice,*" comment gains a whole new significance.

I pause.

Devon just told me that he doesn't let his pleasure-seeker lifestyle spill over to work. Why would he have said that if he was involved with his previous assistant?

Maybe Fanta is just messing with me. A prank on the new girl?

"You're kidding, right?"

Fanta shakes her head then leans into me, whispering. "Rumor has it Devon got his eyes on Hayley and courted her till she gave in. The poor girl fell in love with Devon. Once our CEO grew tired of her company, she was gone."

"That can't be right," I murmur.

Fanta flashes a smile at me as if enjoying my unease. Her smirk—fake and gloating—makes her sharp canine teeth visible. I suddenly wonder if Fanta has a hidden agenda. Does she want to warn me off Devon?

"Ah, you better believe it. Don't you read the tabloids? Our boss didn't build his reputation under false pretenses. Devon Griffin is a chaser." Fanta studies me from head to toe, then clicking her tongue, adds, "But don't worry, you won't be his next victim. He prefers blondes."

A bell goes off in my head.

I know why Fanta sought me out. It isn't to alert me about any lurking danger. It's to mark her territory.

She has a thing for Devon.

As if to confirm my hunch, Fanta smooths down her bob with two hands and says, "Hayley's hair had a very similar color to mine actually. Also, you're too much of a shorty, Laia. Devon likes his girls tall."

I don't exactly know why…perhaps the fact that Fanta is observing me with the same belittling glance I'd so often received in school…but my lips move before I can stop them.

"You know, I hate to crush your hopes, but it's unlikely that Devon would be interested in you either. I'm not sure what his previous attitude on office affairs was, but, only this morning, he reassured me that he wouldn't engage in intimate relationships."

"You *asked* him if he wants to hook up with you? *Bold*!" Fanta snaps her fingers, and the deprecation so evident only a second ago transforms into a sort of admiration.

If I were a cartoon character, this is where steam would start flowing out of my ears.

This chick is insane. Does she seriously think I'd ask such a question of my boss on my first day? Or on any regular day?

My hands fly to my hips. "Your question is so ridiculous I'm not even going to answer it."

Fanta's chin drops at my annoyed tone, but I'm not done with lecturing her.

It isn't only my past frustrations that fuel my outburst, but a new sense of responsibility I feel toward Devon. He told me that one of my tasks would be to control his public image.

Protecting him from malicious comments in his own company's kitchen is a great place to start.

I level my gaze on Fanta. "Besides, I don't think you should be gossiping about our CEO. The salary you receive from him allows you to pay your hairstylist for this dazzling hair color you're so proud of, no? Maybe showing more loyalty to him wouldn't hurt you. Anyway, I don't have time to chat about Devon's alleged soft spot for blondes or his past adventures. I'm not interested in them."

Fanta purses her lips. "I don't believe you. Who wouldn't care to know what her playboy bo—"

I shake my head and hold up my hand, suddenly realizing that the best strategy I can adopt with Ms. Soft Drink is to cut her short.

"Think whatever you want. The only thing I'm concerned with is doing an excellent job for Devon. That, right now, means preparing a coffee for him and then assisting Katja to make his CCF booking."

"Oh? Devon is attending the CFF this year? Will he be going alone?" The eager glint makes Fanta's close-set eyes push closer together, enhancing the foxlike effect.

Without answering, I turn back to the coffee machine to signal that this tête-a-tête is over.

Fanta sniffs. "Huh, so you like to play precious. Well, suit yourself." She strides to the corridor. Before stepping out, she calls back in a haughty voice, "By the way, the water needs to be enabled for the machine to work. *Everybody* knows that."

When she disappears, a growl escapes from my throat.

And here I thought that I would make my very first office friendship. It's clear this arrogant blondie and I will never be friends. Her smug manners catapulted me back to memories that I hate to revisit—times when I felt inadequate and ridiculed.

I press my hand to my chest and suck in a breath.

It's fine. I'm an adult now. I have a good life, a great bestie, a lovely family, and a job. I didn't turn out to be the loser everyone thought I would become.

I might not have a relationship yet, but that's because I don't settle for mediocrity. I want a soul-stirring love with a man who truly deserves my heart. And that's hard to find.

The thoughts about my singlehood bring back the puzzling rumors Fanta shared with me. Devon had seemed honest when he told me he doesn't mix business and pleasure. Should I believe him?

Or should I trust Ms. Soft Drink's gossip? Do those rumors even concern me?

After another calming breath, I decide that they don't.

Whatever the truth is about Hayley, it doesn't matter. I

know Devon Griffin as a man isn't at all what I want or need in my life.

But as a boss, he'll make a significant impact on my future. The guy isn't called a creative genius for nothing. I have so much to learn from him.

I don't care if he had a fling with his former assistant. He surely won't have anything with me.

And not only because I would never get involved with him, but also because, as Fanta had so aptly put it, there's no chance Devon would ever notice me as a woman.

There. Question settled.

I reach around to the side of the coffee machine and make use of Fanta's only helpful comment by switching on the lever that controls the water's flow. I press the button with the cup and two lines, and this time the rattling sound is followed by a strong smell of coffee.

Soon the cup fills up with the brown liquid. I position it on a small plate when it's ready. I add a spoon of sugar and hustle to the corridor, holding Devon's drink straight in front of me.

Despite my resolution to stop mulling over Devon, my thoughts return to his remark about my ugly pantsuit.

Was Devon unconsciously afraid that he might not manage to keep his player self at bay? Is it why he picked a person—namely me—whom he knew he wouldn't feel tempted by?

Katja's voice interrupts me before I can idle any further about this.

"Where have you been for so long?" she asks, furrowing her brows.

"I needed a moment to find my way in the kitchen."

"Really? Only that? Didn't you stop to speak with someone?" She leans forward on her desk. Her lips are straight, and her eyes penetrating.

Holy moly, Katja can certainly look scary if she wants.

Did she come to check on me while I was in the kitchen?

"I met a colleague from HR and introduced myself." In case Katja saw me with Fanta, I don't want her to think I slacked off and lied about it.

Katja nods. "Fine. Be warned, though, most people in our company are nice. But not all. Choose with whom you chitchat. *Wisely…*" She makes a dramatic pause, then points at the cup in my hand. "Now hurry up with that before it gets cold."

"Oh, sure. Yes," I mumble and trot over to Devon's office.

Without knowing exactly why, I smooth down my blouse and run a hand through my hair before pushing his door open.

CHAPTER 10

(Devon)

"Wyatt Harrison is on line one. Would you like to take his call, Devon?"

The phone starts to slip as Laia's melodious timbre surprises me. I squeeze it to my chin to keep it from falling.

I've been without a PA for a few weeks now, so Katja has been taking care of my personal calls. And my secretary's raspy tone could never be described as musical, even with the best of intentions.

Laia's voice elicits an odd sensation in my chest, almost as if my intercostal muscles have decided to contract all at once.

What the heck is wrong with me?

Is it still the aftermath of our encounter in the elevator? Maybe my shock about Laia's new style hasn't worn off yet. No, I can't be this shaken that Laia turned out to be more of a looker than her dingy pantsuit suggested. I knew she was cute when I hired her, despite the ugly clothes.

But if it isn't her new attire, then what is it?

"Devon? Do you want me to tell Mr. Harrison to call you back?"

Laia's repeated question brings me back to reality.

"No need. Put him through, please. Also, when my call ends, I'll be ready to look at the Leonic file with you."

"Very well," she answers.

After a click, Wyatt's familiar baritone greets me. "Hey, mate. What's up?"

I lean back in my chair and swirl it around so that I can look at the landscape from my window while I chat with him.

Along with Pete, Wyatt is my best friend. The three of us were very tight in high school. If Wyatt hadn't been drafted by the NFL and moved away from Arizona, we would still be hanging out together most of the time.

"All is good here, Wyatt. How come you called the office and not my cell phone?"

"I might have misplaced my phone at the last training. That, or an overly enthusiastic groupie snatched it for a souvenir. Anyway, I lost your number." Wyatt's hearty chuckle resounds in my ear.

"I see. And I thought you were too busy even in the off-season to return my calls. Which I would totally understand. Training must come first."

There is a short silence on the line, then Wyatt sniffs. "Ah, yeah, the coach made us sweat like pigs in the mini-camp. But that's not why I've been a ghost. I'm having some problems with the team."

"Problems? Want to elaborate?"

"Not really."

Typical. When my friend is interested in something, he

pesters me as long as needed. His persistence is one of his strengths on the gridiron.

But trying to do vice versa with him never works. It's as if Wyatt believes he's allowed to tackle everyone else, but he never wants to be on the ground—literally and metaphorically.

"Fine, I hope you can resolve the issue. But if you need a hand, let me know." I know better than to press Wyatt on something he doesn't want to share. "So what about today? Did you happen to miss me awfully? Or is there another reason that you rang me up?"

To my surprise, Wyatt replies, "Actually, yes. Is your accountant's villa still available? The one in Glendale. You mentioned that he wanted to sell it some time ago."

"Mike's house? Yep, it's still there. With the stellar price he's asking for it, I doubt he'll find any fool to buy it. Why?"

Wyatt chuckles. "He might just find one person. Me."

"You're kidding, right? Why would you buy a property in the Phoenix area? You're never in Arizona. I've seen you like three times in the past four years. Almost as if you've avoided coming anywhere near Kingman."

I regret this last phrase as soon as it's out.

I know Wyatt took good care of his mother, setting her up in a beautiful mansion that everyone in our hometown admires. The fact that he rarely visits has more to do with the broken relationship he had with his father and the ghosts that still haunt him than with anything else.

"Well, that might have been true in the past. I'll definitely come and visit this summer. Also, there's a vague possibility I'll be spending more time in the Valley of the Sun later. So, just in case that happens, I want to be prepared. You know I hate staying in hotels even for short times. Your accountant's house is in a quiet neighborhood. That's exactly what I'm looking for."

"Quiet neighborhood, huh? The fact that it's close to the State Farm Stadium doesn't come into consideration?"

Wyatt snorts. "I can neither confirm nor deny this."

A grin spreads on my face. I would love nothing more than for Wyatt to move back home. "Well, I'll be happy if you pop over. Pete and I miss your beach-boy grin. Watching you on television isn't the same thing."

"That's because I wear a helmet," Wyatt interjects. "Anyway, will you talk to Mike for me?"

"Sure, consider it done."

"Great, going through an acquaintance will save me the hassle of contracting sleazy real estate agents. They'd only try to woo me with posh high-rises. I know you live in one of those condos, so no offense."

"None taken."

Wyatt might be a pro football player, but he's still a small-town boy at heart.

The ridiculous sum Mike is asking for his property comes to mind, and I quickly correct my thought—a small-town boy with a massive budget at his disposal.

Wyatt clears his throat. "How is Ellie doing?"

"Fine. Busy like a bee, as always. Why do you ask?"

My question is justified. Wyatt and my sister have a tense relationship, and that's putting it mildly.

Cats and dogs get along better than those two. In fact, as far as I know, they haven't even spoken since Wyatt started playing for the Atlanta Kites.

I don't know the exact reason for their clash, but it dates back to Ellie's freshman year in college. I've never wanted to end up in the middle of their conflict, so I just mostly avoid mentioning their names to each other.

After a short silence, Wyatt coughs. "Just that I recently met someone who reminded me of her."

"Did she have loads of freckles and was cheeky as heck?"

"Along those lines," Wyatt murmurs in a pensive voice, then quickly adds, "And you? Anything new on the horizon? You and Pete still hunt every night?"

"Pete, definitely. Me, less and less."

"Getting tired of the mindless fun with ladies, Dev?"

"Something like that." I chuckle, but I realize that what I'm saying is actually true.

"Well…" Wyatt's voice sounds surprisingly somber all of a sudden. "I couldn't agree with you more. My teammates, especially the rookies, are delighted with the groupies we get at the games, but I can't seem to find the pleasure in something so superficial."

"You never could, Wyatt. You're too darned focused. Football is your real mistress. I bet there has never been a woman who could distract you from your goal of becoming NFL Man of the Year."

There's silence on the phone, then Wyatt makes an awkward snort. "Yes, indeed. Anyway, back to you. Is your new, mature self still looking for someone who can cure the hole your treacherous ex left in your heart? Or did you find her already?"

Wyatt never liked Morgan. Which is probably the only thing that he and my sister ever agreed on.

"No, there's absolutely nobody in sight and—"

The door opens, and Laia steps in.

My words stick in my throat.

Her eyes dart to mine. "Sorry, I didn't realize you were still on the phone."

"No problem," I say.

"Is everything okay?" Wyatt asks.

"Sure. It's my assistant. We need to go through an urgent report together." I don't know why I called the Leonic discovery project urgent. I'm not meeting the client until Thursday, so I still have plenty of time to check Laia's notes. But somehow, after seeing Laia, I can't focus on my buddy's voice anymore.

Laia is still standing at the door, undecided whether she should leave.

I gesture her to come over to me. She walks to my desk, holding a folder pressed to her chest.

"I don't want to disturb you any longer," Wyatt says. "But, please do speak to Mike, okay?"

"'Kay, will do," I murmur without paying attention to my words. I could have agreed to convince Ellie to make a cheerleading performance for Wyatt at the Super Bowl. Anything really to cut the conversation with my friend short so that I can finally turn my attention to the report Laia brought me.

Mr. Leonic's company is a crucial acquisition for us, of course. It has nothing to do with Laia's flustered expression that makes her seem so charming.

Laia steps beside me as I lower the phone back to its place.

She puts the papers in front of me. "I've applied the color-scheme we agreed upon. I also took the liberty to look up some background information that you might find useful about the company's previous branding and ad campaigns." She points to the margins, which are filled with round, tightly scribbled letters. "I also summarized some of the passages. Here and there, I added my own thoughts when something appeared important."

My jaw drops. "You did this in only two hours?"

Her cheeks tint with a rosy hue. "Yes."

How is this even possible?

I scan her notes quickly, and my surprise deepens. All of Laia's comments about Mr. Leonic's branding problems hit the nail on the head.

Hayley could spend an entire afternoon on a task like this and only come up with half of what Laia delivered.

I like that Laia's handwriting is neat and easy to read. I can't help but notice she puts little fat dots that look like a heart shape on all her *i*'s. Her calligraphy seems in line with her slightly dreamy personality.

My lips twitch as I stifle my smile.

Laia's face tenses. "Sorry, I probably should've asked if you wanted those comments at all."

She must be thinking that I find her zeal amusing. "Ah, no," I say. "That's not what I'm smirking about."

"Then, about what?"

"The particular way you seem to punctuate your letters. It's very…*girlish.* But not in a bad way," I add hurriedly because Laia bites on her lip.

"I learned to write before I formally started school. From my cousin, Eva, who's only two years my senior. It seems that not even two decades of proper academic training can cancel out the teachings of an eight-year-old role model." Laia smiles, obviously relieved that I wasn't making fun of her initiative.

I roll my chair back slightly so I can peer up at her. "Is your cousin your role model?"

"Partially, yes." Laia nods. "She's a strong, resilient person, and I admire her for that."

"And I admire you," I say but correct my slip immediately, "…your talent of synthesizing. You did a great job with this report. And very fast, too."

"I'm glad you like it." Laia's forehead smooths. "I'm used to reading long texts and identifying the strong and weak points in them. Therefore, this discovery report was fun to do."

"You see, Laia? My gut told me you would enjoy your job as my assistant. And that you'd be good at it. I just didn't expect you to be *this* thorough." I add a grin to show that her overachievement is appreciated.

"You're weird." Laia claps her hand to her mouth. "Oh, sorry, I didn't mean it in the rude way it came out."

"Then which way?" I tilt my head to the side as I observe her.

She licks her lips and swallows. "I just meant that you aren't like I expected a boss to be."

"What was your expectation?"

Laia shrugs. "I certainly didn't think a CEO would give people a chance based on his instincts, especially if those hunches aren't backed up on paper."

"Well, you see…" I straighten because I'd like her to take my words seriously.

She steps back when I get to her eye level and interlaces her fingers in front of her belly. I smile, hoping her defensive posture is only a sign that she's still new here and not because I make her uncomfortable.

"I value personality even more than specific job experience. When things get rough, it's always one's character that pulls them through the hard times." I tap my chest. "Take me, for example. I dropped out of college because I believed that I had an idea worth going after. Many said I was crazy… But look at me now. It worked. And those who doubted me? They had to realize what a mistake they made."

Laia's shoulders go rigid. Her back is so straight it's as if someone were holding her at gunpoint. Slowly she raises her eyes to meet mine. "I think I owe you an apology."

"Why?"

"Because I do. I assumed that…"

"What did you assume?"

The eagerness in my voice surprises me. How bad can what she thought about me be? And why am I so curious to know?

"When you singled me out among the other candidates and invited me to the interview despite my will…"

I wince, and she gives me a small smile.

"Don't worry," she adds, "I'm not complaining that you did. But back then, I assumed you were one of those hotshots who has to have everything they want. The tabloid article I read about you didn't help. It depicted you as someone who believed he was…*la última Coca-Cola del desierto.*"

"Coca-Cola?" I chuckle. "I've never been compared to that. What does it mean?"

"Sorry, when I get nervous, I sometimes switch to Spanish. It's an expression my brother uses. It means the last Coke in the desert…as in…"

"An arrogant dunce?"

She blinks twice. "More or less. Sorry. I took the journalist's words for facts and didn't look deeper."

There's a respect in her eyes that I hadn't seen before now.

Her shy glint reminds me of when Cat realized I wasn't one to mess with and finally stopped peeing in my shoes.

Maybe comparing Laia to my furry companion again makes me feel an unexplainable sense of connection with her, because my chest warms.

I square my shoulders. "It's much easier for people to focus on my social life than on my work ethic."

She nods. "Yes, our *faults* are always more gossip worthy than our values."

I give an imperceptible shrug to ease the tension that settles into my neck.

I don't need to be ashamed about the choices I make in my private life because Laia clearly labeled them as faults.

My eyes flick to Laia's black hair. It accentuates her neckline like a blank canvas that enhances the first stroke of a paintbrush.

A strange prickle invades my palm as if my skin is itching to determine whether her locks are as soft as they look. I stick my hands into my pockets.

Maybe this is a good time to send Laia out for something. I can very well read the report she prepared for me alone.

"Laia, would you mind getting me something?"

"Something?" She rounds her brows.

"Yes. A…uhm, coffee."

Anything really—as long as she's gone, and with her, this unusual flutter in my chest.

Laia's dark brows pull even higher. "*Another* one?" She glances at the cup she brought earlier. Luckily it's empty so she can't see through my excuse.

"Yes, please."

Laia nods. "Of course, I'll be right back." She dashes to the door, making delicious little beats with her shoes.

I call after her. "Take your time, please."

Yes, please take your time.

When she's gone, I slouch back on my chair and massage my temples.

I hired Laia because she looked like the type of woman who would be interested in her job and *not* in me.

So why do I have this sudden pique of interest in her?

CHAPTER 11

(Laia)

I had assumed Devon exaggerated slightly when he promised me that, as his assistant, I'd gain more insight into his company's artistic processes than Fu would during his copywriting internship.

But it's only my second day in the office, and we're already on our way to participating in a preliminary concept evaluation meeting—whatever that means—with the head of the creative department himself.

Devon strides forward energetically, and I trot beside him, trying to keep up the pace.

It's a challenge because my elegant new beige pants keep shifting below my hip bones, creating ruffles just above my shoes. It's probably due to the flatter stomach I seem to have magically acquired.

Well, maybe not so magically.

I did skip lunch yesterday and today, because I've been

running all over the building and assisting Devon. It's unbelievable how much work the man is capable of handling without looking stressed or even tired.

No wonder his company is thriving.

"This is the area where the designers and writers usually hang out." Devon waves his hand around the large room located right below the executive floor.

My eyes open up in awe as I scan my surroundings. This is the first time I'm seeing what happens behind-the-scenes in the agency's creative headquarters. There are no traditional offices in this department, and no walls to cut up the space. The room looks like one giant lodging, flooded with natural light, and chock-full of quirky details, presumably intended to inspire the staff.

"We don't have permanent desks. Instead, the team members are free to roam between the modular work areas, including noise-canceling booths," Devon explains.

"Looks nice. This is where I would be spending my days if I hadn't accepted your offer, right?"

Devon adjusts the collar of his black shirt that he's wearing without a jacket and gives me a slanted glance. "Yes. Do you have regrets?"

"Nope." Indeed, I don't.

I might have thought copywriting would be the most suitable job for me in Devon's company, but I was wrong. If I were an intern here, I could only practice writing ad copies which, though creative, could become repetitive.

As Devon's assistant, however, I can try myself at various new things besides writing. Attending meetings with him is bound to help me with goal #6 from my bucket list: Be more extroverted.

Not to mention that, ever since I started my job, I'm more inspired than ever to write my romance novel. Snippets of dialogue pop into my mind during the oddest possible moments of the day. Before, I could sit for hours and nothing would come to me.

Like this morning when Devon briefed me about our day. I could clearly picture the best meet-cute for my story. It was almost as if Devon's presence had something to do with my muse—when in reality, there wasn't any connection.

There *can't* be any.

I eye the hammocks and the womb chairs placed in the corners, then my gaze moves to the chalkboards suspended from the ceiling.

"These are daily inspirational mantras. We change the quotes on them every week," Devon says.

I study a board that reads, "*The world is like a doughnut. Don't fuss about it. Just eat your part and enjoy it—Bill.*"

"Who is Bill?" I ask curiously, speculating whether the name refers to Bill Gates or Bill Clinton. Or maybe Bill Murray?

"It's the janitor who cleans the upper floors."

When Devon sees my surprised frown, he chuckles.

"Why are you so baffled? Anyone can have motivational nuggets to share. I encourage all employees to submit whatever they would like to display, then Luca, the department head, and I pick the best ones."

"That's kind of a cool idea." I smile at him. "It must give people a sense of pride to see their own words on these boards."

Devon nods. "It's a habit I introduced early on. I built this company to be innovative and fresh, and I'm conscious that to achieve that my employees must feel at ease here."

"At ease or at home?" I tease, pointing at a pink hammock.

"Our offices are often our homes away from home, and

a good office environment can help employees stay engaged, productive, and happy throughout the day."

Devon's words could go straight into a PR leaflet, but the conviction in his voice tells me he genuinely believes what he's saying. It's not lip service. His eyes light up with the specific fervor that only people who truly stand behind their ideas can have.

I suddenly feel proud that he chose me to work for him. He might be a tomcat outside work, but in the office he's a man I can look up to.

A small group of men and women stand around one of the tables, and they wave at us cordially as we approach.

I spot Fu among them. He gives me a bright, ear-to-ear smile, which makes me wonder whether he knows he got his position because I withdrew from our competition. Why else should he be beaming at me like that?

From the corner of my eye, I catch Devon watching me.

"Do you want to go over and talk to Fu? It's okay, I can wait," he says.

But the mild frown and a hint of coldness in his tone suggests impatience.

I quickly shake my head. "I don't want us to be late."

Devon's face smooths. "Good. There's still one place I want to show you before we join Luca and the others. I think you'll like this a lot."

I follow him with a curious anticipation.

"This is our '*Think*' space." Devon points at a raised area with a few armchairs and a massive bookshelf, the kind I'd gladly accept for my bedroom. "I've established this as a sort of inspirational garden where ideas can be invented and sketched out."

My eyes widen as I take in the exquisite collection of books.

They are not only industry-relevant manuals but all sorts of novels. I even spot one of my favorite historical romances by Philippa Gregory.

"You mean these books are for us to *read*? *While* we are at work?" I mumble.

I've always thought that reading helps set the mind free and nourishes creative thinking. I just never met a CEO who shares this vision of mine.

Devon's lips move into a crooked smile. "Okay, the voice you just used would tell me that you're a bookworm even if I hadn't seen your resume."

"Why? What voice did I use?" I ask self-consciously.

"Like an addict searching for her next fix."

The familiar sensation of blushing flushes through me. "I do like reading," I mutter.

"Me too." He winks at me. "I was just kidding. You're welcome to come down here and grab anything you want. You can schedule reading breaks throughout the day to refresh your mind. I know my busy schedule can be overwhelming."

He finishes his phrase with a grin that lures out his dimples.

I'm glad I'm looking at him from a side angle and not standing in front of him. Earlier today, when he flashed the same movie-poster-worthy smirk at me while striding past my desk, my diaphragm flinched so hard I had hiccups for almost twenty minutes.

Devon and I stroll further and enter a corridor that hosts a few glass-walled meeting rooms.

In one of them, five men, all dressed in black pants and crispy white Oxford shirts, are having a heated discussion.

"These guys belong to the accounting team," Devon says. "Though they have their own conference rooms on their floor, they often come up here for their meetings."

Accounting?

I study the blond guy in the group with increased interest. He might be Howard, Chelsea's new flame. She told me Howard is too hot for his own good. Truth be told, the man with long bangs and fleshy lips is pretty good-looking.

Obviously not as hot as Devon, though.

No, wait…where did this thought come from? Devon's dimples must be messing with my brain.

Devon ushers me to a square-shaped room which, except for an oblong table and a few backless, glossy electric-blue stools, has no other furniture.

An enormous cloud sculpture hangs above the door. Devon bows deeply as he passes beneath it.

There aren't many times when I'm glad to be petite, but this is one of them. I'd hate to bump my head on the white plastic fluff or duck down in these shoes.

Four people are sitting inside, three men and a woman.

The woman, a brunette with a short pixie cut and green geometric-print dress, explains something to the others with ample gestures.

As I cross over the doorstep, the cloud above me illuminates and beeps like a metal detector.

I jerk up, my eyes darting to the unexpected noise. However, my legs keep moving, and as a result, I crash into Devon's back.

Great heavens, what kind of workout schedule is this guy on?

It must be similar to the one my brother in the military is subjected to. Otherwise, his muscles wouldn't feel like steel.

I'm rubbing the painful spot on my nose when Devon turns around.

"Are you okay, Laia?"

When I don't answer, he takes hold of my wrist and pulls it gently away from my face. He leans closer, and his breath tickles my cheeks as he bends from left to right, examining me.

"No serious damage, just a tiny red mark. Does it hurt?"

"No, I'm fine." I lie as convincingly as I can. "Though your back is rather hard."

I really just want him to move back to an acceptable social distance. With his face so close, it's hard to ignore tiny details about him I'd rather not contemplate. Like how his stubble accentuates the cleft on his chin, or how he has extremely long eyelashes which, for some reason, instead of curling up bend straight, creating a curtain over his blue irises.

Devon arches his brows. "Well, I was on my high school football team, and our strength coach was big on pull-ups and push-ups."

Football? Of course. I should have known.

Guys as good-looking and self-assured as Devon must have been the stars all their lives.

"I'm not normally this clumsy." I want to assure Devon that, despite the bad track record I've set so far, I'm not accident-prone. "The beeping startled me. What's that cloud anyway?"

"That's our kudos cloud," a voice from the room intervenes.

I turn to find a gangly man with a pair of round glasses and thick auburn hair grinning at me.

"The cloud lights up when one of our clients praises us on social media. It keeps our morale high when we're breaking our brains about a new campaign," the man adds.

"Ah, wow. Clever little thing. A bit noisy, though." I return the man's smile.

He stands up and walks to me, extending his hand. "My name is Rick Anderson. I'm one of the photographers."

His palm is slightly moist as I squeeze it.

"Nice to meet you. I'm Laia Flores. Devon's new PA."

"Pretty name you've got," Rick compliments me.

Devon puts a hand on my shoulder. "Laia, you should meet the rest of the team, too. With Rick, you're familiar enough. We aren't here to share our private lives with each other."

His tone is the coldest I've heard from him since we met.

Not that I want to keep chitchatting with the photographer, but Devon's sudden mood perplexes me.

Many people ask me about my name. Devon questioned me about it the first time we met. So what's his problem? A look at Devon's stubbornly set jaw tells me it's better if I keep quiet about my disdain.

I nod and murmur, "Of course, Devon," and let him introduce me to the rest of the participants.

I learn that the brunette is called Anna, and she's a placement strategist. Anna has large amber eyes and her smile is so vast that it takes up two-thirds of her face. Hugh, a man with a hawk-like nose and frizzy bangs, is the copywriter. Luca, the creative department's head, is a bearded guy who wears red suspenders paired with a yellow shirt. All of them look like they're in their late twenties or early thirties, except for Luca, who must be roughly fifty.

After the introductory round, everybody takes a seat while Devon positions himself at the head of the table, standing.

"Show me what you've got for us, Rick," he asks, and the photographer spreads a few posters on the table.

"These are just the first ideas we're brainstorming about." Luca adjusts his suspenders with his thumbs.

"Yeah, all scripts are dummy copies," Hugh chimes in. "Once we sign off the visuals and the placements, I'll get to work on those sweet words."

I open my laptop and fire up Word, ready to take notes.

Katja warned me that in these meetings, many abbreviations are used. She instructed me to just type 'xxx' each time I miss one, and then ask Devon later what it meant.

I'm not sure if I'm supposed to jot down everything they say or just make a summary of the most important topics discussed. Based on my personal impressions about Devon, though, he'll be more interested in the conversation's essence instead of a word-to-word transcript.

Before I start to type, I take a peek at the posters myself.

My blood chills.

What are these atrocious images for? Do they have a contract to promote a horror movie? Why else would they use pictures of zombies carving their way through heaps of dirt?

I move my glance to Devon.

He frowns at the photos, rubbing the cleft on his chin.

"You don't like them?" Anna asks.

Her voice is as chirpy as a bird's morning song, but there's an anxious undertone in her words, as if she, too, is unsure about the visuals but afraid to speak up.

"I think they're great," Rick intervenes before Devon can utter a word. "The national committee wanted something strong. A bold, new way of reaching subgroups of smokers. These images will surely do that."

The sly smirk spreading on his lips, paired with the sinister images that must be his creation, makes me think Rick could be a perfect inspiration for a villain. A guy who looks normal but has a twisted, darker self.

"Oh, they will give them nightmares for sure," I mutter inaudibly.

Devon must have been looking at me, because while nobody else notices my comment, he does.

He walks over to me and bends down. "Laia, do you have something to say?"

"Nothing."

Warmth rushes to my head in a nanosecond, as all the faces turn toward me.

Shoot, why couldn't I just blabber to myself without moving my lips?

"No, no," Devon protests. "You have an opinion. Please share it with us."

Devon hops down on the empty stool beside me so his elbows rest on the table, and his chest turns toward me.

"Come on, Laia," Anna encourages me. "The Make Room is an honest space. You can say whatever you want here. Right, Devon?"

If that's so, why isn't she expressing her own concerns? I'm pretty sure she has them.

"That's right." Devon nods, his eyes not leaving my face. "I think you have something interesting to say."

I don't. Or maybe just the fact that I believe their photographer needs to see a therapist. The pictures Rick took are sick, abhorrent, and people won't be motivated to stop smoking by looking at them.

Of course, as honest as this meeting room might be, I can't give them my thoughts straight. I kick myself inwardly for starting this discussion.

"Okay, well…I'm not entirely convinced that this direct…uhm, slightly dark visual would appeal to me."

Rick's nostrils flare, and he pushes his glasses higher on his curved nose. "Are you a smoker?"

"No," I admit.

"Then how would you know what a smoker thinks?"

Ouch. Definitely a villain.

"Easy, Rick." Devon's tone is friendly yet categorical. "Let Laia explain."

Rick closes his mouth.

"Laia?" Devon smiles. "Go on."

"Rick is right, I'm not a smoker." I nod at the photographer. "But my mother is, and she would hate these pictures. I get that you need a fresh angle, but there are better ways to give people unexpected wake-up calls than shoving brutal images into their faces."

"Like what?"

It's Devon who asks, and his voice is filled with curiosity. His eyes are sparkling as if what I've said so far is to his liking.

"Like…" *Think, Laia, think.* Suddenly a YouTube video my younger cousin, Juan, showed me once jumps into my mind. "Like the 'Dumb Ways to Die' song."

"Which one?" Hugh brushes his bangs to the side to see me better.

"You know, *Du-uu-mb Ways to Dii-eee…*" I sing the catchy little rhyme to him.

As my jingle fills the room, all jaws drop around me.

Probably none of them expected me to actually chant the song to them, and while I'm doing it I realize it might've been a pretty stupid decision, after all.

I only sing in the comfy security of my shower. I'm not only submitting them to my terrible intonation, but my example probably has no relevance to their anti-smoking campaign.

I quickly cut my performance short and shrug. "I don't remember all the ways the song listed, but there was one about poking a grizzly bear with a stick and another about taking your helmet off in outer space. It's a song that a metro company used, I don't recall where. Maybe in Australia?"

Devon claps his hands. "I know this video. You watch all these adorable cartoon characters dying in the dumbest of ways, and then you get to the moral of the story, which is that the dumbest possible way to die is by slipping at the edge of a train platform or crossing over a train track."

"I know it too." Anna nods. "It isn't a bad inspiration for us. It shows that you can reach people when you do the unexpected." Her eyes move to the ceiling. "I wonder how we could do that with the placement itself. Cigarette packages are old. But so are TV commercials and posters…"

I draw in a sharp breath because an idea is coming to me.

A hint of a smile appears on Devon's lower lip. "I can see you've just had a stroke of genius, right?"

Can he read my face that well?

I nod. "Something popped into my mind, but I doubt it's genius."

Devon tilts his head, his eyes locking with mine. "Laia, why don't you give it a go?"

"Really?" I ask.

"Sure." Devon grins.

I can't possibly say my suggestion aloud. They'll hate it.

As if Devon senses my hesitation, he leans close and lowers his voice. "Laia, I know you didn't originally want this job. But maybe it's just what you need. If you took Fu's position, your opinion wouldn't be asked in meetings like this. But I promised you that, as my assistant, you'll try your wings at many things. So why not take this chance? Don't be afraid. Say what you want. Nobody will judge or belittle you. I promise."

His baritone stirs my stomach.

I'm not used to people taking a chance on me. Fine, I'll just tell them what I think. I wanted to be more extroverted, and this is an excellent chance to practice this skill.

If things go wrong, at least I'm already used to people laughing at me.

I let my gaze travel to the other participants. They, too, seem interested in knowing what I think. Even Rick blinks expectantly, which blue-pencils his previous hostility in my mind.

I return to Devon's blue eyes and nod. "Okay, but please don't laugh."

"Nobody is going to laugh," Anna assures me.

"Just say it. I'm sure it's good," Devon encourages me.

His kind words give me the final push I need, and I draw in a breath to tell them my idea.

CHAPTER 12

(Devon)

After the pre-con meeting is over, Laia gathers up Rick's horrendous photos.

"Where can I put these designs?" she asks.

"Straight to the bin," Rick answers before I can chime in.

"The bin?" Laia's forehead wrinkles with confusion. "But it's your work, Rick."

"I might have taken these pictures, but I can accept when my creation is deemed unfit." Rick flashes a theatrical, I'm misunderstood, grimace at Laia.

Rick's overly dramatic nature never bothered me before. I can usually attribute his preposterous gestures to being an artist and, all in all, a decent one.

Even if his zombie plan is a slip-up.

But today, his whole demeanor is getting on my

nerves. Why is he still *hanging* out here? The rest of the team has already returned to their own spaces, whereas he seems eager to continue the conversation with Laia. Rick's interest in Laia bugs me.

My assistant has a lot to learn about the company, my work methods, and everything. She needs a clear and focused head for that. And mingling with Rick could be a distraction.

I stand up and fetch the posters from Laia's hands. "I'll sort these out. Rick." I give him a somber stare. "I think you should join the others and start brainstorming which visuals could best support Laia's idea. But, please, leave the living dead out this time."

Rick adjusts his glasses and sniffs. "Sure, Devon. You're the boss."

His voice is slightly offended, but I couldn't care less. His primary responsibility is to deliver good campaigns for our clients, and during this meeting he failed to do that.

When Rick is gone, Laia peers up at me. "Are you sure you want to give my idea a try? Like seriously?"

"Why not? It's great." To be honest, Laia's suggestion isn't just great. It's terrific. "How did you come up with it?" I ask.

Laia shrugs. "You know I'm a bookworm, but so is my mom…though, she prefers thrillers, which I don't like. Anyway, I thought, if your ad tapped into the pool of people who like to read, across all genres, that would represent a huge chunk of the smoking market you plan to target."

I give her an appreciative smile. "You thought well. We can slip specifically designed pages toward the end of books, in both paperback and e-copies, which will increase our reach even further. Did you think of a slogan yet?"

A shy glint invades her eyes. "As a matter of fact, I did."

Of course, she did. If this girl isn't a wunderkind…

"Let me hear it."

Laia holds out a hand. "May I write on the back of one of the posters?"

I hand her one of Rick's creations, and our fingers brush against each other. A pleasant glow spreads on my palm from her touch. She really has delicate, soft skin.

Laia flips the poster around, then grabs a pen from the table. She draws a large rectangle, which she divides into two parts. After adding a few refining elements, I recognize the image of an open book.

"Here"—she points to the left page in her illustration—"we should have an exciting chapter ending, somewhere in the second half of the book. So that readers are chewing their nails to discover what happens at the end. Then here"—she drifts her finger to the other page—"would be our message…" She writes something, then pushes the poster to me.

I lift it and read out loud. "If you smoke, your story might end 15% before it should. Quit now." I chuckle. "This is good. Still a bit rough around the edges, but it's an excellent start.

"Really?" Laia's mouth shifts into a full-teeth smile.

I can't help but notice that this display of sheer joy fits her. The yellow dots in her irises dance and her cheekbones are put in evidence.

"Of course. Let's go back upstairs. I'll show you how you can log the details of the meeting and your slogan idea into our system so all team members can access it."

"I'm sure Katja can do that, too. I don't want to slow down your day."

"Nonsense. I've got a free hour, and it's best if you

learn it from me so you can always cater to my taste." I wink.

"To your taste?" Laia jerks back, and her voice jumps an octave.

"Yes. I mean that you can *satisfy my needs*. I'm your boss, after all." I smile.

Laia's face pales. "Which particular needs?"

What is it with her? It seems like my words make her jittery. Maybe she's still overwhelmed by the fact that I put her on the spot during our meeting.

"You know what?" I clasp the posters underneath my armpit. "It doesn't matter. Let's move to my office."

I touch Laia's back to signal that we should move. Her hair feels as soft as I thought it would.

My sister used to have a porcelain doll with similarly silky hair. Laia's petite figure, suggestive eyes, and slender waist remind me of that toy. And so does her aura. There's something sweet and wholesome about my assistant, as if she belonged to the world of fables.

Luckily, Laia moves forward before my mind can elaborate on this entirely fruitless topic.

I make us take the stairs, partially because I want to stretch my legs, but also because I'd like to avoid standing in a confined space with Laia. Last time it happened, her scent had an odd effect on me, and I don't want that again.

Once in my office, we settle on the fluffy black sofa that is part of my office's casual sitting area. Even though the rest of this room is the most traditionally laid-out space in our whole building, I've asked the designer to create this mellow corner where I can conduct agreeable talks with my clients.

It's my conviction that having a large table between me and my conversation partner sets a tense tone—precisely the opposite of what I like to have in my business relationships. Or even with my employees.

Over the years, I've used this sofa on more occasions than I can count. And at six feet of length, it never came across as cramped to me.

Until today.

Does Laia's rigid posture, as if she's afraid our bodies might brush against each other, make me think the sofa is too narrow? Or is it the way her body twitches whenever I bend closer to access her laptop?

"You see, this is the database you'll need to use," I explain, pointing at her screen. "All meetings need to be logged in here."

"Very well. I'll finish typing up my notes and save them." She nods, shifting her weight forward and slightly away from me.

My office door slams open.

The abrupt sound makes Laia flinch and turn her head to the door.

I, on the other hand, don't need to move to know who's walking in. There's only one person who can bypass Katja's impenetrable-guard routine.

Ellie's chipper voice fills the room before her heart-shaped face and bouncy curls appear. "Dev, sorry for the interruption." She treads forward in her sneakers without the slightest sign that she would regret disturbing me.

I straighten from the sofa and amble to her. When she's close enough, she throws her arms around my neck and plants a kiss on my cheek. "Katja said you'd be free to talk."

"Of course Katja would say that," I grumble. "For some reason, my secretary can't resist your charm. It must be those round eyes of yours. She can't see the mischief in them like I do."

Ellie sticks out her tongue, then giggles. "Well, good to know at least Katja is on my side. That snooty, blond assistant of yours always made me schedule an appointment. I'm truly relieved you let her go. Maybe now that you don't have a PA, I can finally visit you more often. Whenever I have lunch breaks, perhaps?"

There's a faint rustling behind my back, which tells me Laia must have stood up.

My sister really can't put a lock on her cheeky tongue. Why did she have to label Hayley as uptight in front of Laia? Now Laia might assume that I berate my employees behind their backs. Which is not true. Even if Hayley had a haughty air, I've never complained about her to my sister.

Except, of course, for that night when—

"Devon, would you mind introducing me?" Laia says.

I point at Laia, who shifts her weight from one foot to the other, eyeing my sister.

"Ellie, I'm sorry to crush your fantasy about blowing in here like a cyclone every time you feel like. In the future, you'll need to book an appointment with Laia…my new assistant."

Laia stands stiff and holds out her hand to Ellie. "I'm Laia Flores. Nice to meet you."

Her voice is less musical than I'm used to hearing from her.

Ellie gives Laia quick head-to-toe, then the corners of her mouth turn up. "Very nice, Devon, *finally* a normal person. Not some stick-legged mannequin."

She grabs Laia's hand and shakes it enthusiastically. "I'm Eloise Griffin, but you can call me Ellie. Everybody does."

Laia's eyes widen and her posture relaxes. "You're Devon's—"

"Sister, yes." Ellie nods. "Sorry for my mean comment about your predecessor. That chick might have been a bombshell, but she was interested in everything, except doing her job." She shakes her head to underline her disapproval.

"So, Ellie, to what do I owe the pleasure today? You stormed in like you had something crucial to discuss," I prompt.

There's a slight annoyance in my voice that surprises me.

I don't know if my irritation comes from the fact that Ellie made me leave my cozy couch, or my sister's comment suggesting I surround myself with top models.

It's not true that *all* my previous assistants were hotties.

My first PA was a man, in fact. And Hayley? I didn't even pick her myself.

I glance at Laia's olive skin and dark hair, and I can't help but feel grateful that I took the time that day to interview my candidates personally. Otherwise, my gem of an assistant would be writing ad copies, and I'd be stuck with one of the girlfriend-wannabees.

"You bet I have," Ellie bobs her head, and her short bangs get all tousled from her movement. She quickly smooths them with a hand. "I need to schedule my holidays for this summer at work. Are you up for a long weekend trip to Mexico in June? I wanted to go there with Cora and Hope. You can even invite Pete if he promises he won't hit on my friends."

"June when? I'm not sure, sis."

"Dev…" Ellie wiggles her finger at me. "You need some rest, just like the rest of us."

I shake my head. "It's not that. Wyatt called me. He might drop by during the summer, but he wasn't sure when…so unless I can also bring him along—"

"Absolutely not. Mr. Super Quarterback isn't invited," Ellie snaps.

"Well, technically, you've known Wyatt as long as you've known Pete. So if you consider Pete a pal…"

Ellie rolls her eyes, which are a similar shade to mine, only with a hint of green. "Exactly *because* I know Wyatt, I have the good sense of *not* being his friend."

Ellie's pocket beeps before she can continue badmouthing. She pulls out her pager and hisses. "Oh, shoot…I need to run back to work, sorry. I thought my new patient wouldn't arrive till later in the afternoon, but he flew in early. Stephanie will kill me if I make a client wait. The pregnancy hormones are making her an even meaner boss than she normally is."

"No problem." I shrug, secretly happy that I don't have to discuss Wyatt with my sister. It was stupid of me to bring him up at all.

Ellie pats Laia on her shoulder as if they're old girlfriends, and she didn't meet her only a second ago. "It was lovely to meet you, Laia. Whenever you want, I can give you a full-fledged user manual to this weird brother of mine."

Strangely enough, Laia doesn't wince under my sister's touch like she does each time I approach her. Instead, she meets my sister's gaze with a bright smile. "Yes, it was a pleasure to meet you."

Ellie gives me a kiss on my cheek. "See you soon, Dev."

Her head snaps to my desk just as she pulls back from me.

"Oh, no! Ellie, don't. Not again." I'm not quick enough.

My sister is already at my table, fumbling and shifting everything around until all of my objects stand in ninety-degree angles to each other, and my pencil holder is placed in the exact geometrical middle line of my desk—a fact that Ellie assures by measuring the distance from both sides twice with her thumb and index finger.

When she's done with her creation, she takes a step back, nods with a satisfied grin, then turns. Just as quickly as she rushed in, she disappears with a loud, "Bye!"

Laia throws me a curious glance when the door closes. "Your sister is super nice. But very energetic, isn't she? And she likes order."

I give out a bemused snort. "That she is. Ellie has an unflagging vitality. She's always been like that. I suspect she has a tick of OCD, too, but don't tell her I said that. She would strangle me before admitting she has control issues or that she's a pathologic neat freak. Especially since she works in a behavioral clinic, counseling others about how to be the best version of themselves. Anyway…" I smile because I want Laia to see that I love my sister despite her quirky nature. "Ellie is great. Sometimes her grit is annoying, like when I didn't have enough sleep. But most of the time, her vivacity is a blessing. There were times in my life where her high spirits kept me literally afloat."

Yes, I couldn't have made it through those years of constant sickness or my breakup with Morgan with my mental health intact, if I hadn't had my sister's support.

I don't understand why I had to share this nugget with Laia. It's none of her business that I had dark periods in my past.

Laia tilts her head, a weird glint filling her eyes. It's a mix of disbelief and sympathy.

Is she sorry for whatever hardship she imagines I might have endured?

I hate anyone pitying me. I've had my share of commiseration for a lifetime.

But Laia clears her throat and surprises me. "It's

important to have your family's support. Especially when life gives you a curveball. I have a sister and a brother. Plus my cousin, who is practically a sister. A pretty big safety net to fall back on. And this knowledge has helped me face some nasty blows, too."

Our glances meet, and Laia gives me a warm smile that assures me she means what she's just told me.

It seems I'll have to learn to interpret Laia's expressions better. She wasn't feeling sorry for me. She was showing empathy. This discovery makes the awkwardness I felt about slipping something personal evaporate.

Laia pivots to the sofa. "I'll get my laptop and finish my notes at my desk." She fetches her computer then glances up at me. "Once I'm done with the file, what can I do for you?"

"When you're ready, just go home. It's been a long second day for you. I'll see you tomorrow morning."

Laia walks to the door. Before exiting, she turns to me.

"Thank you, Devon. For taking a chance with me… you know during the meeting. I appreciate it."

I smile. "No thanks are necessary. You're a superb addition to our team. Don't forget, we start our morning tomorrow with an external client meeting. So dress nice, just like these past two days."

Laia's cheeks turn visibly rosier, and she adjusts the collar of her blouse. "I will do my best."

When the door closes behind her, I march back to my desk and sit down.

Laia's flushed skin still dances in front of my eyes as I turn on my computer. I shouldn't care that the pink color made Laia's eyes twinkle, but I do for some reason.

Laia has proven her worth during these past two days already. I can't start doubting my decision to hire her because I happened to notice her subtle beauty.

Also, it isn't a crime to tease my assistant. It's not like I intentionally made her flustered so I could admire her rosy cheeks. But since she did blush, and I'm not blind, I can acknowledge that bashfulness makes her look prettier.

Noticing it doesn't mean a thing.

CHAPTER 13

(Devon)

"You drive an R8?" Laia squeaks and bolts to my Audi, her heels clicking on the cement in the company's garage.

It's hard to suppress a grin. My car is a gorgeous sight, indeed.

Though not as gorgeous as Laia today.

She listened to my recommendation about choosing her clothes with care. Her twill dress pants are more than appropriate to meet Mr. Leonic in that teahouse downtown.

And they flatter her curvy hips immensely.

Laia is circling around my black jewel when I reach her. Her eyes are wide in admiration. "It's rude to stare when people drive past you, but whenever I spot an R8 on the streets, I can't help myself. This is the perfect gentleman's car."

I know exactly what she means. I had the same reaction each time I saw this model on car shows. Its body is like an expertly tailored men's suit that shows off a chiseled physique. That's why I decided to buy it, even though it eats like a monster.

I walk closer to Laia and point at the engine. "It's not just a pretty face, you know? This car can sprint from 0 to 60 in 3.5 seconds."

Laia nods. "Of course, with the exclusive 5.2 GT, it's no wonder. It must churn out a thrilling 560 hp, no? I bet when you get onramp, it blows by in an orchestral blur of sound and fury."

My thumb freezes on my car key as I fish it out from my pocket.

Laia knows the specs of my Audi?

"Are you a car geek or what?" I ask.

"My dad used to call me a grease monkey, but I guess car geek covers it. He was a soldier and more often in deployment than not. When he was at home, he would often repair vehicles for our neighbors. To impress him, I learned all I could about cars. First it was for him, but then with time, cars became my own interest. I'm even able to perform minor repairs on them."

Laia presses her lips together as if she feels uncomfortable for sharing her private life with me.

But I'm not.

I enjoy how my assistant keeps surprising me each day. I certainly didn't expect that she would genuinely love cars like I do.

I wink at her. "I'm also a fellow gearhead. My passion started when I was in the hospital at the age of eight. My roommate was a teenaged boy who would only talk about cars. We spent so many weeks together his obsession rubbed off on me."

Laia furrows her brows. "Why did you need to stay in a hospital so long?" Then she shakes her head. "Oh, sorry, I didn't mean to pry. Don't tell me if you don't want to."

The reference to my sickness had slipped out.

Women often insist that I should talk more about my past, but I rarely feel the need to oblige. What is it about Laia that makes me let her in on things I don't usually discuss with anyone?

I can't answer this question yet, and since I've already been chatty, I decide to add a bit more explanation.

"I used to have respiratory problems. Between the age of six and eleven, I spent several months in a pediatric unit. It wasn't the most fun part of my life, as you can imagine."

Laia's eyes fill with a compassionate glow. "That must have been hard as a young boy." Then as if she senses I don't like it when someone commiserates with me, she adds, "But at least you discovered a hobby you can still enjoy, no?"

She tilts her head to my Audi.

"Indeed." I grin. "This beauty can trick you into thinking you're charging around the last corner on the last lap to take the checkered flag, when in reality you're just heading to the store for milk."

Laia giggles. "It must be fun driving it. I heard an Audi spokesperson claim that they managed to capture the feeling of sitting down in the tub of a Le Mans race car with this model."

My eyes flick to her shoes. "I'd let you drive it if you weren't in heels."

"I wasn't aware that I'd be driving you around. Otherwise, I wouldn't have put on these shoes." The disappointment on her face is so palpable that I almost back out on my safety rule.

"It's fine." I smile encouragingly and step over to the

driver's side. "Next time we have an appointment in the city, you'll be sure to pack some back-up footwear."

"Wait a minute!" She lowers her laptop bag to the floor. She grabs the purse from her shoulder and ransacks it, before pulling out a black cotton sack. She dangles it triumphantly in front of my eyes.

"If you let me, I can drive."

"What is that?" I ask, a confused frown settling on my face.

She opens it and pulls out a pair of folded flats. "I put these in, just in case. My sandals are so new, I feared—" She claps her hand to her mouth. "Oh, sorry. I'm sure you don't care about my blister-prevention plan."

"No, no. Please go ahead." I chuckle. "It's fascinating to know that my assistant has a tactical vision. If you always treat your work with as much care as your feet, I'm sure you'll never have any problems."

She gives me a lopsided grin, then takes her flats into one hand. With her other hand, she reaches down and slips out of a sandal. She wobbles on one foot, while her glance bounces between the shoe she has just taken off and her flats.

I snort.

She looks like a stork trying to take a one-legged nap. Or rather like a cute, confused flamingo in her salmon-colored top.

Her eyes move to mine, and her lips curl up. "I look ridiculous, don't I? I'm afraid if I move, I'll skid."

Her smile has the same intense quality that a streak of morning light carries when it shines on someone's closed eyelids. Suddenly, from darkness, there is day.

And what a day.

"Maybe you should have done this in the car," I say,

still focused on channeling my thoughts away from her mouth.

"Sure, that would have been better. Could you maybe…?" She throws me a pleading glance.

I drop my bag, tuck the car key away, and step over to her.

I snake an arm around her waist so she can lean on me and finish changing her shoe.

The moment I embrace her, her scent envelops me. Though I've sensed the delicately sweet notes a few times before, I can only now decipher what they resemble.

Honeysuckles…

As I inhale, I'm grateful for the breathing reeducation I endured as a child, because without it I wouldn't be able to enjoy Laia's enticing bouquet.

Before I can stop myself, the words tumble from my mouth. "What perfume are you using?"

Her back muscles tense. "None, actually. I get prickles from any type, so I stopped using them a while ago." Her glance moves to my hand on her side. "You know, I actually meant whether you could open the car for me so I can…"

Why didn't I think of that? It would have been easier than embracing her. And more appropriate, given that I'm her boss.

I grab my car key, and when my Audi beeps, I say, "I'll help you hop over without stumbling, okay?"

Luckily, we only have a few feet to cover. After that, I can release her and reinstall the due distance between us.

As Laia lowers herself to the driver's seat, I force my eyes away from her legs and stare at my hands.

Laia changes into her flats, stashes her sandals in her bag, and gets up. "I'll just put this in the trunk with my laptop bag. Are you keeping yours with you?" she asks.

With her heels gone, I remember how short she is.

Being petite suits her. She doesn't need the heels to make her figure leaner. She's fine just the way she is.

"Yes," I answer.

My mind is occupied by the realization that I've never dated anyone as small as Laia. This might explain why I feel so protective of my assistant.

Laia slams the trunk and comes back to me. "All done. Do you want to sit in the back? Shall I hold the door open for you?"

I roll my eyes. "I prefer to sit in the front, and I can get the car door for myself. You don't have to behave like a professional chauffeur."

"Did you let your previous assistant drive your car?"

I narrow my eyes at her. Why is she interested in what Hayley did or didn't do?

Katja reported that she saw Laia talking to Fanta in the kitchen that first day. That woman not only has the oddest name of all my employees, but she's also the gossipiest one. I've wondered whether Fanta could be feeding information to the tabloids about my company. Some magazines have started to include precise details about my work when they babble about my private life.

The "Just for You" article Laia showed me this morning mentioned that I would be participating in the CCF gala. The reporter couldn't have learned about that from an official source, because the list of attendees hasn't been published yet.

But when I shared my suspicion with Sarah, my head of HR said I was paranoid. For some reason, Sarah likes Fanta despite her big mouth. Perhaps because the woman is a wizard of PowerPoint and not just a chatterbox.

I give Laia a warm smile, which I hope shows I'm not the jerk she might have heard I am.

"No. Hayley didn't know as much about cars as you do. I'd only let another fellow aficionado behind the wheel of my Audi."

Laia grins. "Then, I'm honored."

"We should get going," I say, grabbing my bag from the floor.

When we're both inside and buckled up, I ask, "So, how does it feel? Like Le Mans?"

Laia caresses the leather beside her legs and runs a finger over the fancy dashboard. She reaches for the levers on the side with an experienced hand. She adjusts the inclination of the backrest and raises her seat. She takes her time to find the perfect angling for the mirrors, too. Once she's done turning the driver seat into her own little universe, she blinks at me.

"Well, I've never driven a race car, but this R8 rolls around you, not under you. It's fabulous."

The dreaminess in Laia's voice is baffling. I certainly never heard it from any women while discussing cars. Morgan only got excited like this when she raved about Tiffany's new collection.

The absurdity of comparing my assistant with my ex-fiancée dawns on me. To avoid wondering how my mind could go so haywire, I turn to Laia. "Come on, switch it on. Otherwise, we'll be late."

Laia throws me a questioning glance as if she wants my final blessing. When I nod encouragingly, she lights up the engine.

My Audi gives out its usual roar, resembling a lion who is poked awake despite its will.

"What a sound. It's pure seduction," she giggles excitedly.

She looks as happy as my sister when Mom bought her

a hamster—minus the fact that said hamster bit Ellie's finger the first time she caressed him.

I set the GPS to the meeting's address, and we roll out of the garage.

Laia is so absorbed by driving that she doesn't say a word during our entire ride to the teahouse.

I don't mind our silence. It's a thrill to watch Laia handle my car, especially the content smile stretched on her lips. Without the distraction of small talk, I can focus my attention on how she switches gears and rolls the wheel.

She definitely has more grit as a driver than I'd have assumed based on her sweet, and sometimes shy, character. Though she stays in the speed limits, she deepens her foot on the gas whenever she can, obviously enjoying the Audi's horsepower.

The sight of her makes my belly buzz with a certain warmth. We share the same passion, so I can relate to her pleasure.

Or at least I hope it's only that.

We arrive at the Okinawa Teahouse all too soon. As Laia parks the car, I'm almost sorry that we must get out.

Devon, concentrate! You have a crucial negotiation now.

The reminder is much needed, because if I were to follow my gut, I would cancel the meeting with Mr. Leonic and ask Laia to take me to Los Angeles. Or anywhere else far enough so I can watch her drive for a few more hours.

CHAPTER 14

(Laia)

Ever since I read the *Memoirs of a Geisha*, I've wanted to travel to Japan for my honeymoon. But given that my soulmate is taking his time showing up, the Okinawa teahouse is probably the closest I'll get to this fantasy for a long while.

The place possesses an authentic charm with some East meets West flare. Stone, bamboo, and pictures depicting the flower arrangement used in tea ceremonies are thoughtful reminders of nature everywhere.

The tables are swooping booths, and each sitting area is mirrored by a cylinder of wood attached to the ceiling to create the sensation of trees in a forest. The tiny spotlights above them mimic the effect of the sun filtering in through the treetops.

A waitress in an elegant kimono leads us to a booth close to the large windows providing a dramatic panorama to the desert landscape.

We order Jasmine tea, and it arrives in a hand-painted ceramic tea pot featuring a panda.

Mr. Leonic is a man with a reddish beard and half-moon shaped glasses. He either has a nervous tick or feels uncomfortable about the branding changes Devon is proposing, because he keeps adjusting his blue tie even if it sits impeccably.

After listening to Devon for a few minutes, I decide it must be the former. There's no way Mr. Leonic doesn't see the pure genius in Devon's plan.

Later, as if to confirm my deductions, Mr. Leonic announces, "Devon, I'm impressed. You captured our image problem perfectly. I agree that we need to stop focusing on depicting singlehood as a problem. And I love the hopeful message that finding love is an adventure."

Devon nods. "Are you ready to move forward with the creative brief then?"

"Oh, yes." Mr. Leonic taps on the table. "The sooner, the better."

"Great." Devon exchanges a triumphant glance with me. "Then, let's discuss the details on how to continue."

My heart makes a small jump at the sight of Devon's smile.

After seeing him handle this deal, I have an easier time understanding how he could build Hudson Communications from scratch.

Devon is more than just an above-average handsome guy. He has strong magnetism. This has to be the key component of his successful career.

Where does his charisma come from?

Is it the way his chin darts forward decisively when he nods? Or is it the *I know what I'm talking about and I'm your savior* gleam in his blue irises?

Yes, this last aspect is definitely part of his charm.

If you glance into his eyes when he talks—or, in my case, watch from the side while paying meticulous attention to keeping my jaw from gaping—you get the feeling that Devon could be the man you need to solve all your problems.

The only man you'd ever need.

I pinch the skin above my wrist underneath the table to snap myself out of the moony haze. What am I even thinking?

Devon has the perfect manners to present his business ideas and a ravishing smile that accompanies them; it doesn't mean I should fall under his spell.

I must remember I'm only allowed to appreciate him as my *boss*.

As a *man*, Devon couldn't be farther away from my ideals. His man-about-town lifestyle is the antithesis of how I view relationships. Had we met outside of work, I'd have probably run the other way.

I'd better focus on this each time I feel these annoying butterflies in my stomach.

"… with all these details cleared, I'll head back to my company and announce the good news to my associates." Mr. Leonic takes the last sip from his cup then stands up.

What? Is the meeting over?

I peek at my watch and realize we've been sitting in the teahouse for over an hour. It seemed so short. Maybe because I spent a chunk of the time pondering about Devon?

Devon straightens and shakes Mr. Leonic's hand. "Happy to have you on board."

Mr. Leonic turns to me. "It was a pleasure to meet you, Ms. Flores. Thank you for the great meeting."

His good-bye is so warm I almost forget my role was about equal to the decorative cushion on the bench.

When the man leaves, I glance at Devon. "Shall we go?"

His eyes move to my cup, which is still full. "Why don't we sit back and finish your tea first? Or aren't you thirsty?"

"No, I am." In truth, my throat is parched. "I just thought that if I couldn't contribute in any meaningful way to your presentation, at least I should avoid bothering you with my loud gulping."

He eyes me with his brows arched. "You can't be serious, Laia. Didn't you hear how much I borrowed from the background research you did on the dating company? I even quoted one of your comments: '*Finding love can't be a burden, it must be viewed as an adventure.*'"

My cheeks warm as Devon repeats the words I scribbled on his report. "The idea of rebranding the dating company unleashed my romantic side. I clearly let myself get carried away. I'm sure those words weren't the decisive factor for Mr. Leonic."

Devon lowers himself back to his seat, and I follow his example.

He pushes my cup to me but keeps studying me with a perplexed grimace. "I think your phrase, though sappy, resolves the entire problem Mr. Leonic had with his firm's image. Why dismiss what you wrote? You don't like to give yourself credit, Laia. You aren't proud enough of what you do. Of how great you are."

Now my skin literally burns.

I gawk at my interlaced fingers. "I'm not the most self-assured person when it comes to my achievements, that much is true. Though I'm working on becoming more confident. It's just difficult because"—I raise my head to meet Devon's gaze—"there aren't that many things I can boast about."

His eyes widen. "What are you saying? You have a

great degree. You have an excellent work attitude. Superb instincts with creative stuff. Besides, you're a total catch." He pauses and clears his throat. "I mean professionally, of course."

"Of course. How else?"

I press my lips together, angry at myself that this bitter tidbit could escape. And for the ridiculous frustration that brews in my stomach after Devon's well-meaning words.

Did I wish he'd say I was a catch as a woman?

I can't be *that* stupid, can I?

Devon stares at me. "Laia, I…"

"Devon Griffin! Oh. My. Golly. If this isn't a coincidence."

The soprano belongs to an all-legged blonde wearing a scarlet top, knee-length boots, and shiny black pants. Her thighs are so perfectly sculpted I wonder whether she's a model for ThighMaster.

Devon pales.

He jumps up, and his hasty movement shakes our table —lukewarm droplets of tea land on my hand.

The blonde is already in front of our booth, bouncing on her offbeat heels, her zebra-striped coat casually thrown across her forearm.

Why she needs a coat, I can't imagine. The outside temperature surely doesn't call for it. It must be part of that statement-making fashion strategy Chelsea always chews my ear about.

"Aren't you even going to greet me, Dev?" The blonde peers at Devon from under her lashes, her mouth pulled into a feigned pouting, which evidences the Marilyn Monroe mole above her upper lip.

"Hello, Morgan," Devon says.

The blonde smiles. "That's better. It's been a long time

since we ran into each other, huh? A couple of years, I think."

"Four," Devon answers. "How is Theo?"

"Good. Always on some business trip." Morgan rolls her eyes and makes a dramatic wave. "So work, work, work. Pretty boring."

"Oh, I see," Devon murmurs.

Morgan brushes her waves behind her ears. "I'm meeting a friend here, but she's late. Do you mind if I sit with you while I wait?"

Devon's face tenses. "Actually, we were just about to go."

Were we? I thought I was supposed to drink my tea. Though there's probably not much left in my cup anyway after Devon spilled half of it.

My eyes bounce between their faces.

Who is this woman? One of Devon's flings?

If so, then why does she seem happy about seeing him, while Devon looks as if he swallowed a fishbone and it stuck in his throat?

Morgan exchanges his words with a smirk, but she doesn't move. "Why are you in such a hurry? I'd love to catch up. We could do that at the upcoming CCF gala, but—"

"CCF? How do you know I'm attending it?" Devon's eyes widen.

Morgan bats her lashes. "I heard it from Theo. He's invited, too."

"The attendees' list wasn't released yet," Devon says.

Morgan's lips open and close. "Theo read in a newspaper that you'll be there."

The small, local tabloid story is the only one to run this story so far, so unless her husband is a fan of female gossip magazines, this is a lousy lie.

On my first day, I set up a permanent search option for Devon's name and Hudson Communications on my laptop. It trawls all relevant newspapers, industry journals, and even those publications that I usually consider bush telegraphs—a necessary addition, due to Devon's lifestyle. I think Morgan spotted this information about Devon herself, but for some reason, she doesn't want to admit it.

Devon either doesn't remember me showing him the article this morning or he doesn't want to call Morgan on her fib. In any case, he simply replies, "I see. So, Theo is going?"

Something in Devon's voice tells me he isn't thrilled about the prospect of bumping into the guy. Could it be that Devon had an affair with this woman behind her husband's back?

Morgan rolls her eyes. "Unfortunately not. Why should my workaholic hubby participate in a luxurious event that might finally be fun for his plus one? No, Theo chose to travel to Alaska that week to represent some boring food company."

Devon's tight jaw relaxes somewhat. "CCF isn't a big deal for lawyers anyway. Theo isn't missing out on much."

"The same can't be said for me."

The bitterness in Morgan's voice is palpable, and for a brief second, I feel sorry for her.

A sensation that dissipates immediately when she peers down at me with a challenging look on her face.

The daring glint in her eyes forces me to stand up.

A smirk appears on her lower lip as if she's satisfied she made me do something without having to utter a word.

Suddenly, I get the distinct feeling this woman has been the queen bee for a good chunk of her life. Which is probably the reason she's upset about not getting her way with her husband.

Girls like Morgan made my school years miserable.

Keeping her green eyes locked with mine, Morgan asks Devon, "Don't you want to introduce me to your girlfriend?"

My scalp prickles.

First, because I'm super irritated that she doesn't even address me.

And, second, her insinuation that Devon and I could have something other than a business relationship doesn't unleash the inner protest I believe it should.

I'm about to correct her about her false assumption when Devon says, "I'd rather not. You'll have to excuse us, Morgan, but Laia and I need to go."

When I don't react, Devon puts his hand between my shoulder blades and gives me a gentle nudge. Then he withdraws his hand, picks up his bag, and steps out from our booth.

Without his touch, my mental fog clears, and I gather my own things. I throw a quick glance at Morgan and mutter an, "It was nice to see you, bye," before hurrying out behind Devon.

Morgan calls out, "Nice running into you both."

Devon doesn't turn, but I make a quick swirl and catch Morgan squinting at my computer bag. Then her eyes wander to Devon's back, and a longing glint fills her eyes.

Why didn't Devon tell Morgan I'm his assistant?

Devon doesn't let me ponder this mystery. After swiping his credit card at the counter, he goes straight to the door and holds it open for me. I'm not sure why, but I scurry outside like a mouse being chased by a cat.

As I pass Devon, my shoulder brushes his chest. It's lucky I switched my heels to flats because I get wobbly knees from the brief contact with him.

We walk to Devon's Audi in silence.

Should I ask him what his behavior was all about? Would it be unfitting for me to inquire about who the woman was or why he didn't tell her the truth about me?

My curiosity wins the battle.

As soon as we settle in his car, with me in the passenger seat this time, my question is out.

"Who is Morgan?"

Devon clicks his safety belt shut, but he doesn't say a word. Just when I think he won't answer at all, he says, "She's an old acquaintance. No one important."

"An old acquaintance who needs to think I'm your girlfriend?" My tone comes out throatier than I'd prefer.

Devon's eyes dart to mine. "I didn't say you were my girlfriend."

Oh, fudge. It's true, he did not.

"But you didn't deny Morgan's assumption either. Were you trying to make her jealous?"

Devon's jaw steels. "No. I just didn't want to waste time with useless chitchat. I'd rather get back to the company and finish up."

"Of course," I mumble.

As if he considers our discussion closed, he adjusts his seat and mirrors to their original position and switches on the engine.

I'm so ashamed of my last question I can't even enjoy the smooth style with which Devon steers us toward Hudson Communications.

It was silly to assume Devon might have been trying to make a stunning woman like Morgan green-eyed with my company.

This idea shouldn't bother me, but it does.

While we move through the traffic, I dare a quick, slanted glance at Devon. He looks sunk in his thoughts which, based on his brooding expression, must not be cheerful. Why is he so grumpy?

Is it because of Morgan? Who can she be?

I should ask Chelsea if she knows her. My friend has read every available tabloid article on Devon. Maybe she came across the woman's name somewhere.

The thought of Chelsea reminds me what my roomie told me about my good judgment toward men. She was confident that I'd remain unaffected by Devon.

I had been so convinced Chelsea was right.

But what about now? What is this mushiness in my belly?

CHAPTER 15

(Devon)

"Why can't I just focus on these wretched numbers?"

My annoyance is so intense I speak loudly despite being alone in my office.

It's Friday, and I want to start my weekend. But for that, I need to finish this darned report. A task that seems impossible due to my lack of focus.

I lower my pen and rub my eyes.

When I reopen them, a line on a graph, which should simply state the forecasted sales our campaign predicts, reminds me of a black tendril.

A growl leaves my throat.

Great, now I'm not only speaking to myself, but I'm also unable to get through this budget estimate without envisioning Laia's dark curls as patterns on my graphs.

What's going on with me?

My cell phone vibrates.

I flip it open, and my sister's frustrated voice thunders

at me. "Did you speak to Wyatt? When can I finalize our vacation plan?"

Ellie's question manages to push Laia's face aside in my mind. I shift back on the chair and put my elbow on my desk for support.

"No, I didn't have a chance to talk to him yet. But I will, I promise."

"You better," Ellie growls. I hear a few loud knocks and clinking sound on her end.

"What are you doing, sis?"

"Me? Nothing. Just dusting a shelf in one of the therapy rooms." Her voice sounds distracted, as if part of her brain is absorbed by her cleaning task.

I stifle a laugh and suppress the question of whether she lost a bet with the janitor.

My sister is a neat freak who keeps her kitchen appliances in perfect order—we're talking containers stacked by shape and color, and then arranged concentrically. The idea of a book out of place or a dusty shelf might not be a tragedy to me, but to my sweet unconventional sis, it certainly is.

"I'll try to reach Wyatt this weekend," I say soothingly. "I just had a strange day yesterday so—"

"Wait, what happened?" Ellie's responsible therapist hat is back on. "I should've picked up on the weird tone of your voice straight away."

"There's nothing weird about my tone," I snap, proving her point.

There's silence on the line, then Ellie asks, "Did something happen with your assistant?"

"My assistant? For heaven's sake, Ellie, why would you arrive at this conclusion?"

"Well, when Hayley tried to seduce you, you also sounded this troubled. Not that I blame you. I'd have been the same if a co-worker came at me with the monthly finance report, while dressed like a sex-bunny." Ellie giggles.

Why did I ever confide in my sister about what Hayley did?

"It's nothing to do with Laia," I sigh. "Laia is great. More than great. Hayley's bravado is the last thing I'd expect from her."

Even if, Laia would probably look incredibly hot in a costume like—

I kick myself inwardly before my pathetic brain can continue with this idea.

"Ah, I'm glad to hear this," Ellie says. "Your new assistant seemed very nice. I'd be disappointed to hear if she turned out to be dopey."

"So what, liking me would make Laia a moron? That's what you're implying?"

I don't know why my question has a sharp edge.

Ellie chuckles. "Look who got all touchy-feely. Don't worry, that's not what I meant. I think you're a good guy, brother. It's a pity you don't let anyone see it. At least not since that witch, Morgan, broke your heart."

Mentioning my ex makes me recall yesterday's meeting.

"I bumped into Morgan yesterday. We spoke."

"Don't tell me you're rekindling with her?" Ellie's voice is alarmed.

"No, of course not. She just happened to be in the same teahouse where Laia and I had a client meeting. She's still married to Theo."

"That dullard, ah yeah."

Her comment lures a smile to my lips.

Ellie is incredibly loyal, as a friend and as a sister. Even if she used to like Theo, as soon as she learned that

Morgan cheated on me with him, my sister totally wrote the dude off.

"So how was it seeing Morgan?" Ellie's chirpy tone is tuned down to a softer timbre that somehow reminds me of Laia's way of speaking.

"Nothing special," I say automatically, because my thoughts are revisiting the first time I heard my assistant's voice.

"Really?" Ellie gasps. "You sound like you mean it."

"I do," I answer, and while I utter the words, I realize they're correct.

Then why did I feel so sullen after the teahouse? If it wasn't Morgan's presence, then what?

"I'm happy for you," Ellie says. "That girl was the worst thing that ever happened to you. She turned you into a commitment-phobic. But you're not like Pete. You're—"

A loud alarm resounds on the phone.

"Ah, dang it, I need to go," Ellie grumbles. "We're having a general fire training in the health center, and apparently, I'm supposed to be heading to the nearest exit."

"Go, go. Hone your rescue skills. I'll wrap up here and then head out."

"Okay, have a good weekend, Dev. Speak to you later."

"Later, sis."

I switch off my phone, thanking my lucky stars that Ellie's establishment made the entirely unreasonable decision to organize a fire drill on a Friday evening. It saved me from listening to a lecture.

Whatever my sister thinks about Pete and the kind of life he introduced me to, it sure helped me get over Morgan.

For good it seems.

I was bewildered to see my ex, but I didn't feel enraged, hurt, or even mildly attracted.

I did think her hairdresser went too crazy with her highlights. Was it because Morgan stood close to Laia?

A flashing symbol on my screen draws my eyes. I have a new email from Laia. I click it open, and my jaw drops.

She's already finished the briefing documents I assigned this morning. This girl is truly a treasure. I should go congratulate her on her quick work.

Just as I stand up, I hear chatter in the corridor. Katja must still be in the office.

I lower myself back into my chair. I'd prefer to give my kudos to Laia when my secretary is gone. Probably because Katja pointed out that I seem to check on her and Laia way more often than I used to with the others.

Which is not even true.

Or perhaps it is.

But I have more things to discuss with Laia than with my previous assistants. In a week, she has made herself a valuable resource I can lean on and whose opinion is worth listening to.

I'll check a few spreadsheets and wait till Katja leaves.

Then I can go out and compliment Laia.

CHAPTER 16

(Laia)

Katja zips her large brown handbag and shoulders it, while her free fingers strike a few keys to shut down her computer.

I take this as my cue that the day's about to end and let out a relieved sigh.

It's going to be my first, well-deserved weekend as an employed woman.

I stretch my arms above my head and roll my head in small, circular motions. I've been sitting at my desk almost the entire day, and my body craves some movement.

Though the task I've been assigned to was enjoyable, I don't mind calling it a night.

Just as I push back my chair, Katja stands up and looks at me.

"What are you doing, Laia?"

"Getting ready to go home?" I reply, phrasing my words more as a question than a statement, because something in Katja's startled tone makes me suspect I might've misinterpreted the situation.

"Laia, *I'm* going home, but as his assistant, you must wait till Devon is done. He might have sent you home earlier on Wednesday, but you won't have that privilege all the time."

She gives me an earnest you're-not-to-leave nod that makes her trademark braids drift forward.

Once again, I'm surprised just how similar she looks to how I pictured Ranyevskaya's character in *The Cherry Orchard*. One day, when we're on friendlier terms, I'll ask her where her family is originally from.

"No problem." I smile as if her request didn't weigh on me, then trying to hit a casual tone, I add, "Just out of curiosity, how long does Devon usually stay? I hope not too late, right?"

Almost an hour ago, Chelsea messaged me that she'd already finished her day and asked me to go out for a cocktail and dinner with her colleagues from accounting.

From the winking smiley she added to her text, I deduced that the famous bulging-suit Howard will be with her.

Since she'll probably stay out until late, I can use our comfy sofa to curl up, set the living room stereo to a jazz station—which Chelsea hates, but I love—and get on with writing my romance novel.

Katja opens her arms. "It depends. Hayley used to stay till very late with Devon..." A frown appears on her forehead, then, as if something just occurred to her, she strolls over to my desk and leans toward me. "Laia, let me give you a piece of advice. Watch out with Devon, okay?"

Her voice is low and has, for the first time ever, a hint of motherly concern.

"Why?" I ask, puzzled.

Katja gives me a *there's no use pretending* look. "My dear, I may be old enough to be your mother, but I'm still very sharp. The change in your clothes didn't escape my attention. But I need to warn you like I warned Hayley. Devon Griffin isn't what you need. As a boss, yes, he is great. But you should not get dreamy about him as a man. Hayley didn't listen to me, unfortunately."

Again, this Hayley.

I might've decided that what Devon did or didn't do with his previous assistant doesn't concern me, but after Katja's comment, I can't avoid getting to the bottom of this gossip.

I straighten from my seat and level Katja's gaze. "What exactly happened to Hayley?"

Katja inhales, then releases the air with a loud swish. "Hayley had a major crush on Devon. I cautioned her not to get involved with him emotionally, but she laughed at my concern. Then one morning, I came into the office, and Hayley was gone."

"Gone? Just like that?"

Katja gives me an uneasy smirk. "Devon decided to let her go."

My stomach tightens.

Katja either doesn't know all the details, or she doesn't feel like sharing them with me. In any case, what she said so far doesn't contradict the rumor I heard from Fanta.

"Do you think I'm like Hayley?" I force my voice to sound disdained by her accusation, even if my innards are cramped with a pang of odd guilt.

Katja throws a quick cross on her chest. "Heaven forbid, no. Hayley was a whole different ball game. I see that you're here because you want to work, and you do an excellent job."

"Ah, thanks."

"But"—Katja lifts a finger—"I also noticed how you look at Devon each time he steps out of his office."

I shake my head. "I don't ogle him if that's what you're implying."

Really, I don't.

I might've forgotten my glance on him once today, when he handed a document to Katja, but that was only because…I don't know. Probably my eyes were exhausted, and they'd glazed over.

Katja sniffs. "Perhaps not. Then call me overly chary. Still, I think it's wiser if I warn you. I've worked for Devon for five years now. The man has a bone-deep appeal that could charm the spots off a Dalmatian. Don't tell me you didn't perceive it."

I shrug, avoiding Katja's gaze.

I can't deny that I know what she is getting at. Not after the thrills Devon's proximity triggers in me.

"Okay, so Devon has that certain, *je ne sais quoi*. So what?"

"So what?" Katja throws me a concerned glance and pats my shoulder. "So, he's a dangerous guy to be around."

"But you just told me I need to wait till he finishes work," I snap, confused.

"Yes, you're his assistant, so you don't have a choice. But limit your interaction to professional topics when you're with him, okay?"

I swallow and meet Katja's light-blue eyes. "I know how to protect myself against charming guys like Devon."

Katja gives out an amused snort.

There's a loud noise from Devon's office, as if he dropped a book or something. Katja's eyes flick to his door, and she waits a few seconds before answering. "Our boss isn't a real womanizer, you know. Just someone who thinks fleeting pleasure is the preferable choice. I doubt he ever means to hurt the women he gets involved with."

I put a finger to my chin. "Didn't you start this whole discourse to make me wary about him?"

Katja chuckles. "You're right, Laia. But I don't want you to assume that Devon is mean. He isn't. Exactly because he is a great guy and has this innate kindness and amiability, he manages to disarm women. But falling for him would set you up for heartache, so please keep your head leveled around him. Don't play with a player, or you will get hurt. Be an exceptional assistant to him, but nothing more. Then your future in the company will be bright."

She sears me with an I-don't-want-to-see-you-hurt stare.

I plaster on a smile I don't entirely feel. "I wasn't planning on anything else, but thank you for your concern."

Katja gives me a relieved glance. "Great, now I feel calmer leaving you here." She turns and walks to the elevator.

I slouch back in my chair.

I can protect myself from Devon and his smile. I can.

But as his last charming grin pops into my mind, a warm glow starts in my chest and flares quickly to a decisive heat. The more I savor the memory of his dimples, the more the puzzling hotness migrates to my belly. I press my hands on my abdomen, trying to offset the unfamiliar feeling that brews in me.

Given my lack of experience with men, desire is uncharted territory for me, so I'm not sure what to make of the sensation.

To change my thoughts, I take a notepad from my drawer.

I'll just scribble down my rough ideas for my romance.

I can flesh them out into proper paragraphs when I'm at home.

I focus on the white paper and abandon myself to the love story shaping in my mind. The words flow from the tip of my pen, and my previous worries quiet down.

Perhaps I should be grateful for the sensations Devon stirs up in me, since they seem to help me depict the attraction my protagonists feel for each other.

After I'm done recording everything, there's still no movement from Devon's office.

My stomach growls, signaling what I already know. It's late, and the best thing would be to go home and have dinner.

I straighten and grab the tea mug I brought to the office. It shows my favorite scene from Disney's *Beauty and the Beast* remake—the dance.

The cup was a gift from Eva. My cousin joked that if I drink from it every day, it will remind me that I shouldn't settle for anything less than my own fairy tale.

I trot to the kitchen. Some warm liquid in my belly should curb my appetite. I choose the Winter Nights tea blend, because I'm attracted to its Christmas-y fragrance, and pour hot water on it.

Chelsea always scolds me that I use too much water for one teabag. She claims it dilutes the aroma. But I can't help it. I have an esthetic need to see a cup full. Not filled to half or two-thirds, but brimming.

I inch toward my desk, wondering when Devon will decide to call it a night. My chest stutters as I imagine his tall figure stepping out of his office. I squeeze my mug tighter and blink at the cartoon characters.

Yes, I'll settle for nothing less than my own fairy tale. Definitely not for a fleeting sensation of heat.

CHAPTER 17

(Laia)

"Careful or you'll spill it."

Devon's voice spooks me, and it's only by a miracle that I don't slosh the hot liquid on myself. I lower the mug to my desk and glance up.

He's sitting in my chair, legs crossed, back in a relaxed posture. And, horror of horrors, he has a piece of paper is in his hands.

My piece of paper. My outline.

I silently pray that he hasn't had time to read anything yet.

But as my eyes move to his scrutinizing expression, I know my prayer is in vain.

Devon holds out the paper and his lips curl up. "I didn't expect the briefing about the HGT Sportswear campaign to sound this…huh, what's the word…*romantic*."

Heat rushes to my head, and I launch forward, snatching my notes from him. I hide the paper behind my back, while I drop my gaze to my keyboard.

"The HGT briefing is done, and so are the other two files you requested. I uploaded them all to the server and sent an email to notify you."

"I know. I read your message."

"You did? Then why did you snoop around at my table?"

I didn't intend for my voice to sound quite so accusing. Devon is the owner and, as such, has every right to check what I, or any other employee, is doing at their desk. I can only blame my harsh tone on my embarrassment.

Devon read through my romance notes. I could sink into the ground.

Devon jumps up from my chair. "I'm sorry, Laia. I didn't mean to pry into your private business. I wanted to congratulate you on finishing your briefing documents so fast. But since you weren't here, I decided to sit and wait for you. Then that interesting title drew my attention. *Love's True Power…*"

He murmurs the provisional title of my book with such a throaty baritone that the little hairs on the back of my neck rise.

He tilts his head, his eyes searching mine. "Are you writing a novel?"

There is no point in negating the evidence. He's already read my whole plot outline.

At least I've switched the hero's eye color into a trustworthy brown, instead of the cornflower shade I initially envisioned.

I slide my mug toward my screen, so I can lean my hip on the desk without the risk of capsizing my tea. When I feel the support of the massive wooden table, I peek up at Devon.

"Yes, I'm trying to put together the first draft. Writing a

book has always been on my bucket list. It's a romance, but you must've figured that out from the title."

Devon nods. "I have. Interesting…so you want to become a romance writer?"

His tone is full of curiosity, and there's no hint of reprimand in it, even if it could be understandable. He caught me working on a private project during my working hours.

I decide to answer honestly. "I'd love to write the stories that are in my head, yes. Do I want to become a full-time author? Maybe. For now, I'm just treating my novel as an occasion to turn a dream into reality. Once it's ready…or rather, if it ever gets ready, I'll think about what to do with it."

Devon furrows his brows. "Why the 'if'? Your outline seems pretty detailed already. Having a strong story grid is a substantial step for a great novel. A bit like a briefing document for an ad campaign."

"Yeah, well, it isn't so much the plot, but the characters that will give me pain." I lower the paper to my desk.

"Why is that?"

I shrug. "I'll only be able to draw upon my fantasy when I can describe—"

I stop just in time, realizing my lack of experience with men isn't a topic I should be discussing with Devon.

First, because I'm his assistant, so my extra-curricular activities (or the entire lack thereof) don't concern him.

Second, Katja warned me to stick to professional topics with Devon.

And, third, that unsettling warmth in my belly I thought I'd banned for good is back now, stronger than ever.

"Describe what?" Devon's smile grows bigger.

He obviously isn't out of his element in this discussion.

"Describe how…" *It feels losing oneself in the kiss of a man.* "…how a man, uhm thinks."

Devon lifts a brow. "How a man thinks?"

"Yes." I hurry to consolidate my excuse. "I'm planning on using dual points of view, so I'll do chapters from the heroine's and from the hero's angle. But I fear that depicting how a man reasons could become a challenge."

Phew, I think I managed to correct my slip.

And what I said is even real. I do fret how I'll be able to identify with a male protagonist.

Devon pulls my notes closer to him and scans my writing. "Why don't I help you with that?"

"With what?"

His eyes leave my outline, and his gaze locks with mine. "Teaching you how a man thinks."

"That's not possible," I mumble, inching backward ever so slightly.

"Why not? I'm a guy."

"Yes, I know that you're a guy." I force my voice to sound even.

We are, after all, discussing my ambition to write a book, and not something that should make me blush, even if the warmth is already oozing into my skin.

"But you're also my boss. It would be bizarre to pick your brain about how I should set up my male protagonist."

Devon stares at me as if he doesn't see a problem with it at all. "I, on the other hand, think it could be fun. I love artistic challenges, and there are only a few things more creative than conceiving a novel out of thin air."

I shake my head. "No, it's not worth your time."

"Nonsense," Devon waves, "you said that writing a book is on your bucket list, right? If you embrace your dream, you'll reap great benefits. You can even channel your creativity into your work here. So, as your boss, I feel obliged to help you. What do you say? Can I coach you to become an expert on men's thoughts?"

CHAPTER 18

(Devon)

My offer isn't that big of a deal, really.

When the idea of Hudson Communications first popped into my mind, I didn't have anyone to bounce my ideas off. It was a lonely, agonizing process of birth.

Much like what Laia will face if I don't give her a hand.

It won't cost me much effort to introduce her to a male's perspective on life and women. But it'll make her feel empowered when she writes her story.

Laia stands still, glaring at me.

I meet her gaze as nonchalantly as I can while I wait for her answer.

"I don't know, Devon." Laia shakes her head. "I'm trying to write a love story."

I nod. "Yeah, boy meets girl. Girl meets boy. They make love. I know what romance entails."

"Do you really?" The question pops out of her lips so abruptly, it's as if it hijacked her conscious approval process.

My hunch is confirmed when her eyes widen, and her fingers fly to her chest, spreading into a fan. "I'm so sorry. I didn't mean for it to sound as it did. I don't want to insinuate that you don't know what romance is. In absolute terms, at least. Though I do believe that you aren't the kind of man who knows much about the romance *I* like and want to write about."

"And what type of romance is that?"

"The only real one, I suppose…" Laia avoids my gaze and picks up her mug from the table. Her tea must've cooled off because she drinks four avid gulps before continuing. "The finding your soulmate kind."

I snort bemusedly. "That's not very realistic on your part. There is no such thing as a soulmate."

Laia sets her half-empty mug back on her desk and crosses her arms over her chest. "Of course there is."

Her naivety is disarming and annoying at the same time.

I shake my head. "I probably have more experience under my belt than you do, so take it from me—soulmates don't exist. If you want to use this mushy concept in your novel, go for it. Unattainable fantasies attract people. Just know that what you're describing doesn't exist in real life."

Laia's nostrils flare. Her chin tilts up with determination. "Devon, excuse me for my harsh words, but that is one of the most patronizing *and* cynical things I've ever heard. And believe me, I've been talked down to a few times in my life."

Guilt worms through my chest.

I should have phrased my comment more carefully. I didn't want Laia to feel snubbed. "Laia, I—"

"By the way, just because you didn't find your soulmate yet, it doesn't mean that you should doubt her existence."

My meeting with Morgan and the total absence of any kind of longing toward the woman I used to worship pops into my mind.

No, I'm sure there are no such things as soulmates.

It pains me to be brutally honest with Laia. I can tell from the emotion tinting her last phrase that she really believes in this I-was-made-to-love-you bunkum.

At the same time, I don't want to see her get hurt over her childlike beliefs. I've become strangely attached to her.

"Laia, what you're saying is a thing of Hollywood blockbusters." I pat her elbow soothingly.

A tingling invades my palm and I pause for a short breath. I drop my hand and let it hang lose behind me while I add, "In reality, you don't have a person you're destined to be with. You might meet someone attractive and enjoyable. You may even decide to spend your life with that person, for lack of a better alternative. But that doesn't make him your soulmate. I'm sorry."

Laia's gaze darkens.

Right now, her eye color doesn't remind me of Cat, but instead of a wild animal. Perhaps a deer.

The glint in her eyes is innocent but enigmatic at the same time. As if Laia is privy to some kind of secret I'm not.

"It's not me you should feel sorry for. You enjoy women's company only when there are no strings attached and—"

"Please, don't say I should feel sorry for those women. My partner always knows what she can or cannot expect from me. I do pleasure and fun, but no emotions. I don't pretend to want the happily-ever-after deal."

Laia snorts. "Not that your sincerity makes it less hurtful for anyone, but I wasn't talking about your flings. No, I think the person you should feel sorry for is *you*."

Me?

"Please enlighten me. Why."

Laia picks at her nails. "I think we should stop this conversation, Devon, and agree that we disagree. I'm your assistant, and it's not my place to tell you what you should or should not do in your private life."

"It's a little too late for that, don't you think?" I bend slightly closer to her capturing her gaze. "You've dropped a you-should-feel-sorry-for-yourself bomb on me. You got me curious."

"Okay, if you really want to know…robbing a relationship of commitment and emotions is wrong. It turns it into something shallow and pointless."

"Well, it isn't entirely pointless, you know…"

"Yeah." Laia snorts. "You're in it for one thing only." A delicate color seeps into her cheeks, but her voice doesn't waver. "There is nothing exceptionally deep or meaningful about *that*."

I want to shoot back a resentful comment, but my eyes flick to her mug, and my irritation fades.

A princess and a monster…

Laia is clearly a hopeless romantic. That explains the wholesomeness I admire about her. I'm not sure I want to say anything more to challenge her idealistic view of love.

"Well, Laia, you might be right. Let's agree to disagree."

Laia nods. "As I said, it was kind of you to offer your help with my romance, but I think it's better if you don't."

"I understand. Our opinions on relationships are abysmally different."

Laia nods. "They are, indeed."

We glare at each other, and the air between us becomes dense.

Or at least, so it feels to me. It's like the particles are loaded with the intensity of our gazes, and they float around us with tiny sizzles.

I'd probably keep staring at Laia in silence, but she interrupts me by peeking at her watch. "Devon, it's getting late. Do you need me to help you with anything else?"

"No, you're free to go, if you want."

I don't really want her to leave, but it's Friday evening, and Laia must be anxious to get the heck out of the office and do…well, whatever is that she does in the evenings.

"Okay, thanks." Laia sighs with relief. She pivots to her desk and fidgets with her keyboard until her screen goes dark.

Curiosity flares in my chest about Laia's plans for the weekend, but, luckily, I'm sensible enough to stop myself from inquiring about them.

"Okay, then have a great weekend," I say, and meander back to my office.

It's time to get back to my own life. I have better things to do than just chitchatting with my assistant. Especially since she clearly dismissed my offer to help her.

Pete has invited me to be his wingman on a double-date dinner. The girl I'll need to entertain is supposedly hot.

Once in my office, I lie down on the sofa.

From the corridor, I can hear the sounds of Laia's shoes. I listen to the rhythmic clicks trying to imagine what she could be doing.

Now she's going to the kitchen to wash her mug. Now

she's back. And now she must be picking up her bag and tidying up her desk. The noise reaching my ears sounds like pencils shifting back and forth in a pencil holder.

Shortly after, there are clicks on the floor again, signaling that she's on the move. The thuds get fainter and fainter, telling me Laia must have left for the elevator.

I sit up and pull my cell phone from my pocket.

I have no idea why, but out of the blue, I'm no longer in the mood to go out. I don't want to show a good time for a woman I've never met, even if she looks like Heidi Klum.

A long night in a club doesn't tempt me either—which, knowing Pete, would be the unavoidable continuation of our soiree.

I compose a message.

"Hi, pal. Let's take a rain check for tonight. Some important work stuff came up. It'll take my whole evening. Greet your new friends from me. Catch you next week, Dev."

I hit send and put the phone away.

It's superfluous to ponder about why I'm deserting Pete. My buddy will do well without me. He might even thank me later for the double pleasure package my absence granted him.

Besides, it's not like Pete never bails on me. He refused to come with me to the car show on Sunday. And I even got a ticket for him from Vanessa.

Does Laia know there's such a cool event in town?

Maybe I should've offered her Pete's ticket. Like a gift, from one aficionado to another aficionado.

I shake my head and stand up.

Well, that ship has sailed anyway. I didn't mention the show to Laia, so she might or might not be there.

CHAPTER 19

(Laia)

"Remind me again why we've been standing in this boring line for over an hour now? It's Sunday, and it's hot. Why don't we go to the swimming pool instead?"

It's Chelsea's third attempt to dissuade me from buying us tickets to the Phoenix Car Show's Special May Edition. First, she said we should get a mani-pedi instead, and shortly after, she proposed an impromptu visit to the mall.

As if any of these options could be mentioned on the same page as the thrill of seeing Audi showcase its RS 6 Avant, their dashing Euro-wagon.

I quickly count the number of people in front of us.

Forty-six. Not that bad.

"Don't worry, we're almost at the counter," I console her. "Come on, it'll be fun. Did you know that you can test drive anything you like?"

Chelsea stares at me as if I'm an alien. "Why didn't you bring your brother instead of me?"

Yes, Luis Miguel would have been more enthusiastic company for sure. Both of us got infected with my father's love of cars, so he would be excited about this event.

"He's still in deployment overseas. But I think you'll like this show, too." It's my job to instill a sense of anticipation in Chelsea, so I ponder what might convince her that I'm not subjecting her to torture. "There will be cute guys who are good with their hands."

Chelsea grins. "Now that's more of an argument for your case, but"—she glances at her watch—"I'm meeting Howard for dinner. Will we get home in time? I need to do a proper waxing."

I roll my eyes. "Of course. The show closes at six. Your skin is already hairless anyway."

Chelsea smooths her miniskirt and blinks at her long, lean legs. "Yeah, most of it. But I need all areas of my body to be spotless. Who knows where tonight will lead, right?" She wiggles her brows at me.

I hold up my hand. "I don't need to hear this. Anyway, you barely know the guy, Chels, and he's your supervisor."

Chelsea purses her lips, then shrugs. "He likes me. I like him. Also, we are mature adults. We don't need to be soulmates to hit it off."

She sounds just like Devon.

My chest tightens as I recall his disillusioned view of relationships.

Usually, I feel sorry for people who don't recognize the importance of love, but in Devon's case, my emotion was different. I couldn't help but feel disappointed about the way he spoke.

Not that it should be any of my business whether he wishes to be one person's true love or a paramour to many women.

"OMG, is that our CEO over there?" Chelsea squeaks and points behind me.

I grab at her arm and push it to her side without turning my head. "It's impolite to point at people."

"It's really him, Laia. Look," Chelsea insists.

I whirl around.

Oh goodness, it *is* Devon.

The odds of him showing up weren't unfeasible, given that we share a passion for potent engines and propulsion dynamics. Did I fantasize about running into him at this event?

No, absolutely not.

Or perhaps just a little. One fleeting thought when I picked my favorite flowery blouse and paired it to my best-fitting blue jeans instead of my comfier pants.

This is the first time meeting Devon outside of the office, and I'm taken aback by how different he looks.

Correction, different and same.

He has the same stubborn jaw, the same muscular legs, and the same broad shoulders, but he's wrapped his chiseled muscles into a jeans and polo shirt combo that makes him appear very approachable.

Apparently too approachable, because before I realize what I'm doing, I find myself waving at him.

Devon notices me and gives a dazzling smile.

"He's coming to speak with us," Chelsea whispers and grabs her lipstick from her tiny clutch purse. She applies it to her mouth with brisk strokes.

"What are you doing?" I ask, keeping an eye on Devon.

"There's no harm in freshening up. You want some?" She holds out the bright red color to me.

"Shouldn't you spare your good looks for Howard?"

My phrase comes out a bit too hissy, almost as if an insecure, covetous creature had control of my vocal cords.

Chelsea doesn't miss it. "Hey, Laia, is that jealousy I hear? Don't worry. I withdrew my claims on Devon the moment I realized he wasn't interested in me. That's the biggest turn-off I can have. But you, girl, why are you all tense? Is there something you're not telling me about our dashing boss and you?"

"Sshhh, be quiet," I hush as Devon enters into earshot distance.

Chelsea gives me an *I'm so going to squeeze you about this later* glance but stops her inappropriate interrogation.

"Hi, ladies." Devon greets us with a smile that's friendly and flirty at the same time.

Maybe I'm just projecting flirty into his gesture, though. Because of the way the breeze tousles his hair and because his teeth glisten unrealistically white.

"Hi, Devon. What a surprise to see you here," Chelsea purrs beside me, and I almost kick her knee for sounding so sensual.

Isn't she planning on hooking up with Howard tonight? Then she should stop imitating Beyoncé's timbre.

"Well, I love cars as much as Laia." Devon winks at me, and my knees almost buckle.

"You do? *Interesting*." Chelsea squints at me, and I can see how she observes the teased ponytail I spent over twenty minutes creating.

"Do you also need to buy tickets?" I ask, hoping that my voice doesn't sound too excited.

As my brother would say, it's no Valhalla if I get to stand in the same queue as Devon for a couple of minutes.

Devon's forehead creases. "I already have my entry cards. I happen to know the PR manager of the venue, and she slipped me two free VIP passes."

Though he doesn't put an accent on the *she*, I can't stop myself from wondering whether he and the venue's probably gorgeous PR have a history or not.

"Two passes?" Chelsea chimes in. "So, are you here with someone?"

This time I'm thankful for Chelsea's big mouth because I was curious about the same thing but wouldn't have dared to ask.

"Nope," Devon shrugs. "It seems I don't know any fellow car lovers except for my assistant."

"So why don't you give your free pass to Laia then?" Chelsea asks with an innocent smile.

I burst into a fit of coughing from the saliva I just choked on when hearing my friend's blunt proposal. What is she even thinking?

Devon's brows arch, and he throws me a worried glance.

Chelsea pats my back, while she continues to lay the groundwork to whatever diabolic plan she's come up with. "Laia has been raving about this show for weeks, but the tickets were sold out online. I'm not even sure we will get one standing in this line so—"

I manage to gain back control of my lungs. "Nonsense, of course we'll get tickets."

Devon's eyes bounce between Chelsea and me. "I'd be more than happy to give you my free pass, but I fear I only have one extra ticket, so I'm not sure…"

Chelsea waves. "That's no problem. I'm not a car lover anyway. Laia can go in with you, and I can head home to prepare for my date."

I turn to Chelsea. "But you aren't meeting Howard until eight. Don't you want to come and see the show?"

"Howard?" Devon furrows his brows. "As in Howard Wright from accounting?"

I clasp my hand to my mouth.

Why did I need to out my friend's private life like that? Devon might be dressed casually, but he's still the CEO of the company we work for.

Chelsea throws daggers at me, probably recalling how Devon explicitly stated that he doesn't like to mix work with relationships.

"Yes, it's *that* Howard," Chelsea answers.

"You know it's against the rules, right?" Devon says, but his voice doesn't sound particularly troubled by the prospect of an intern dating one of his managers.

Chelsea, however, takes his question as a call to war.

I wince as I see the challenging glimmer invade her eyes. My friend has a way of getting cheeky whenever she thinks someone is questioning her unjustly.

I try to poke her to remind her that she should keep cool, but she leans forward, and my fingers grip the air.

Chelsea puts her hands on her hips and narrows her eyes at Devon. "Howard and I have a dinner plan together, that's all. Whatever happens between us won't impact our collaboration at work, I promise. There won't be any intervention needed, like with your ex-assistant."

This time I aim correctly, and my thumbs lands between her ribs.

"What?" Chelsea throws me a half-guilty slant. "I just heard some rumors."

Of course she did. I spilled the beans to her about my chat with Fanta and Katja.

Chelsea flashes a smile that says *I'm mortified if I stepped on his toes, but he deserved it.* "I'm not saying that *any* of the gossip is true, but I'm hoping Devon might grant Howard and me a break as long as we don't create drama at work?"

Devon's jaw quivers as if he's gritting his teeth, then his

eyes flick to my face. An undecipherable emotion washes over his face but dissipates quickly.

He blinks at Chelsea and clears his throat. "Well, as it so happens, I've been pondering my strict rule concerning relationships at work. I might need to be more tolerant. So, yes, as long as you and Howard don't create problems for the other employees or our business, I don't see an issue with you meeting outside work."

Chelsea grins. "Perfect. Thanks so much. I'll tell Howard tonight. I think he's been reticent, because he feared he might get fired."

"Chels," I whisper.

Chelsea giggles. "Sorry, too much information. Anyway, I'll leave you to enjoy this spectacular car show. *Together*."

I would like to pinch her for the emphasis she put on the last word.

But Chelsea pivots away and strolls toward the parking. After a few steps, however, she looks back. "I almost forgot. Laia, are you okay with taking the bus to your sister's? Or shall I leave the car for you?"

"No, I'm fine taking—"

"I'll take Laia wherever she needs to go after the show. Don't worry."

My eyes dart to Devon.

I want to protest about his generosity. He really has no obligation to drive me around, just because I can't afford my own vehicle yet.

But Chelsea accepts his offer on my behalf before I can utter a word. "That's so nice of you, Devon. Thanks. You're a great boss. Have fun!"

After announcing the words that tie me to Devon for the duration of the show and beyond, Chelsea sashays forth.

"You have a perky friend," Devon says.

I roll my eyes. "You've no idea."

"Do you mind that she accepted my ticket and my offer to chauffeur you around?"

His expression is slightly timid, as if he actually fears I will say yes. This unexpected vulnerability is disarming, especially because he tops it with a lopsided, boyish smile.

"No, I don't." I shake my head. "Both are awfully nice of you to propose. I'm excited about this show. Chelsea might have exaggerated about us not getting tickets, but without a pass, it would probably take another hour before I could get inside."

"That would be a shame. I don't know if you heard, but Audi is on a wagon jag. They brought their e-tron Sportback to Phoenix. It's all-electric. It might not have the elegance of the R8, but I'm dying to check it out."

Before I can stop myself, I blurt, "Me too!"

"Well then…" Devon fetches the two silver VIP passes from his back pocket. "Let's go admire all the new models, shall we?"

We saunter to the entrance, side by side. To anyone watching, we have to look like a couple. It isn't even the fact that such an idea occurs to me that startles me. Rather that it carries an astonishing giddiness that makes me smile like I won the Karma Revero GT—the highest prize in the drawing at the show.

Oh, boy, I think I'm moving into dangerous territories this afternoon…

CHAPTER 20

(Devon)

"Look, here's the RS 6! Let's check it out!" Without realizing what she's doing, Laia grabs my wrist and pulls me toward the Audi's wagon shimmering on a rotating stage to our left.

My skin lights on fire where her fingers touch me.

I follow her, keeping my arm stretched in just the perfect angle so her pull is neither too hard, nor too easy. I'm afraid if I tweak our contact in any direction, she might release me from her grip. For some reason, I want to enjoy our physical connection as long as it lasts.

If we weren't at the car show, I'd ask myself what this strange attraction means, but we are here, and the salesman has already zeroed in on me.

"Welcome!" He dashes forward, flashing an all-teeth smile. "Are you interested to learn more about this special wagon?"

The guy is a young fellow with freckles on his fleshy nose and perfectly styled hair. He might not appear old enough to buy a beer in a pub, but I know I shouldn't dismiss him as a greenhorn based on his puffy cheeks and hairless face. A big player like Audi would never let flunkies run their booths at an event like this.

"Ah, yes. We absolutely are," Laia replies instead of me.

Her happy-go-lucky gleam warms my heart.

We've spent the past two hours going from one stand to another, exploring redesigned models and futuristic car concepts.

In the beginning, Laia seemed intimidated by my presence. She strolled quietly beside me. But as time passed and the sights distracted her from whatever was holding her back, her eyes started to sparkle with that exceptional glint that makes her face irresistible—wholesome and darned sexy at the same time.

As I throw a side-glance at her, my pulse picks up the pace despite my best judgment.

"That's fabulous news." The salesman, whose name tag reads Richard Cleve, grins. "The RS 6 Avant has been a forbidden fruit for us Americans for many years."

He jumps into his pitch, his glance ostentatiously set on my face even though it was Laia who answered him.

"In the past"—he points at the car—"if you found this model, it was either a custom-built or black-market shipment from Europe. But in only a month, Audi will start to roll out this gem in our country too. Want to take a closer look?"

"Yes."

Laia speaks again, but the guy pretends it was me. He puts a hand on my shoulder, guiding me toward the stage.

As we step closer, the rotation stops. The salesman climbs up and waves for me to follow him.

Laia stands there with her lips pressed into a line. It's clear she dislikes the way the man is ignoring her.

"Ladies first." I smile at Laia and hold my hand out to her.

Though she isn't wearing heels, but flat sandals, the podium is much higher to her than it is to me.

Laia's lips curl up, and she takes my hand. She lands on the stage with an agile jump.

I try not to focus on how her blue jeans tighten around her hips as she moves, but even with my best effort, I forget my eyes on her curvy lines a second too long. Just enough time for my heart to give a beat out of sync.

While I get on to the stage myself, I begin to fear something is seriously wrong with me. I've known numerous women, but none, including Morgan, has ever messed with my cardiac rhythm as far as I can remember.

Maybe I'm having a relapse of my childhood condition? That would explain my unusual shortness of breath.

If it's not that, then…then that would mean that I'm beginning to desire my assistant.

Could this be the reason I gave permission to Laia's friend to date Howard?

The salesman finally decides to give Laia some attention and smiles at her. "What do you think, miss? Are you picturing this all-season family hauler in your house? You could drive your kids to soccer practice in it. I assure you, all the other moms would be totally envious."

A deep purple spread on Laia's cheeks.

I don't know whether Laia feels uneasy because Richard assumes we're a couple planning a family, or if she's bothered that he thinks her only interest in this vehicle is to show off in front of soccer moms.

The phrase that Laia said about being used to people talking down to her pops into my mind, and I curse myself for not exploring her puzzling statement any further.

I expect Laia to correct Richard's misconception, but she surprises me by giving the guy a flat-lined smirk.

"Yes, that's *exactly* what I have in mind," she replies.

What?

Laia seemed irritated when I insinuated to Morgan that she was my girlfriend. And now she's accepting that a salesman has us married? Isn't she going to negate that we're in a relationship?

The fact that Laia goes along with this roleplay puts a smile on my lips. I grin at her and wiggle my brows to show that I'm game.

When she exchanges my gesture with a wicked smile, I know she's plotting to grill poor Richard a bit.

The sight of the unexpected naughtiness in her irises makes me question why I used to think tall, blonde women were the prettiest. Brunettes and tiny frames are way more appealing.

"Are you sure, honey, that this wagon will be large enough for us?" I ask Laia, then shoot an apologetic glance to the salesman. "We only have one boy for now, but we'd like to have a large family."

Laia struggles to keep a straight face but tops my comment by adding, "Yeah, a bit like *The Brady Bunch.* Though I suppose, for the first few years, this car could be okay."

Richard's tense face smooths out. "You won't find a better one in this entire car show."

Laia points at the engine and bats her lashes, as if she can't count to two. "How fast can this vehicle go?"

Richard caresses the car's top. "The performance is bewildering. I don't want to annoy you with exact numbers, but let's just say you'll feel like you're in a race car."

Laia bobs her head and pretends to murmur just to

herself, but her voice is loud enough for us to hear. "Audi quoted a 0-62 mph sprint of 3.5 seconds and a 0 to 124 mph run of 12 seconds, but with the top speed being electronically limited to 155 mph…it's not race car range." She peers up at Richard. "But if we got an optional carbon-ceramic brake package, we could up that limit to 190 mph, right?"

Richard stares at her, too flabbergasted to even say a word.

I chuckle and pat the salesman on his arm. "Don't take it personally, Richard. My wife can put any man in his place when it comes to cars. That's why I make her decide any time we invest in a new ride."

Richard's eyes fill with new respect, and he begins to explain the cylinder specifications, price packages, and all optional benefits to Laia.

After a thorough presentation, where all Richard's efforts are focused on Laia instead of me, we wave good-bye.

Laia giggles as we leave Richard's stand behind. "Oh, that was fun. Do you think he believed that we didn't purchase because we're waiting for the ultra-exclusive 25th Anniversary Edition to come out?"

"I think he realized he was dealing with a real aficionado in your person. When you said you adored the bright Nogaro Blue in which those vehicles will be painted, he probably bought your fib."

Laia's expression turns somber. "Oh, by the way, I'm sorry I invented that whole story about our wedding taking place at the Monaco Grand Prix. Or even having said that you and I were a couple."

I stop and reach for her elbow. I turn her to me. "Don't apologize. I had as much fun as you did. You weren't the first one who pretended that we're more than just a boss and his assistant. But we aren't more...or are we?"

Laia startles me by saying. "Well, maybe we are."

Her eyes lock with mine, and there's a shy smile on her lips.

My mouth turns dry.

So she, too, feels this magnetism between us?

"Yeah." I hit the most seductive tone I can muster, despite the itchiness in my throat. "Do you want to tell me what we are?"

Laia cocks her head to the side, without releasing my gaze. "Future friends, perhaps?"

Despite my will to keep my features composed, my face falls.

Laia's eyes immediately widen. "Oh, sorry, I didn't mean to be inappropriate. I just thought since we have some things in common, that maybe someday..." She adjusts her ponytail with a hasty motion.

I had been picturing Laia's naked flesh, and *she* thinks she's inappropriate by suggesting that we could be friends? How can this girl be so danged sweet?

I would enjoy hanging out with Laia outside of work. Our afternoon so far has been the best fun I've had in a while. But she unleashes some pretty intense physical reactions from me. I care about what she thinks and what she likes.

Would this draw I feel for her grow stronger if we became friends?

I don't want to arrive at a situation where I'll become so desperate to woo her that I'll squeeze myself into a bunny costume like Hayley did with me.

Before I can answer, a cheerful squeak interrupts us. "Ah, Devon, love! I'm so glad you could make it." Vanessa's blond bob appears beside us from out of nowhere. To be fair, she could have been standing here without me noticing. I was too absorbed by my conversation with Laia.

Vanessa wears a white top and a black pencil skirt. Her hair is side-parted and meticulously flat-ironed, which accentuates her pointy chin.

She casts her arms around my neck and leans in to give a short smack on my mouth—her usual greeting each time we meet.

I turn my head so her lips land on my jawline. I don't know why, but I would hate for Laia to see me act flirty.

Laia stiffens as she eyes Vanessa's arms around my neck.

Vanessa releases me and introduces herself to Laia in her buoyant style. Laia shakes her hand formally.

I thank Vanessa for the tickets once more, and we exchange a few shallow words. After the minimal courtesy, I excuse us.

Unoffended about being cut short, Vanessa says she needs to get back to her PR duties. She salutes us with an energetic wave before hurrying off to one of the stands to talk to a hotshot reporter.

Laia and I walk to the exit in silence.

As we reach my car, Laia says, "You could have told me you got the ticket from your…uhm, current companion."

"Vanessa and I aren't seeing each other. We had a thing at some point, but it's over. Now, we're kind of friends," I explain.

Calling Vanessa a friend may be a bit of a stretch, but I'd like Laia to see me as a man who isn't only capable of entertaining flings. I want to show her I'm not as superficial in my interactions with women as she might have thought.

Laia shakes her head. "You don't have to justify yourself in front of me. You obviously aren't thrilled about the idea of becoming *my* friend so…"

Her words bug me enough to disregard my previous doubts. "No, on the contrary. I'd love to."

"Really?" Laia's mouth moves into a little circle. "Even if you're my boss?"

"Sure." I can't back out on my own stupid words now. "Also, who knows how long I'll be your boss, right? Once you become a best-selling romance author, you'll surely quit Hudson Communications."

"Ah, that's still further down the road, but yes, there might be a point where I can't stand working for you any longer. Uhm… keep. I meant *keep* working for you. This heat confused my tongue," she adds with a short chuckle.

"Shall we get into my Audi then?" I point at my car. "The AC should cool us off fast." While I propose this, I realize my afternoon with Laia is about to come to an end.

"Ah, that would be lovely." Laia smooths down her blouse, and her movement accentuates her upper body's silhouette.

My throat feels parched at the sight of her.

I search desperately for a good excuse to extend our time together, but when Laia takes her first step to my Audi, I still haven't found one. So I blurt out the first idea that comes into my mind. "Before going to your sister's, we could drop by my apartment. I corrected your briefing reports yesterday, so if you'd like, I could give them to you right away."

"You corrected my documents on your free day?" Laia's brows arch. "But they weren't that urgent."

Why couldn't I invent something smarter than persuading Laia to work on a Sunday?

"Well" I shrug nonchalantly—"I wanted you to have my feedback as soon as possible. But if you'd rather wait till Monday, no problem. Your sister might be waiting for you, right?" I hurry to make my silly offer as easy as possible to refuse.

She shakes her head, giving me a smile. "No, that's super kind of you. I'd love to read your comments today if the detour to your house isn't too much trouble. Alicia isn't expecting me before dinner, anyway."

The way Laia's lips curl up sends my blood racing in my veins, and I can't stop myself from trying to lift her mood even more.

"What do you say if *you* drive?" I hand her my car keys.

Laia gapes at me then bobs her head. "I'd love to."

As the warmth in her voice triggers a familiar, delicious pull in my belly, I wonder why I offered her the wheel again. But I choose to leave this puzzle unsolved.

For the benefit of my soul.

CHAPTER 21

(Laia)

"Okay, so we go to your place then?" I light the engine and pivot to Devon.

He is checking something on his phone, but as he hears my question, he jerks back. "Excuse me?"

"I asked whether we go to your place then," I repeat.

Devon's lips move into a mischievous grin, and he winks. "Sure, let's go to *my* place."

That's when I realize that his saucy playboy brain is joking about the way I phrased my sentence.

I know I should feel irritation, but the only sensation his tongue-in-cheek remark unleashes is a certain longing that he meant it for real.

I'm really going nuts here.

First, I propose to my boss that we should be friends. *Friends*! As if I could ever be pals with a man whose values about love are in diagonal opposition to mine, but whose fleeting touch makes my bones all mushy.

And now I even feel disappointed that Devon is only

inviting me into his apartment to give me back my reports, instead of… No. I need to not think about this any further.

I step hard on the gas, forgetting I'm sitting in his Audi and not in Chelsea's Pontiac. The engine howls, and we shoot out of the parking with the force of a jet.

"Huhu, slow down a bit, Laia! I'm glad you're feeling more in your element. You looked a little tense a moment ago. But we shouldn't get a ticket, if possible." Devon chuckles.

"What makes you say I was tense?" What reason would I have not to feel at ease?

Just because I can sense his tantalizing cologne, a clean musky scent with a hint of green, without even trying to? Or because his body irradiates such a heat toward me that I feel like fanning myself?

No, all is good with me. *Peachy even.*

Devon clears his throat and points at my hands.

I follow his gaze. My skin plays in a bluish-white as my fingers clutch the wheel. I release the pressure and roll back my shoulders. "Okay, maybe I had a pang of jitters because…mhm…I'm nervous about the remarks you made on my briefing reports."

My professional responsibilities couldn't be further from my mind as we roll through the traffic, but it's a plausible excuse.

"No need." Devon reaches out and pats the hand I just moved to the gearstick. "You did a good job with them."

His gesture is friendly but sends tingles up to my shoulder.

"Turn left here, please, then take the second to the right." Devon points. His arm almost brushes my shoulder, but I press back to my seat to avoid the contact.

If I get any more thrills on my skin, I'll feel like I'm

sitting in the middle of a termite mound—a bizarre sensual kind.

We arrive at a high-rise, and Devon calls out, "Stop here. That's where I live."

I park the Audi near his building.

Devon lives very close to the Arts and Willo Historic District, my two favorite areas in this city. I would trade our flat in Laveen Village for this location in a heartbeat. And I'm sure Chelsea would too.

Devon can literally walk to theaters, museums, and art galleries, and he has countless fancy shops at his disposal, a fact that enthuses me less but would probably be the primary motivation for my roomie to move here.

An elderly doorman keeps watch in front of his place. He greets Devon with a wide smile. Devon exchanges his cordial salutation with a friendly wave.

Once we're in the hall, Devon pauses. "Wait, Laia, let's go back for a second."

We trot to the door, where Devon puts his hand on the doorman's shoulder. "Philip, this is Laia. Laia, this is Philip, my building's guardian."

Philip and I shake hands, both of us somewhat taken aback by this spontaneous introduction.

Why does Devon's doorman need to know my name? I'm not planning on coming here frequently.

Philip has white, thick locks, cut short like a sheep's fur. His face is covered in deep-creased wrinkles, but his eyes glimmer with the spirit of youth.

"It's a pleasure to meet you, Ms. Flores," he says, his full lower lip twisting upward. "It's good to see that Mr. Griffin finally has some company. I've been wondering whether I should introduce him to one of my nieces so he won't get lonely."

Lonely? Doesn't Devon's doorman read the tabloids?

"Oh, no." I shake my head. "I'm just his assistant. We're here to pick up some documents."

Philip blinks at Devon with disapproval, while he taps at his own cheeks with both hands. "Mr. Devon, only an assistant? What will Ms. Ellie say to this? She frequently inquires whether I see you with someone, and I always have to say no and no."

Philip turns to me, a warmth overtaking his features. "And when I finally meet a pretty, young lady at your side, it turns out that it's all work-related." He rubs his neck. "Oh, my, oh, my…"

"No need to worry about me, Philip." Devon touches the doorman's hand but doesn't comment any further on his complaints. "Have a great day."

Devon guides me back to his building and toward the elevator.

As we wait and watch the bright red numbers decreasing on the monitor, I have a hard time wrapping my head around what's just happened.

The doorman's voice didn't hint at a joke, and his face was more concerned than mocking when he scolded Devon.

Devon studies me with furrowed brows. "Everything okay with you, Laia?"

"Sure. I'm just wondering about something."

"About what?"

I'm tempted to say that it doesn't matter, but number eight on my bucket list, "Become as feisty and strong as Eva," comes to mind. Biting back my questions is certainly not helping me with this goal.

"Why did Philip say he should find you a date? Aren't you one of the city's ultimate playboys?"

Devon's expression steels, and a vexed glint seeps into his eyes. "Is this what you think of me?"

"I…I…" I play with my left earlobe, not knowing how to formulate my next phrase. I know it should be an apology, but I can't seem to find the right words.

What has gotten into me? My label for Devon was too harsh.

There's a difference between being courageous and spirited and blabbing out things without checking their level of hurtfulness first.

Could my blunder be the work of that Lilliputian fraction of my soul that still feels resentful about seeing Vanessa almost-kiss Devon?

Devon shrugs, withdrawing his glance from me. "You know, things are never as black-and-white as they seem."

The elevator arrives, and Devon enters.

I march behind him, while my cheeks burn as if I just opened the oven on those delicious cinnamon rolls my mother used to prepare for us as afternoon snacks.

Only this time, my churning stomach isn't caused by the yummy fragrance but by my foolish behavior.

It's not just my poor choice of words that makes me feel guilty. My hasty comment betrayed that I'm more than interested in Devon's private affairs.

As the doors close, the air seems to densify around us, and I struggle to breathe.

Elevators always accentuate social weirdness to an unbearable level. Maybe it's due to the restriction of space, or the neon lights, or the feeling that I'm not anchored to the ground.

Without knowing why I'm even speaking, I begin to prattle. "Did you know they did an experiment where a man stood with his back to the elevator door while everyone else faced forward?"

Devon's impassive face tells me he couldn't care less about what I'm jabbering.

But since speaking seems to ease the lump in my throat, I continue, “You know what happened? Everybody got nervous because the man was acting differently than expected. People made self-soothing gestures, and they only calmed down once the man turned to look at the door, too.”

“Self-soothing gestures? Like?” Devon lifts a brow.

“Mhmm, like hugging oneself, playing with one’s shirt, fiddling with the strap of a bag or…” I chew on my lip, thinking what else I could add.

I’m glad my story finally gripped Devon’s interest and distracted him from his grim mood.

“Chewing on one’s lip?” Devon reaches out and brushes his thumb against my mouth without actually touching me.

His finger is so close I can feel his warmth on my lower lip.

I swallow. “Yes, that too.”

“Are you nervous now, Laia?” Devon takes a small step toward me.

Why is it so sultry in here? Did somebody switch off the air-conditioning?

“I’m not nervous,” I mumble.

Devon captures my gaze and inches a half-step forward. “Still not nervous?”

I shake my head because I can’t trust my voice.

Devon is standing in my closest socially acceptable circle. One more step would put him into unacceptable proximity. One where I’d feel his breath on my cheeks…

Devon takes another half-step.

“And now? Not nervous at all?” he asks.

Yesssss. “No,” I whisper, while I peek up at his face

“Strange…” He cocks his head to the side, his eyes not leaving mine. “I would have thought standing this close to someone who's supposed to be only about seducing women…an *ultimate playboy*…would make a person with your impeccable moral standards uneasy."

"My impeccable moral standards? What are you talking about?"

Devon sniffs. "You're not the only one who's made assumptions about the other. I also sized you up, Laia, based on our talk on Friday." My name is but a soft caress from his lips.

"And what conclusions did you draw?" I force myself not to drop my gaze.

I brought this confrontation on myself, and I don't want to be the usual coward and back out of it without understanding what Devon thinks about me.

"I think you're someone who won't settle for anything but perfection. You want your relationships to be magical, the swipe-me-off-my-feet, make-me-swoon-and-promise-the-sky kind of thing. I wonder how many times you found that kind of bliss…" He brushes a tendril behind my ear. "Not too many, right?"

His fingers sear on my skin, and there's that coquettish glint in his eyes as if he were challenging me into something—something that I realize I want more than anything.

I gawk at him, while a crazy urge to bend forward builds in my chest.

Am I such a hot mess because I have no real experience with men? Is my decision about waiting for the right one biting me in the butt and turning me into a horny teenager?

However disturbing this idea sounds, I still like it better than the other option. The one that would mean that my desires are explicitly related to Devon's persona.

And my budding feelings for him.

"No. I didn't find whom I'm looking for yet," I say. "But true love is worth waiting for."

His eyes widen, and his lips part a little. "Waiting? Are you saying that you…? That you *never*…?"

My silence answers his question.

A troubled frown settles on his face.

"I'm sorry, Laia. I don't know what came over me." He shakes his head. "It must've been your comment about me being a playboy…it made my blood boil. I wanted to…" He rubs his neck, dropping his gaze. "I'm sorry."

He recoils to the opposite wall of the elevator.

How did I end up in this conversation? I never meant to discuss my virginity with him.

But it's not only what I revealed to him that squeezes my belly like I've been kicked in the guts. It's the realization that Devon acted provocatively because I infuriated him with my judgmental remark.

I'd contemplated how it would be to kiss him, while he was only taunting me with his player charm to school me.

"It's okay," I say, but almost gag on the humiliation that closes up my throat.

Devon holds out his hand. "Forgive me?"

"Yep. No problem." I put my hand in his, though I know it's bound to make me feel worse.

And it certainly does.

The buzzing in my palms and the leftover flutters in my chest make it clear I'm more than just a victim of my hormones. There's something more to my reaction.

The elevator beeps. Devon lets go of my hand and dashes out.

I stay behind and press my hands on my cheeks. How could I assume Devon was being genuinely flirty with me?

So dumb of me.

No, I need to stop whining. This is something the old

Laia would do. But I'm trying to build a new me, a stronger and more resilient one. And to do that I need to find the positive points in everything.

I take a deep inhale.

Looking at it from another angle, this humiliating exchange with Devon has been useful. It showed me that even if I were to disregard us being opposites, I still couldn't become his love interest.

Which is no surprise. He dates women like Vanessa, Morgan, and those others from the tabloids.

This is an empowering realization. I don't have to interpret my unsettling feelings about Devon.

I should be ecstatic that this burden is off from my shoulders. But as I step out and follow Devon to his door, the only thing I feel is my belly knotting with bitterness.

CHAPTER 22

(Devon)

Pete once told me that elevators are places of in-between, and as such, they are the perfect setting for heated interactions that wouldn't otherwise be allowed. Rooms where the rules of the game can be reinvented.

Did I buy into his wacky reasoning?

It seems that I did, otherwise, why would I have come at Laia like that? Throwing some Don Juan act on her…in the name of what? Hurt pride?

The memory of her face as she admitted just how innocent she really is, makes me cringe, and I accelerate my pace.

I need to get away from that steamy little box where my words and actions turned into my worst enemies. A swishing noise behind me tells me that Laia must be only a few steps from me.

I exhale and turn the key in the lock.

The only thing I can do is to admit it happened. I apologized to Laia, and she accepted. Perhaps she'll forget soon just what a colossal jerk I've been.

With this thought in mind, I push the door open.

"Oh, *cielo mio*, is this cute thing yours?"

Laia's soprano makes me whip around. She's staring at something between my legs. A weak meow signals to me that she must've discovered my little companion. I point at the furry, black ball sitting on my travertine floor. "Yes, that's Cat."

"I can see it's a cat. What's his name? Or is it a she?"

"It's a she. And *she* is called Cat."

Laia snorts. "Did you call your cat Cat? That's just….mhmm." She wrinkles her forehead. "Very original, to say the least."

"Yeah, I'm not big on naming pets. Hudson was an exception." I smile, and my heart leaps when Laia exchanges it with one of her own.

Desperate to make the atmosphere between us agreeable again, I blabber on, "Technically, the kitten isn't even mine. It's Ellie's, so I shouldn't have had to name her. But since the beast has lived in my apartment for the last six months, I had to come up with a way to call her."

We enter, and the sleazy animal goes straight for Laia's legs. Cat circles around her purring like a turbocharged engine.

Normally only the sight of Ellie unleashes this level of enthusiasm from Cat. Me returning home certainly never qualifies for such a show.

Laia kneels down and lifts Cat gently. "Oh, heavens. Look at that! What a sweet kitty." Laia rubs her underneath her chin and throws me a questioning look. "I didn't figure you as a cat person."

Cat relaxes into her arms as if it's the place she's

always intended to be. I didn't think her purring could get any louder, but it does.

"Why is that?" I ask, a curious inclination in my voice.

It seems the episode in the elevator wasn't enough for my entire brain to get the memo that it would be best if Laia and I stay in a strict boss-employee relationship.

"I don't know." Laia tilts her head. "Maybe from the dedication to your work and your busy social life." She clears her throat. "But also because of Hudson. I assumed that if you did have a pet, it would be a dog."

"Actually, if it depended on me, I probably wouldn't have chosen to care for a cat. But my sister begged me to adopt Cat after one of her roomies refused to put up with the noise. Apparently, *I* am just supposed to be fine with that."

"Aww, that's really sweet of you." Laia giggles.

The sound of her laugh makes Cat's eyes spring open.

I wasn't mistaken when I compared Laia's gaze to my cat's. Now that the two pairs of yellow-brown irises are staring at me, they look eerily similar to each other.

Laia furrows her brows. "What are you gaping at? You look like you've seen a ghost."

"Nothing, just surprised to see Cat like anyone besides Ellie."

"Isn't she usually this well behaved?"

"If you call peeing into my shoes, scratching my bed, and ignoring me royally after I've just fed her then, yes, Cat is the best-behaved pet ever."

Laia laughs, this time whole-heartedly. It's so contagious I chuckle with her.

Cat, recognizing the only word of interest to her from our conversation, jumps from Laia's arms and bolts to her plate in the kitchen.

"Oh, oh. I think someone is hungry," Laia says.

"Yes, this is partially why I needed to stop by, besides giving you the briefing reports. Normally my neighbor lady takes care of Cat's afternoon snacks, but today she's visiting her niece."

"Do you want me to feed Cat while you gather your papers?"

"Sure, that would be great."

Though I don't want to ask favors of Laia, having a few minutes alone would be a much-needed break. I have to reorganize my thoughts and rid my body from the desire her closeness awakened.

"Where can I find her food?"

"Cat's stuff is in the white cupboard to the left when you enter the kitchen. The beast drinks only sparkling water." I lift my shoulders and drop them. "Don't ask me how she got into that weird habit. Probably Ellie spoiled her for life before abandoning her to me."

"White cupboard, sparkling water. Noted."

Laia leaves for the kitchen, and I go straight to my study. Just as I enter, my landline rings.

"Hey, man. What's up? Finally, I manage to catch you," Pete's gruff voice echoes on the phone.

"I was busy yesterday when you rang me."

"I hope with someone ravishing and not with some stinky work stuff." Pete chuckles.

His familiar banter relaxes my shoulders. "I wish, my friend. I've been buried in a mountain of documents."

My statement is a partial fib. When Pete called last night, I'd already finished correcting Laia's reports. But I didn't feel like going out, so instead, I ordered in some Chinese and spent the evening watching a Mexican serial about narco-trafficking. I even managed to pick up a few Spanish expressions which I could show off to Laia when—

"Don't you have an assistant who can help with that? The hot young Salma Hayek?"

Pete's comment is so relevant to my line of thoughts that I give out a nervous cough. "Pete, you old fox. Your wheels always turn in one direction. I told you, Laia is purely a professional help in my life." I'm glad my buddy can't see my chin harden.

"Sure, Dev, I get it. But old habits die hard. You might have dialed back on clubbing with me, which I don't particularly like, but the instincts I've helped you groom still brew the same way, don't they? When you see a woman you like, you can't help but tempt her, no?"

Shame curls through my chest.

I'd like to contradict Pete, but he's right. I'd almost claimed Laia's mouth only minutes ago. If she'd taken only a second longer, I might have actually made my move.

"Maybe," I murmur, "but not when it comes to my employees. Anyway, why did you call? Is it about Friday?"

Before Pete can answer, I hear a faint bang, a noise similar to slamming of a door. I hark to see whether Laia needs help with something, but since I don't hear her call, I redirect my attention to Pete.

"Yep. I ran into Jimmy, and he asked me to check with you whether you'd help him out. Harry, one of the pianists, has the flu. Jimmy couldn't find anyone to replace his slot on such short notice. I told him you'd be fine with a few rounds on stage."

I shrug. "No problem. It's not the first time."

"Perfect. I'm looking forward to it. And you know what? I have an idea. Why don't you invite your assistant? I'm not her boss, and I could use some sweet Latina company while you play us cool songs."

My stomach twitches despite knowing Pete is messing with me. Jimmy'z is just as much a sanctuary as my apartment. Neither Pete nor I have ever invited a girl to our favorite jazz club. It's a venue reserved for our male bonding and letting off steam.

"Ha ha, you're so funny. I'm hanging up now. See you on Friday."

"Fine. Don't you dare ditch me this time, 'kay? Bye."

The line goes dead, and I put the phone down.

Pete's comment about Laia sets an odd tension in my stomach.

How absurd is that? How can I be troubled about losing a woman I didn't even kiss to my buddy, who has never even met her? I can't be jealous.

I'm just protective of Laia. Now that I know that she's looking for a white knight and saving herself for him, I can't even envision her being courted by someone like my buddy.

Or me.

This afterthought sneaks up on me without warning and leaves a bitter taste in my mouth.

Indeed, by no definition am I a white knight. More like a dark warrior who doesn't need a woman to feel whole.

Even if the girl happens to have the most incredible eyes and kindest smile in the whole world.

This is just who I am.

If I know this, then why am I still hung up on a yearning to kiss Laia?

CHAPTER 23

(Devon)

As I head back to the living room with the reports under my arm, Laia's sweet giggle reaches my ears.

Huh, she must be having fun with Ca—

Cat's head appears from her fancy black cat toilet that I transferred this morning from the balcony to the corridor.

I freeze mid-thought. If my kitten isn't in the kitchen, who is Laia laughing with?

A second sound echoes through the walls, but this time in a chirpier soprano. The memory of the slamming door comes back to me, and I suddenly remember that my sister still has my spare keys.

If she came to bring me back those, her timing couldn't be more convenient…*for her.*

A soft murmur tells me my sister must be chatting with Laia, but from where I stand, I can't catch a word of what they're saying.

"Psst, Cat," I whisper, trying to lure her over to me. "What is my crazy sis up to, huh? Do you know?"

Cat, as always, lacks any sign of cooperation.

She even seems to take offense that I dared to call out to her while she's doing something as crucial as licking her paws clean. In answer, she huffs, then dashes back to the kitchen.

I drop the documents on the beige sofa and tiptoe behind her as quietly as I can, hoping to catch a bit of the conversation without the girls realizing my presence. I suspect it can't be a coincidence that Ellie turned up in my apartment at the exact same time that I brought Laia here.

I flatten my back against the wall beside the kitchen's door and peek inside.

"He's pretty fine now, but boy, was it bad when we were younger," my sister says, leaning against the black granite counter. Her coral-colored blouse blends in nicely with the tile backsplash.

There's no doubt whom or what she's speaking about.

As if to confirm my hunch, Laia answers, "I didn't know Devon's health problems were so severe. He mentioned he'd been hospitalized a few times, but I didn't want to pry."

She faces away from me so I can't see her expression, but I get to admire how her hair sways as she shakes her head.

Ellie's eyes widen. "No way, Dev told you that he was sick? It's not a thing he tells anyone."

"Really?" Laia's voice is higher than usual and has a startled timbre.

I'm tempted to slam my forehead on the jamb. It's not true that I keep my childhood condition a secret. I might not go around flashing a T-shirt that says, "I used to suffer from severely recurring bronchospasm," but Wyatt knows about it. And Pete, too.

So there you go…I didn't give Laia the kind of special treatment that Ellie implies.

My sister pulls her dainty nose into a pensive grimace, while she vigorously scratches her left earlobe. It's her trademark expression for *I'm about to mount a new rescue mission* and usually means trouble.

Ellie just can't help her inner drive to fix others.

Especially me.

As if to prove I should've listened to my gut and revealed my presence before she could utter another word, Ellie leans toward Laia in a conspiratorial manner. "You know, I think Dev's past challenges might be an unconscious factor in his zeal to play the lady's man. It's compensation for his past deprivations."

Ellie touches Laia's arm and smiles as if they've known each other forever.

I can't blame Ellie for her warm, forthcoming manners. My sister is not only a very expansive person, but Laia has something in her that makes you like her on the spot. A quiet, understated charm which, the longer you remain exposed, the more it seeps into every inch of your being.

But I can definitely condemn my sister's gossipy remark.

The moment to intervene has come.

I need to stop my sister before she depicts me as an unfortunate victim of circumstances in Laia's eyes. Or worse, before she arrives at her favorite hypothesis about why Morgan could fool me.

I cough shortly to draw their attention, then I step into the kitchen. "Ah, Ellie. What a surprise, little sis. I didn't realize you kept my spare keys the last time you stayed over."

Ellie doesn't flinch at my comment. Instead, she darts to me and jumps into my neck. "I'm so happy I popped by. It's a funny coincidence, really. I happened to pass by in front of your building, and Philip stopped me. He mentioned you were upstairs with Laia to fetch some work stuff. I thought it would be a lovely time to catch you and give back your keys."

She pulls back from me and grabs the keys from her pocket. She dangles them in front of me with an innocent smile.

Her feigned candor doesn't fool me. There's something seriously off in her story.

Did she tip Philip to give her a call if he saw me with a woman?

No, that would be too much, even for Ellie.

She might have sworn to bring me back to the path of virtue, but she wouldn't spy on me with the help of my doorman, or would she?

I take the keys and deposit them on the kitchen counter. "Thanks, Ellie. But you could've just given me these another day. There was no need to come upstairs."

Ellie points at Laia. "No, brother. It's a perfect time. Otherwise, I would have missed out on chatting with your lovely assistant."

"And filled her up on old and meaningless stories about me?" I grit my teeth.

"Devon, I didn't mean to…" It's Laia who chimes in, with a soft, almost frightened tone.

I capture Laia's gaze. "Don't worry. I know you didn't press my sister for information on me. Ellie is…*uhm*…a smooth talker."

Ellie taps my back. "Thanks for that, Dev. For the record, we only touched upon your health because Laia found your salbutamol spray in the cupboard."

Laia's eyes fill with a guilty glint. "I did, sorry. It was right beside Cat's food, and I didn't know whether it belonged there. I asked Ellie what it was, and if I should move it somewhere else."

"Agatha must have shifted it around. She's the neighbor I mentioned to you," I reply.

"After spending a week at work and a Sunday afternoon with you"—Ellie gives me a coy smile as if to drive home the point that she knows I was at the car show with Laia—"I'm sure your assistant didn't need my help to interpret your facade for what it is: a wall you build against the world."

Grrr, again this psychobabble.

"Ellie, please…" I lower my voice to a menacing hiss. "Don't embarrass me like this. Also, it's wrong to assume that our past defines us. It certainly doesn't define me."

Laia steps closer and puts her hand briefly on my arm. "I don't think that's what your sister meant, Devon. She just wants you to recognize that certain patterns in your behavior could be impacted by what happened to you. But it doesn't mean you're the result of your past. All of us can choose who we want to be or want to believe in. In every moment. We *can* break patterns."

She sounds a bit like a motivational bestseller.

Also, what patterns should I be looking at?

Tingling in the weirdest possible way when Laia touches me?

That will be a tough one to break away from, given that when Laia withdraws her fingers, I almost grab them and pull them back to my skin.

Ellie watches us from the corner of her eye, her mouth twisted upward. "Dev, before I go, I have one more thing to say."

I snap my head to her. "Tell me quickly, because I need to drop Laia at her sister's house."

Ellie's glance ricochets from me to Laia. A calculating grimace flashes on her symmetric features. "Laia, didn't you say earlier that you have no plans for next Friday?"

Laia squares her shoulders. "Yes, I'm free. Why?"

I narrow my eyes at my sister, suspicion settling in my chest.

I sincerely hope she isn't going with this where I think she is.

Before I can come up with a suitable way to disarm her, Ellie pops her question with a casual wave. "Do you want to come with me to a nice jazz club? I'd love to go, and it would be fun with some gal company."

My fingers itch with the need to strangle my sister. There's no doubt about which club she is referring to.

Laia's face relaxes, as if she's happy that Ellie's proposal turned out to be a simple invite to an evening between girls. "Ah, that sounds nice."

Nice? Not really. Rather diabolic.

Of course, Laia doesn't know what Ellie's real intention is. I, on the other hand, can see through my sister's scheming.

"Laia probably doesn't even like jazz," I grumble, throwing an I-know-what-you're-up-to glance at Ellie.

To my surprise, Laia exclaims. "Oh no, I *love* jazz. I played the saxophone in my school's music team. I wasn't very good at it, though."

What? Laia and I like the same music? Most women don't like jazz. Morgan certainly didn't.

This sidetracks me just long enough to allow my cunning sister to seal her deal.

"Perfect." Ellie grins at Laia. "Then I'll take you to Phoenix's best jazz venue. It's called Jimmy'z Jazz Haven."

"Great," Laia answers with a bright smile. "I don't usually go out. My roomie loves to go to dance clubs, but those aren't my thing. I'm not a dancer. This place, however, sounds fun."

I clear my throat loudly, in lack of a better way to signal to Ellie that she needs to abort her insane plan.

Ellie, mistakenly or deliberately—the latter knowing her—takes my gesture as a sign that I want her to inform Laia that I will also be present.

"Oh…" She pats Laia's arm. "I almost forgot to mention. Dev will also be there with a buddy of his. I hope that's okay."

Laia's eyes dart to me, then move back to my sister. She chews shortly on her lower lip, before saying, "Of course, yes. No problem at all."

Put like that, what could Laia say?

I'm her boss, after all. She can't back out on an invite she accepted after learning I would be there. And my foxy sister knows this.

Which becomes evident when Ellie claps her hands. "Super, I'm glad it all works out. I've been looking forward to chatting with Pete, too." She winks at me.

We both know it's a fib. There's only one reason she would say what she just did. She's planning to get Laia and me alone somehow.

Panic fills my stomach. I can't allow Ellie to bring Laia to Jimmy'z.

I've already decided that Laia and I need to stay in a strict business relationship. I can't become her friend or hang out with her.

It's hard enough adhering to this, due to the elemental craving I feel for Laia. But it might become near to impossible if Ellie deliberately tries to bring us together.

And in my favorite jazz club no less.

I'll have no choice but to cancel on Pete.

Oh, snap, except I can't. I've already agreed to jump in for that missing pianist. The owner would be disappointed if I bailed on him when he needed me.

My eyes wander to Laia, who is speaking about the logistic details of the evening with Ellie. My throat thickens as I watch her smile and nod to my sister.

I suddenly realize that if Laia comes, she'll hear me play the piano.

My sister once told me that luring out enticing music from any instrument is a man's most attractive trait.

The vision is tempting. Maybe if Laia saw me on stage, she would reassess her opinion of me.

D'oh, my obsession with Laia is getting out of hand.

Ellie gives a thumbs-up to Laia, then turns to me. "I've cleared everything with Laia, so I'll go now. If not earlier, then see you on Friday."

"Okay, it was good to see you, sis," I mumble.

Even if you put me into a mess that you can't even imagine.

As if she heard my unspoken thought, Ellie gives me a peck on my cheek and whispers, "It'll be fun, you'll see."

She kneels and picks up Cat, who has been rolling back and forth on the tile between us. She snuggles her cheek to the animal's fur. "Keep being a good girl with Dev, okay?"

Cat gives out a treacherous meow, which we both know can't count as a promise.

Ellie lowers the animal back to the ground. She waves to us, then rushes to the entrance. Before disappearing, she yells back, "By the way, in case you missed it during your reverie, I told Laia you would drive her to Jimmy'z. I'll be coming straight from work, 'kay?"

She doesn't wait for my answer but slams the door shut.

I gape at the empty corridor, shaking my head. Ellie is

more astute than I gave her credit for. She used my moment of distraction to her advantage. If I didn't like her as much as I do, I would surely come up with a plan to torture her.

Laia touches my shoulder. "Do you have my files?"

"I left the folder in my living room. I'll go and get it."

Laia waits for me in the corridor. She's saying good-bye to Cat by tickling her below her ear as I return.

My furry companion purrs in sheer pleasure, and I can't suppress the pathetic wish of trading places with my pet.

Before my fantasy can get any weirder, I step over to the door and open it. "Let's go, I'm all set."

CHAPTER 24

(Laia)

As I stroll toward the printing room, only the faint murmur of a vacuum cleaner interrupts the silence.

No sounds of fingers tapping against keyboards.

No clicking of staplers.

I'm not surprised by this quietude. Most employees, including Katja, are long gone, even if it's only six o'clock in the evening. The cleaning staff must have taken advantage of this particular Friday to begin their work sooner.

Despite their earlier shift, I know I'll stay undisturbed for a while. Bill, the janitor responsible for the top floors, knows I tend to stay later than the other employees—the price I pay for working in close contact with our CEO.

Even if not so close this week.

These past few days, I've seen much less of Devon than I would have wished.

Which is a pretty shameful truth to admit, but it's true.

Devon rarely left his office, and when he did, he didn't

ask me to accompany him to meetings or brainstorm about client projects.

Instead, he ordered me to spend entire days at the creative hub, in accounting, and even at HR, shadowing the respective department heads.

When I asked him why this was necessary, he told me I needed to gain insights and hands-on experiences in every area of the company so I could perform my duties better.

Though his explanation sounds logical, I still can't shake the suspicion that Devon regretted spending Sunday with me and has decided to re-establish boss-employee boundaries.

Which is probably for the best.

Ever since Ellie told me about Devon as a young boy, my thoughts have been swirling around him even more.

His sister gave me a very different angle on his character. Though her interpretation could be flawed, something in her assumption about the why of Devon's behavior spoke to me.

Maybe he *is* compensating for some past deprivation with his libertine lifestyle. That would explain how a man so witty, generous, and kind could behave like such a dullard in his private life.

I tap on my forehead to stop the spiraling of my senseless conjectures. I'm only looking for excuses to justify my crush on Devon.

And it's pathetic.

I switch on the lights in the printing room and walk to a printer. I enable the proper settings and hit Enter. As I wait for the papers, I decide to call Chelsea to kill time.

"Hi, Chels. It's me, Laia."

A male voice replies, "Hi, Laia. It's Howard."

Shoot, why did I forget that my roomie would be out with him?

Before I can apologize for disturbing them, Howard holds the phone away from his mouth, which makes his baritone muffled. "Chelsea, sugar, it's your friend."

In a second, my friend's familiar voice echoes in my ear. "Laia? Did you see it too? It's weird, isn't it?"

She doesn't sound troubled that I interrupted her romantic date. Her eager tone, which she usually reserves for significant gossip, surprises me so much I forget my original intention of hanging up as fast as I can.

"Saw what, Chels? I've no clue what you're talking about."

"Aren't you calling about *True Facts*?" she asks.

My jaw drops.

"Why would I call you about a tabloid? Especially one that releases articles that contradict its name more often than not?"

Chelsea gives out a bemused snort. "Because it published a piece about our boss whose public image you're supposed to be curating?"

"That's not possible." I shake my head. "I did my regular news search this morning, and the list was empty."

"Weird, the article appeared online yesterday. I discovered it this afternoon, browsing on my phone."

Fiddlesticks, how could I miss this?

The article must contain something incredibly juicy if my roomie assumed I was calling about it.

I tap the printer's dashboard, and the shuffling of papers pauses. I quickly restart its flow, then ask, "How bad is it?"

While waiting for Chelsea's answer, I squeeze the phone between my shoulder and chin and race over to the computer in the corner of the room where employees can change their printing requests without having to walk back to their desks. I can use its browser.

My pulse drums in my ears as I type in my password and unlock the screen.

I type "True Facts Devon Griffin," and the first result that comes up reads, "Did the Hudson Communications' CEO have a change of heart?"

Chelsea's right. The timestamp is yesterday. I click on it and hold my breath.

"It's not bad at all. That's what makes it so odd," Chelsea says.

"What do you mean? What does it say about Devon and the company? Be specific, Chels. Do they mention any of our recent campaigns?" I snap at my friend because the tabloid's page is loading slowly, and I'm getting more nervous with the minute.

When I created my search settings, I thought I included all local gossip magazines, but it seems I must have missed *True Facts*.

Chelsea chuckles. "About the company? Nothing. It's all about Devon and what's happening to him."

Just as she says this, the website decides to cooperate, and the article appears on the screen.

After the bold headline, there are two photos of Devon laid side by side.

In one, he's in a press conference and looks absolutely ravishing as he speaks to the journalists. The other picture shows him in a fancy restaurant having dinner with a gorgeous blonde.

My heart squeezes as I look at how flirtily the girl smiles at him.

Then I read the caption. "Now and then. What's happening with one of our town's best tomcats? Did he give up on the chase for good?"

"Exactly," Chelsea exclaims, and I realize I must've spoken the words out loud instead.

"Are you looking at the article right now?" she asks.

"Yes, I am." My eyes fly through the lines.

It's a short text written in a sassy, almost obnoxious tone. The reporter speculates about why Devon hasn't been spotted clubbing in the past two weeks and presents two hypotheses.

Number one suggests that Devon is having a change of heart and wants to settle. While number two explains Devon's untypical behavior with a secret business deal that Hudson Communications will be announcing soon.

"So, what do you think? Interesting stuff, no?" Chelsea says. "Pretty much in line with what I—"

"Certainly not," I hurry to cut her off. "Please don't speak about your whacky gut feeling. Especially not when you're with Howard."

Chelsea told me that she perceived Devon's interest in me when we met at the car show. She went so far as to say our boss might be more indulgent about office affairs because he's got his eyes on me.

I refuted her insane idea, but without confessing what happened in Devon's elevator, I couldn't entirely dissipate her crazy theory.

"Of course not. I'm always very discreet. You should know this." Chelsea sniffs.

Chelsea being very discreet is as much of an overstatement as saying the Sahara supplies the entire world's population with fruits and veggies. But since I know my bestie never intends to harm with her chattiness, I don't contradict her.

"Anyway, you're right. There's no information about our company in the article besides a vague conjecture. Thanks for telling me about this, though. It completely slipped my attention."

"I'm glad I could help." Chelsea's voice clears from

resentment. A wonderful quality of my roomie is that she isn't able to hold a grudge with me. "When are you meeting Devon's sister?" she asks.

"As soon as my documents print."

And Devon decides to leave.

I bite back this last part just in time.

It was a conscious decision to hide from my friend that Devon is driving me to the jazz club, or that he will even be there at all. I didn't want to ignite Chelsea's misconception about our boss and me any further.

Partially because I feared that her claims could instill dangerous hopes in my heart.

"Great. Going out will do you good. You can't always be a homebody." Chelsea pauses and makes a coughing noise, but it sounds like she's trying to whitewash a sensual moan. A playful giggle bubbles up from her throat, and she adds, "Sorry, sweetie, I need to go now. Howard has special plans for us, and he's ready to reveal them, I think."

"Sure, don't keep him waiting. Bye, Chels." I hang up before I need to witness anything from Howard's surprise.

I gather my printed documents and go to the kitchen to make myself a black tea.

Ellie seems super enthusiastic about our evening. She texted me at least twice already to ensure that I wouldn't cancel on her. I'm not a night owl, and without some boost, I risk yawning all night. I return to my desk, balancing my steaming beverage in one hand, while in the other, I squeeze the papers.

I keep my eyes on my mug because I don't want to get myself dirty. Before going to the printing room, I changed into my jazz-club attire—a purple top and a pair of thin, black jeans.

As I amble forward, my thoughts return to the tabloid article.

Since I know there's no concealed business deal on Devon's agenda, I wonder whether the reporter's first claim could be correct.

Could Devon be considering a lifestyle change?

The talk we had about my romance book certainly didn't suggest that.

I know I shouldn't be concerned with what Devon does or doesn't do after leaving the office, as long as his private life doesn't taint his business image.

But I am.

As much as I hate to admit it, I wish the gossip magazine's author was right. No man has ever occupied my mind this intensely as Devon does.

At least no real men.

I've fantasized about movie heroes or my favorite book-boyfriends for entire nights, but my obsession with Devon is even wor—

Ouch!

My forehead bumps into something hard. A warm swish of air brushes my skin at the same time as a loud "*Careful!*" cuts through the air.

The unexpected sound and proximity of Devon's voice startles me, and I jerk my head up.

The movement makes my mouth land only inches away from Devon's lips and shakes my hand enough to spill most of the hot liquid from my cup.

On to…

I drop my glance and jump back as if hit by a current.

The fudge berries, I've splashed tea on Devon.

All. Over. Him.

The large yellow spot on his chest grows bigger by the second as the liquid seeps into the white fabric of his shirt.

Devon curses and drops the folder he's been carrying to the floor. He begins unbuttoning his shirt.

My jaw drops. "What are you doing?"

His eyes meet mine, but his fingers don't stop. "What does it look like, Laia? I'm taking off this darned, wet thing. Your tea burns like fire…"

His voice isn't as angry as it should be, considering I've probably ruined his Oxford shirt and risked giving him third-degree injuries.

His tolerance of my clumsiness only enhances my embarrassment.

I'd like to make myself useful somehow, so I quickly set my empty cup and printed papers on the floor and launch forward.

"Here, let me help!" I exclaim.

My hands land on his arm.

I only realize how objectionable my action could look after I start pulling his shirt toward me.

Devon's fingers close around my wrist, and he gently peels off my fingers. "I appreciate your effort, but if you don't move your hand, I won't be able to take it off. I first need to loosen the cufflinks." His voice has an amused undertone as if my zeal entertained him.

"Oh, yes, of course. I just wanted to help…you know, to diminish the risk of injury," I mutter, recoiling quickly. My sheepish tone may as well translate as *I'm ready to die from mortification*.

He undoes the two silver knobs while his glance moves to my face, which must be the reddest it had ever been.

Devon flashes me a crooked smirk, while he slips out of his shirt. "Don't look so flustered, Laia. I didn't assume that your fervor to undress me was triggered by anything other than your wish to save me from a burn."

Indeed, by nothing else.

Definitely not by the sight of so much sheer muscle.

I retreat two steps more, hoping the distance will help me direct my gaze away from Devon's upper body.

But as I move back, I have an even better view of his bare chest and abs—that, if my fleeting glance doesn't betray me, could very well be a solid eight-pack—so I really don't know where to focus my eyes.

His legs are still covered, but staring at his pants would be equally awkward.

In the end, I settle my gaze on his face.

Devon's lips are still set in a curve. He holds his shirt in his arm—*when did he have the time to fold it this neatly?*—and he's watching me.

As our glances interlock, his irises darken.

He shakes his head as if to clear it from a bothering thought and asks, "So…uhm…Laia, are those documents you printed for the casual footwear campaign?"

His business phrase contrasts his shirtless posture so absurdly that a nervous giggle escapes from my throat. I cover it up with a nod, as assistant-like as I can. "Yes, they are."

While I speak, I realize that due to the distractive exposure of his manliness, I forgot to excuse myself for pouring hot tea over him.

"Devon, I would like to say how sorry I am that"—I wave toward his shirt—"I risked scorching you. I was caught up in my thoughts about…a chapter of my novel."

Plotting my romance in my head is a far better excuse than admitting what occupied my mind.

"That's fine. I was distracted too. I'll watch where I walk from now on," he replies, smiling.

Yeah, don't walk around bare-chested unless you want your female employees to have a heart attack.

I suppress this idiotic phrase just in time, but, unfortunately, a similarly crackbrained one slips out. "Luckily, there's nobody else around. No danger of getting a mean vanilla doughnut smashed on you."

The image of whipped cream on his muscles is the last thing I should have brought up, dang it!

Devon's eyes widen at my goofy comment, and his lower lip twitches. "Shall I deduce from this that you don't like doughnuts? Or just vanilla ones?"

My cheeks boil. "No, I love doughnuts. Any kind, really. I have a sweet tooth. Though chocolate is probably my favorite of all…"

My babbling stops as Devon's hint at a smile grows into a full-blown grin.

"Ah, that's good to know," he says in a serious tone, but his eyes keep laughing at me. "Once a month we have a treat-day in the office. You may bring any sweets you like."

He's making fun of me.

But I guess I deserve it. I'm behaving like a complete moron.

Why did I have to tell him I like chocolate more than vanilla? Devon doesn't care.

I drop my gaze to the floor. "Okay, sure. I'll bake something nice for that day then."

I need to say something to demonstrate that my brain didn't get spilled with that cup of tea. Something that can re-establish a more office-type atmosphere between us.

I clear my throat. "So, are you done with work for tonight?"

Devon nods. "We can leave here in twenty minutes if that suits you. Ellie wanted to meet you at Jimmy'z around seven, right?"

"Ah, so you didn't forget," I say.

Devon furrows his brows. "Forget? Of course, not. Ellie checked in with me several times to ensure that I would take you." There's a trace of irritation in his tone, as if he isn't happy that we need to drive together.

I raise my glance to meet his blue irises. "I can take the tube, instead. It wasn't my idea that we go to the club together. Your sister—"

"Don't worry, Laia," he interrupts me by putting up a hand.

I want to ignore how his pectorals flex, but against my best will, my glance dips to his chiseled chest.

"I know my over-zealous sister. She…uhm…" Devon scratches his neck. "Ellie thinks I need help in the dating department."

"What? Why?"

Devon certainly doesn't need a hand with meeting women.

"Ellie holds similar values to you, so she's never satisfied with my choices." His face moves into a boyishly flustered grimace, and that's when I understand what he's getting at.

"Wait, Ellie wants you to find a *real* relationship? With *me*?"

Why did my stupid voice waver at this last word?

Devon shrugs as if his sister's plan isn't worth discussing. "Something like that. But don't worry. I'll tell Ellie to leave you out of her matchmaking attempts. My sister has a hard time accepting that I don't need a woman to be happy."

"Everyone needs somebody to love." The words rush out of my mouth like air leaving a holey balloon, instinctively and unstoppably, probably fueled by the disappointment Devon's statement awakens.

Devon rolls his eyes. "Are you going Solomon Burke on me?" He folds his arms across his chest, which makes his shoulders as broad as an athlete's. "And where do you get this wisdom? From your countless past experiences?"

I gasp, and his face softens immediately.

He steps closer and reaches for my arm. "I'm so sorry, Laia. I shouldn't have said that last part. It was wrong of me on so many levels."

"Don't worry." I keep my voice as stable as I can. "I'm used to people belittling my take on love because I have no experience. But you, Devon"—I square my shoulders—"you have plenty. And, still, you're just as clueless as I am. Despite your countless flings, you've never *truly* loved, right?"

Devon looks as if I slapped him.

"As a matter of fact, I have. Once. But it turned ugly. It's not something I'd ever want to repeat."

His short but bitter declaration is honest. There is no shadow of doubt about it. Only a person who had his heart broken could pronounce these words with such fervor and iciness at the same time.

He withdraws his gaze and bends to collect his folder from the floor.

I stand paralyzed.

I shouldn't have assumed that Devon has never loved anyone. I've completely misinterpreted him. He doesn't prefer short flings to meaningful relationships because he's afraid to commit. He's scared to be hurt again.

"You have a spare shirt for me, right?"

His question jars me out of my thoughts.

"Yes, yes, of course. I got three of them from the dry cleaner on Tuesday. I'll come and show—"

"No, thanks. I know where we keep them. I'll go and change. Meet you in the garage at quarter to seven?" he asks without looking at me.

"Yes, that would be fine."

"Good." Devon turns and saunters back to his office.

As I stare at his absolutely perfect back, my throat closes up. I wonder whether he's so upset about my comment that he can't even stand to ride in the same elevator with me.

I recall the night when he offered his help for my romance novel. His voice had a disillusioned undertone when he spoke about soulmates. Why didn't I pick up on it?

Instead I was judgmental and jumped to the conclusion that he's a playboy with a cynical worldview and loose morals. Guilt floods my chest as Devon's hurt glint dances in front of my eyes.

My sense of culpability is coupled with another feeling, too.

An entirely hopeless desire. A wish to teach Devon to believe in love again.

CHAPTER 25

(Laia)

"My sister might be here already." The hopeful edge in Devon's voice is so palpable I cringe. Devon can't wait to hand the baton to his sister and stop being in my company. During the drive, he didn't utter more than three words to me despite my attempts to jumpstart a conversation.

As we walk on the long and narrow underground corridor of Jimmy'z, I pray we find Ellie downstairs.

As we descend a mysterious blue staircase with a curved ceiling that takes us thirty feet down from street level to the club area, I accelerate my pace to be at his side.

I take a peek at his somber frown.

There's no question that Devon's facial features were made for a brooding hero look. The way his lips harden in a line and his eyes glimmer is how I imagined the male lead in my romance during the scene where he realizes he's lost his love forever.

Ah, Laia, you need to stop this. Now.

I already have too many moods that I find irresistible on him. Adding the vexed man to the collection wouldn't be wise. Especially after his revelation about his broken heart.

"So, what's the deal with this place? Why is it so special?" I ask, hoping to clear my head by speaking.

Devon gives me a slanted glance then shrugs. "Wait till we're downstairs. The club might not look much when you enter, but the owner's love for music really comes through in the main performance space."

Just as he finishes his phrase, we arrive in a room that has an impressive volume.

It hosts a stage that's larger in width than depth, eschewing the traditional shoe-box layout. Besides a giant Steinway piano, which seems to be a permanent piece, there's enough empty space for an entire band to fit on the podium comfortably. The whole is framed by a 20-foot-long, velvet maroon curtain, a signature backdrop for any genuine jazz club. But it's the tiny details of the room that make me understand what Devon meant.

Musical elements are everywhere, like the handmade wooden piano key details in the bar or the chandelier above, featuring two hundred plus trumpets.

My glance wanders to the carved Gothic pews that create a front row before the round, more conventional tables.

"These facilitate better views of the live gigs," Devon explains, pointing at the benches. "Jimmy didn't just build a trendy club, he—"

"He conjured a sanctuary for jazz lovers," I murmur, because the pews remind me of the seats in the church my mother goes to.

His eyes widen. "Yes, that's correct."

There is a sort of astonishment in his voice, but I don't pause to question what it might mean. I'm just happy that we're on speaking terms again.

"Come, let's sit at the bar while we wait for my sister," Devon says.

He orders us two glasses of sparkling water, and we settle on the leather stools.

Just as the barman places the drinks in front of us, Ellie's chipper voice draws my attention.

"Devon, Laia, here I am." She hurries over with a bright smile on her face.

Her curls are tamed with a thick, green hairband that plays up the emerald hue in her eyes. The corners of her mouth almost reach her ears as she greets me.

"It's going to be fun tonight. Right, brother?" Ellie pats Devon on his back.

"Hi, sis. Good that you're here." Devon nods to his sister and stands up. "I need to go backstage to speak with Jimmy. He wants me to play at eight, and it's almost time. If Pete comes, please keep him company."

Before he turns, he blinks at me. I detect a hint of concern in his eyes. "I hope you'll enjoy the music, Laia."

Without waiting for my answer, he whips around and leaves.

What was that? Was it his way of showing that we're good?

Ellie points at my glass. "Did you guys seriously order these? I go out so rarely I need something far tastier than just plain water when I finally do."

"I imagine Devon didn't want anything that would make him sleepy before he plays." I feel the need to protect her brother's choice, though I'm not sure why. I'd had the same thought as Ellie when I heard Devon order the waters.

Ellie rolls her eyes. "Let *him* be serious then, but you and I, we're here to have fun. What do you prefer in cocktails, sweet or fruity?"

"Both, I guess. I'm not big on names, though. Pick something. I trust your taste."

Ellie grins as if my answer is just what she wanted to hear. She waves the bartender closer and hops up on the barstool beside me. "Can you fix us two Strawberry Bellinis, please?"

She bats her lashes, and the guy immediately jumps to the mixer.

"Coming right up," he says.

Ellie holds up her hand. "Wait, let me tell you how I want them first, okay? I know some use *any* type of sparkling wine, but I'd love *real* Prosecco in it. Also, if you use fresh strawberries, make sure to wash them thoroughly. If you only have frozen ones, then blend them a tad more than you usually would. I hate to have chunks of fruit in my drinks. "

As I listen to Ellie, I can't help but recall how she rearranged Devon's desk in less than a minute. I admire that she seems to know exactly how she likes the things around herself to be and acts upon those preferences.

I, too often, let others' wishes come before my own because I'm afraid to be assertive. The reason why speaking up for myself landed so high on my bucket list.

Though I thought I was making progress on this front since starting my new job, my gaff with Devon demonstrates I still have much to learn before I nail this giving-others-a-piece-of-my-mind thing.

The barman's mouth opens at Ellie's explanation, but he nods. "Of course, I'll make it just the way you want it." He accompanies his phrase with a smile that betrays that he'd love to prepare something more than just a cocktail for Ellie.

Ellie smiles at him, then turns back to me. "Sooo…how is everything in the office? Do you enjoy working for my brother?"

I'd love to answer a simple yes, but something in Ellie's friendly face and freckled nose makes it hard to lie. "Yes, though it's a little confusing sometimes."

Ellie's brows arch suspiciously. "Confusing, how?"

Good job, Laia.

Why couldn't I choose a less questionable word? Who labels her interaction with her boss confusing?

I shrug, feigning nonchalance. "Devon is a good boss. He's…he's great at what he does. So prepared, and driven. I've already learned a lot from him, but…"

Ellie shifts closer to me, lowering her voice. "But? Was he mean to you? Offended you?"

I shake my head. "Oh, no. Not at all. I think it was me who might've offended him just before we came over here."

The urge to share with someone the embarrassing details of my blooper becomes so strong that I can't resist.

While we sip our cocktails, are all we could have hoped for—pink and gloriously yummy—I tell Ellie everything about our hot tea incident.

Well, everything *except* the wild fantasies her brother's shirtless sight unleashed in me.

Ellie nods as she listens, clicking her tongue once or twice.

I recite the exchange Devon and I had about true love, and as I get to the point I'd wish to change the most, she claps her hands.

"Ah, still Morgan. I can't believe this. She might've

been the homecoming queen, but she was such a tart. I could never understand what my brother saw in her."

Morgan?

Long slender legs, thick blond mane, and perfectly sculpted porcelain-doll features pop into my mind, together with a taunting smile and extravagant zebra coat.

I met the woman who destroyed Devon's faith in true love, and I didn't even realize it.

"Did they split a long time ago?" I inquire.

"Yep." Ellie sighs. "Just when Devon started his company. I guess he has Morgan to thank, partially, for Hudson Communications. After they broke up, Devon started to focus only on work. He didn't go out, and he didn't date. His dedication paid off, because in less than a year his company booked the first big client."

Didn't go out and didn't date?

This doesn't sound like Devon.

Ellie points at my wrinkled forehead. "I can see you're second-guessing me. Do you happen to be an avid tabloid reader?"

Wow, Ellie is pretty good at reading minds.

Since I'm busted, I have no other choice but to tell the truth. "Avid? Absolutely not. But my roomie is. Thus I've seen my share of articles about Devon. Also, your brother told me he only enjoys relationships as long as there are no strings attached."

"That's what my brother wants everyone to believe—even himself. For the first two years after Morgan, Devon worked like a madman. I feared he would become a workaholic and suffocate himself in his career. So, when Pete convinced Devon to start clubbing with him, I was glad. I hoped Devon would meet a girl who would break Morgan's curse. But instead, my stupid brother developed a taste for the womanizing lifestyle and began equating relationships to few-nights-stands."

Morgan's image in my head gets enriched with a magic wand. I see her place the jinx of "no-love" on Devon.

"What did Morgan do?" I ask.

Ellie purses her lips and takes another sip from her pink beverage. "Mhmm, this is delicious."

She gives a thumbs up to the bartender who's been throwing admiring glances at her. The man's face drifts into a grimace of joy.

Ellie pivots back to me. She smooths her cocktail napkin carefully with her free hand, then places her glass on the counter. "Morgan cheated on Devon. When Devon found out, he broke up with her, dropped out of college, and began working full time on his own company."

"Cheated? Oh, that must have been awful," I say with more emotion in my voice than I'm comfortable revealing.

Ellie throws me an appraising glance. "It makes you see Devon under a different light, doesn't it?"

Despite my best effort to keep up a barrier against Devon, another stone loosens in my heart's wall. How can I blame him for his disillusioned view of love after what he's been through?

My compassion for him gives my brain permission to release some suppressed thoughts. Thoughts that make my breathing grow shallow.

I reach for my glass and drain my cocktail, hoping the sweet liquid will wash away my previous misconceptions about Devon and the mushy sensations currently brewing in my stomach.

It doesn't quite manage to do that, but somehow the agreeable warmth of alcohol spreading into my belly makes me feel better.

Ellie watches me with narrowed eyes. "You were thirsty, huh? Shall I order us another round?"

Her cocktail is still half-full, but I could use another of these delicious pink miracles.

An unexpected giggle jumps from my throat. "Oh, I'd love that."

Ellie grins and stands up. Instead of waving to the bartender, she walks over to him, probably to motivate him a little.

While she's gone, I close my eyes and enjoy the woozy but pleasant sensation of weightlessness that settles around my toes and fingertips.

I've never been one to hold my liquor, never even practiced it much, to be honest. The one time I had three glasses of sweet sherry on a New Year's Eve, I only felt sluggish and sleepy.

Now, however, my facials muscles are prone to smiling without any conscious effort. The tip of my nose feels like it doesn't belong to my body, and I find it extremely funny.

Maybe tonight could become a fun experience after all.

Who would have thought so, after my hot tea fiasco?

The image of a shirtless Devon comes back to me, and the cocktail must have brought down all my healthy defenses, because I don't discard the vision.

I let the memory of his muscles linger in my mind and create a never felt buzz in my chest. I don't chide myself for it, just let it stir up all that it wishes, while a delightful smile spreads on my lips.

CHAPTER 26

(Devon)

Jimmy greets me backstage with a wide grin. "Dev, thanks so much for jumping in for Harry. You've no idea how tough it is to get a pianist as good as you on short notice."

I smile at the chubby, round-faced man who, as always, wears a black shirt with the club logo embroidered on his chest.

"No problem, Jim. You know I like to help whenever I can."

To be honest, I was more than happy to leave Ellie and Laia alone for a while. I wouldn't be great company to the girls anyhow. My chat with Laia put me into too much of a grim mood for that.

Jimmy scratches his thick, white beard, which I know he keeps growing, despite his wife's sheer dislike of hairy men, to honor his favorite baritone saxophonist. "But it's such a special evening for you. I hate to tear you away from your lovely companion. She does have something of Magos Herrera's charm, doesn't she?"

Jimmy compares everyone to musicians. The fact that Mexico's jazz prodigy reminds him of Laia—though I can't trace any objective likelihood between the two—is the highest compliment he can pay to my assistant, at least in Jimmy's terms.

"Yes, she's an exceptional girl," I murmur without realizing, while my mind wanders back to the fierce glow in Laia's eyes when she accused me of not knowing what true love meant.

It was rational for Laia, without knowing about my past, to believe I'd always been a ladies' man.

Still, her words stung like yellow jackets, and even remembering them sends a hot, smoky, almost irreverent pain billowing through my chest.

My grief has nothing to do with my ex, and everything to do with the realization that Laia doesn't believe me capable of real devotion.

Jimmy's fleshy lower lip moves into a smirk. "It's good to see you bringing along a girl for a change. I'd much rather see you with lots of kiddos who'll inherit your gift for music than drinking booze with Pete." He winks at me. "Though don't tell our Elvis imitator I said that. I like him just as much as you, but I know he won't change, while with you I still have some hope."

Before I get the chance to correct Jimmy's assumption about Laia, he taps my back. "Gotta get back outside, Dev. Pick some nice song for the lady of your heart."

He rushes away, leaving me with a mood darker than I had before we spoke.

I rub my cheeks and draw in a big breath. Lucky I'm about to play the piano, because this activity always clears my head.

As I exit to the podium, my eyes immediately search for Laia and my sister. I have no doubt they'll get along fabulously, but I'm worried because I couldn't coax out of Ellie what her secret plan for tonight is.

And I'm sure she has one.

I first find Ellie who is hard to miss, given that she's gesticulating with ample movements to the barman.

My glance shifts further to Laia, still sitting on the same barstool where I left her. Her eyes are closed as if she's wrapped up in some inner fantasy. Whatever she sees, it must be good, because a ravishing smile plays on her lips.

I settle to the piano, but my gaze is still on her face.

She looks absolutely stunning and unusually relaxed. I would give anything to see her this happy more often.

It wasn't entirely illogical for Jimmy to assume that when I finally show up with a woman in his club after years of frequenting the place alone the person I come with would have a special meaning.

Still, his misconception frustrated me.

Now, admiring how the spotlights of the bar illuminate Laia's face, making her skin sparkle, I realize my irritation about Jimmy's theory wasn't caused by the right reason. I wasn't bothered that he assumed Laia and I dated. I was troubled because his remark made me want that he *didn't* have to misinterpret our situation.

"Hey, when are you starting?" A man from a nearby table jars me out of my reverie.

I nod to him to signal *right now* and blink at the massive music sheet holder that contains the full repertoire Harry was supposed to play.

I like Bud Powell and Miles Davis, but before getting into their groovy rhythms, I'd like to play one special song.

I don't even need the notes for it, since I know it by heart.

Will *she* understand why I picked it?

Do I even?

Before I can change my mind, I press my fingers on the keyboard.

As the first strings strike, sending a bittersweet melody floating around the room, Laia's eyes spring open.

For a moment, despite her eyelids not shading her spectacular irises anymore, she still appears to be elsewhere…in a sort of trance, maybe. But then her gaze moves to me, and her lips part slightly.

I would never confess it to Ellie—the instigator of my demise—and I have a tough time even admitting it to myself, but as my eyes lock with Laia's, the whole club seems to brighten up.

I didn't want Laia to come tonight. I've been angry with my sister for inviting her. But having Laia at Jimmy'z, listening to the song she inspired me to pick, feels good.

Like Laia belongs here.

In the very hideaway to which I ostentatiously refused to invite any women.

Could this be a sign that Laia could fit my life, too?

A powerful emotion surges through me. Desperately afraid to trust it or even decipher what it might be, I shove it aside and deepen my fingertips on the keys.

Yes, sublimating these scary, exciting feelings into this song will surely help rid my soul of them for good.

CHAPTER 27

(Laia)

The sounds that Devon lures from the piano swirl around the room like magical serpents, wiggling their way into the listeners' souls.

His music must be the reason I feel suddenly breathless.

The snake must be crashing my ribs against my lungs as it dances through my chest.

The first three buttons of his shirt are open, giving just a glimpse at his collarbone. His fingers run up and down on the white and black keys with such grace, it's as if he were born to do this. The melody, familiar, captivating, but above all played to perfection, fills the bar.

Just when I think I'm not able to take his music's beauty, Devon begins to sing.

I can't see if he has a mic attached to his shirt, or maybe it's clipped to the piano in a way that's invisible to anyone not on stage, but he must have some kind of amplifier, because his voice reverberates from the walls of the bar with sheer force.

And what a voice.

How did I not catch this before?

When Devon speaks, he has a deep and pleasant baritone. But when he sings? His intonation is so sensual and purring, I feel like I've just eaten a full-blown, decadent chocolate cake with strawberry topping.

Satisfied but craving for more.

I lean forward on my seat, not realizing when Ellie comes back and plops down beside me. My whole attention is focused on Devon.

Slowly the words he sings make their way into my mind. Up until now, I've been so caught up with the acoustic of his voice that I didn't recognize what song he was playing.

Everybody needs somebody to love…

It's more a soul than a jazz song. I wonder why he picked it. Is it a joke to me? A provocation?

Devon glances up while his hands continue playing. His gaze travels to me, and I spot a mischievous glint in his eyes.

That, or I've drunk too much.

But I like the idea that it's there—more than I probably should.

Ellie hands me another glass, and I take it, murmuring a quiet, "Thanks."

She bends closer and whispers, "I used to tell him that if a woman heard him play, she would ultimately fall in love with him."

I snap my head to her, because her words are too spot-on to be coincidental.

Can she see how my heart is jumping around in my chest? Or is my ragged breathing betraying me?

"Is that why you invited me here?" I ask Ellie. "Devon told me you're trying to fix him up. But he doesn't like it."

Ellie twirls her glass around and a piece of strawberry on the rim falls into her drink. "Devon doesn't know what he needs, but I do. He needs a good girl he can fall for. Only that will heal his soul."

At the unmistakable conclusion about who she has in mind for her brother, my neck begins to itch.

I wouldn't mind being *that* girl.

Especially now that I'm listening to Devon's voice singing this utterly romantic song.

The problem is all evidence suggests I can't be. Even if I tried…

I lift my glass. "Well, cheers to that. But please don't place your bets on me. I'm not the right person to save your brother." I quickly swallow a few gulps from my drink because saying these words out loud makes me sad.

This second cocktail is more potent than the first; it burns my throat and sends a direct heat into my stomach. But at least it also dissipates a bit of my sorrow.

Ellie smacks her lips. "We'll see about that. Something tells me you could be exactly the right person for this job. And my hunches are usually good."

Except this time.

I'm way out of my league with a man like Devon. I was with Bobby, my high-school crush, and he was…I can't even mention him on the same page with Devon.

Intellectually. Charisma-wise. Or physically.

Ellie flutters her hands above her head as if signaling to somebody.

A blond man with an Elvis haircut walks to us.

"Hi, kiddo," he greets Ellie with a kiss on her cheek. Then he turns to me. "Hi, Laia."

I stare at him wide-eyed.

The guy indeed looks like "the King" only in blonde, but even if his face seems familiar, I'm sure I've never met him.

"I don't think we've met," I say.

He grins. "No, we haven't. But I do know you. I'm Pete, Devon's friend."

Ah, the friend under whose wings a heartbroken Devon turned into a careless playboy.

"Your boss has told me many great things about you," Pete adds.

"Did he?" I answer, while my eyes wander to the stage.

To my surprise, Devon is staring at me.

His brows are set in a furrowed line, even as he plays a new song, a classic from Bud Powell.

I don't know what has gotten into me, maybe the Bellini's naughty kick, but I give Devon a long, lingering glance before I turn back to Pete.

From the corner of my eyes, I see Devon's still watching me. I exchange Pete's smile with a flirty one of my own. "Well, that's lovely to hear. Though I'm not sure I deserve so much praise."

My voice is drenched in that faux-modesty that I've often observed Chelsea use with men when she wants to trick them into complimenting her.

Pete shakes his head. "Oh, no. My friend didn't exaggerate one bit with his words, I assure you."

Ellie clears her throat and puts a hand on my shoulder. "Is your cocktail good?"

While I confirm that it indeed is, Pete intercepts Devon's gaze. He smacks his lips, spreading his fingers like the petals of a rosebud.

Devon's face tenses, and his fingers miss a note, which makes the refrain of "Bouncing with Bud" edgier than it was supposed to be.

My chest warms at his mistake. I can't help but hope my coquettish behavior contributed to this slip.

Pete pivots back to us, chuckling. "So, beautiful ladies, what are you drinking?"

I hold up my cocktail. "I don't remember the name, but it has perfectly blended strawberries and lots of bubbles."

Pete wiggles his brows. "Sounds just the right kind of drink then. I'll also get—"

Before he can continue, Ellie jumps up. "Before you do that, Pete, there's something important I'd like to discuss with you…in private. Do you mind if we step outside?"

Pete looks bewildered at first, then shrugs. "Of course, kiddo. I know better than to contradict you when you have this determined glint in your eyes. Your wish, my command." He blinks at me. "Will you be fine on your own, Laia?"

"*Suurrre.*" Okay, this last 'r' rolled off a bit funnily. Maybe my tongue has gotten larger in the past minute?

"Devon will stop playing soon and keep her company," Ellie chimes in. "*You* and I surely won't be missed."

Pete gives Ellie a suspicious glare then nods. "Ah, I see. See you later, Laia. *Maybe.*"

Before I can make sense of why he added this weird 'maybe', he turns and walks toward the exit.

Ellie leans close to me. "Laia, may I ask you a favor?"

The wheels of my brain turn slower than usual. "How can I help with that?"

Ellie smiles. "Simple. When Devon is done with his performance, keep him occupied so he doesn't come looking for us. Got it?"

I want to answer, "*got-it-what-if*," but I manage to stop myself.

She wouldn't find it particularly funny. And it probably

isn't. Only the devilish pink liquid in my belly makes me think it is.

So I just nod.

Ellie flashes me a smile then hurries off after Pete.

My eyes roam back to the stage, where Devon has started a soul-stirring jazz ballade. His eyes are lost on the horizon, and his jaw is set in a frown.

I lift my glass and empty the last drops of my drink.

I'll need all the giddy I can get if I'm to keep Devon busy and away from his sister and his friend.

CHAPTER 28

(Laia)

The song comes to an end, and Devon is greeted with a round of applause.

I join in as well, utterly surprised that my palms make such vivid noise. I never noticed I have *such* a talent.

Maybe if my job for Devon falls through, and I can't publish my romance novel, I should try casting for some talk show. My particular skill might be appreciated in the audience of Oprah, for example.

Yeah, I could even become the clapping champion of—

"Laia?"

Huh, Devon's mic is truly terrific. It sounded almost as if he were standing next to me.

"Laia?"

This time Devon's hand taps gently on my shoulder. Two of his fingers land on the bare skin of my neck, making me sizzle at his touch.

My eyes dart to his, and a wide grin spreads on my face. "You were just…wow, Devon. Like wow, *wow*…"

I sound like a total moron, and I see that my lack of proper vocabulary is as puzzling to him as it is to me.

Or maybe more to him.

I actually find it mildly funny. Why do I need to use sophisticated expressions and elaborate metaphors? A '*wow, wow*' is just as good, right?

One of his brows lifts as he eyes the cocktail glasses on the counter. "Have you been drinking? And where is my sister?"

"Huhu!" I raise my hands in protest. "Is this a firing-squad or what? Too many questions at once."

Devon's cherry-colored mouth twitches, hinting at a smile.

Though perhaps raspberry would be a better fruit for his lips' color. Cherries can be too dark, and Devon's flesh is…

I bend closer to him, letting my gaze linger on his mouth.

Yes, definitely raspberry.

The sweet and ripe kind, not the ones my mother used to buy from Señor Gonzales—

"Are you *drunk*?"

Devon's lips move, and I realize how close I am as his breath tickles my nose.

"Of course not," I jerk back and straighten my spine to prove my point. I even jump up from my seat for emphasis.

Despite a slight sway, I manage to stand straight in front of him.

Like I wanted to demonstrate, I'm *perfectly* sober.

Devon sighs, but the corners of his mouth curve up.

"You're not used to alcohol or going out. It shows. You should have stuck with the sparkling water I ordered."

Isn't he a reputed party king? Why is he so shocked that I had one or two little bubblies?

I pick up a glass from the counter. "It's just some yumminess your sister picked out for us. It's so delicious that even Pete wanted to taste it. Want me to order you one?"

His face becomes serious, and he shakes his head. "No, I'm fine. Thanks. Where is Pete?"

He puts a weird emphasis on his buddy's name, but I ignore it, together with his question.

I'm busy thinking about how I could cheer Devon up.

We need to bide our time before his sister and friend return, and that won't happen for a while, judging by Ellie's secretive behavior. I can't spend the whole evening walking on eggshells around Devon.

I blink at my drink as if it can give me an answer and notice there's still a strawberry sitting on a bit of pinkish delight in the bottom of my glass.

This might just be enough.

I press closer to Devon.

He doesn't retreat, but his eyes widen. "What are you doing?" he asks, somewhat alarmed.

"You really have to taste this. It's *sooo* good. Come on, just a teenie-tiny sip." I hold up my glass to him and lick my lips as if to demonstrate how amazing the flavor is.

Devon's gaze travels to my mouth, and his pupils dilate. His blue irises become two thin circles around the giant black holes as they expand.

"Fine. Give me the strawberry." His voice is challenging with a smooth, almost seductive edge.

Like in the elevator, only this time I'm not intimidated or flustered by it. I suspect it's probably the courage of the two Bellinis that makes me act so cocky, but I reach for the fruit and lift it from the glass.

"You wanted this?" I wiggle my brows.

Devon stares at me and slowly, *oh-so-very-slowly*, nods.

My last grain of rationality desperately shouts that I'm playing with fire. Still, its warning is inaudible due to the loud, unruly voice urging me to reach out and caress Devon's cheeks to see whether the stubble sprouting on his jawline is soft or tickly.

"All you need to say is please, and it's all yours," I tease.

Devon's gaze holds mine. "*Please.*"

This single word triggers a cascade of warmth in my belly. To distract myself from the sensation, I try to recall which bucket list items I'm currently conquering.

But his eyes are blazing enough to fry my brain, and my neurons can't ponder anything other than the depth of his blue irises.

Laia, you said A, now comes B...

I guide the strawberry to him, and when his mouth opens to take hold of it, my thumb brushes against his lower lip.

I think I hear his breath hitch, but I could be mistaking my own ragged inhale for his.

The brief contact makes a flicker of reason return in my deserted mind. I take a step back and place my glass on the counter.

"So, your verdict?" I ask, trying for a voice that's calm but comes out husky.

Devon chews on the strawberry and after swallowing gives me an enigmatic smile. "You were right. It would have been a pity not to try *this*."

Devon's cell chimes. He takes it from his pocket and peeks at it.

And so do I.

A calendar reminder flashes on his screen. "*Cora Tuesday night!!!*"

I'm surprised I can read the upside down script through my slightly blurred vision.

Devon swipes the note to silence the alarm and blinks up at me. "I'm sorry for this interruption. What were we saying?"

All the coy wooziness dissipates from my chest. 'Cora Tuesday' canceled out whatever special moment we might have had.

Correction, I've had—*in the singular*.

A high-strung snicker bubbles up from my throat at the realization that I almost made a fool of myself.

It was silly to assume that a man who has female names in his calendar for every weekday could be enticed with me.

"What's funny?" Devon asks.

"Nothing. Everything. *This*." I point at him then at me.

"I'm not sure I understand." His brows round.

"It's funny that I felt there was something sizzling between us when there wasn't, right?" I ask.

Devon inhales then exhales loudly. "Laia, the truth is—"

"No problem. I know I'm not *Laia Friday*." I force out a giddy chuckle.

Best to pretend my reason escaped to the safe harbor of tipsiness, then maybe Devon won't question why I tried to act like a femme fatale.

Devon's gaze darkens. "That's not what I wanted to say. But it might be better if we pick up this conversation another time when you're not…" He scratches his chin, and the five-o'clock-shadow I admired makes a rustling sound. "Where are Ellie and Pete anyway?"

"Outside." I point toward the stairs. "Ellie asked me to keep you occupied while she speaks with Pete. *Privately*. I think your sister may be in love with your friend. Isn't that romantic? Maybe she can teach Pete that one woman is enough..."

My own words stir up an unsettling image.

I see Devon planting a feathery kiss on my mouth while whispering, "*You are my media naranja, Laia.*"

I don't even bother to decipher why my illusory Devon uses the Spanish equivalent to declare that I'm his soulmate. I'm just shocked such a vision could bypass my control in the first place, even with the alcohol.

Devon's chin hardens. "I'll text Ellie to check what's going on."

He pulls out his phone and types quickly.

After only a minute, during which I rub my mind clean of my derailed fantasy, his phone chimes.

His brows furrow as he reads his sister's answer. "It seems Ellie decided to turn the tables on us for real. She and Pete won't be coming back to the club."

I give him an I-told-you-so glance.

He snorts, but his lips hint at a smile. "I'm confident it's not what you think, Laia. There is no one Ellie is less likely to fall for than Pete. Well, maybe just one."

"I know, I know." I give him a coy smirk. "Your friend, Wyatt. I heard how much she dislikes him. I can't fathom why, though. He's one hunky football player."

"I didn't know you follow football," Devon says in a perplexed tone.

"Oh, I don't. Chelsea made us google Wyatt last week after he called you in the office."

Devon's eyes widen. "Did you just admit to me that you've spoken about my private call to Chelsea?

"Oh, shoot, I guess I just did." I tap on my forehead.

"Which is utterly stupid, given that I'm your PA, right?" Maybe mentioning my job title jumpstarts my responsible self for a second because I add, "It was a slip, I'm sorry. I was too excited after my first day, so I overshared with my friend. I don't usually talk to Chelsea about these details. I mean *ever*."

Devon's face softens. "It's not a state secret that Wyatt and I are friends, so no harm done. And since I believe this information isn't something your sober self would have blurted out, I think it's time for us to go. We don't need to wait for Ellie and Pete, so I can take you home to rest." He takes hold of my elbow.

Despite the fantastic zing his fingers give me, I wiggle free from his grip. The fact that he spoke to me as if I'm a drunk fool makes me annoyed.

"I'm not ready to go just yet. I think I'll stay and get another drink. One that's *not* sparkling water."

Devon sighs. "Laia, please, it's better if we go. You'll have a bad headache as it is tomorrow. Trust me."

I hold my temples with my palms on both sides and rock my head side to side. "All fine, see?" But just as I finish bragging, a spasm sizzles through my temples. My face contorts into a grimace.

Devon steps to me and cradles my cheeks in his hands. A worried glance fills his eyes. "You're starting to get a throbbing already, aren't you?"

His tone is filled with concern, and his sweet attention depletes my previous flare of rebellion. Or it maybe it's the heat of his touch that seeps into my skin with light ripples.

Whatever it is, I don't feel like contradicting him anymore.

I peek up at him and nod. "Fine. Let's go home."

CHAPTER 29

(Devon)

I don't like women who drink too much.

I don't even like *myself* when I drink too much. I hate when my judgment becomes clouded through alcohol. That's why only a handful of people have ever witnessed me even inebriated.

I should be put off by Laia's confused state.

But I can't help it, I find even tipsiness darned sweet on her.

And if it were only that…

As I put my hand on Laia's lower back to assure she won't trip on the club's stairs —even though she performs her slightly unstable ascent with her chin up, she can't fool me. I know she must be feeling dizzy— that daring glint with which she gave me the strawberry flashes through me.

And I'm once again robbed of breath.

A muscle was bunched on her neckline when she

retreated, almost as if it cost her to back off. It sure as heck cost me not to reach out and haul her to my chest.

If that silly reminder Ellie programmed into my phone about her roomie's gallery opening hadn't come between us, I'm not sure I could've stopped myself from claiming Laia's mouth this time.

"*¡Andale*, Devon! Gimme your car keys. I can totally drive us." Laia's addled timbre snaps me out of my mindtrip.

She holds out her hand to me as we reach my Audi. The menacing frown with which she tries to coax me into handing her my keys makes her look cute as a doll.

Her words, despite preserving their jingling quality, roll heavier than they did inside the club. The cocktails must be fully spread throughout her bloodstream by now.

"No, no, Laia. I'm driving."

She reaches for my hand and tries to snatch the keys. Her fingers miss and land on my chest, triggering thrills in my entire torso.

To hide the manly warmth I feel from her innocent touch, I fall back on a tone that I practiced with Ellie when she went through her unreasonable adolescent years, and our parents were at their wit's end with her. "It's not safe for you to drive, so let's not start a discussion about it. It's getting late anyway."

"How late is it then?" Her eyes flick to her watch, and as she stares at her arm, her eyes glaze over.

I'm pretty sure she isn't able to read the numbers. Judging by the giant yawn she covers up with a hand, the only thing she should be doing is hopping into her bed to sleep.

I take her wrist and point at the hour hand. "It's almost nine. Not too late, but for you and your pink bubblies, late enough."

I add a smile to show I'm not chiding her. I noticed that she didn't like it when I commented on her tipsiness.

She watches my fingers on her arm, then slowly raises her chin. "Did you realize you can wrap your hand around my wrist, and there's still some space between your fingers?"

She's right. Her wrist is so delicate my hand closes easily around it.

"That's because you have the bone structure of a bird." I chuckle, ignoring how the spot where we touch sends licks of sizzles up to my shoulders.

She narrows her eyes. "Take that back. I'm no bird. I'm…I am…"

Her eyes drift toward the sky, and for a second I think she's lost in the sight of the stars. Then as if she's just remembered her thread, her glance flicks back to me, and a triumphant smile stretches on her lips.

"I'm a woman. A *mujer*, Devon. MU-JE-EER. You get it?"

Something in the way she says this makes me pause and release her hand.

It's not just the alcohol speaking.

No, there's a certain edge in her voice that suggests she actually believes I've never noticed she's a woman.

Where has Laia been the past half-hour? Or the last two weeks, really? How can she think I'm unaffected by her confusingly innocent and entirely disarming charm?

Laia takes my silence as confirmation of who-knows-what insane theory she's formed about me, and she taps my chest with her palm.

"Your problem, Devon, is that you waste your time with Tuesday Coras, Thursday Jessicas, and Sunday what's-her-names, while—"

"Laia, Cora is Ellie's friend. *Not* my date," I insert.

Laia stares at me wide-eyed then waves. "One swallow does not make a summer."

A suspicion forms in me, and its bare possibility makes my chest buzz. "Were you bothered by the thought that I would have a *date* on Tuesday? That's why you're upset?"

Her mouth opens and closes. "No. Of course not. And I'm not upset."

Oh, yes, she is.

My lips curve into a smile, because her frustration confirms the magnetic pull between us is a mutual sensation.

Laia's nostrils flare, and she pulls her hands to her hips. "Stop grinning at me with your player smile. *I* am not the problem here. That one is you and your obsession with the past. That *Morogan* cheating on you? It's her loss, don't you see it?"

My jaw goes slack. "How do you even know of—?"

Laia presses her finger on my mouth. "*Ssshh*, the how isn't important. I'm teaching you something here. Something you can't seem to grasp, Devon."

Our gazes lock, and I'm lost in her irises, twinkling in the streetlamp's light.

"You're stupid to let one delusion dictate your actions. I believe you can't…you shouldn't…you…" She stops, and then as if she hadn't been addressing one of my most private topics, another giant yawn escapes from her mouth.

I want to be mad at Laia. I really do. What right does she have to judge me based on the information Ellie gossiped about?

I'll need to kill my sister for sharing my story. Laia even said Morgan's name wrong.

But this detail doesn't bother me in the slightest.

What does is that Laia believes I don't know she's a woman, when each fiber in my body is all too aware that she is. That she thinks I'm still hooked on the playboy life when, in reality, since she walked into my office, I haven't been on a single date.

As I stare at her, the desire to show to her what I think swamps my chest. I want to grab her, pin her against the car, and silence that mouth of hers with a desperate kiss.

It's an action I'll probably regret later, but the urge is too strong.

Just as I'm about to haul her to me, Laia closes her eyes and shrugs.

"Ugh, I'm tired," she mumbles.

She actually looks exhausted as she stands there, rubbing at her eyes with her fists like a cartoon character.

The weird carnal desire that took possession of me dissipates, leaving space for another sensation that's equally, or perhaps even more, puzzling.

A sense of intense protectiveness.

I want to get Laia in bed.

But not the way I fantasized about a second ago. I want her tucked in, relaxed, and able to recover. Her safety and well-being are all that count.

When did I start to care for her *this* much?

I proceed with my planned gesture, but instead of grabbing Laia's waist and pulling her to me, I simply put my arm around her shoulders and gently guide her to my car. I open the door and settle her into the passenger seat.

Laia moans softly and closes her eyes.

I bend over her to close the safety belt.

Her eyelids quiver, and her breathing slows, signaling that she isn't far from a deep REM. I take a deep, conscious breath and move back from her.

Since the first time we met, her perfume has been my Achille's heel. The enticing scent does things to my insides I'd better avoid feeling. It entices prospects and what-ifs that would be wiser to avoid, and I can't help but contemplate them anyway.

"Laia?" I ask softly. "Where do you live?"

No answer. Only a steady stream of air. I sigh and take her purse.

A gentleman—and despite what some might think, I am one—never goes through a woman's bag.

Unless it's an emergency.

I rummage in her black leather bag for her wallet and take out her driver's license.

I furrow my brows. This can't be right. I distinctly remember from Laia's application file that she doesn't live far from my place. This address in Laveen Village must be an old one.

I rearrange her wallet and stuff it back in her bag. While I do, my hand brushes against the cover of a book.

My lips curl up, because even if I didn't think of it consciously, I expected to find a novel in here.

I pick up the book, interested to see what kinds of topics occupy her mind.

I expect a cheesy romance. Like the one she told me she'd love to write.

But the book is some acclaimed motivational guide. *Success Lies Within Us*. Is this what inspired Laia to build up her bucket list?

I thumb through it and find it's a pretty exciting read despite the slightly new-age tone the author uses.

I put the book back, fetch Laia's house keys, and stick them into my pocket.

I close the passenger door with care so I don't wake Laia and saunter to the driver seat.

After hopping in, I take my phone and log into the app that stores all my employee data. I scroll through the list of names until I get to the letter 'F' and copy Laia's current address into my GPS.

In less than ten minutes, we arrive at her house. The street where she lives is indeed close to my condo. If I wanted, I could walk to visit her one of these days.

I freeze mid-thought.

Why would I walk to Laia's apartment? It seems Laia's scent has wrecked my neuronal connections.

I shake my head and get out of the car.

I want to open the entrance door before carrying Laia inside. Once she's in my arms, I don't want to be fiddling with locks.

I disregard the anticipation brewing in my stomach when I think that soon I'll lift Laia and press her soft curves to my chest.

Instead, I hasten to her building and try all her keys.

But none works.

Mhmm…weird.

I check the names on the intercom. On the third row, there's "Flores" so we're at the right place. But why can't I open the door?

I step back to check the windows, but all are dark. The inhabitants are either out on a Friday night or already sleeping. In neither case can they buzz me in.

Just as I'm about to walk back to my car, a fifty-something woman with pockmarked cheeks and a wolfish face passes me. She throws me a quick, suspicious glance then scurries to Laia's building's door.

Great, I'll ask her to let us in.

The woman fumbles with her keys while her eyes fly to me then back to the lock.

I amble to her and clear my throat.

The woman whips around, her eyes wide in alarm.

"Excuse me, would you—" I break off as something

sharp lands on my sternum, knocking the air from my ribcage.

I need a second before I find my voice, and the first sound that leaves my lips is a painful *ouch*, as I clasp at the tender spot on my chest.

The woman pulls back her arm, revealing a bunch of heavy keys that sway on a swing ring similar to Ellie's. Only this woman's string is blue instead of pink.

Despite the discomfort I still feel, an amused snort escapes my throat.

Huh, I clearly underestimated my sister's gadget. This darned thing can truly hurt if appropriately used.

The woman yells, "Back off now, or I'll charge again."

"I'm sorry," I mumble. "I just wanted to—"

The woman lifts her rubber chain as if to show that she isn't playing. "I. SAID. BACK. OFF."

I turn around and retreat to my car without another word. I'd like to avoid another metallic punch into my flesh.

Also, I realize that even if I get into Laia's building, there's no guarantee I'll be able to open her apartment door. Since Laia's keys didn't match the gate's lock, they might not work for her flat.

I can't risk being spotted again by this paranoid neighbor while trying to force a door open. She'd surely call the police on me. The last thing I need is a another tabloid story that I've been arrested for breaking into a flat with my unconscious assistant in my arms.

I hear the building door close with a loud bang.

Good, at least the crazy lady is gone.

I stop beside my car's window and stare at Laia sleeping.

There's only one option left.

I have a spare bedroom in my house, and currently, it's

only Cat who enjoys the king-sized bed. She won't mind sharing it with Laia. My kitty seemed to be a fan of my assistant.

What worries me isn't whether I have enough space.

No, it's the hitched breathing I get from the idea that Laia will stay over at my place.

I cough twice and thump at my chest with my fist.

Okay, better.

The mean jab from that lunatic woman's keychain must have messed with my respiratory reflex.

Even so, as my eyes dip to Laia's slightly open mouth, my heart stutters.

CHAPTER 30

(Devon)

When we arrive at my building, Philip has gone home, and the night doorman is on duty. Not a single muscle twitches on his well-trained face as he sees me carrying Laia in my arms. He pulls the door open and wishes me a polite "good night."

We get into the elevator, and I use my elbow to push my floor's button.

I try to avoid peering down at Laia while she's so close, hoping if my eyes don't feast on her sleeping innocence, it'll be easier to tame the jitter in my stomach. However, as the elevator doors close, my determination becomes an absurd mission due to the mirrors lining the walls. It might just be better to see the real thing than her four silvery reflections.

I lower my glance and gasp, because Laia's eyes are half-open.

She peeks up at me from below her lashes and not in a bewildered, *what the heck am I doing in your arms*, kind of way. No, her eyes are warm and calm.

"It feels good, Devon. Soo goooood..." she murmurs and closes her eyelids again.

I realize she isn't awake at all, but probably dreaming. *Am I in her dream? Am I?*

Before this puzzling realization can sink in, the doors open.

Cat, as if she knows I'm not alone, makes loud meows before I turn the lock. Her yellow irises illuminate when she spots Laia in my arms, as if I'd given her fish pâté.

The little beast is happy to have Laia back at my house. And if I'm honest, so am I.

I throw off my shoes and carry Laia to the spare bedroom. I lay her gently on the bed and take off her flats.

By the time I take her shoes to the corridor and return, my furry companion has already settled herself in the curve between Laia's shoulder and neck. She leans her head on Laia's collar bone.

I stare at them, and a smile makes its way to my lips.

They look precious together.

For a second, I wish I had a fairy grandmother who could turn me into a kitten so I could join my cat and snuggle against Laia's warm body.

Cat would probably scratch my face if I approached them, though.

I fetch a blanket and want to put it on Laia, but Cat lifts her chin and scoffs at me.

"I'm not taking her away from you, Cat. I just want to tuck her in," I murmur.

As if the animal understands me, she lowers her head and starts to purr.

I arrange the checkered cover so it wraps Laia's entire body up to her chest then I walk out of the room.

I go to the kitchen to get a glass of water and make a

sandwich. There's not much left in my fridge, so I leave the two eggs and bacon untouched, despite feeling famished. Laia will need those fatty calories more when she wakes. It's clear she isn't used to pulling late nights or gulping down cocktails, so I'm afraid she'll have a splitting headache.

As I finish eating, my phone beeps.

It's a text from Ellie.

"Sorry Pete and I had to leave. Thank you for getting Laia home safely. xoxo"

I doubt my sister had anything urgent to discuss with Pete. My best guess is she wanted to remove herself and my buddy from the picture so Laia and I would be forced to spend an evening together.

Which is probably for the best, at least where it concerns Pete. I didn't like the sweet glances my buddy gave to Laia while I was on stage.

Laia's lecture about Morgan comes back to me, and I sigh.

I'll still need to scold my sister for telling Laia about Morgan.

At least after tonight, Laia knows I wasn't lying to her when I said that I had loved.

I finish washing my plate and glass.

On the way to my room, I can't suppress the urge to sneak in and take a last peek at the two sleeping beauties.

Once I'm in my own bed, it's still early, so I browse the latest news on my phone. I need something to distract my mind from Laia's presence in my house. I do a quick search for any current rumors circulating about me. I don't expect to find anything, since Laia hasn't mentioned any new articles, and I know she monitors my public image with care.

But to my surprise, a result from yesterday comes up.

The headline makes me sit up.

I scan the article and pause at the phrase, "*Did something or someone remind our carefree playboy that his life is empty without a meaningful relationship?*"

"That's exactly what happened," I murmur as my phone drops to my lap.

I imagine the author must've decided to venture into such idling about my behavior because he lacked any other concrete, juicy piece to fill his column.

Still, I'm sure glad he did.

Though unwittingly, the writer captured into words what occurred when Laia came into my life.

Isn't it strange that this article appeared in front of me at just the right time?

With the peculiar sensations Laia unlocked in me tonight, I'm finally ready to admit that I'm fed up with my old life. I've had enough messing around. I'm tired of flings.

I want *strings attached*. To someone special, with whom I feel at ease—a person who interests and excites me.

I already know who that woman should be.

Yes, I *want* Laia.

And not just in the you-look-so-gorgeous appreciation I usually reserve for other women. It's not a fleeting desire, what I feel for her.

Something in Laia I still can't pinpoint makes me want to spend time with her, protect her, and long for her more than I have for anyone.

Do I stand a chance with her?

I know she's drawn to me. After our moment in the club, there's no question about that. She might have been tipsy, but her eyes spoke of real desire toward me.

However, it's likely only a physical attraction. Laia has already expressed to me that I couldn't be further from the type of man she would date.

But that's *precisely* what I would love to happen.

I want to court her, date her, get to know her, and let her know me.

I rub my temples, as a long sigh escapes my chest.

Is there a way I could make Laia change her mind?

CHAPTER 31

(Laia)

I wake to a rough, warm, and humid *something* licking my face.

I turn my head to the side and almost jump as Cat's yellow irises meet mine.

It's useless to ask myself where I am. The kitty by my side is a perfect clue.

The question is *why* am I here?

Cat lets out a demanding meow, and I tickle her below her chin.

"Hey, buddy, did you sleep with me?" I murmur, lifting myself to my elbows.

My head immediately protests, sending jolts all the way to my toes. A groan escapes, and I squeeze my eyes shut for a second.

If I listened to my body, I'd lie back until the pounding in my temples ceases, but I know I can't do this.

I need to get up from this amazingly soft bed—probably the comfiest I've ever slept in—and start acting like a good employee should in her boss's house.

I open my eyes, and my glance drifts to the blanket enfolding me neatly like a wrapped sausage. Though my mouth feels sticky and parched, the ultimate reminder that last night wasn't my greatest moment, my stomach still growls at the idea of minced meat.

It figures. I didn't have dinner before going to the club, which must be why those pink drinks hit me harder than they should have.

I lift the cover and peek beneath it.

I sigh in relief when I realize I'm still dressed, and only my shoes are missing.

My bag is on the night table beside the bed, its long handle folded into an immaculate little bundle.

Did Devon do that? Did he tuck me in this nicely, too?

But more importantly, *how* did I end up in his condo at all?

My memories of last night are hazy, to say the least. A big chunk is missing. As soon as I hit the seat of Devon's Audi, heavy tiredness had descended, and I couldn't fight it back.

Well, frankly, I might not have tried. It was far easier to suffocate my fuzzy feelings for Devon in the silence of sleep than face them.

And, since I'm still not ready to analyze my own stupidity—because what else could I call my forlorn crush on Devon—I decide to size up my current situation based on the facts I *can* be sure of.

1. I'm in Devon's house.

2. Devon, for some reason, decided to take me to his place instead of my house.

3. He tucked me in with a checkered blanket.

4. I've apparently slept here.

5. Devon is awake, because I can hear his footsteps.

6. He must be making breakfast, because the mouthwatering smell that reaches my nostrils can't come from anything but bacon and eggs.

That's about as far as I can get without summoning the humiliating image of my tipsiness.

I sit up, and Cat protests as I shift her from my lap to the bed. I press my feet to the floor to get some mental anchoring.

A soft music filters in from the living room. It's a remake of a popular Aretha Franklin song, "Son of a Preacher Man." The melody brings back memories without me consciously calling upon them.

Devon on stage, playing piano.

His voice filling my soul with an indescribable pleasure.

Him coming to me after his performance and me…

I freeze.

Blimey…did I do what I think I did?

Did I really study Devon's lips close up, tempt him to eat my strawberry, and then called him stupid, screaming, "I'm a woman"? I might have even spelled it out in Spanish for him.

Panic locks up all my muscles. Why did I do that? Why?

He'll surely fire me now.

I bury my face in my palms as desperation spreads in my chest. Hudson Communications is my best (not to say only) shot at getting some much-needed business experience, and it could land me with a permanent contract.

And let's not forget that the new situations I face at my job are like a gold mine for my creative muse. Ever since I started working in the company, my mind has been in full throttle, romance-writing mode. If I continue like this, before the official internship period is over, I could have a first draft nearly ready.

No, no, I can't stop working for…*Devon*.

My breath catches as the final consequence of my termination comes to me.

If Devon decides to send me away, I'll have no excuse to see him each day. The fear this last point unleashes hits me like a bucket of icy water.

I lower my hands to my side, pondering the puzzling realization.

I would miss *him*—more than the job itself.

The draw I felt last night wasn't just the effect of the bubbly drinks and watching Devon sing like he was friggin' Sinatra. It's something more than that.

Cat sneezes, then blinks at me as if she's surprised by what just happened. Her face is so comical I break out in a giggle.

There's a knock on the door. "Laia? Are you awake?"

No, I'm not.

Devon's baritone sends me into a frenzy, and I jump up. I'm not ready to face him. First, I need to make sure that the looney voice that suggested I'm falling for my boss won't be back again.

I run to the closet and open it. It's full of cartoon boxes and men's suits. No, I can't squeeze myself in here.

I scurry back to the bed and kneel. Perhaps I could fit underneath? Not likely. I might've lost a few pounds since I started the job, but I'm still not that skinny.

I straighten and grab the checkered blanket. I'll just pretend I'm still sleeping until Devon leaves for the office.

Cat sniffs as if to remind me it's Saturday.

"Laia! I'm coming in." The door opens before I can find a suitable escape. I'm frozen in front of the bed, my hands gripping his blanket.

His face moves into a smile—a rather friendly one considering the misery I put him through last night.

"How are you feeling?" he asks.

I drop the blanket and comb through my hair with my fingers. Jeez, I must look a mess with all the knots.

"Good. Just a bit of…" I start, but when his brows furrow, I decide to go with the truth. "Fine, I feel like a tomahawk just landed in the middle of my skull."

"That kind of throbbing is gruesome," he chuckles.

Isn't he upset with me for getting tipsy in his favorite jazz club and ruining the night for him?

"Come," he waves to me, "I've made some breakfast. Food will help with the pain." Without waiting for me to react, he turns and walks out.

I throw a side-glance at Cat, half-expecting the animal to advise me on what to do. Cat is licking her paws and doesn't answer, so it's up to me.

I opt to follow Devon.

At some point, I'll need to leave his guest room anyway. Also, the delicious smell seeping in from the kitchen is almost unbearable for my empty stomach.

Devon has set the large oval table in the living room. There's a white plate filled with various yummy treats on a red tablecloth. His scrambled eggs look like they're cooked to perfection.

I take my seat and press my palms to my thighs because my fingers want to immediately grab the fork.

Devon sits down, too, and pours himself a coffee. He doesn't have a plate. Has he eaten already? Does it mean that I can start without waiting for him?

Devon grins at me. "Dig in before it gets cold. I'm already done with breakfast."

He doesn't have to tell me twice. I'm so hungry it takes all my willpower not to fetch the bacon with my bare fingers.

I'm just chewing on a delicious piece that's as crispy as if my mother made it when Devon asks, "By the way, did you lose your house keys?"

"What? Did I? Oh, no."

Chelsea will kill me when she finds out. We've already changed the lock once when I forgot my keys in San Sebastian after visiting my family.

Devon opens his arms and shrugs. "I'm not sure. I tried the ones from your purse last night. They didn't work. That's why I brought you here. I didn't want to wake your neighbors."

Then it hits me. I swallow my bite. "You must've taken me to Luis's flat. That's not where I live."

Devon's jaw drops. "Who is Luis?"

"He's my brother. A soldier. He currently serves at a military base in Germany. I listed his house on my resume. In reality, I live together with Chelsea. When we came to the interview, we decided to give separate postal addresses."

"Why?" Devon inquires.

"We feared that being roomies might be a problem in the selection process."

"Well, it wouldn't have been. But it could have saved you from spending a night in the company of my cat." Devon winks.

"Oh, I didn't mind. Your bed was very comfortable. Your guest bed, I mean," I add.

"I'm glad." He flashes a bright smile. "When I bought my place, I imagined my parents would come to Phoenix more often after they retire. That's why I set up the spare room. But my folks prefer to stay put and have Ellie and me visit them."

"So you're not from Phoenix?" I arch my brows.

I somehow assumed that a popular man like Devon must've lived his whole life in a big city.

"No, I was born in Washington State, in a small town. Before starting high-school, after my breathing therapy finished, my family decided to move to Kingman, Arizona."

"Kingman? Get out? You lived there?"

Devon arches his brows. "You know it? It's not a famous place."

"Well, not according to my father. He's a fan of the Route 66 Museum, primarily their cars exhibit, of course. He dragged our family there once when he was on leave. For years, I used to have a picture in my bedroom of a Studebaker I snapped during that trip."

Devon's eyes widen. "Huh, that's still a place I often hit when I go home. Especially since they added their international electric vehicle exhibit. There's a 1912 CT commercial truck on show. It's not like any duallys you've ever seen. It boosts triple-wide, solid rubber tires mounted on wooden spoke wheels. It basically makes the driver sit ten feet in the air…it's a real monster!"

"Ah, I'd love to see that," I say because Devon's description gives me the goosebumps. "You know, I have a hard time believing you come from a small town like I do."

"I guess we have more things in common than you thought."

"I guess so, too. This could be the reason I—" I bite my lip just in time.

Devon cocks his head. "You what?"

Oh dear, this fun chat about our shared passion almost made me slip how much I like him.

I pick up a small piece of bread from my half-empty plate and shape it into a ball before I raise my eyes to meet his. "I like working for you."

"*Just* working?"

My eyes widen. "What do you mean?"

He shrugs and gives me a lopsided grin. "I thought you might enjoy spending time with me outside of the office, too. Our afternoon at the car show was fun, no? Maybe you should come to Kingman someday. I'd love to take you to the museum and show you the new vehicles they've got."

My jaw drops. "You would?"

"Of course. Why wouldn't I?"

Doesn't he remember last night?

"Because of what happened in the club. I ruined your evening." I meant to excuse myself for my behavior sooner, but the smell of bacon must've hijacked my reason. "I want you to know I'm mortified. I don't usually…well, I've never actually gotten drunk in my life."

Devon adjusts his coffee cup and shakes his head. "No need to excuse yourself. You're a cute tipsy person. A tad more daring than your usual self, but…" He pauses as if he remembers something. He clicks his tongue before he continues, "It wasn't a burden to chaperone you. On the contrary."

"So you won't fire me?"

His eyes widen. "Fire you? No, why should I?"

"Because…I said things I shouldn't have. I called you stupid."

"You did." Devon nods. "But you were right, I might have been stupid."

It's my turn to look surprised. "Why would you say that?"

"My sister told you about what happened with Morgan, right?"

He stares at me, and the intensity of his gaze is such that I can't bear to make a sound so I only nod.

"I figured as much. Did she also mention I asked Morgan to marry me before finding out that she'd cheated on me?"

I clasp a hand to my mouth to suppress a shocked gasp.

"So Ellie didn't dish everything." Devon's voice isn't annoyed, only sad. "Well, I did. I proposed to Morgan, and she accepted. But only a few hours after I became her fiancé, I learned that she had an affair with a friend of mine from the college faculty."

"With a friend of yours? Oh, that's horrible," I whisper. "My closest experience to being betrayed was when Bobby, my prom date, whom I used to be head over heels about, admitted to me that he'd only accepted to show up in public with me because Chelsea promised she'd go out with him if he took me to the dance."

Devon tilts his head, his mouth agape.

"Oh, sorry. I don't know why I came up with this silly example," I mutter. "My high school heartache is nothing compared to the treason you've suffered."

Devon's gaze heats with something that makes the blood thicken in my veins. "Please don't depreciate your experiences. I might've made that mistake myself, but I'm not going to repeat it again. Also, just for the record, your prom date had to be a giant dullard if he couldn't recognize just what a treasure you are."

His statement takes my breath away.

"Thank you," I mumble because nothing wittier comes to mind.

"No, thank you," Devon says. "Your speech last night

got me thinking. I've been replaying parts of it in my mind this morning."

Oh, dear heaven…which parts?

"Really?" I squeeze the sound out with considerable effort.

Devon leans forward, planting his elbows on the tablecloth. "Yes. And you're right. I shouldn't chase empty relationships. In fact, I decided I won't. Not anymore."

With each word, my chin drops lower. "Are you Devon?"

Devon chuckles. "Yes, it's still me. I just had a…an epiphany. Come to think of it, I could even propose you a little deal concerning it."

"A deal?" I chew on my lower lip.

"Yes. I'll stop going after meaningless flings if you quit putting yourself down and finally realize you're much better than what you think, or what pricks like Bobby made you believe."

I gape at him, wide-eyed.

Is he serious? Or did the aliens kidnap him while I slept?

"So what do you think of our deal? Are you game?" he asks.

"Well, I could surely use a final push to abandon my harsh self-critique but… I'd like to understand…did you have a change of heart just because of what I told you?"

Devon sighs. "Not only. You remember the teahouse? The woman we met there was—"

"Morgan."

"Yes. I haven't seen her in a long time. But when I saw her in Okinawa, I wasn't particularly touched. This clearly means that, despite the love I had for her, Morgan wasn't *the* love of my life. Thus, her mistake shouldn't make me doubt the importance of soulmates."

I grab my glass to take a sip because my throat is suddenly parched.

When I lift it, I realize it's empty. Devon immediately grabs a bottle of water and pours my glass full.

Like real full, up to the rim.

"Oh, sorry," he says. "I like my glasses almost brimming. Shall I throw away a bit so that you can more easily drink?"

"No, that's perfect."

Devon and I both like our cups full?

This fact, coupled with his admission about wanting to believe in soulmates again, does more damage to my soul than a dumdum bullet could.

How am I ever going to convince myself that I'm not falling for Devon?

Devon, unaware of my inner battle, clears his throat. "Anyway, my new behavior isn't something that will come easily to me. I've spent way too many years being cynical about love. That's why…" He throws me a speculative glance. "I thought you could help me."

"Meeee?"

Heat rushes to my head, and I feel dizzy at the possible implications behind his words.

"Yes." Devon smiles. "You're the person with the most unshakable belief about the importance of true love that I know. You'd be perfectly equipped to teach me how to become a believer. I'd like you to coach me on my road to being a reformed playboy." He adds a wink to his last word.

I wish I could react to his self-ironic joke with a smile, but my features are frozen. I'd thought he meant I could help him because…

Of course, hc wouldn't mean it like that. Devon only

wants me to coach him into a dream man so that he can find his dream woman.

Who, obviously, is not me.

Devon stares at me expectantly. "So, would you be up to it? I could lend you a hand with your self-confidence in return. This way, we would both nail our goals."

"But-t-t I'm your assistant," I stutter, flashing my job title as armor.

"Ah," Devon waves, "I wouldn't propose lessons at work. We could make time for them on the weekends, like today, for example. We could go to a park and then—"

"Park!" I squeak, suddenly remembering the promise I made Alicia last Sunday. I'm supposed to watch her twins while she and her hubby run some errands.

I peek at my watch and realize I barely have time to run home to shower and change.

"Everything okay?" Devon asks.

I jump up. "I'm sorry I need to go. I'm meeting someone at Margaret T. Hance Park at two."

"A date?" Devon's face tenses.

"Sort of," I shrug. I don't want to confess that it's just babysitting duty.

Devon straightens. "Ah, okay, then I won't keep you."

I flash an apologetic smile. "I'm sorry. Can we discuss this coaching idea of yours later?"

Or better, never.

I don't think I'm strong enough to coach Devon in his metamorphosis. I'm too involved emotionally.

Way too involved.

"Sure, okay," he answers.

I scurry to the corridor where I find my flats laid out nicely beside the entrance. Did Devon polish them? The soft leather glimmers more than usual. I decide to ignore the odd detail and slip them on.

Devon is behind me. "So, you're going to Margaret T. Hance Park? Which part then?"

"Uhm, not sure." I place my hand on the doorknob as if it could bring me closer to being out of Devon's house and his bewitching closeness. "Near to the giant panda, I think."

Yes, that will be the perfect spot for the twins. It's got plenty of shade.

"Have fun. See you soon," Devon says.

"Yes, see you on Monday. Bye-bye." I slip out of the door and head straight for the stairs.

I don't want Devon to wait for the elevator with me. I might need to burn twenty-three floors, but it's still better than being forced to look at his handsome face any longer.

CHAPTER 32

(Devon)

"Are you sure you don't want to come with me?" I implore Pete on the phone, using my most persuasive tone.

"I'm sorry, Dev, but I've planned a soccer-watching, chill-out session after last night's heavy hitter. Thanks, by the way, for throwing me at the mercy of your sister. Ellie pestered me for at least an hour about how you and I should quit behaving like party-obsessed adolescents."

I can imagine Ellie's arguments and Pete's reaction to them all too well. I'm sure glad I didn't have to participate in their discussion.

But I still feel like apologizing to Pete. He's fallen victim to my sister's deadly matchmaker-slash-savior complex.

"I'm sorry, mate. But if it's any consolation, we didn't stay in Jimmy'z too long either. Laia didn't feel well, so I had to take her home."

I carefully avoid mentioning that the home I'm referring to is actually my own house. I only called him to see whether he is up to a run with me, not to entrust him with my secrets about Laia.

"She looked fine to me when I saw her before Ellie dragged me out of the club. More than fine, in fact. Sizzling hot in that purple top. I sure wouldn't have minded taking *her* home either. Your assistant got all her curves at the right places, no?" Pete smacks his lips, and I can picture him spreading his fingers like a budding flower, as he usually does.

Irritation courses through me.

"Pete, if you forgot, I'm her boss, so I can't allow you to talk about her like that. Not now, not *ever*."

Pete snorts loudly in my ear. "Hey, tune it down a notch, mate. I was just kidding. I didn't mean any harm. Jeez, what's going on with you lately? You haven't been clubbing for over two weeks. You give me the lamest excuses for your absence. When you finally agree to meet up, you invite your assistant *and* your sister to our jazz club, and now you jump down my throat because of some manly humor? If I didn't know any better, I'd consider your inconsequential behavior as a sign that you're in love…"

His mocking tone makes my blood boil.

"And what if I am?" I snap.

"What if you are," Pete repeats, chuckling, but then breaks off. "…wait, are you serious? You've fallen in love with someone?" When I don't answer, he adds, "With your assistant?"

"No," I mumble, but my tone suggests that the answer is a yes.

I decide to man up and own up to my feelings. At least if Pete learns I'm smitten with Laia, he won't try to hit on her ever again. "Okay, I might not be in love with Laia just yet, but I'm walking on very thin ice toward that."

Pete draws in a few sharp breaths. "*Woauha*, that's… uhm, surprising but not unexpected. I knew sooner or later you would yoke your head and settle. Not everyone is a true free spirit like me."

His comment draws a smile to my lips. "Yes, Pete, you're unique."

"Thanks, buddy, for recognizing it," Pete replies, his voice dripping from smugness. "What's the deal? Does Laia love you back or what?"

"No, unfortunately not. She's attracted to me physically, but—"

"What, but?" Pete interjects. "If she wants a piece of you, that's your window of opportunity right there."

I sigh. "No, Laia isn't like that. She is all about fairy tales and shiny armored heroes. And we both know I'm nowhere near that. Even if she were interested in an affair, which I repeat she isn't, I don't want just a fling with her. I want to *be* with her. But I couldn't be more different than her idea of a fitting boyfriend."

"Ah, you've landed yourself a major crush, pal. But for what it's worth, I think your sis believes you have a chance with your assistant. That would explain her possessiveness when I flirted with Laia."

Pete can seem superficial to some, but he has a bewildering talent to deduce hidden behavioral motivations in women. Probably because he has honed his skills with so many.

"Yes, for some reason Ellie thinks mine isn't a lost cause. That's why she invited you. She wanted to give Laia and me some alone time."

"Did you put her up to it?"

I snort. "Like I could ever convince my sis to go along with a scheme like that unless it was her idea. Nope, I didn't even know Ellie would ambush you."

Pete laughs. "Well, it wasn't an entirely wasted evening. After Ellie was done with her lecture, we had a pleasant meal. Anyway, what are you planning to do about Laia? Will you just silently adore her while you keep acting like her boss?"

Disappointment washes through me as I think about the disastrous ending at breakfast.

And to think it started out so well.

I'd prepared a nice meal and managed to steer our conversation to the topic of love without Laia becoming suspicious. But then…

My stomach hardens as I think how Laia is on her way to meet someone right now. "Laia has a date in a park this afternoon," I grumble.

"A park, huh?" Pete's tone is beyond suspicious, and I can hear how he's putting two and two together. "That's why you proposed this spontaneous jogging to me. Not because you wanted to make up for last night. Also, you usually go to Encanto Park, not Margaret T. Hance Park… It's all so clear now."

"Yeah," I admit, shame curling through my chest. "I just wanted to take a look at the man who's lucky enough to spend time with Laia. Are you sure you don't want to come with me?"

"Nope. You're a racehorse, and I hate doing sports with you. Wyatt has gotten you too obsessed with your physical performance, I tell ya. Also, it would be much better for you to go alone. If Laia dislikes playboys, it might not be the best move to bump into her while you're with me."

Pete has a point, unfortunately.

Also, it's almost two o'clock. The park is at least twenty minutes walking distance from my building, and with Pete's usual pace, we might miss Laia and her mystery date.

"Okay, fine," I say, determined. "I'll go alone then. Enjoy your soccer game."

"I will. And, you, go and charm that assistant of yours. Unbury all the good boy stuff from deep in your heart, and onto which I helped you toss a thick protective layer, and you should be all set."

I smile at Pete's encouraging words.

I know he's sorry I'm quitting our common lifestyle, but I appreciate that he backs me up even if he doesn't agree with my choice.

"Thanks! Speak to you later, Pete."

I hang up and at the speed of light change into my workout clothes. I sprint down the stairs to warm up my calf muscles. I greet Phillipe at the entrance, then take the road toward the park where Laia must be with the guy I already hate.

CHAPTER 33

(Devon)

I dash by an old lady dragging a cart for her groceries and a young woman dressed in a miniskirt who throws a dazzling smile at me.

From the corner of my eye, I check her out, and despite realizing that she's pretty, there's not one fiber in my body that would want to stop and chat her up.

I guess I left my player self behind for good.

Now my only task is to convince Laia about this, too.

When the crosswalk light pings, I push my way through the afternoon crowd loitering on the sidewalk and hurry to the other side of the road.

I don't know Margaret T. Hance Park well, because, as Pete has so cleverly pointed out, I never jog there.

I've only been there once during a jazz festival. I remember seeing a lovely pathway that goes all around the park and thinking that the tall buildings as a backdrop looked suggestive when the band played. But I have no idea where that big panda Laia mentioned could be located.

I enter the park, and thick green grass greets me, together with a couple posing for their wedding pictures. I lose a few precious minutes as the photographer set up the camera with a wide-angle, and unless I want to end up in their family album, I need to wait until they take a break so I can pass behind them.

I peek at my watch. Two-ten. I need to hurry up, or I risk Laia and her date changing location.

I'm glad for the fluffy clouds that tame the sun's power to a bearable, almost agreeable level because without their help, I would have arrived at the park drenched in sweat instead of only slightly out of breath.

My intention is to jog past Laia and her guy without being seen so I can take a good look at him. After that, I could maybe circle around and—

I freeze mid-thought because a giant bronze sculpture of a mama bear and her cub comes into sight.

I slow my pace and scan the area.

I don't need to look for Laia long.

There's only one blanket on the grassy clearing that stretches behind the statue, and it's occupied by the woman who managed to turn me inside out in less than two short weeks.

Laia is with a man and two small children. One kid is sitting on her lap and the other on the guy's knees. The two of them are engrossed in an animated discussion.

My heart rate picks up, even though I've slowed my tempo. It beats so fast in my throat it's as if I've just completed three Iron Man competitions in a row.

Laia is dating a man who has kids?

I'm so distracted I don't realize that my legs keep moving, bringing me closer.

Suddenly, as if Laia felt my glare, she glances up, and her eyes travel to me. Her face moves into a grimace of utter bewilderment. I think I can even read a shocked, "*Devon*?" on her lips.

Her companion turns, and I notice that he's more or less my age. He has light-brown hair in buzz cut and, as far as I can tell, a rather robust frame.

The little girl in his arms reaches up to the man's chin and grabs at it. He encompasses the child's hand in his palm and blows a kiss at it, but his eyes remain fixated on me.

I decide to go and greet them.

I mean, what else can I do now that my spying act is busted?

I approach, trying for a relaxed three-fingers wave that could demonstrate I'm just as surprised to see them here as they are to see me, while also stating that I'm totally cool about our encounter. Unfortunately, since my entire body is locked up with tension, my movement comes out awkward.

"Hi, Laia," I exclaim, determined to make up for the ridiculous gesture with an upbeat tone. "What a coincidence!"

Laia peers up at me, her dark eyebrows drawn together. "But I told you I would be in this park."

The man gives me a narrow-eyed glance. "Who is *he*, Laia?"

Ah, so far along in their relationship that the guy feels entitled to know who I am? Has Laia been dating him this whole time, and I didn't know?

Laia shifts the small brunette, whose hair color matches the blanket, and raises herself to her feet.

I notice she's wearing a delightful orange spaghetti dress that leaves her shoulders bare and flatters her complexion.

"Brian," Laia points at me, "this is Devon Griffin, my boss. Devon, this is Brian Smith."

Brian immediately jumps up, lifting the child he's holding to his hip as he straightens. He extends a hand to me. "Oh, I've heard about you. It's a pleasure to meet Laia's boss. You've got an extraordinary girl on your team, I can assure you."

He winks at Laia, and she blushes.

I press my teeth together to stifle a growl. What does this man think? That I don't know how precious Laia is? I know it *much* more than he does.

Since I can't act on my jealousy, I shake his hand. "Thank you for the reminder, but I know Laia is a gem."

My comment earns me a smile from Laia, and her cheeks darken a shade more.

"So, Brian," I clear my throat, "are these your children?"

"Yes, they are. This one"—he pats the cheek of the girl in his arms—"is Sandy and that other trouble maker is Mila."

"They're adorable," I say politely. Truth be told, the two little monkeys look extremely cute, but the fact that their father is seeing the same woman I desire makes it impossible for me to engage with them.

"What are you doing here, Devon?" Laia asks.

Her voice has a suspicious edge, which makes me shift my weight and square my shoulders.

I point at my sneakers. "I decided to jog. You know, to keep in shape. This park is amazing for a run."

"Ah, really?" Brian chimes in. "I thought the trails were better at Encanto, no?"

"Are you an expert on running locations?" My timbre comes out slightly harsh, but Brian doesn't seem to make much of it. Maybe because little Sandy distracts him by pulling on his ear.

"I'm sorry it took so long, guys!" A soprano interrupts us.

It belongs to a short woman who has Laia's dark hair color and a similar shade of skin. She trudges towards us with both of her arms stretched out and goes straight to the child sitting on the blanket. She picks her up and starts planting kisses on the kid's neck.

"Did you miss mommy, Mila baby? Huh, did you?" Then, as if she's just realized I'm here, she turns to me. "Oh, hi, I don't think we've met. I'm Alicia Flores. And you are?"

Brian throws a warning glance at the woman. "Ali love, this is Devon Griffin. Laia's *boss*."

I stare at them, dumbfounded. "Flores? You're Laia's sister? And Brian is…"

Alicia smiles at me. "Yes, my husband."

My chest expands with relief, and I'm finally able to hold my shoulders without feeling like an elephant is crushing my trapezius muscles.

So Laia's mystery date isn't really a date…it's her brother-in-law.

Best. News. Ever.

I exercise superb self-control and stop myself from pumping my fist in the air and screaming a triumphant "yes."

I beam at Alicia. "It's lovely to meet you."

Laia holds out her arms to Alicia. "Want to give Mila to me? You and Brian will never get your list done if you don't leave now."

Alicia and Brian exchange a glance.

"Are you sure you are up to it, sis? I mean, your boss

has just arrived here so…" Alicia gives Laia a questioning glance.

Laia shakes her head. "Don't worry, I said I'd watch them, and I will. I suppose Devon needs to get on with his workout anyway, don't you?"

She turns to me, and there's an almost challenging glint in her eyes, as if she's daring me to either commit to my lie or drop my pretense altogether.

Before I react, Alicia shoves Mila into Laia's arms with a relieved smile. "Ah, good. I really must get a haircut, and Brian is in *desperate* need of some new shirts, but I don't trust his taste enough to let him go alone."

Brian rolls his eyes at his wife's comment while he sets Sandy on the blanket.

"I'm glad I can help, sis." Laia smiles at Alicia.

Alicia plants a kiss on Laia's cheek and strokes her daughter's hair. "We should be back in two or three hours. I'm sorry I couldn't bring the twin strollers. Otherwise, you could have gone walking. There's a small doughnut festival further down in the park. I saw it when I came in."

A genial idea comes to me.

"Wait," I exclaim. "I can accompany Laia to the festival. I can carry little Sandy, so we can taste those treats."

"What?" Laia squeaks.

At the same time, her sister yells, "Excellent idea! I'm always worried about leaving poor Laia alone with our two daredevils. I sometimes can't handle them alone, and I'm their mother."

"But aren't you here to jog?" Laia asks.

"I can jog later. Or tomorrow." I kneel down to Sandy. Now that I know her father isn't my rival, I'm more than happy to make friends with the chubby munchkin.

I hold out my hand to the little girl. Sandy smiles at me

and pulls on my wrist as if to show that I should lift her up. I follow her orders and straighten with her in my arms.

"You see? I don't think I'll have a problem with your daughters." I wink at Alicia and Brian.

Brian chuckles. "Don't be fooled by their pink cheeks and large Bambi eyes. These two ladies know what they want, and they'll make you lose your head in a second. All Flores women have this capacity."

Especially one.

I blink at Laia, who stands with her brows furrowed, while Mila is doing acrobatic movements in her arms.

Alicia and Brian wave good-bye and walk away.

"Are you sure you made the right trade for your *spontaneous* workout?" Laia asks with a mischievous glint in her eyes.

"Oh, yes. Absolutely. I just hope the doughnut stand has some sweets with mean vanilla cream. Those are *my* favorites."

Laia gives out a bemused snort that could also be a giggle covered up, then nods. "Fine. Then let's pack up and head over there."

CHAPTER 34

(Laia)

"Here you go, sweetheart, two regular doughnuts with chocolate and vanilla dip and two plain, baby-sized ones." The vendor hands me the scrumptious treats on a tray and tops my order with a friendly smile.

I get out of the queue and saunter toward the small playground where I left Devon with the twins. It's nestled in the shade of four giant Indian Rosewoods, and the place is cool enough to safely allow my nieces to explore the play area.

The sweet fragrance of fried pastry, mixed with the mouthwatering scent of dark chocolate, tickles my nostrils, but despite their typical allure, my stomach doesn't growl. It sits frozen into a tiny ball that shrinks further with each step I take.

What is Devon *really* doing here?

I *know* he didn't forget that I told him I was coming to this park.

My eyes travel to his wide-shouldered figure. He squats on the grey stone frame of the giant sandbox and waves the twins to approach, while Sandy and Mila trot further away like small, disobedient cubs.

A smile jumps to my face as I observe Devon's concerned expression.

Mila, after a squeaking, "Da-da-da," plops down and gets busy digging a hole.

I pause to watch Devon's reaction.

The only rule I set for him was to keep the girls out of any burrowing activity before we eat because I couldn't find any wet wipes in the diaper bag Alicia left me. How will he make the two daredevils respect my instruction?

Devon's face contracts into a grimace of frustration as he observes Mila fumbling with the sand. Then he jumps up and rushes to her. He lifts the little troublemaker into the air and, before Mila's mouth can curl down, he begins to wave her body right and left while puffing loudly like a helicopter.

Mila's happy guffaws reach my ear.

Sandy watches with amazed eyes, then reaches her arms toward the sky, screeching loudly for her turn.

Devon chuckles, and without lowering Mila to the ground, he picks up her sister too. He secures both of them on his shoulders, engulfing their torsos as if they were two tiny sacks of potatoes and carefully twirls them around.

I can't suppress a chuckle.

I know I shouldn't be surprised by how well Devon is handling my nieces. As a creative person, he must still be in touch with his inner child.

However, what astonishes me is the almost unconditional admiration Sandy and Mila show toward Devon after only an hour together. It's as if Devon's appeal and extraordinary magnetism on women can be felt at any age —even in toddlerhood.

I can just take our stroll to the doughnut stand as an example. Usually, Sandy and Mila can't get enough of me and love to be cuddled by their aunt. But this time, both of them wanted to be carried by Devon, and Devon only.

When I tried to peel one of them away from him, they began to howl. In the end, Devon wound up toting both kids—one in each arm.

I can't say I blame my nieces.

If it were up to me, I'd love to nestle into those strong, muscular arms and press my head against Devon's chest to inhale his scent.

That would definitely unfreeze my belly and spark a potent fire in it.

I redirect my attention to reality before my brain can embark on a journey to fantasyland.

"Hey there, guys! I'm back, and look at what I've got." I raise my tray to the girls' eye level.

"You see, kiddos, I told you your auntie would return, packed with goodies." He slowly releases the girls to the ground and pats their heads. "What do you say if we climb out of this sand before you become any dirtier, and I get scolded?" He winks and flashes a boyish I-did-what-I-could smile at me.

As if I could ever reprimand him for being adorable with my nieces…

I point at the nearest bench, right below one of the trees. "We could sit there."

The twins, persuaded by the sight and smell of sugary rings, toddle out of the sandbox and follow me like two tiny ducklings.

Devon lingers behind them with his hands stuck into his white shorts' pockets.

I settle on the bench, placing the tray on the wooden surface. I forbid my glance to wander to Devon's brawny thighs, sculpted calves, or the chest muscles that are nicely visible in his tighter-than-usual navy workout T-shirt.

Instead, I watch Sandy and Mila. They reach past and go straight for the adult-sized doughnuts.

"No, no, you two little mischiefs." I lift the treats I bought for Devon and myself. "Those two smaller ones are yours."

Mila and Sandy seem slightly disappointed that their sweets don't have toppings and are only one-third the size of ours, but after a moment of pouting, they pick up their doughnuts and bite into them.

Devon hops down beside me, and I push the tray back to give him more space. Despite my best effort of shoving the platter to the bench's extremity, his body lands so close to mine our hips touch. His bare knees graze my own.

Devon doesn't seem bothered that we're squeezed into such proximity. He smiles and asks, "Can I have mine?"

I hand him his vanilla cream delight.

He attacks it with a hungry appetite. "Mhmm, this is delicious. I was famished," he murmurs.

"Didn't you have lunch?" I ask.

"Nope," he answers between chomps. "Not even breakfast."

"What?" I turn to him, which makes my entire thigh press against his warm legs. "Didn't you eat before I woke up? I thought you said…"

His eyes fill with a flustered glint. "I might have told a small fib there. I forgot to refill my fridge, so I only had enough ingredients to prepare one meal. And I wanted you to eat, so…"

Devon preferred to nourish me instead of himself?

That's just…ahhh…

My heart stutters long enough for me to notice. "Thank you, but that wasn't necessary."

Devon shakes his head. "Of course it was. I'm not a drinker, but I've been tipsy enough times to know what it entails. If we hadn't gotten your stomach filled, you would've had a massive headache the whole day. By the way"—he lifts a hand and traces two fingers from my temple toward my ear—"how is that throbbing doing?"

The effect of his gesture is devastating.

My stomach fills with butterflies—the giant, tropical kind with a wingspan that stretches almost a foot across—and the buzz sends ripples through all my cells.

"It's much better, I think," I mumble, grateful that any sound makes its way out of my parched throat.

"Ta-taa-ta." Sandy intervenes in our conversation by leaning on Devon's knees and attempting to capture the last bite of his doughnut.

"No, Sandy," I say and break off a piece from my untouched sweet. "Eat this instead."

My niece is apparently happy about the trade I offer—not only larger, but also covered with thick chocolate—because she immediately comes over to me and snatches my gift.

"La-la da-da-da," Mila chants.

"That translates into 'Laia I want some, too.'" Devon chuckles.

He's probably right, so I hand a piece to Mila, too.

The girls chew on their prey with joyful grins, and once they've stuffed everything into their tiny mouths, they waddle to the sandbox again.

I don't stop them this time since now they can get filthy. Alicia has a germ-obsession, and she'll bathe them as soon as they arrive home anyway.

Without the twins' presence, I'm again too aware of

the heat emanating from Devon's body. It becomes so unbearable I shift a few inches farther from Devon. Enough to breathe normally, but not so far he'll wonder why I changed position. The last thing I need is for him to realize just how smitten I am with him.

Devon has already finished his doughnut, but his eyes still have an eager glint.

"Do you want the rest?" I hold out what remains from my own treat to him.

"No, thank you."

"Are you sure? You still look hungry."

One of his brow arches. "Do I? Well, maybe I am. Just *not* for doughnuts."

My jaw drops, but before I can ask about his odd remark, he continues, "You told me you have a sweet tooth and that chocolate is your favorite flavor."

I wince as he recites my embarrassed jabber from last night.

"What's wrong?" he asks.

"Nothing, just I didn't expect you to recall that."

"I remember *all* the things you tell me, Laia." The intensity of his gaze is such that my ribcage roils.

Does his emphasis have a meaning? Or is he just boasting about his great memory?

While I try to convince my brain not to jump to any hopeful conclusions about his potential double-meaning, Devon continues, "Like, I didn't forget what you said about being used to people talking down to you. What did you mean by that? I've been wondering about it a lot."

"It was nothing but a peeved slip." I wave, wanting him to drop the subject.

But he doesn't.

"Please, Laia. I'm curious."

The honesty in his voice makes me think he really wants to know about my past, which is weird.

Is this interest more than just a boss's concern?

I move my glance to Sandy and Mila, who are building a sort of castle or a large hill—depending on the point of view.

"You know…" I start while keeping my eyes glued on the twins, "I'm the youngest in my family, and as such, my opinion always counted less than that of my siblings. Not in a mean, *you are silly so we won't listen to you* way, rather in a *we love you, but you're so naïve* one. Enough, however, to stop voicing what I used to feel or believe. This habit of keeping in my shell accompanied me my whole life, but recently I started to get fed up with it."

As I say it, I realize it might have been my real motivation for giving that motivational guide a shot and starting that bucket list in the first place.

Yes, I wished to land a job, but there was more to my decision than just frustration over my refusal letters. I wanted to change into a better, stronger version of myself.

Devon nods. "I can relate to that. I think Ellie struggled with the same problem when she was younger. It's the curse of the little sisters."

The old Laia would respond to his emphatic interruption with a shy smile and then shut up, afraid she'd already given away too much of herself. But because I'm suddenly aware that, thanks to Devon and his choice to take a chance on me, I'm actually on the rocky road to becoming a more open person, I push myself.

"If I'm honest, it wasn't just my family. At school, I wasn't popular. Not that I am now, but back then I used to be a kind of outcast." I pause, unsure how to continue.

Then I draw in a sharp breath and let the words rush to my tongue, without any filter. "I was a chubby Latina girl who always had burritos for lunch instead of trendy lettuce sandwiches. I wore my sister's hand me down clothes and had no earrings or necklaces. I loved to read literary classics, while my companions were obsessed with reality shows and manga characters. I wasn't good at sports but had good enough grades to be branded a nerd."

"It's hard for me to believe you weren't always this stunning." Devon's voice cuts through the demons of my past.

"Well, you better believe it," I say with a bitter smile, while a fragment of my mind registers that Devon has called me stunning. "I didn't have girlfriends until high school. That's when Chelsea's family moved into my town, San Sebastian."

"Ah, so you and Chelsea go way back?"

"Yes. Chelsea was the first person at school to look beyond my social reputation, and we became besties. Before that, I only spent time with my cousin Eva. Chelsea's friendship turned things around for me because she was adored by many, especially by boys. Hanging with her allowed me to bask in her positive aura."

Warmth invades my spine as Devon's palm lands on my upper back.

I should move away if I don't want my bones to liquefy into a gooey mess, but the sense of protection and pleasure I get from his touch is too irresistible.

So I stay put and turn my head to him.

When our gazes cross, he gives me a bright smile. "For what it's worth, I happen to be a great fan of *your* aura."

CHAPTER 35

(Devon)

My fingers itch to slide up to Laia's nape and graze the soft skin on her neck. Especially because I can see in her eyes that my touch is to her liking. Following through with my desire would come naturally to me. I'm used to giving the green light to my body's needs while my mind takes the backseat.

But if I want Laia to start seeing me as something more than just her player boss, I *need* to show her I'm more.

I need to let her into my past. No matter how raw and vulnerable it will make me feel.

So I withdraw my hand from her back and say, "By the way, having been a pariah is just one more thing we have in common."

"In common?" Her brows rise.

"Yes. Did you assume I was a popular guy all my life?"

"Actually, I kind of did," she admits. "How could I not?

Ellie told me Morgan was homecoming queen. Only the coolest guy in school gets to date the hottest girl, no?"

Her reasoning isn't far off.

Conquering Morgan was a status symbol for me. As her boyfriend, I managed to chase away all the ghosts of my sickly childhood. Because she accepted me, I finally believed that I wasn't an underdog anymore.

I nod. "Yes, I was a rather well-known guy in high school, mainly in my senior year. But in elementary and middle school, I lived my days as a wretch. I spent weeks, or sometimes even months, at home or in the hospital. I could rarely play outside, due to my severe respiratory condition. As a result, I was weak, pale, and shy. Just imagine, Ellie was my only friend, and even her bestie didn't like me."

My glance moves to Laia's giggling nieces. Sandy shovels sand on her sister's lap with both palms, while Mila throws the dirt back to the ground with a gurgling laugh.

"How terrible." Laia sucks in a breath. "I can't believe I didn't even consider the ramifications of your disease… Girls may pay attention to perfect lunch boxes and pretty accessories, but I know from Luis that boys measure popularity in speed and strength."

"Yes, and I lacked both of those back then."

I blink at Laia. She chews on her lower lip, and my heart squeezes at the sight of her unease. It wasn't my intention to rub it into her face that she made false assumptions about me. I just wanted her to know me better…and maybe *like* me better.

"Don't worry. My story, like yours, has a turning point. For me, it was our move from Washington State to Arizona."

Laia cocks her head to the side. "What happened? You

arrived in Kingman and became the new hottie, like Chelsea in my school?"

I like the teasing edge in her voice but even more the implication of her words.

"I'm flattered that you would describe me as a hottie, but no, it wasn't an overnight thing. In the beginning, I was still mostly invisible. But I started to do sports, and the more I worked out, the fitter I became. At the end of my freshman year, I joined the athletic team, and that's when things turned around."

"How so?"

"That's where I met Wyatt. He was part of the football team. He convinced his trainer to take me on board. I wasn't nearly as talented as Wyatt, which is why he's a pro now and I'm not, but I liked playing in the team and enjoyed the social exposure it gave me."

"Yeah, girls are dazzled by football players," Laia chimes in.

"Wasn't your dullard prom date a sportive too? A basketball captain, no?"

Laia's cheeks flush. "Yes. I guess I'm pretty much like all the girls then."

"No, you're not."

Not one bit.

"Right." She nods. "I'm probably the only female you know who wants to wait for…" She pauses and waves. "You know what I mean."

Since she offers the topic on a silver platter, I can't stop myself from asking the question that's been on my mind ever since my foolish behavior in the elevator.

"Is it because of religion that you…?"

Laia's eyes dart to me. "Why are you interested?"

She doesn't need to know yet that I'd like to become a man with better relationship values because of her, so I shrug. "I asked you to coach my social life into a more meaningful pattern. Understanding your motivation could be my first lesson."

Laia gives me a smile that's sweet but shy at the same time. "Okay, then the answer is no. I was raised a Catholic, but I don't feel that I'm bound by religious rules about chastity. I just…" She sighs. "Ah, you'll find it silly…"

"No, please. I know I dismissed your principles as naïve in the past, but now I want to hear them. Try me."

Laia's eyes flick to her nieces, but when she sees they're still happily occupied, she rubs her hands together as if the gesture could help her organize her thoughts.

I listen to the swishing sound with a growing expectation. I want to learn what makes her believe in the importance of waiting for true love.

She starts out with something I don't expect.

"I know our bodies have their instincts. When we see someone attractive, we react to him or her, right?"

Our glances cross, and I give her a lopsided grin. "Till here, you've got me on board."

She blushes at my comment, and I can ascertain just how right her words are because my cells drift into a state of arousal at the sight of her rosy cheeks.

"Today, many think it's stupid, if not even unhealthy, to resist these urges. On the other hand, I believe if we give in to them too soon, we deprive ourselves of something important." She tells me this with a tone of somebody who has reflected on the topic a great deal.

"Of what?"

"Physical pleasure can transform into something powerful when it's shared with the person you love. Then it's not just an act to derive momentary euphoria, but a true unification between souls."

To my surprise, her reasoning speaks to me.

Maybe because I've already experienced how much more satisfying a brief, casual touch of Laia's skin can be compared to a night spent in the arms of a woman I don't care for.

"And what about passion?" I ask because I want to understand how she can manage to dominate her physical needs.

"Passion?"

"Yes, that irrepressible longing that connects the body to the soul. Sometimes it can be a gateway from one to the other, no?" My chest brews with the very sensation I'm trying to describe.

Laia snorts. "Right. How many of the women you've slept with managed to reach your soul?"

Her snappy answer leaves me speechless.

She's absolutely right. After Morgan, I knew only volatile pleasure. I didn't even wish to go beyond that with anyone.

Not until Laia came along.

As if Laia can read my thoughts, she says, "You see? I think true intimacy is a major act of love. So, it shouldn't be an alternate ending to a club night."

How can this philosophical and charmingly innocent discourse sound so sexy from Laia's lips?

I capture her eyes and try to channel all my admiration into my gaze. It's too early to express what I feel for her. She could think I'm trying to play her to get my way with her, which couldn't be further away from my intentions.

Okay, fine, I do long for her body, too—a lot. But it isn't *the* reason I want Laia.

I'd like that real intimacy for us like she's just described. For the first time in my life, I want to be with someone whose wit and values I admire and who understands and shares my hobbies.

A person who could be my soulmate, for all I know.

Laia stares at me with lips slightly parted, and she's either perceiving my affection or our interlocked gaze stirs something in her, too, because her pupils dilate.

Her breathing becomes deeper. I can hear her heavy draws of air, despite her nieces' content baby talk and the pulse slamming in my ears.

If I leaned in, my lips could press against her soft mouth. It would be so easy and so *very* satisfying.

But that's not how I want our first kiss to be.

I don't want to steal it from Laia in her moment of weakness. I'd like to do this properly. Maybe at a candle-lit dinner or something.

Like a hero worthy of her romance books.

So despite feeling like I'm tearing out my guts, I point at her nieces. "Shall we get them out of the sand and start walking back to the meeting spot with your sister?"

Laia blinks twice, then jumps up. "Ah, great idea. Yes. We need to head back. Alicia and Brian always take less time than they actually plan for. They think they want to be alone, but then they miss their kids so much, they hurry back to them. But that's just normal parenting, no?"

My eyes dip to her lips.

Why can't I stick to my resolution, dang it! I said I wouldn't kiss her here, so I need to stop staring at her mouth.

To jumpstart my brain, I stand up and grab the tray. "I'll throw this away. I'll be back for the two angels in a sec."

Laia smiles. "Good, because I think Mila and Sandy will want to be carried by you. I hope you won't have back pain tomorrow."

"No, the girls are feather-light. It's a pleasure to hold them." I grin.

I turn away before I can add that the one person I'm dying to hold is the little monkeys' aunt.

As I walk to the bin, swaying the tray back and forth in my hand, my heart is filled with giddy optimism.

I could see that Laia wanted me to kiss her. Which means she might be starting to see that I *could* be that special person she's waiting for.

Just as this thought crosses my mind, I know with absolute certainty that I want to be him.

I love Laia, and I would want nothing more than for her to love me back.

And I might just have the perfect stroke of genius about how I can stack the odds in my favor.

All I need is more time with Laia. *Alone.*

CHAPTER 36

(Laia)

I lift the grey carry-on to my bed and spread it open.

What shall I take for three days in Tucson?

Chelsea enters my room with a cocktail dress thrown over her arm and a smug expression.

"You've given me short notice, but I think I managed my mission. What do you think?" She lifts her purchase and holds it out to me. "Will this dress be suitable for the gala?"

"Oh, my gosh, Chels," I squeak as my eyes travel to the pale-blue fabric that seems so soft I want to rub my cheeks against it. "You outdid yourself. If you ever need a fallback profession, being a personal shopper would be a career to consider. You've the most amazing taste!"

I don't know where Chelsea found this attire, but it's perfect. The A-lined delight looks comfy but chic at the same time. And, as always, Chelsea nailed my body shape and size.

My friend basks in my compliment but pretends to be modest. "Ah, it wasn't that hard, after all." Then she drops her act and grins. "I'm so glad you like it. And it's totally in the budget you gave me."

"You're a lifesaver. I don't know what I'd have done without you." I step over to her and give her a hug.

I called Chelsea this afternoon and begged her to come to my rescue after learning about Devon's revised agenda for the CCF.

CCF stands for "Celebrating Creative Folks" and it's a yearly gathering for hotshots who work in the advertising field. It's mostly a networking event and is usually organized in breathtakingly fancy hotels.

I already knew he was participating after Katja made his hotel reservation my first day in the company. What I didn't know, however, was that he would extend a last-minute request for me to join him on his trip.

Chelsea pouts her lips. "I think Devon should have given you more heads up. If I'd known sooner that you were going, I'd have ordered you the same pumps I have from Taryn Rose. They're lightweight with responsive cushioning. You could wear them for twelve hours and not notice."

"That's okay," I reassure my friend, "I'll be fine in my own sandals."

The truth is, I'd have loved to know about Devon's change of plan earlier, too. But, as it appears, he kept Katja in the dark about it as well.

His secretary was just as surprised as I was when Devon broke the news to us this morning. Even more so, because Devon changed the reservation details himself instead of asking Katja to do it.

Katja told me that, for the past four years, Devon has always shown up solo at the CCF. The suspicious glance with which she accompanied her revelation did nothing but increase my jitters about tagging along with Devon on a three-day-long journey.

I don't know why Devon wants me to accompany him, but I fear it might have to do with his crazy idea that I should coach him.

I don't know how to help him without accidentally revealing the way I feel for him…

Chelsea brushes her finger on the tip of my nose. "You're thinking about your feelings for Devon, aren't you?"

"Maybe," I mumble.

Ah, why did Howard need to visit his cousin on Saturday?

With him gone, Chelsea stayed home and saw me return from the park all flustered. She didn't buy my excuse that Sandy and Mila got me this worked-up. Ultimately, she coaxed me into letting the cat out of the bag about my crush.

"Well, I was thinking of Devon too, when I chose this dress." Chelsea wiggles her brows. "I wanted either a bodycon or a bandage-style dress with a stylish belt to draw attention to your tiny waist and yummy hips. But since for now you only have an unofficial date with Devon, I went for a classic look with this fifties-style outfit."

I cringe as she labels the gala a date—even if an unofficial one.

Chelsea must think I'm unhappy that she picked a more sober look because she grabs the dress and presses it to me. "Don't worry, though, this flared skirt and well-defined midsection will show off your succulent curves all the same."

I sigh. "As puzzling as it is that you call my hourglass-shape succulent, that's not why I winced. I don't want you to insinuate that tomorrow is something more than it is. I know very well it isn't, and any hope in the opposite direction risks fueling my emotions for Devon. And that's not the healthy mental state I need for surviving this impromptu business trip."

"Ah." Chelsea waves with her hand. "When are you going to admit the big boss is courting you?"

"He isn't, unfortunately."

Chelsea gives me a you're-selling-yourself-short look, which she's perfected throughout our teenage years. She's so good her glance is often enough to shake me out of my self-commiseration.

As if Chelsea realizes her usual encouragement won't cut it today, she drops my cocktail dress onto the carry-on and puts her hands on my shoulders.

Her gesture makes me suspect I'm about to receive sassy preaching about why her take on the situation is the right one and why I'm entirely mistaken.

This time, however, she'll find me ready to counter all her points.

Not because I don't wish with all my soul that Chelsea is right. But because I fear if I buy into my friend's idea, I risk a more significant heartache than the one I'm already destined to have.

"Laia, Devon offered to help you with your cheesy romance book—"

"It was nothing but creative interest in my project," I chime in before Chelsea can twist this unrelated information into evidence to support her wacky theory.

Chelsea furrows her brows. "Let me finish first, then you can tell me your verdict. Okay, let's ignore his offer to support you with your book. We still have his invite for the motor show—"

"You basically forced him to give me his VIP pass…"

This turns into an inaudible mumble as Chelsea presses her palm to my lips.

"I said *listen*, Laia. Besides the car show, there's the fact that he took you to his house to get some reports he could've given you at work. Next up is the jazz club. And"—she holds up her hand as she sees me opening my mouth—"I know it was Ellie who proposed it. But Devon said his sister is a matchmaker. Maybe he recruited her to drop the invite?"

"Unlikely," I murmur, but a weak flicker of doubt awakens in my chest.

Though I could force myself to find a plausible explanation to almost all the details Chelsea's recited so far, I must admit that stringing them all together makes it sound like Devon is going out of his way to spend time with me.

Chelsea, who knows me enough to recognize my shifting mood, continues with increased enthusiasm. He brought you to his house. He made you breakfast and stayed hungry so you could eat. And last"—Chelsea makes a dramatic circular wave, then points her index to the ceiling—"he shows up in the park where he *knew* you would spend the afternoon and volunteers to babysit your annoying nieces."

"Sandy and Mila are adorable," I retort.

"Ah, I know that, of course." Chelsea sighs. "I was just putting myself into the shoes of a rich, single playboy. Isn't it weird that a man like Devon does all this for his assistant? To me, it's like a giant, blinking sign that he is *very* interested in you, Laia. And not as an employee, but as a woman."

Without wanting, my lips curl up and my chest begins to buzz with a sense of lightness. "So you think he might be falling for me?"

Chelsea shrugs. "Well, I'm not sure if we should frame

his feelings like that. Let's call it a bodily crush, or a *flirt-mance*. Like what Howard feels for me."

"Do you mean Devon wants me for a fling? Like his ex-assistant?"

The idea that this is what Devon could desire from me is even worse than the thought that he doesn't care for me at all.

I sink to my bed and bury my face into my palms.

Chelsea sits down beside me and rubs her temples. "That Hayley chick?"

"Yes. I've never really found out what happened to her, but there had to be something." I raise my head as a suspicion wiggles itself into my mind. "What if Devon really had a fling with her, which ended badly—aka the girl fell in love with him—and he fired her?"

Chelsea examines her nails as if those could provide an answer to my question. After a second, she peers up at me. "I'm not sure what that was about. But I think you shouldn't even care. The past is the past. That's what I always tell the guys I date. You only need to focus on what's happening between you and Devon and what might happen on this trip. Is your room going to be close to his?"

"Jeez, Chels." I roll my eyes. "I have no idea. I didn't speak to him about that. I only know we're leaving tomorrow from the office and we're supposed to be back Friday evening."

I'm lying. Devon told me he booked two adjacent rooms for us.

But I don't want to encourage my roomie's fantasy about what I should do while in Tucson. She doesn't seem bothered by the idea that Devon's interest in me is only physical.

I place my hand on top of Chelsea's head. "Anyway, I

might be smitten with Devon, but I don't want to get involved with him unless he feels the same way about me."

Chelsea smacks her lips. "Laia, what you aspire to only happens in the movies. In real life, people meet, get together, hit it off—or don't—and *then* they maybe develop profound feelings for each other." She pokes me in the ribs. "Wouldn't it be worth loosening up on your rules a little, given that you're *smitten* with him?"

"No," I murmur, but my tone is only half-convinced.

I would never want to sacrifice my values for a guy.

But if there is a man for whom I may risk doing precisely that, it's Devon Griffin.

CHAPTER 37

(Devon)

"Oh, my!" A quiet gasp escapes from Laia's throat as we enter the Paradise Point Four Seasons, Tucson's best five-star plus resort.

I glance at Laia's face and my chest warms.

She clenches her carry-on's handle and scans the lobby with large eyes. The coffered ceiling has knife-edged planes fitted with LED strips. The yellow blouse she wears enhances the specks in her irises as the lighting reflects her gaze.

It's an interesting sight, but not nearly as gripping as Laia's enthusiastic face.

"It's not too shabby, right?" I smile at her.

Tucked away amid the Sonoran Desert, this hotel was picked as the location for the CCF gala twice in the past five years. This isn't surprising considering the beauty of the Tortolita Mountains that the resort's outdoor venues overlook, and the luxurious yet modern feel its indoor spaces offer.

"Are you kidding?" Laia waves toward the custom-made reception desk that's backed with a giant expressionist painting. "This place is fantastic. By far, the most gorgeous hotel I've ever been to. I love how it pairs glamour and contemporary implementation."

"I'm so glad you like it," I say.

And I am.

After all, I've booked us a three-day-long stay, despite suspecting that most event attendees will leave the next day after the gala. If I'm entirely honest, I actually counted on the participants' early departure.

Small luxury establishments don't accept overlapping events, so I expect the hotel to become quiet once the CCF's crowd clears out. It'll be an ideal location for some alone time with Laia.

CCF isn't a critical business event where I need to focus on acquiring clients or brainstorming with fellow creatives. Instead, it's a laid-back celebration of our profession, topped with great food and decent live bands. So I'll be able to dedicate all my attention to Laia and make her see that I can be the man for her.

This trip is a chance to reveal my feelings to Laia. My only problem is she doesn't know yet that there are no work activities planned for us, other than tonight's gala. I haven't found a way yet to tell her my plan, without the risk of sounding like I wanted to kidnap her and keep her in Tucson without a legitimate reason.

But I'm hoping that, as the day progresses, I might see further proof that she's attracted to me. That would give me the courage to spill the beans and propose a mini-vacation with me.

"Devon, I forgot my laptop bag in the car." Laia's voice cuts through my contemplation.

"Do you want me to get it for you?" I offer, but she shakes her head.

"No, that's okay. I'll ask the valet boy to fetch it for me if you give me the car keys."

I dig out the keys from my pocket and hand them to her.

As she takes them, our fingers brush. It's a brief, involuntary gesture, but it makes my arm pause mid-air all the same.

Laia's eyes dart to mine, and I'm sure she must be feeling the same pangs of electricity as I do. Her flustered gaze and sharp inhale point to that.

"Well, then I'll go and…"

"Sure. You go and…" *Sticking to my pledge of courting her slowly is so hard.* "I'll check into our rooms in the meanwhile." Yes, doing something useful will help me reactivate my brain.

Laia blinks at her luggage. "Can I leave this with you?"

"Of course, no problem."

She smiles, then walks away while I grab both of our bags.

I stride over to the reception desk. After a closer look, I decide it must be a Rottet design. Not many designers could pair brass, myrtle burl, and marble in such an enticing combo. I make a mental note that if I ever decide to re-look my company I should contact the talented Texas architect firm.

The young receptionist steps over to me. "Welcome to Paradise Point, Mr.…?"

"Mr. Griffin. Devon Griffin. I'm here for the CCF with my plus one, Laia Flores."

I ignore the giddy smile that wants to push its way to

my cheeks as I call Laia my plus one. I'm really getting ahead of myself, but I can't help it.

That short connection a moment ago left my insides flaring with hope and joyful anticipation for the next days.

The receptionist's well-trimmed goatee shifts into a polite smirk. "Yes, of course. Give me just a second to check." He peers down at his screen and types on his keyboard. "Ah, yes. I have you here. Mr. Griffin and Mrs. Flores. Perfect." Then his bushy brows drift together. "Oh, wait, we have a tiny problem."

"What problem?" I ask, alarmed.

The receptionist rubs his chin, and the squishy sound of his beard is unnerving.

"One of your rooms was given away to another participant. The one you booked for Ms. Flores."

"What? How could this happen?" I bark and take absolute satisfaction in watching the guy pale.

Nothing was supposed to go wrong. *Nothing*. And now this lad tells me Laia doesn't have a room?

"I'm not sure." The receptionist hits a few keys, and his eyes speed back and forth as he reads his screen. "Ah, okay, I have it. We had a special request from a lady who has anxiety issues when placed on the top floor. A colleague of mine switched Ms. Flores' room with hers. Thanks to this change, Ms. Flores can stay in a suite with a breathtaking view of Wild Burro Canyon." He flashes me a relieved smile, apparently proud that he managed to clear up my problem.

"Only not on the same floor as I am," I murmur.

"Well, no. I'm really sorry about that."

For his benefit, the receptionist does seem sorry, so I decide not to pester him any further. It's not the end of the world if Laia and I need to sleep on a different floor. Maybe this distance will even add a touch of the romanticism Laia likes.

After dinner together, I'll accompany her to her level as if I'm giving her a lift home and then wander back to my own floor. I'd like her to have the best possible time in Tucson, and staying in a suite instead of a deluxe room might contribute to that.

"Here are your keys, sir." The receptionist hands me the cards. "Do you need someone to take up your luggage, or will you manage?"

"It's fine, I'll take care of them. Thanks."

I slip the cards in my jacket pocket and pivot around to search for Laia. She should be back already.

But instead of her dark hair, blond tresses teased into a high bun obscure my view.

Morgan struts towards me, her boot heels clicking on the graphite tiles with each step. Her hands are in the pockets of her pink blazer, the same hue as her lipstick.

"Hey there, Dev," she purrs when she reaches me, pulling her shoulders back so her white top's neckline becomes more plunging. "How great to see you again. How are you?"

"All is good," I answer, then decide to cut to the chase. "What are you doing here, Morgan? I thought Theo and you couldn't make it because of his Alaska trip."

Morgan's hooded eyelids, a trait she hates on herself but learned to mask with eyeshadow, flutter. "Well, yes. Theo is indeed there. But I asked him to confirm my presence for this gala before he left."

My eyes widen. "Theo agreed for you to come to his work event without him?"

Morgan shrugs. "Like you said in the teahouse, the gala wouldn't have been an important gig for him anyway. As for me, well, let's just say I didn't give him much choice.

I really wanted to be here. And I can be *very* persuasive when I set on mind on something."

I shake my head. "I remember that. But as far as I know, you don't have a job, other than being a socialite. Why would you want to participate in an ad industry event that's of no concern to you?"

"Well, I wouldn't say it's of no concern." She gives me a coy smile. "You are here, no?"

"Me?" My brows jump almost to my hairline.

"Yes. I've been thinking about you since our meeting at the teahouse. About how things went down between us. I wanted a chance to catch you alone and chat about that. I have regrets, you know." She bends slightly closer, and her perfume's potent cloud wafts over me. "Do you have them, too?"

I take a step back because her fragrance tickles my throat. "Regrets? About us, you mean? No, as a matter of fact, I do not."

Morgan sniffs. "I get it. We have a lot of peculiar memories, right?"

"Peculiar isn't the most adequate word to describe them."

"Ah," Morgan sighs, "don't be so rigid, Dev. I know I've made a mistake. A big one. But in my defense, you weren't particularly fun in college. Not like you used to be in high school. There, we had a blast together. But as soon as we moved to Phoenix, that changed. *You* changed."

I square my shoulders as she recites the same lame excuse she gave me for her betrayal years ago.

"What you mean is I couldn't be at your service non-stop anymore. I was preparing my business plan for Hudson Communications, tracking down potential clients, and studying full-time, Morgan."

She nods. "I understand now. I might have been shortsighted to think you were wasting your time with your company idea. I should have placed my bets on you and not on Theo."

"Well, it's a unique type of apology. I'm not sure Theo would be happy to hear it."

Morgan rolls her eyes. "I'm not even sure he would care. I never thought becoming a wealthy lawyer would turn him into the boring guy he is now. All he cares about is his business. He doesn't go out to clubs like you do. I feel like I'm married to an old man."

I'm amazed that talking with Morgan about our past doesn't even trigger a mild annoyance. Much less the bitterness I used to feel.

I've lived in the aftermath of my failed relationship with her for many years. I told myself it was better never to commit again because I'd been burned by love.

But as I stare at Morgan, it dawns on me that I lied to myself.

I've never really loved Morgan.

At least not the way I love Laia.

I mistook the sense of pride that came from being with Morgan for a sense of bliss. I thought I cared for her deeply, but I never felt at ease with her like I do with Laia. I didn't admire her soul or share her same interests.

I was wrong to ever propose to her. We would have never been happy together. Under this light, I'm lucky Morgan cheated on me. And even more fortunate I found out about her affair before we could tie the knot.

This realization makes me give Morgan a warm smile. I have no reason to hold a grudge with her.

"It's probably just a busy period for your husband. You have that in any business. But concerning us, no worries. It's all in the past. We can start with a clean slate. I'm not mad at you for what happened with Theo."

And I'm not.

All trace of past resentment is gone. My love for Laia burned it all.

Morgan beams at me. "A fresh start? Go, figure. It's just what I have been thinking about ever since I read that article about you in *True Facts*. And this hotel could be just the right setting for that, no?"

"For what exactly?" I ask.

Morgan rolls her eyes. "For our new beginning, silly. Don't tell me our coincidental meeting wasn't the reason you dialed back on clubbing? The timing is eerily perfect. Did seeing me make you realize that flings weren't what you wanted?"

She fiddles with her earlobe, but it doesn't come across as if she were genuinely flustered.

I'm not surprised Morgan is aware of my latest tabloid article. She already slipped that she follows gossip about me when she admitted back in the teahouse that she knew I was attending CCF.

What I didn't expect, however, is for Morgan to jump to such an erroneous conclusion about my feelings.

I rub my neck, trying to find a polite way to tell her that her happiness isn't my concern anymore.

I level her gaze. "Morgan you're a married woman and I—"

Morgan dismisses my words with a wave of her manicured hands.

"Marriages can be undone. I haven't been happy with Theo for years now. Perhaps never as happy as I was with you." She gives me a coy smile. "Dev, don't think I didn't see through your lie in the teahouse. That girl you were with? Her laptop bag and clothes told me the story. She isn't your girlfriend. A colleague or an assistant, maybe?

You wanted me to believe you two were dating so I'd get jealous."

"That wasn't my intention. I'm not after a second chance with you."

Morgan's eyes widen, and for the first time, she looks uneasy. Then she shakes her head. "Of course. I didn't expect that we'd hit it off here in the reception. Too many years have passed. We need more time to reconnect. Don't worry, we'll have the occasion to do that. This morning when I arrived, I switched the suite Theo booked for me for the room beside yours."

A lightbulb goes up in my head.

"Are you the lady with the fear of heights? Doesn't Theo own a penthouse?"

"Okay, I might not suffer from anxiety attacks on the top floor, but the room beside yours was already assigned to someone, so I needed a good excuse to convince the receptionist. She was a woman," she adds with a one-shoulder shrug as if to show that, had it been a man, no fibs would have been necessary.

Which is probably true. Morgan can always get what she wants with men. But not with me, not anymore.

"Did you even bother to ask whose room you were taking?"

"What does it matter? It'll be far easier to spend time together if we sleep in adjacent rooms. You're here alone, and I'm here alone, so we—" She stops, and her eyes zero in on something behind my back.

I whirl around, and Laia's perplexed expression greets me. She holds her laptop bag clutched to her chest, and her eyes bounce between my face and Morgan's.

"Devon, I'm sorry it took so long," she mumbles. "Hi, Morgan, nice to see you again."

From her tone, I can decipher that she isn't particularly

thrilled about seeing my ex. I pray that her annoyance is fueled by her growing feelings for me.

Morgan narrows her eyes at Laia. "Hi." Then she turns to me. "You didn't say that your colleague is here too."

"Laia and I came to the event together, yes." I try to pronounce my phrase casually so I don't startle Laia with its deeper meaning, but with enough emphasis for Morgan to understand that whatever plans she had for us won't happen.

I'm not sure if Morgan understands my point, but she swallows and nods. "I need to go now. Let's continue this later, Devon." With this enigmatic promise, she prances off.

"So, uhm…" Laia clears her throat. "Your ex decided to show up for the event, after all? And I see she knows that we work together."

There's a cool timbre to her voice as if the appearance of Morgan has washed away all intimacy that had sprouted between us. Panic seizes my belly as I realize Morgan's presence could undermine my efforts.

I capture Laia's gaze. "I didn't know Morgan would be here. She came here without her husband because…I don't know. Maybe she needed a five-star spa treatment. Frankly, I don't care why she's here."

"Right," Laia murmurs, but her mouth presses into a line of disbelief.

"No, seriously, I don't. I've gone through some soul-searching, and I realized my relationship with Morgan went down exactly as it should have. No correction." I lift my finger as Laia's mouth opens. "I shouldn't have asked her to marry me in the first place, but since I did, it was just as well that our engagement went up in flames."

Laia's eyes widen. "Are you serious?"

"Very." I nod. "Now, please, let's ignore that this

conversation ever happened. The gala is in a few hours, and I'd like to show you the property before we need to get ready. I suggest we find our rooms, drop off our luggage, and go for a walk."

Laia eyes me with a questioning look as if she can't decide whether she should insist on the subject of Morgan or not. Then her lips curl up. "Okay, let's go for a tour. I spotted some giant Saguaro cactuses while waiting for the valet outside, and I'd love to admire them closer."

CHAPTER 38

(Laia)

I pull the clips from my hair with a discouraged sigh.

I wish Chelsea were here. Or Eva…

That was my third try at a twisted up-do, but I'm giving up. I can't tame my mane into any style other than a ponytail, a braid, or a messy bun on my own, and none of those hairstyles are worthy of the fantastic dress my roomie picked for me.

Maybe I should leave my tresses loose?

I glance into a mirror to check and run my fingers on the skirt's fabric, which is slippery and soft.

Yes, not bad at all. I actually like what I'm seeing, which is a rare happening for me.

The silhouette of this dress plays up my strong features as Chelsea anticipated it would, while it also graciously hides almost everything I feel unsure about.

Let's hope Devon will like it, too.

Faint music reaches my ear, and I walk to my private balcony and peer outside. I must be in the wing located just above the gala hall because the jazzy tunes floating from below are exceptionally clear.

Despite the upgrade—and boy, if my suite isn't fabulous! Starting with the indigenous-inspired textiles, the amazing natural materials and earth tones, and ending with the magnificent canyon view I can enjoy from my terrace, it's all like in a dream—I was sorry when Devon announced that we're sleeping on different floors.

I'd already started to fantasize about how it would be to sleep, knowing that just a thin wall separated us.

The rational part of me, however, knows that some breathing space from Devon is a blessing. I still don't know what he wants from me, and even if I have my hopeful suspicions, it's better to safeguard as much clarity as possible when we're together.

Especially now that his ex-fiancée has turned up in the hotel without her husband.

Devon seemed sincere when he said he didn't care about Morgan being here. Still, her presence disturbs the blossoming confidence in my chest.

The melody from downstairs changes to a groovier rhythm, and its upbeat tone lifts my mood.

I raise my chin and let my eyes feast on the lush greenery below.

Besides the Wild Burrow Canyon, my suite also faces the hotel's garden. Although calling it simply a garden doesn't do justice to the enormous green landscape that hosts an extended parterre, a life-size chess set, and a beautiful rose field. They must invest a lot of time and considerable resources to keep these plants alive despite the heat and dryness of the surrounding desert.

Memories from our stroll in the park surface in my mind, and my pulse immediately pumps harder in my veins.

Our afternoon was magical. Devon showed me the surrounding area on foot, and we also made a quick drive to visit a nearby spring. We spoke and joked like real friends, but there were definitely sizzles between us.

I can't wait to see how tonight will evolve.

With this thought in mind and nerves dancing a jig in my stomach, I hurry back into my room.

I slip on my sandals, the only genuinely high-heeled pair I possess. I've had them for a long time, but it's the first time I'm actually wearing them.

Should I happen to dance with Devon—which I may or may not have fantasized about this afternoon—I'd like to be able to peer up at him without straining my neck.

My feet waver as I find my balance on the beige carpet. If I really can't stand the pain in my toes later tonight, I can always sneak upstairs and change into my flats.

I exit my room and head toward the elevator, while I pre-savor the vision of how I'll lean on Devon's arm and sway to a romantic song with him.

CHAPTER 39

(Devon)

I enter the large hall hosting the gala and scan the crowd for Laia.

Respecting the event's laid-back style, and emphasizing the spirit that creative people aren't stuck-up businessmen, there aren't any fixed table arrangements. Instead, the hotel created a large sitting corner from comfy leather couches and plush armchairs. There are low stands scattered around, where one can easily place the food that is served in the sumptuous buffet lining the wall next to the entrance.

Laia isn't anywhere.

I'd considered walking up to her room and knocking before coming downstairs, but then I recalled how Ellie used to hate being rushed when dressing.

The ambiance lighting in the room is a mélange of bright pink and silver spotlights. It harmonizes with the open bar's design, which has a large shelf filled with sleek candles in the shade of cotton candy.

The barman is busy mixing cocktails, all his movements visible thanks to the counter's glass planes.

My eyes drift further because I'm not looking for a drink, nor do I want to offer one to Laia.

She was the most adorable tipsy person, and I liked the bold, uninhibited way she spoke to me, but I'd prefer to achieve the same ease in her without the help of an external substance. Using only my words and actions.

There's a large but relatively low stage close to the terrace door, and the musicians are already playing.

I'm happy about the choice the organizers made. The members of Pale Blue Mornings are talented folks. I had the pleasure of listening to them one night at Jimmy'z. I'm sure they'll delight us with relaxing blues and jazz songs—just the kind Laia and I like.

That's, if she finally gets here…

Someone taps my shoulder, and my heart jumps into my throat.

There she is…

An almost foolish smile spreads on my face but freezes on my lips when I turn.

"Ah, Morgan. It's just you."

Disappointment drips from my voice, and it doesn't miss Morgan's attention.

"Just me?" Morgan lifts a brow. "Who were you hoping it was? That mousy colleague of yours?"

"What right do you have to call her mousy?" I snap.

Morgan shrugs. "Because she's dull, isn't she? I wonder what she'll put on tonight. Probably a pantsuit or something."

She adjusts her strapless black evening gown that has a steep cut on one thigh. She's the only female in the room who upgraded the casual cocktail dress code into a white-tie event.

"Whatever Laia wears, she'll look lovely in it," I answer.

Morgan cocks her head to the side and observes me. "Huh, so I got it wrong, didn't I?"

She certainly did—many things. I just don't know which one she's referring to. "What do you mean?"

"That tabloid article. It wasn't telling the truth. You didn't give up your lifestyle. You brought along your co-worker for some extra-curricular activity. I didn't realize you had a fetish for the boss-employee setup."

Her words bug me because they are partially correct, though not in the sense Morgan means.

I have no desire to discuss my feelings for Laia with Morgan, so I shake my head. "It's none of your business why Laia is here. The only thing you should deduce from her presence is that whatever you imagined would happen between us in this resort, will *not* occur."

A vexed glint invades Morgan's eyes, and I wonder for a second whether my words were too blunt. But she really irritated me with her dismissive remarks about Laia.

She sniffs. "You know, Devon, it might be time for you to come down from your moral high horse. *I* might have hooked up with your buddy in college, but at least I married the guy. I'm not an egoist playboy like you."

Before I can interject that only this afternoon she said that she was ready to blow up her marriage, Morgan turns on her heels and rushes out of the room.

I stride over to the bar, hop up on a barstool, and order sparkling water.

As I watch the bubbles rise to the surface in my glass, Morgan's last words swirl in my head.

I used to protect my conscience by telling myself I wasn't hurting anyone as long as I was transparent with my partners about what they could expect. That I could do no harm, because I never pretended to want anything more than what I was capable of giving.

But perhaps my ex is right.

I was selfish. I focused on what *I* wanted. I never bothered to question what would be best for the women I dated.

With Laia, I can't make the same mistake.

Where is she, anyway? I hope she didn't get lost.

"Why are you looking so grumpy?"

Laia's voice jars me out of my self-doubt. She stands beside me with a concerned expression.

Her dulcet timbre acts like a spell, dissolving the dark cloud of worry at once.

Morgan's comment about Laia's dress couldn't have been farther off. Laia looks absolutely breathtaking in her flared skirt and tight bodice with a sober but still charming neckline. The light shade of blue accentuates her skin's glow and sparkles against the dark cascade of her hair.

"You're…pretty. Very, very pretty."

Laia blushes. "Thanks. But it's Chelsea who found this dress for me, so I can't take credit for it."

"Maybe not for the dress, but the rest is all you. And that's the most important part. The part I like the most."

Her jaw drops, and an alarmed glint invades her gaze.

Oh, perhaps I need to go slower with these kinds of compliments. I don't want to scare her off.

I pick up my glass and take a sip. The cold water eases my throat.

"Do you want me to order you anything?" I ask, pretending my previous comment wasn't a confession at all.

"No, I'm fine. You remember my bubbly accident, don't you?"

"They have plain water, too," I point at my drink, but she shakes her head again.

"No, I'm really okay, Devon, thanks."

I wave to the band. "Do you like these guys? They're awesome, no?"

The singer is singing "Ain't Misbehavin'" from LeRoy Holmes, and her deep contralto reverberates in the air around us.

"Yes, they're great. Since the reception mixed up your booking, I could listen to them while I got ready. Would you like to dance?" Laia's voice is filled with an anxious undertone.

I'd love to be carried away by the singer's sensual voice while Laia leans against my chest, but I can see Laia's unease.

She really didn't lie when she told Ellie she isn't a dancer…

I decide to propose something different.

I point to the terrace door. "I'd prefer to take a walk in the garden."

A soft whoosh of air leaves her lips as her mouth moves into a surprised *oh*. "Sure, okay. Go. I'll…I'll just see what's at the buffet and then—"

Does she think I want her to stay?

"I meant you and me. *Together*." I stand up and shake my legs as if to prove that they indeed need some movement.

Laia's brows move into a confused frown. "Oh, right. Okay, sure…I can come with you if you like."

"Let's go then." I grin at her and put a hand between her shoulder blades.

CHAPTER 40

(Laia)

The evening air's flowery scent wraps me in a protective embrace, as I step from the terrace onto the garden's pebbly road.

It grants me a brief break from my frustration of not understanding Devon's behavior.

"Where would you like to go? Toward the rose garden where we went this afternoon? Or the small pond on the other side of the chessboard?"

Devon's voice comes from much closer than expected. His hot breath rakes my skin with a tempting pleasure, freezing my brain cells.

I take a second before I turn and peer up at him.

"We can go wherever you want." I aim for my voice to sound lighthearted and score on the medium-high end of the success scale. "It's you who needs to loosen up your legs."

Dcvon points to the left. "Then let's go to the roses."

He stretches his arm toward me. "You want to lean on me?"

"Why?"

"Because of your heels. They are rather high." He smiles at me warmly. "I don't want you to break your neck because of my fancy."

I'd love nothing more than to hold on to Devon, but *not* because I'm afraid to fall.

And that's the only reason he offers his arm, apparently, so it's better to avoid touching him altogether.

"I won't," I say confidently.

At least not my neck.

My heart is a different matter…

The labyrinth of roses is more beautiful than it was when the afternoon sun illuminated its bushes. The petals glisten in a silvery halo, and the contrast between the shadows and the delicate moonlight creates a magical fairyland feel.

There are no artificial streetlights here, only candles at the windows of the small chapel that stands at the center of the maze.

Devon ambles to the building and waves to me. "Come, the view is amazing from here. You can see the entire rose garden, the canyon, and the hotel at one glance."

I stagger over to him. The lack of proper lighting might contribute to the fable-like atmosphere, but it also makes the path more challenging.

Confusion pulls in my belly with each shaky step I take.

Chelsea had convinced me that Devon's puzzling behavior might mean something. I even thought I saw confirmation that my friend was right during our afternoon together. But then when I invited him to dance, he refused me. *Point-blank.*

If he wanted a chance to cozy up with me, he surely wouldn't have done that, right?

The slow beats of a song from the ballroom drift around us, and a silly disappointment surfaces in me once more. I'm tagging along on his walk like a clumsy puppy, without even understanding why he wished me to accompany him on this trip in the first place.

That's enough, Laia.

The voice of confidence I've been nurturing over these past weeks finally makes its appearance.

And it's right. I have to stop beating myself down. What I must do, instead, is clear the situation with Devon, once and for all.

"Why am I really here, Devon?" I blurt out when I reach him, even if I didn't make a conscious decision about confronting him.

Devon turns to me, his arms opening as his shoulders pull up in perfect synchrony with his brows. "You're here to see the garden with me."

I square my shoulders before leveling his gaze. "No, I mean why did you invite me to Tucson? I don't think you really needed me here as your assistant."

Devon shakes his head, his tone still baffled. "Yes, of course, I did. Your company here means *so much* to me."

Again these ambiguous words.

Is he doing it on purpose? Can't he see how easy it is to misinterpret what he's saying?

I draw in a big breath as I gather my wit.

Maybe Devon can't help himself. Perhaps flirting is in his blood. But if he's playing with me, even if unwittingly, I need to know. *Now.*

"Why didn't you want to dance with me?" I ask.

Devon's jaw drops, then he throws back his head and

laughs. "Oh, heavens, is this why you look so sullen? You wanted to dance with me?"

Hold your ground. "And what if I did? Is that a crime?"

His face becomes serious, and his eyes lock with mine. "No, it's not. Why did you want to dance with me, Laia?"

I take a step back and land against the wall of the chapel. I fold my arms in front of my chest.

Embarrassment and a strange boldness war for space inside me, but I somehow manage both with equal aplomb—which makes me wonder how much I've truly changed since meeting Devon.

This contemplation becomes fact when the words the old me would never have dared to utter find their way to my lips. "I wanted to dance with you because…uhm…I think I fancy you."

I describe my feelings with a non-committing word, even if my ribcage drums. Despite my impulse of courage there's still enough of the shy Laia left in me.

Devon's eyes widen, but before he can respond, I add, "And based on some of your late actions, I assumed you might fancy me. But—"

His lips curl up. "But now you think I proposed a walk instead of accepting your invitation to dance because I'm not interested in you."

His voice is soft and thick with a rough emotion—a bit like a sour punch straw candy. Below the zest of acidity, I can sense its sweet taste.

I nod.

He deduced my thought correctly. Now the ball is in his court.

Devon gives me a bold, sweeping gaze. "So, you believed I refused to dance with you because I didn't want to have you in my arms…" He takes a step toward me. "…feel your warm body pressed to my chest…" He approaches even more. "…or have your mouth only inches away from my own?"

He's so close I can see the tiniest details on his face in the glow of the candlelight.

"Something like that," I mumble.

He tilts his head, but his eyes don't leave mine. "Well, Laia, you've got it all wrong."

"Do I?" I whisper.

He wiggles his brows and nods. "Absolutely. Because I'm interested in you. *A lot*. And not just as my assistant, but as a woman. Because," he chuckles shortly, "despite what you reproached me for at Jimmy'z, I'm all too aware that this is what you are. I know as your boss I'm not supposed to be feeling this way about you, but I do."

He smiles in a boyish, I'm-guilty-but-I-don't-mind way.

I stare at him, my mouth opening and closing.

Am I awake or dreaming? "But I'm not skinny, blond, or tall," I say as if my brain struggled to accept Devon's abrupt confession.

He sighs. "No, Laia, you're not. And yet, you set fire to me like no one ever could."

As if Devon can read my doubts, he leans in so his breath caresses my ear and adds, "You, Laia, are nothing I could have ever imagined wanting, yet you arouse every sense, every thought, *heck*, every feeling in me."

He brackets my waist with a palm on either side, and then rubs the tip of his nose against mine.

I search his gaze, and what I find nearly has me swaying.

Devon isn't lying about his attraction to me. I read the molten desire in his eyes, taste it in the ragged pants of his breath.

Warmth swirls through my belly, yet I stand motionless as our lips almost touch.

However, as soon as Devon brushes his mouth on mine, gently as if he's asking permission, a sharp, wild need sizzles through me. My fingers yearn to touch him, and my lips to taste more of him. It's a potent sensation I'm entirely unfamiliar with, yet it seems so natural… so *right*. Its raw power clobbers my inexperience.

My hands snake behind his nape without hesitation, hauling him closer to me.

My fervor wrenches a moan from Devon, and his kiss becomes deeper and more demanding. He slides his arms behind my back in a hungry hello.

My soul does triumphant somersaults at the delicate trail of kisses he leaves on my neck as he moves up to nuzzle on my ear.

But despite the joy, there is also a flicker of fear.

Devon didn't speak of love. Only of liking, arousal, and desire…

What if he's only driven by sheer lust and nothing more?

Maybe this is just a regular make-out session for him, while it means *everything* to me.

The anxious thought tries to overpower my mind, but the bewitching energy that passes between Devon and me proves stronger. It forces my doubt back into a hidden corner where it can't disturb me.

A yearning to surrender entirely to Devon's sweet teasing blots out all my reason and I abandon myself to our mingling breaths.

I hope that wherever our kiss will lead me, I'll be fine.

CHAPTER 41

(Devon)

My lips are probing Laia's soft mouth, and her choppy breaths devour my will to resist her body's sweet temptation. All my control flees, leaving only the madness of desire I feel for her.

I'm dazzled by the licks of electricity racing through my veins, but the warm glow that fills my chest is even more amazing.

Only, in this moment, do I understand how right my innocent Laia has been…and how wise.

I can surely testify now that, when you love a person, intimacy—be it only a kiss—becomes something indescribably profound.

As Laia's skin brushes against mine, making me go mindless with an insatiable craving for her, it's not only our bodies that explore each other but also our souls.

Which is a bone-tingling, heart-pumping, wanting-to-embrace-the-world kind of experience that I never dreamed existed.

My hands move up to her hair, tracing the fine line of her spine. I immerse my fingers in her black mane, massaging her scalp with my fingertips.

A hum of pleasure slips from her lips and, in a trice, all my cells vibrate with the manly desire to pin her against the wall and discover every secret inch on her neck, ear, and beyond.

But as much as I want to indulge my longing, I know it's the moment to stop. If not, I'll go too far and drag Laia with me.

I slowly pull back.

As her eyes flutter open and I take in her surprised glance, I almost curse myself for my chosen path.

"Why did you stop?" she asks with a timid but lustful voice that hints that maybe, *just maybe*, I could have gone a tad further with her if I had only tried.

But I didn't want to.

Not this way. Not yet. I need to do this right with Laia.

I caress her lower lip with a thumb. "Believe me, if it were only my morals at stake, I would have scooped you up already and brought you to my hotel room. But it isn't only about me, or what I want. I don't want to rush you into anything."

Laia's cheeks become rosy, and she drops her gaze to the ground.

I love the adorable embarrassment that she fails to hide from me.

After the declaration of our mutual attraction—which is, of course, the understatement of the century concerning my feelings for her—she shouldn't feel abashed by my comment.

Most of the women I used to date wouldn't.

But the fact that Laia feels at unease makes her even more special in my eyes.

She raises her chin, her eyes traveling to mine. "And you don't mind…you know that I won't…?"

I sigh. "You want me to be honest with you?"

"Always," she replies promptly.

"Then the answer is, I do. I *do* mind. Every fiber in my body is aching to have more of you. From the very moment you walked into my office for the interview, I guess. I just took a while to recognize and acknowledge my attraction."

Laia's eyes widen, and her lips move into a tiny circle.

"But," I say and softly tap the tip of her nose, "one of the reasons I find you so bewitching is your character. I respect your strong values. I appreciate that you're someone who wants to save herself for the person who will be the love of her life." *And I would like to be that person.* I omit this thought from my discourse and add, "I know well the flesh's yearning, and our chemistry is… what shall I call it? Mind blowing?"

A smile spreads on her face. "Well, that pretty much describes it from my side."

Her cheeky comment does nothing but instigate my wish to capture her mouth again, but instead of giving in, I finish my discourse.

"Yes, from my side, too. I'm afraid I might not be able to stop if I get any more blinded by the heat of passion. And that's not what I want."

Laia draws in a deep breath as if she's summoning her strength or courage. "And what is it you want? From me, I mean."

I want you to love me the way I love you.

"I want to…uhm, date you? I'd like you to see I'm more than just a player."

Laia raises herself on her tiptoes and leans close to me. Her lips brush against mine as she whispers, "I already know you're more than that. If not, I wouldn't like you the way I do."

She plants a feathery kiss on my mouth.

The tingles she leaves behind, and probably the unexpected boldness of her words and gesture, make me lightheaded, and I blurt out, "Laia, you're the woman I always desired."

Her eyes widen, and, in a second, her lips are back on mine.

The contours of the world blur around us and I give in to the joy of having her breath uniting with mine.

When she moves back, she grins at me. "I'm sorry. I didn't want to test your self-control. I just couldn't resist doing this after what you said."

"You know, I might have better willpower than I thought. Maybe we could give it a few more nudges."

My phrase lures out that delicate pink hue I've come to worship on her skin. She giggles. "Why don't we go back and have a dance instead?"

"So, you like dancing? But in my kitchen, you said you weren't a dancer."

"Well, I'm not, but I'm not wooden-legged either. I said what I did because I needed a reasonable excuse to explain why I preferred being a homebody to going out with Chelsea. Other than being a bookworm, I mean."

A smile spreads on my face. "Very well, then. Let's go dance. But on the way back, I'm keeping you close to me. I hated to watch how you struggled on the pebbles."

Laia winks. "Deal. If I'm not mistaken, the band has just started playing a Solomon Burke. If we hurry, we might catch the end."

We meander to the building hand in hand. I tease Laia about how, after all, I might turn out as an inspiration for her romance book.

As we chat and joke, and the warmth from Laia's fingers seeps into my palm, I'm almost able to rid myself of the question of whether I'm what Laia really needs and whether I'll be good enough for her.

CHAPTER 42

(Laia)

I switch off the light in my suite and snuggle into the luxurious silky bed sheets, while a sigh leaves my throat. My head is full of swirling thoughts about Devon, and my chest hums.

I suspected my feelings for him were more potent than a simple crush, but only now, in the quietude of my room, do I have the time to catch my breath (not only figuratively speaking) and recognize just how deep I've fallen.

There is no question. I'm in *love* with Devon.

Strangely, this devotion is more off-kilter than I could've imagined. Thanks to the countless romances I've read, I thought I'd know what it felt like to be in love. I expected a gushy feeling that would plaster a crazy, big smile on my lips. A kind of "cloud nine" sensation.

And while I'm definitely grinning in the darkness as I remember Devon's kiss…kisses—yeah, definitely plural—there is so much more to my emotions than just euphoric giddiness.

When Devon held me in his arms on the dance floor, I felt whole.

As if a part of me I didn't even know I was missing was hidden in his gaze. As if, with him in my life, I could build something I couldn't have seen or known before.

I press a hand on my chest to keep my heart from jumping. But it's a fruitless endeavor.

I inhale deeply and sit up. I'm too electrified to sleep. I turn the light back on and reach for the book on my nightstand. Perhaps reading a chapter from my motivational guide will help me settle down?

As if per serendipity, the book opens up on a page titled "Sharing and Showing Your Love."

It's the section dedicated to the various love languages. It argues that when we deliberately choose to disregard the style we're most comfortable using because of another person, that's a potential sign of true love.

Though I read this chapter some time ago, my breathing quickens when I scan the lines.

Devon is most at ease with showing his attraction physically. He's even a true master of it, as I could attest to tonight.

I ignore the thrills the memory of Devon's touch unleashes in me and focus on the detail of how he clearly decided to respect my boundaries even if it meant frustrating his own manly desires.

Could this be a sign that Devon feels as strongly about me as I do about him?

One of his phrases comes back to me.

Laia, you're the woman I always desired.

It sounded like an honest slip. Something he wasn't ready to reveal to me yet, but did it anyway because he got caught up in the moment.

The possibility that the book is right, and thus Devon

might love me, sends me on a dreamy mind trip. It involves lots of white fabric, my and his families and friends, and an enormous cake with chocolate frosting.

When I get to the point in my vision where Devon and I are about to exchange our vows, I shake my head.

I don't need this fantasy. What I need is to reciprocate Devon's considerate gesture in my own way.

I want to surprise him. Make him see I'm ready to step out of my comfort zone for him. I secretly hope it might prompt him to be more verbally forthcoming about his potential feelings for me.

I shut the book and drop it to the bed. I jump up, fish my slippers from beneath the bed, and put them on. I grab my room card and head straight to the door.

In less than a minute, I glide with a quiet rustling on the stairs.

I hope nobody will be sportive enough to use the staircase in the middle of the night when there's a perfectly well-functioning elevator.

Though Devon and I were among the last to leave the gala, there could still be some guests looming about.

I'd like to meet as few people as possible in my striped pajama pants and T-shirt that reads, "*I like to party, but by party I mean take naps,*" which is courtesy of my all-so-funny brother.

I foretaste Devon's bewilderment when he sees me at his door. I hope he'll like the glimpse of my less timid, more flirtatious side and appreciate the special good night kiss I plan on giving him.

My wish is that it will keep him dreaming of me.

And me of him, of course, but that's a given.

I push the glass door leading to his floor open, and it creaks despite my conscious effort to exercise as little pressure as possible. I scurry along the toffee-colored carpet of the corridor when, suddenly, I hear a chirring noise.

CHAPTER 43

(Devon)

I kick off my shoes and take off my black jacket. I drop it on the large queen bed and throw myself down beside it.

I stare at the white ceiling and listen to the water gurgling in the pipes within the walls. Even this banal noise is music to my ears, due to the caffeine-like, happy buzz coursing through me.

This night couldn't have been any better if I'd prayed for it to happen. I not only managed to confess to Laia that I can't consider her a mere employee anymore, but learned that my gut wasn't deluding me. My hunch about her interest in me was spot on.

Accompanying Laia to her room and leaving her there without asking to be invited in was harder than I would've thought. Probably because she got naughty and probed my resolution to be a gentleman with more than one toe-curling kiss.

Elation suffuses my chest as I ponder our time in the ballroom.

If tonight is a preview of how Laia and I could be as a couple, we're truly meant to be together.

We had so much fun dancing, talking, and just being in each other's company that the four-hour-long reception flew by in an instant.

I smile as I realize tomorrow I'll be able to reveal my surprise to Laia. I might've worried how she'd feel about spending two days alone with me in Tucson, but after tonight I'm confident that the quietness of the hotel will be to her liking.

I sit up and unbutton my shirt. I take it off and let it fall on top of my jacket.

I'll get my clothes sorted out later. First, I want to check what kind of soft drinks I have in the minibar. I could really use a ginger ale or a tonic water.

Just as the suction of the fridge gives in to the pressure of my grip, there's a knock on my door.

Maybe Laia wants to give me a last good night kiss?

My heart skitters with sweet anticipation.

In my most husky Chris Hemsworth imitation, which Ellie and her roomies claim could make reading out of a telephone directory sound sexy, I say, "Just a sec, I'll be right there."

I grab my shirt to slip it on again, but then I decide against it.

Two can play the cheeky tempting game.

I know Laia's self-restraint is probably stronger than mine, but I can still try and tease her a bit, no?

CHAPTER 44

(Laia)

The door of the room beside Devon's opens.

I spot a room service cart containing someone's untouched midnight snack. It's been conveniently placed to my right side and is large enough to hide me. I quickly crouch down behind it on the floor. If I'm lucky, Devon's neighbor will walk the other way and won't spot me.

Otherwise, I'll have to pretend I just stepped out of a nearby room to collect my dish, instead of dawdling about in my nightwear. I peek out from behind the white tablecloth to check whether the air is clear.

But to my surprise, it isn't.

A slender blonde stands in the corridor with her back to me.

First, I think she's still wearing her evening attire. At a closer look, I realize she's dressed in a super sexy, probably costly, kimono—the kind Chelsea orders from Agent

Provocateur whenever her father gives her a fat birthday envelope.

Underneath the kimono, the woman has a long, silk nightie so fitted it would rip on my hips if I ever dared to try it.

Huh, and I was afraid to look inappropriate in my top and pants!

Just as the thought pops into my mind, the blonde turns, and I see her face.

I freeze.

Morgan is the guest who took my room? Why is she out here in her show-more-than-hide lingerie?

Morgan's next move answers both questions.

She knocks on Devon's door with a breezy movement, then pulls back her hand to her hip, shifting her lean legs into a flattering pose.

Devon appears in the doorway.

From the shadow cast by Morgan and the door, I can't see his face, but I get a good glimpse at his bare torso and those muscles that made me speechless. My stomach shrinks to the size of an M&M.

Do these two have a late-night date?

It seems so because Morgan sashays forward and Devon moves back to leave her space to enter. The door slams shut behind her.

I wait for a second in my hideout, then straighten with trembling legs. I press my back to the beige wallpaper, but I struggle to keep my posture on my wobbly knees, even with the support.

That's why he didn't get upset with me for not sleeping with him…

Devon wasn't putting my needs in front of his own when he didn't insist. He simply had another plan in mind for tonight.

With his ex. The woman who betrayed him and whom he said he didn't care for anymore.

Didn't care, my eye!

I sprint back to the staircase, forcing my brain into an artificial numbness until I reach the safe harbor of my room. Once inside, I dash to the bed and lift the treacherous adviser that made me assume Devon's behavior was a sign that he loved me. "Stupid, stupid book," I exclaim and throw it against the door with all my force.

It tumbles to the floor with a loud thud.

I stare at its crumpled pages, then stagger over and place it on the table beside the door. As much as I want to blame a lifeless object for what happened, I know the fault lies with me. And me alone.

How could I hope a player like Devon could change for me? Want *me* and nobody else?

I shuffle back to the bed and slump down. I slide my hands up and down on the crisp, lavender-smelling sheets as a suspicious thought occurs to me.

Maybe it was Devon who made the reception switch my room? It can't be a coincidence that Morgan ended up sleeping beside him.

Well, technically with him.

The cynical voice makes me almost choke.

I swallow and keep the wheels of my mind turning, though I know they'll lead me down a painful path.

If Devon upgraded me to the suite so Morgan could be close to him, then he must've decided to rekindle with her as soon as he saw her at the reception. A new wave of nausea hits me as I realize Morgan wasn't at the gala tonight. At least I didn't see her there.

Maybe she and Devon made arrangements to only meet at night? This seems reasonable. The woman is married, after all. Perhaps she fears the scandal.

But how can Devon accept to be with her after she stomped on his heart? Is it just a physical desire he has for her, or is he still smitten with his ex?

What does this mean for me?

Was I just a distraction to Devon? A warm-up for his night of passion with Morgan?

The hungry glint in Devon's eyes when he embraced me flashes through my mind, and I shudder.

Whatever Devon's reason for kissing me, it can't be an honest interest in me. It was lust that I saw in his gaze—and only a temporary one at best.

It can't be more, given that he's now in bed with Morgan.

The sobs erupt from my throat with the violence of a volcano at this humiliating thought.

I throw myself on the bed and let my tears free flow. I hug my torso and squeeze my eyes shut. What hurts most isn't that Devon is still the playboy he claimed he didn't want to be or that he might have feelings for his ex.

No, the most painful part is the realization that even though Devon will never love me, my heart will belong to him forever.

CHAPTER 45

(Devon)

"What are you doing here, Morgan?" I ask.

Staying in place would mean I'll be forced into close contact with her negligee-covered body, so I take the safer approach and back off a few steps.

Morgan passes the threshold into my room and pulls the door shut behind her. "Do you know what I'm up to, Dev?"

"No, but I reckon you're about to go to sleep. That's a nightgown you're wearing, no?"

This is not my best guess about why Morgan showed up here, but I hope if I pretend not to understand her real intentions, Morgan won't actually spell it out, and I won't be forced to act like a jerk with her.

"Indeed, it is. You like it?" Morgan purrs, and from the taunting way she wiggles her brows, I fear my feigned ignorance won't save me from what's about to come.

She runs a hand on the contour of her see-through

kimono, apparently unaware that my mind isn't hung up on her figure.

"It's nice. A gift from Theo?" I ask.

Morgan winces as I mention her husband's name, and for a second, her gaze drops to the floor. Then she shakes her head and raises her chin again. "As a matter of fact, it is. But he didn't even see it on me yet. No time between his many business trips."

The bitter edge of her voice is hard to ignore.

I can see that Morgan is in a confused place right now. From what she told me about her marriage, she must not be particularly happy.

But I'm not the solution to her boredom.

My heart beats only for one woman, and she's probably sleeping like an angel a few floors above me. But even in my most hardcore playboy days, I would have never considered fooling around with someone who was spoken for.

I decide to be more explicit. "Morgan, I don't claim to know why you came here to wish me good night in person. But I have the feeling you weren't motivated by the *right* reasons. So…" I let my voice trail off, giving her the chance to back off with her dignity intact.

Morgan eyes my bare chest—I curse myself for not putting on a shirt right away when I spotted her—and a weak smile plays on her lower lip. "Perhaps. But then again, perhaps not." She tilts her chin up so her green eyes meet mine. "You know I've been angry with you here at the gala."

I snort. "I realized that. You stormed out on me in a rather dramatic way."

Morgan sighs, then lifts her shoulders and purses her lips in such a harmonious flow I wonder whether she practices this particular gesture in the mirror.

"Well, what can I say? I'm not good at taking refusals. Also, I was shocked because you could never resist me in the past." Her eyes drift to the ceiling.

"Much has changed since we were together," I murmur.

Her gaze darts back to my face. "Yes, indeed. That's what I realized once I was back in my room. I started thinking and arrived at the conclusion that I might've expected too much of you."

"Come again?"

She runs a hand through her blond tresses. "I thought you were ready to settle down like that tabloid article suggested. But what if you aren't? Being a playboy isn't the worst thing in the world. I shouldn't have chided you."

I could start a discussion with Morgan about how I'm not a playboy anymore. But any additional information I bring up may prolong her stay in my room, and I would prefer it if she left.

I shrug. "Okay, thanks for this."

Morgan smiles. "No problem. Your preference for fleeting pleasure actually made me see an alternative solution for my problem. Maybe I don't have to leave Theo. I just need to create some fun in *my* life, then it will be easier to handle my husband's shortcomings."

"I'm glad you decided to salvage your marriage, Morgan," I say, but I can't help the cautious undertone in my voice.

The new direction of Morgan's thoughts seems as troublesome as her idea of getting back together with me.

Morgan takes a step toward me. "So what do you say? Want to lend me a hand?"

"In what exactly?"

"Spicing up my life, of course."

"You leave me speechless with this offer," I say while I think of the least brutal way of refusing her again.

Morgan might've cheated on me in the past, but I also betrayed her.

I didn't love her the way I love Laia. Still, I acted as if I did.

So for me, our scores are even. I wouldn't take pleasure in hurting Morgan any more than necessary for her to realize that she and I are never going to happen.

Morgan runs a finger on her collarbone. "We don't need words. I'll be satisfied if you put your mouth to a different use." She launches forward, pressing her palms on my chest.

I snatch her wrists and lower them gently but firmly to her side.

"Morgan, I'm not interested in *any* of this."

She points at my empty bed. "But why? I could hear through the wall that you came back alone from the party. This means that seducing your mousy colleague didn't turn out as you hoped."

"I've told you not to speak about Laia in these terms." I keep my voice even but add a menacing edge to it.

Morgan rolls her eyes. "As I said, I'm not here to judge. If you want to get into Laia's pants because she has a certain schoolgirl charm, I'm not saying you shouldn't. But tonight you won't be able to. So why not take advantage of us being in a room together, away from the prying eyes? You used to be pretty crazy about me, no?"

As I stare at her expression, which is an odd mix of self-confidence and self-doubt, an unexpected feeling settles in my chest.

I'm sorry for Morgan.

My ex clearly doesn't know who I am or what I want, but I'm sure she doesn't understand herself and her own wishes. That's why she cheated on me in college, and that's why she would be ready to betray her husband with me now.

Not knowing your real needs is a dark place to be in.

I should know. I wasted several years in this smug ignorance until Laia taught me that I need to change and have the power to do so. I ignore my initial flare of hostility that Morgan's snarky remark about Laia triggered, and go for pure honesty.

"Laia isn't a lustful fantasy for me, Morgan. I love her. That tabloid article you read? It was right about me. I am ready to settle. With Laia."

Her jaw drops. "You love her? But she is short and so…*plain.*"

"No, she isn't plain. She's witty, kind, and incredibly sweet. And she's beautiful to me. Inside and out."

Morgan's lips curl down. "So that's a no for us then?"

I nod. "Indeed. But it would've been even if Laia weren't in my life."

"Huh, want to twist the knife of rejection deeper, huh?" Morgan asks with a hurt glint in her eyes. "Are you punishing me because I cheated on you? I thought you said you forgave me."

"I did," I say. "I just meant that I'm not the same man I was in college, so I would turn down your offer anyway."

Morgan sniffs. "Certainly. In college, you loved slender, tall, and blonde. That's clearly not your taste now."

Though her words are cynical and probably meant to vex me, I don't get irritated because I see she's only lashing out due to her hurt pride.

I shake my head." Morgan, I know you won't restore the magic you miss in your marriage by hopping into bed with me, or with anyone else who isn't your husband. I've been down the road of volatile pleasure. I never managed to fill the void in my chest with flings."

While one single kiss from Laia, the woman I love, gorged it entirely.

This proves that the act of love without actual emotion only brings brief happiness at best.

Morgan snorts. "Quite frankly, I would take volatile pleasure over no pleasure in a heartbeat. It's not my fault Theo became dull. I won't feel guilty for wanting to have fun while I'm still young."

Morgan needs to realize that her past actions led her to the present she's living, and if she's unsatisfied with her life, then first, it's her who needs to change.

Like Ellie told me, *to find someone special, you need to start acting like you're worthy of it.*

But I'm not the right person to teach Morgan this lesson, as I'm still just a student of it at best.

Also, I have the feeling my ex isn't ready to listen to such advice anyway.

I cock my head toward the door. "Morgan, I think it's best if you returned to your room now. We'll pretend you were never here."

She works her jaw then nods. "Fine. But just for the record"—she gives me a weak, bitter smile—"it's *still* your loss."

"I know. But I can live with that."

Morgan snorts and, her chin high, sashays to the door and pulls it open. "Good-bye, Dev. Thanks for the…chat."

As the door shuts, I realize I'm the one who should've thanked her for this discussion.

Talking with Morgan made me see even clearer how right the path I've chosen with Laia is.

Rushing Laia wouldn't only force her into something for which she isn't ready yet, but it could leave me feeling empty. I would miss out on savoring each vital step on the way to really getting to know her.

Yes, waiting for my love isn't just the demonstration of my feelings to her as I first believed.

No, it's also for my own benefit.

CHAPTER 46

(Devon)

The next morning, after a night spent with marvelous dreams, I'm ready to start the first official day of my relationship with Laia.

I take a shower and proceed with shaving. I catch myself grinning foolishly in the mirror, but I can't help it.

The water has never felt so good on my skin, and no fluorescent bathroom light has ever shone this enchantingly. I'm aware that my exuberant mood might be distorting my perception of things, but I don't mind it one bit.

I pass the razor at least three times to make my chin extra-smooth. I wouldn't want to irritate Laia's soft skin with my stubble.

I rinse my face and dab it into a white, fluffy towel. I put on a pair of dark jeans and am about to slide on my polo shirt when a loud knock echoes in the air.

Afraid to be played again by Morgan, I tiptoe to the door and peek out though the keyhole.

When I see Laia's long black tresses dancing around her elbow—the only part of her body I'm able to peek at—my heart stutters.

I yank the door open.

"Laia!" From the over-zealous accent I didn't intend to have, I know it'll be a fierce battle to play down my actual feelings for her today.

Sooner or later I'll have to confess to her that I don't *only* like her.

Laia's eyes dart to my chest, then her eyes scan the room behind me. "Are you alone?"

"Yes, of course," I reply cheerfully. "I'm just getting ready for breakfast."

"Well, start with putting on a shirt, will you?" she answers in a very efficient, assistant-like manner.

"Don't like what you see?" I wink playfully but shove my head through the blue polo's neck. After I'm done putting it on, I blink at Laia.

Her expression is perplexed, as if my previous comment bothered her.

Oh no, I hope she didn't think I was trying to tempt her about her resolution…

"I'm sorry, Laia, I was just joking with you. I'm in too much of a good mood after yesterday night, you know."

"I can imagine," she murmurs, but her glance, despite being directed at my face, seems to travel through me instead of actually seeing me.

Why is she acting like a robot around me?

"What happened to you?" I ask, not even trying to hide the concern in my voice. "Where did you leave the giddy young woman I kissed good-night?"

My phrase seems to break through the spell, because her features reanimate.

"May I come in?" she says.

"Of course," I respond, feeling like an idiot for not inviting her in.

As Laia walks inside, I notice she has her carry-on with her. The grey suitcase had been hidden from my view by the jamb.

"Why do you have your stuff with you?"

Laia rolls her luggage to the brown table beside the fridge, then turns to face me. "Because I came to tell you good-bye."

"What?" My brows reach my hairline.

"I said, I came to greet you in a farewell kind of way. I'm taking the bus back to Phoenix," she announces in a calm but emotionless voice.

Her eyes are fixed on my chest.

I launch forward and grab her shoulders. I hold her firmly until she's forced to peer up at me.

"What's this all about, Laia? Why are you acting like last evening didn't happen? And why do you want to leave?"

Laia stares at me, the yellow dots in her irises shimmering like small fireballs. "Devon, I'm sorry, but this—whatever it is you think we have between us—isn't going to work."

My heart drops.

"Why would you say that?"

Laia sucks in a breath. "Let me answer your question with another question. Were you alone last night?"

"Yes, of course."

Laia's eyes flutter shut, and she shakes her head. "At least you could have the decency to tell it straight to my face."

"Tell what?" I snap at her, irritation bubbling up in my chest from her unreasonable behavior. But just as the words leave my lips, a suspicion awakens in me.

"You know about Morgan? How?"

Laia opens her eyes and they glimmer with a deep sadness. "It doesn't matter. But I know you invited her over after you took me to my room. And to think, I fell for your I-don't-care-about-my-ex act…"

The disappointment in her words slaps me so hard I forget to protest her conclusion's erroneousness.

Laia takes my silence as a sign of admitting my guilt because she nods. "I should have known better. But I wanted to believe you could change. That you could leave your past behind. You know why, Devon? Because I don't only like you—I'm in *love* with you."

"You're in love with me?" I jerk back, unable to process the full meaning of her words. But after a second, a euphoric grin spreads on my face. "That's wonderful news, Laia because I—"

Before I can finish, Laia's palms whack me hard on my chest. "I'm not interested in hearing another lie or sweet-talking from you. What is it with you, anyway? Do you have a craving for getting what you can't have? Is that why you tried your charms on me?"

"No, Laia! I truly meant what I said last night—"

Laia's eyes narrow, and she squeaks, "I don't believe you."

"But I do," I insist.

"Liar!" Laia is almost screaming now. Her body angles away from me with a rigid posture. "Stop playing with me!"

Desperation and irritation are splintering my heart in equal measures.

Dang it! This is not how I envisioned admitting to her what I feel.

A frenzied wish to make Laia see the myriad of profound things I harbor for her overhauls me. I need to make her see how wrong she is about my feelings. But how can I do that if she won't listen?

Laia exhales loudly and bites on her lower lip.

With her gesture, I have my answer.

I reach out and cup her face. "You don't believe me? Then at least believe this."

I haul her closer with a brisk movement and press my mouth on hers with an urgent moan.

She tries to resist at first. Her hands flex against my shoulders, pushing me to back off, but her fingers don't have real power.

Almost as if only half of her heart is in her refusal.

This gives me hope that the other half wants exactly what I want.

I steel my hold on her jawline, paying attention not to grip her delicate bones too forcefully.

My lips launch into a demonstration of my devotion to her, which she stubbornly refuses to acknowledge.

After a few seconds, her resistance softens, and then it ceases entirely. Her arms fall to her side, and her lips open up for me. I slide my hands to her nape and squeeze her closer to my chest.

The bright sunlight filtering through the window disappears, and so does the humming of the room's AC. There's nothing else but Laia's hot breath, soft skin, and my pulse that slams in her heartbeats' rhythm.

We're lost in a hungry exchange of breaths, but all too soon, Laia pulls back.

She wiggles free from my embrace.

Her breathing comes in short pants, and her cheeks are flushed. Her lips are swollen from my nibbling, but her eyes burn with an angry flame. "Why did you have to do this?"

"To prove to you that I love you," I murmur sheepishly.

Laia shakes her head. "You only proved that you desire me. But that's not love. If you loved me, you wouldn't have made a booty-call to your ex right after dropping me off."

My jaw sinks. "You think I *slept* with Morgan?"

"Well, didn't you?"

"No, I did not." I control the outrage in my voice, even if Laia's assumption stings.

She shrugs, and with this subtle movement, her sullen attitude melds into a quiet resignation. "It's hard for me to believe, given that you arranged for Morgan's room to be right next to yours."

My throat dries out, and no words come out.

"Also…" Laia squares her shoulders. "I heard the story about your former assistant, Hayley. That you fired her because she fell in love with you while you only wanted a fling with her? Would this have been my destiny, too?"

The mention of Hayley snaps me out of my self-induced impotence. "Laia, I said I loved you. Why do you think I would say that?"

She shakes her head. "I don't know. Maybe because you thought that's what I'd need to hear to jump into your bed?"

I narrow my eyes. "Where did you even hear this nonsense about Hayley and me?"

"From someone at the company. I didn't want to believe it at first. I told myself it was mean-spirited gossip, nothing more. But after what happened between us, and between you and Morgan…I'm not so sure anymore."

My stomach churns. "You said last night that you knew I was more than just a player. That you saw *more* in me."

Laia's chin quivers. "Yes, I did. But maybe I was mistaken."

Her words cut deep into my soul like sharp blades.

I could contradict her on all of her accusations. I didn't sleep with Morgan. I never touched Hayley.

And I certainly didn't tell Laia about my love to get into her panties.

So then why don't I argue my case?

Maybe because of the way Laia is staring at me. With her brows furrowed and her lips in a hard line, as if her belief in my flawed nature is unshakable. Or perhaps it's because of my own plaguing doubts about my character.

Perhaps it was foolish to hope I could cancel out my past and deserve to be loved by someone as pure as Laia. To wish that Laia would ignore my previous mistakes and trust me.

"I'm sorry if this is what you think of me," I murmur.

Laia's eyes fill with tears. "I'm sorry, too."

The sight of her sorrow is more destructive than any of her previous words. I don't want to see her sad, and the realization that I'm the cause of her distress shreds my insides.

If I were to insist on my truth with Laia, I might convince her.

Would that be the best choice at this point? Am I really and truly the right one for her?

I know it in my bones that she deserves that—the best man who will make her happy.

But what if I'm not him?

The air escapes my lungs in a loud whoosh, as if I were tackled by Wyatt's impressive frame during a high school football match.

But it's the sobering truth that causes my ribcage to crash.

Maybe my greatest act of love for Laia should be to give her up.

Laia said she loved me, but maybe she has fallen into the same trap she accused me of. I know I'm not just attracted to her physically, because I have more than enough experience under my belt to see the difference.

But Laia does not.

What if her feelings for me are magnified by our potent chemistry?

If so, with me out of the picture, Laia could have a better chance of finding someone who's pure like her.

Not a rotten apple like me.

I need to push Laia away. For good.

I capture her gaze. "You're right, Laia. Perhaps once a player, always a player. I probably have a sick attraction to the boss-employee romance trope, despite the rules I impose in the company."

Morgan's recriminations taste foul on my tongue, but I continue anyway. "Also, I've been curious to see how someone so innocent like you would behave with someone like me. But it was a lapse of judgment from my part. You want, and clearly deserve, more than just a fling with me."

Laia's eyes widen.

It's almost as if despite her flaring anger and fiery comments, she still held onto a straw of hope about my character, which I, with my answer, have set on fire.

"I think I'll go now, Devon," she mumbles, dropping her glance to the floor. Her voice is throaty with the sobs she must be biting back. "I'll email you a formal resignation letter as soon as I get home."

"Very well." My words seem to float around me like they don't belong to me.

That's not what my heart wants to tell Laia.

But since this is what my brain needs to choose so she can be happy in the long run, I roll my hands into fists and watch Laia fetch her carry-on.

I open the door for her in a last gallant gesture, and she thanks me for it quietly.

"Live well, Devon," she whispers before stepping out into the corridor.

I lean to the jamb, paralyzed and empty, as the weight of what I've just done settles on my shoulders.

I did a good thing for Laia, and this knowledge must be my consolation. But I also lost the person who managed to make me see the world differently and taught me what true love could feel like.

As I stare at her disappearing silhouette, I know the scar this good-bye will leave behind will stay with me forever.

CHAPTER 47

(Laia)

"Well, if this won't cheer you up at least a little, I'm going to start to worry." Eva dips a spoon in the chocolate fudge ice cream she brought me this morning and holds it out.

I shake my head. "No, thanks."

Though the top layer is melted creaminess and the toffee splinters wink invitingly at me, my stomach won't accept anything. My belly has been in a knotted, petrified state ever since I exited Devon's hotel room.

Two days, six hours, and forty-three minutes ago.

Not that I'm counting. Or at least not consciously.

But my soul is frozen in that moment when Devon admitted I was but a dalliance for him—a game he played to satisfy his curiosity.

Eva arches her perfectly trimmed eyebrows, then lowers the spoon. She walks around our kitchen island and sits down beside me on a chair.

"Laia, *querida*, you need to eat something. You never

refuse Tio Mario's ice creams. They're your favorites. That's why I carried them in the cooler with me."

I pat my cousin's hand. "It's so sweet of you to be here and babysit me while Chelsea is at work, but it isn't necessary. You should get back to San Sebastian. To Nathan and to your school."

Eva twirls a finger beside her temple. "*¿Estas loca o que?* Yeah, you must be crazy if you think I'd leave you alone with your heartbreak. Don't you recall how you helped me through my rough patch with Nathan? No, *querida*, I'm here. I will stay as long as I need until you feel better."

I recall the intervention I had to perform when Eva found out about her husband and his brother's crazy bet about her back while they were still just dating.

But her situation then, and mine now, are entirely different.

"Eva, you were in a relationship with Nathan when all hell broke loose. My heartache compared to yours is just silly. It's the fruit of stringing together my ludicrous hopes about Devon into a fantasy. I knew he was a playboy, and playboys aren't interested in relationships, especially not with hopeless romantics like me. But that still didn't stop me from dreaming."

Eva pulls back her black tresses, almost as long as my own, into a ponytail and blows the air from her cheeks. "First of all, Laia, quit this self-blaming act. If anyone is to be chided, it's your irresponsible boss. He should have never toyed with you if he didn't have serious intentions. It was just mean of him. Even if…" Eva's voice trails off in a meaningful way.

My eyes fly to her face.

She's studying me with a calculating glance.

"Even if, *what*?" I ask, slightly irritated.

My cousin should know better than to play with my nerves and patience right now.

She inhales and shrugs. "Even if we need to consider the hypothesis that Devon lied to you about something entirely different."

My mouth moves into a confused frown. "What are you even talking about?"

"Well…" Eva adjusts her pink blouse's top button. "I'm just pointing out that the events you described to Chelsea and me don't really add up. Why would Devon kiss you, spend the evening in a lovey-dovey mood with you, and hop into his ex's bed? Why would he say he loves you and then deny the very statement in the same conversation?"

"Because he's a player. He was just messing around with me."

Eva narrows her eyes. "Do you really believe this?"

"Yes," I blurt out, but there is an almost imperceptible shake in my snappy answer.

My mind drifts back to our last kiss.

I ignore the thrills that race through my veins at the memory of his lips, and focus on his last words before his mouth captured mine.

If you don't believe me, then believe this…

Eva brushes back a string of hair behind my ear. "You see, *querida*, you yourself have doubts about what went down with Devon. If you learned anything from mine and Nathan's example, then it should be that things aren't always as straightforward as '*I love you, and you love me*'. Or better, in the quintessence, it's always that simple. But we are often too wrapped up in our messy realities and ghosts of the past to accept and admit our feelings for what they are."

I fold my arms across my chest. "I did recognize what I felt for Devon. I was even enough of a dimwit to tell him."

"Perhaps." Eva bobs her head. "But at the first shadow of a doubt, you backed out on him. Which kind of proves my point. You're stuck in your own inferiority complex and self-doubt, as well as being a prisoner of your unrealistic aspirations about Prince Charming."

My nostrils flare. "You're the one who told me I shouldn't settle for anything but my own fairy tale. You even gave me that mug to remind me of that."

Eva chuckles. "I did. But you can have a fairy tale with someone who isn't perfect like Prince Charming. Someone who has a tormented past."

"I know that," I growl, "but is it too much to ask that the man who drops me off after the most incredible evening I've ever had doesn't run straight into another woman's arms?"

Eva ignores my annoyed tone and, instead, leans forward. "Are you absolutely certain it was Devon who invited his ex to his room? That they did anything except talk? She wasn't there in the morning, was she?"

"No. She was not. But I'm sure—"

Eva holds up her hand. "Didn't you say, and I quote, 'He even had the nerve to ask me with a genuinely baffled expression whether I thought he'd slept with his ex'?"

"What if I did?"

Eva shakes her head. "Don't you think Devon was bewildered because you accused him wrongly?"

"That can't be." I tap my hand on our table with a loud thump that also hurts my palm. Eva only smiles at me coyly as I rub the tender spot with my thumb.

"Can't it?"

Her provoking tone bothers me, but I have to admit her reasoning isn't entirely off. If I'm honest, Devon's horrified expression when he asked me if I believed he'd been with Morgan was a detail I glossed over, and each time, it confused me. I explained his reaction by blaming his potential shock that I exposed his double game.

Could I have been wrong? Maybe Morgan went over to Devon's, but he didn't touch her?

"Right, like any man in his right mind could resist a woman of Morgan's beauty, especially when dressed in that racy robe," I mumble out loud the curveball that my inherent uncertainty throws at me.

Eva sighs. "You forget that a man in love is different from a normal man. He reasons with his heart and not with…you know." She wiggles her brows at me.

A man in love.

Eva's words seem to trigger my fable-loving inner goddess because, for a moment, I allow myself to ponder whether I accused Devon erroneously and if he hadn't betrayed my trust.

Desperate to fight back the mushy warmth that takes possession of my chest and spreads toward the rest of my body, I concentrate on the rest of the events that confirm I'm right to feel deceived by Devon.

"Okay, we don't know what went down with his ex. But the story with his previous assistant? He also had an affair with her. Which, you must admit, is a clear sign I wasn't anything special to him."

Eva twists her mouth from left to right, which makes her look like a pensive squirrel.

Just when she opens her lips to answer, the lock of our entrance door clicks.

Chelsea trots inside with a card box in her arms. "Hi, you both!" she greets us and drops her package on the kitchen counter.

"What's that?" Eva asks.

"Laia's office stuff. She asked me to collect it for her, so I did."

Chelsea's voice is high-pitched and trembling, a quality it only acquires when my roomie is about to explode with some exciting news.

My heart gives a beat out of rhythm.

Did she bump into Devon when she gathered my belongings? If so, did he ask about me?

He hasn't answered my resignation email yet. So it's been two days, seven hours, and ten minutes that I haven't heard or seen him.

Before I get a chance to scold my brain for keeping track of the time again, Chelsea walks to the other side of the table. She bends forward, resting her weight on her elbows, a mysterious smile stretching on her face.

"You won't guess what I discovered today," she announces in a dramatic voice.

"Come on, just spill it quickly. I'm in the middle of a psychotherapy session with Laia," Eva says.

Chelsea purses her pink-painted lips. "About Devon, I suppose?" Without waiting for our answer, she adds, "Perfect timing then. Because my information is about him."

Eva gives me a slanted glance, and then as if she realizes I won't have the strength to inquire, she asks, "What did you find out, Chels?"

Chelsea's green eyes fill with the same zeal she gets when she narrates a story on her YouTube channel. "So, it happened like this…I went upstairs to get Laia's things, but Devon was out of the office. His domesticated dragon—"

"Katja, his secretary," I chime in, seeing Eva lift her brows. "Chelsea calls her that."

Chelsea giggles. "That's because she's fearsome. Like horror story kind. Especially with those stiff braids. Anyway, so Katja told me that Devon called in sick today. She said he had a migraine or something."

Eva throws me a meaningful glance. "You see? He

might feel terrible about what happened between you two."

"Or he just went out last night to a club and got his eardrums busted," I mumble, but I don't believe my own cheeky remark either.

Chelsea seems bothered that we derailed from her tale and coughs twice to reclaim our attention. "Ladies, could I continue? I'm still not at my crux."

We nod, and Chelsea clears her voice. "Okay, so Katja asked me what happened to you and why you decided to quit so unexpectedly."

My jaw tightens. "Oh, gosh, Chels, I hope you didn't tell her why."

Chelsea rolls her eyes. "Of course I didn't. Or at least not everything. Only major brushstrokes."

"Not everything? Chels!" I exclaim, but my roomie exchanges my irritation with a charming shrug.

"Wait till I tell you what I found out, okay? Then you can get all banshee on me."

I lean back on my chair. "Okay, finish what you started. But count that as a proper scolding. You really need to learn how to be more discreet."

Chelsea brushes off my critique with a little sniff and dives back in to her narration. "I thought Katja would be indignant when she heard how Devon tinkered with your feelings, but instead she jumped to his defense like a lioness. She told me that from what she knew, Devon would never get back with his ex. She claimed you must have gotten confused by what you saw."

Eva claps her hands. "Just what I said."

I poke Chelsea's arm. "Didn't you say you hadn't gotten into the nuts-and-bolts of what happened? Mentioning Morgan seems pretty detailed to me."

Chelsea's face assumes a somewhat guilty look. "Have

you tried to tell a half-truth to that woman? It's an impossible task. Also, she may or may not have used Russian interrogation techniques on me."

Eva begins to giggle, and despite my annoyance, I can't help the smile that forces its way to my lips, hearing my roomie's lousy excuse.

"Is this all you learned?" Eva asks.

"No, here comes the beef." Chelsea pauses and bounces her gaze between Eva and me. When she's convinced both of us are curious enough, she continues. "Katja got so worked up that she called Devon's sister to check whether she knew what happened."

"Ellie? She spoke to Ellie?"

Mortification grips my chest as I imagine how that conversation must've gone down.

"Yes, they spoke while I was there. And guess what? His sister not only confirmed to Katja—and me, given that I was listening closely—that Devon didn't hook up with his ex…but she also revealed what really happened with that Hayley chick. *All* the dirty details."

My diaphragm contracts so abruptly I almost slip from my chair.

"Is Hayley Devon's ex-assistant? What about her?" Eva is gripping Chelsea's wrist as if it will bring my roomie to spit out the truth faster.

"Nothing happened with her," Chelsea replies, and when she sees our widening eyes, she nods. "*Nada*, absolutely nothing. Devon let her go because she tried to seduce him one evening, and he didn't wish to get involved with an employee. But he fixed her up with a new job at a different company. So he didn't just put the gal out on the street, so to speak."

I stare at my roomie, my mouth hanging. "Are you serious?"

Chelsea nods. "I heard Ellie say it, honey. I think you might have made a bit of a gaffe with Devon after all."

A gaffe?

No, I made a disaster.

"Oh, dear heaven. I accused Devon of being a liar and a boss with a fetish for his assistants…and none of that was true…" I bury my face into my hands.

Eva rubs my back. "On the upside, cousin, it probably means that Devon actually loves you, like he said he did."

Devon *loves me…*

Eva's words hover in my brain like grains of sugar in a glass of water. The more I stir and turn them, the more they dissolve and seep into me, releasing a sweet gushiness I thought I could never feel again.

My lips move into a smile. "You think he loves me?"

Eva and Chelsea both nod.

"The only question is," Chelsea says, "why he decided to lie to you."

"It's because I hurt him with my lack of faith in him," I answer without hesitation, raising my head.

As soon as the words make their way to my lips, I know they must be right.

I've failed Devon. I impeached him when he was innocent. And all because I saw Morgan in a sexy nightgown enter his room. I accused him of being shallow, but the one who was shallow was me.

Eva sighs. "Well, then we need to find a way to make him see that you believe in him."

"You're right," I mutter. "I have to speak to Devon and apologize for my prejudiced behavior. Even if he might not be interested in what I have to say. Maybe I've lost his interest for good…"

Chelsea clicks her tongue. "Nonsense. The guy must be heartbroken like you were a minute ago. You think he won't care if he learns that the woman he loves actually trusts him and wants to be with him? I don't think so."

Eva nods. "Indeed. I might've said I wasn't interested in what Nathan had to say after I thought he betrayed my trust, but actually I was dying to hear that he loved me. You need to confess to Devon that you misjudged him and ask him to forgive you."

"Yes, but I don't want to bother him at home or at work…"

I'm only finding excuses. I'm chickening out over the possibility that I blew my chance with Devon.

Chelsea grins. "I have the perfect solution. You call Ellie and convince her to take her brother out to dinner. Then you show up instead of his sister and boom! You have a gorgeous, cozy setting for your grand gesture."

Chelsea's idea isn't bad.

Devon could just ignore the doorbell once he sees it's me at his doorstep or at work. He could duck into a meeting. But in a restaurant…

I jump up and scurry to my phone charging on the kitchen counter and lift it. "I'm going to do this," I say while already clicking on Ellie's number.

"Don't pick Italian though," Chelsea warns me. "You can't make a love confession while eating spaghetti or dripping from pizza sauce. My tip is sushi, clean, quick, and a bit of sake that will loosen your inhibitions."

"Sushi, got it." I flash a smile at my roomie.

If my day, and perhaps my life, turns around, it will be entirely thanks to her and her big mouth. I'll have to excuse myself for rebuking Chelsea for her indiscretion.

But first, I need to concentrate on making my apology to Devon.

Let's hope he'll forgive me for being such a dork…

CHAPTER 48

(Devon)

I silence my vibrating phone and take another sip from my drink.

"Shouldn't you answer Ellie's call?" Pete asks me with a concerned glance.

"Nah, she surely wants to speak to me about how stupid I've been with Laia, and I'm in no mood for such a chat. I want to forget and have fun."

I wave toward the stage where Harry, the pianist I jumped in for, is playing a soul fusion song.

Pete tilts his head to the side, and his hair, combed into a carefree coif tonight, bounces from his movement. "Man, I understand the advantages of the head in the sand strategy. I do. I'm usually all for it. But in this case, I—"

"*Shhh.*" I press my finger to my lips. "Not another word about what happened. It was my conscious decision to lie to Laia, and I did it to make her happy."

Deep heart-to-hearts aren't Pete's forte. He must feel

strongly about my behavior, because, despite his usual that's-just-life attitude, he shakes his head.

"You said Laia friggin' cried. That's not a sign of joy. Also, your idiotic fib is making you miserable, dude!" Pete shifts uncomfortably on his barstool. "Dev, I'll give it to you straight. You made a colossal blunder. It's hogwash that Laia will be better off without you. Especially if she's in love with you."

I twirl around on my chair and lean my back to the bar's counter.

And here I was hoping that by avoiding Ellie, I could escape the sneaky, self-blaming inner voice that's been insulting me ever since I got back from Tucson. The one that suggests I took the easy way out. That my giving up on Laia wasn't a noble gesture, but the manifestation of my ultimate fear of commitment.

Now it seems that I've unwittingly signed up for Pete's rescue mission.

My buddy also turns to the stage and kicks the flooring with his brown brogue. The ground is paved with black-and-white stones that mimic piano keys. On each dark strip, the name of an iconic jazz singer is engraved, and Pete's sole is currently pestering Nat King Cole.

"I'd like to give you a piece of good advice, but I'm not much of a love guru, pal," Pete tells me in a pensive voice. "Heck, I probably know less about women than I'd like to."

I tap his shoulder. "What do you mean? Your house has more female visitors than the White House."

Pete flashes me a lopsided grin. "That much is true. But you know as well as I do that I don't deal with hearts. A bit like Wyatt, though his reason is his ambition, while my excuse is the sheer joy I find in non-commitment. In all cases, I'm not well-equipped to guide you. But"—he lifts his finger—"I do know one thing. If I ever happen to find a woman I fall in love with, I won't care what has happened in my past. I won't let any paranoia about having been a womanizer spoil my bliss. I'll just concentrate on my future with her."

My eyes dart to Pete. I didn't expect him to say something this profound.

He winks at me. "I haven't found my special one, yet, of course. But you get what I mean? You ought to put things right with Laia. Don't take away her choice about whether you're good enough for her. Let her decide. I think if she knew the truth, she'd—"

"Here you are, you wacko! Why won't you pick up when I call?" Ellie storms over to us, panting.

Her bun is in unusual disarray, and her cheeks are flushed as if she'd been running. Her untypically disheveled look makes me think Jimmy'z might not be the first place she so tempestuously searched for my presence.

As if to confirm my suspicion, she says, "I've been to your house, in your gym, checked the supermarkets you usually go to…and even went to that horrid Red Heaven club where the hairy bouncer tried to hit on me. Yuck!"

I give her a soothing smile. "Here I am. It's Friday, no?"

Ellie taps on her forehead. "Shoot, why didn't I think of that? I just figured this would be the last place you'd come, considering that last time you were here was with…"

She breaks off and gives me an alarmed glance.

"Laia. You can say her name. Pete's been chewing my ear about what a dullard I've been anyway, so your complaints won't spoil my evening."

Ellie shakes her head. "We don't have time for this, Dev. You need to come with me."

"Come with you? Where?"

Ellie's eyes move to the counter, to Pete's shoes, then back to my face. "Uhm, dinner."

"I already had a sandwich, but thanks."

Ellie stares at me. "I don't care. You're coming with me," she says, then grabs my arm. "Sorry, Pete, but we have to bail on you."

Pete chuckles. "Don't worry, I'm getting the hang of that lately. I'll just go upstairs with you and then drop by the Red Heaven. The hairy bouncer definitely won't hit on me, but the cute redhead who serves the drinks might."

He stands up and throws a few bills on the bar for our drinks.

Ellie pulls on my arm. "Come on, Dev, we're going to be late."

"Late for what?"

"For dinner," she repeats slowly and articulately as if I have trouble hearing.

"I've already told you I'm not hungry. I'd rather stay and listen to Harry play another few tunes."

Ellie's grip doesn't soften on me. "Devon Griffin, stand up right now and walk with me. Or else I'm going to…" She thinks for a moment, then her face illuminates. "…go out and use that lipstick knife you discredited so much on your beloved Audi's gloss."

My jaw drops at her blunt threat, but I straighten. A suspicion that wherever we're going Laia will be there spreads in my chest and my heart rate picks up. "Okay, fine. I'm coming with you. But you're behaving like a nutcase, you know that, right?"

Ellie grins. "I know. But let's go now. We're already way too late."

Late? So there is indeed an appointment with Laia?

Panic grips my stomach. I don't want us to miss Laia.

As every fiber of my body lights with the desire to see her again, I realize just how big of a lie I've been telling myself these past days.

I can never let go of Laia. I love her—more than life itself.

I grab Ellie's arm. "Then let's hurry up, sis,"

I pull her to the staircase so fast that Pete struggles to keep pace with us, which is something because his legs are longer than mine.

My gut is lodged in my throat as we mount the stairs and my heart hums with a mix of fear and anticipation.

If Laia agreed to play along with Ellie, then maybe it's not too late to correct what Pete called the biggest blunder of my life?

CHAPTER 49

(Laia)

I'm pacing like a hunted animal on the restaurant's terrace.

Ellie told me to be here at nine, but it's already nine-thirty.

Why are they late? Maybe she blabbed to Devon about my plan, and he decided not to come?

A waiter with impeccably slicked-back hair comes up to me, for the third time since I've arrived. His red-and-black waiter uniform makes him look more like a karate master instead of a server. Or maybe it's the impassive, I'm-at-peace-with-the-world expression with which he observes me—I can't quite decide.

"Are you sure you don't want to come inside and take a table, Miss?" he asks in a polite voice.

I take another peek at my watch. Another five minutes have passed.

Devon isn't coming…

A bitter tang fills my mouth, but I force myself to

plaster on a smirk I don't feel. It isn't the waiter's fault that I single-handedly ruined everything with Devon. I might never be at peace with myself due to my brainless, mistrustful action, but I can at least pretend I know how to answer a stranger in a socially acceptable manner.

"No, I think I'll just go. It's a nice restaurant, though. Your sashimi and nigiri look excellent from what I could see through the glass. Lots of tuna. The spicy kind, which is good. I like spicy."

The man is either trained well, or politeness is simply coded in his DNA. Either way, he ignores my obviously embarrassed jabber and the maniacal way I'm picking my nails and nods.

"It would be our pleasure to welcome you at Kona Grill anytime you like, miss."

I wave to him and walk down from their terrace to the small street where the restaurant is located.

I had Chelsea drop me off, hoping my evening might end on a positive note with Devon. Now I'll need to take the bus home.

There isn't anyone around, and I'm grateful for the quietude. The evening is unusually warm, even for May, but there's also unusual moisture in the air. Thick, grey clouds cover the shrinking moon's cusps.

As I trudge toward the bus stop with slumped shoulders, droplets moisten my skin, leaving wet smudges on my black skirt.

A loud thunder echoes through the air.

Well, it seems that even the sky knows that tonight is one to earmark.

Why else would it call upon an untypical, late-spring storm?

I stop and turn my face upwards. If this were my

romance novel, this would be the perfect moment for the estranged lovers to reunite.

There's just something incredibly fulfilling about rekindling in a tempest. It's almost as if rain has the power to not only cleanse away literal dirt, but also any metaphorical impurity, to clear the path for a new, brighter future.

But I'm only interested in a future with Devon. And that's not going to be happening, no matter how much water falls on me…

Numbness infuses my body, and the tears that were dwelling in my eyes while I waited in the restaurant find their free flow. Lukewarm rain drizzles on my cheeks and mixes with my own salty drops.

Eva was right.

My self-doubt and inferiority complex made me think that when faced with a choice between Morgan and me, Devon would surely choose her. Instead of giving Devon the chance to explain what happened, I drew conclusions based on my prejudices.

Why couldn't I trust his actions and words? Why did I need to give credit to my foolish thoughts and fears?

I let the hollowness take possession of my innards. I don't fight it; I indulge in it. I deserve to feel wretched. I hurt Devon. Badly.

I let the water bathe me, praying that it may blue pencil at least part of my guilt and misery.

My crying eventually calms down, and I open my arms and just stand quietly in the rain.

A short cough resounds behind my back.

Oops, my self-flagellation must be blocking someone's path.

I quickly lower my arms and step to the side.

But nobody passes.

"Laia?"

My jaw plummets to my knees, and I whip around.

Devon's cleft chin, pulled into a confused frown, greets

me. He holds a red umbrella with the symbol of Kona Grill in one hand, while his other is hooked into the belt of his slim-cut, grey chinos.

"What are you doing here, Devon?" I ask.

"Ellie coaxed me into accompanying her to a sushi restaurant. When we arrived, she made me wait outside while she went in to consult with a waiter. Allegedly to inquire whether they had chicken katsu rolls. Then she dashed outside, shoved this umbrella into my hand, and sent me down this road to check when the next night bus is leaving."

Despite the shock Devon's appearance triggered, a small giggle escapes from my throat. "And you followed her whacky instructions?"

Devon snorts bemusedly. "I guess I did. I figured that Ellie had a hidden agenda, and I wanted to see what it was. Anyway, if I didn't comply, she would've invented a way to make me, so it was easier to go with the flow. "Also…" He shrugs. "I kind of hoped you'd be her ulterior motive…"

He *hoped* his sister would lead him to *me?* Does this mean…?

Despite his perplexing phrase, Devon's expression remains steeled.

Desperate to make him reveal something more, I ask, "Aren't you upset that Ellie tricked you into meeting me?"

Devon tilts his head to the side but, instead of answering, his eyes wander slowly along my body. He walks to me, shifting his umbrella so it now covers me, too.

His sudden closeness and the intimate feel of being under the same umbrella awakens a tempest in me and threatens to buckle my knees.

To find some grounding, I press my hands firmly to my skirt. That's when I notice it's soaked.

I peer down at my own top, which is sticking to my bosom like a second skin.

My hair drips, and I can only imagine how the make-up Chelsea and Eva so masterfully smeared on my face must look.

"You're wet. What were you doing out here in the rain?" he asks.

"I was…I…" *Why does my mind shut off at this crucial moment?*

There's so much I need to tell Devon. I've perfected my apology for hours with Eva and Chelsea. But now that I'm face-to-face with him, I can't seem to muster a word.

I close my eyes and reopen them, hoping this brief exercise will jumpstart my brain.

It certainly does, but not in the way I'd have wished. Especially after my glance dips to Devon's mouth.

Instead of my practiced plea, the thoughts that rush to my mind are either memories of how deliciously he tasted, or a yearning to savor him again.

"Laia? Why were you out here alone? If I'm interpreting this puzzle correctly, you were supposed to be in that restaurant, no? That's why Ellie wanted me to go there with her?"

A weak smile tugs at his lower lip as he studies me.

Devon's question finally cuts through my emotional haze.

"Yes, I called Ellie and asked her to help me arrange a dinner with you. But since you didn't show up, I thought you wouldn't come."

His brows round. "If you wanted to eat with me, why didn't you invite me directly?"

"Because of what happened between us in the hotel."

Devon nods slowly. "Yes, I see." But then he pauses. "No, wait a second, I don't. Why *did* you want to dine with me at all? You quit your job and wished me farewell. I thought you never wanted to see me again. That's what you wrote in your email."

I suck in a breath and lower my gaze to his chest.

"I know I wrote that, but it's not true. I shouldn't have acted the way I did." My voice wavers, but I steel myself to continue. Devon deserves my full-fledged disclosure. Even if my stomach is frozen in fear at his potential refusal, I'm going to come clean with him. If there is one person I'm ready to abandon my shell for, it's Devon. "I know I've been wrong about Morgan and Hayley—"

Devon jerks back. "Wait, how do you know that?"

I play with my fingers instead of giving an answer.

Devon lifts my chin till our gazes meet. "Who told you that? Was it Ellie?" His voice isn't angry but insistent.

"No…and yes. I heard it from Chelsea, who heard it from Katja, who heard it from Ellie, who heard it from you."

"Ah, so it was a very straightforward gossip chain then." He rolls his eyes. "At least it delivered you the correct information, unlike that previous rumor."

"Why didn't you correct me when I accused you unjustly, Devon?" I blurt out.

"I was caught off guard. You accused me of sleeping with Morgan. And then you jumped out with Hayley's story."

"I'm so sorry, Devon," I mumble.

He shakes his head. "Don't be. Though your allegations were entirely false, I realized I deserved your harsh words."

"No, you didn't!"

Devon rubs his neck. "No, I did. Not for what I did with Morgan or Hayley, but for how I lived my life before meeting you. I've been a selfish jerk. I toyed with others' feelings. Unwittingly, yes, but I still did. I hurt women. Many."

"You've changed, Devon. I know that."

I brush a finger on his cheek, and he flinches as if my touch burns him.

He pulls back from me and sighs. "Yes, I did. But that isn't enough. I'll never be a truly wholesome person like you. I can't make my past undone. Laia, you're the purest and most wonderful creature I've ever met. You deserve someone better than me."

My jaw drops as the meaning of his words settle in.

Devon didn't lie because he was offended by my unwarranted incrimination. He kept me in the dark because he thought he wasn't the right one for me.

I want to snuggle up to him, but the umbrella is in my way. I grab it from him and drop it to the ground.

"Why did you do that?" Devon asks.

"Because I want to do this." I launch forward and snake my arms around his neck. I raise myself to my tiptoes and pull my face so close to him that my forehead caresses his chin.

The rain, which has turned from a drizzle to a downpour, cascades down on us, the licks of water drenching us and tickling our skins.

I tilt my face upward as he bends down. Our lips align but don't touch.

"I'm not the man for you," he whispers, a painful glimmer in his eyes. "Lord knows I want to be him. But you need someone more—"

"Hush," I press a finger on his mouth. "You're *exactly* what I need. And the only person I want. You don't have to change or improve in any way. You're perfect for me. Please forgive me for not believing this before."

CHAPTER 50

(Devon)

Laia's lips curl up, and she breaths the three magical words into my mouth softly. "I love you."

My eyes widen. "Do you mean this?"

"Yes, Devon. I don't want anyone else but you."

Her words swirl in my head, coating my soul with a joy I didn't think possible.

Laia thinks I'm good enough for her. She wants me. She loves me. *Me*!

My arms close around her hips, and I lift her gently in the air.

She gasps then giggles. "What are you doing? I'm too heavy!"

"You're not. And I can't stop the joy that overcame me. Not when I know that you love me. Because I love you too, Laia. More than anything in this world. If there is such a thing as soulmates, I'm sure you are mine."

Without lowering her to the ground, I slowly close the

gap between our lips. She cups my face, and our mouths mold into one.

The suppressed longing sweeps over me. It's like a current that first percolates timidly, but with each shared breath it grows stronger. Before I know it, the sweet pleasure of her embrace enters every crevice in my soul, canceling and mending all the sorrow and past hurt.

The gushing rain rumbles around us with rhythmic cadence. Its music creates the perfect underpinning for our hammering heartbeats.

Suddenly I feel like dancing. I feel wholesome and happy with Laia in my arms.

I swirl Laia around slowly as if we were swaying to the storm's melody, while we fight a playful battle to demonstrate who missed the other more.

I think I'm almost winning it when Ellie's cheerful yell breaks our bliss.

"Here you are!"

We both turn our heads to my sister standing a few feet away under a red restaurant umbrella.

I lower Laia to the ground but don't release her.

An ear-to-ear smile stretches on Ellie's face as she winks at us. "Please, carry on. It was better than a blockbuster movie. Far more moving. I swear you looked like the couple on the cover of *The Notebook*."

Laia's cheeks blush, but her arms remain around my torso.

I'm glad she doesn't feel bashful about showing her feelings anymore, because I'm sure not shy to shout to the whole wide world that I want to be with her.

"Did you worry about us?" I ask my sister. "You shouldn't have. Your masterplan went down perfectly."

Ellie wipes her forehead in a theatrical gesture. "Huh, I'm relieved. As time passed, I wondered whether you might've missed Laia and actually set out to check the bus schedule."

"No, Devon found me," Laia replies. She throws me a slanted glance, then grins at my sister. "And I was lucky because he forgave my stupid behavior."

"There was nothing to forgive." I wink at Laia. "And I'm the lucky one."

Ellie giggles. "I guess my comparison wasn't that far off. You really are a gushy couple in love now, how sweet!"

My chest warms at Ellie's voice. It's almost as euphoric as if it were her who found the love of her life. Ellie is such a good sister, and if Laia and I are together, it's also her merit.

I wiggle out from Laia's embrace gently and step over to Ellie. I hug her and plant a peck on her cheek. "Without you, Ellie, it wouldn't have been possible. I owe you a big thank you, sis."

Laia comes and embraces Ellie also. "Yes, Ellie, thanks for seeing what was best for us before we even realized it ourselves."

"Guys, you are *so* welcome." Ellie sucks in two rapid and then one long breath, her go-to strategy to fight back overwhelming emotions, then she clears her throat. "We should probably get you dry. You'll catch a cold in these wet clothes. Let's go back to Dev's car."

"Being out in the rain is fun," I chuckle giddily. "You should try it, too."

Laia gives me an approving smile as if she understands perfectly what I'm saying.

Ellie, on the other hand, scrunches her nose. "No, loverboy, I'm fine under this umbrella. And I think it's enough of a Nicholas Sparks romance for now. We don't want you or Laia to kick off your relationship with a runny nose, or worse, a fever." She gives us her serious I-know-what-I'm-talking-about glance.

"Right," we answer in a chorus, water dripping from our noses and eyelashes.

I fetch the umbrella Laia tossed to the pavement and close it. It doesn't make sense to protect ourselves from the water, given that we're both already soaked. I take Laia's moist fingers, and we saunter behind my sister, hand in hand, to the restaurant's parking.

"You make me happy," Laia whispers to me.

"And you turned me into the man I never knew I could be," I reply and plant a kiss on the top of her head.

While we walk, I bask in the elation that circles through my veins.

Ellie might be worried that we'll get sick, but the glow in my chest could brighten any weather. I could be out in a snowstorm and still feel fuzzily warm, as long as Laia and I are together.

I guess that's what it feels like having a soulmate, after all…

EPILOGUE

(Laia)

As soon as I step into the lobby at Hudson Communications, Steve's and Chuck's smiling faces greet me.

"Good day, Ms. Laia," Chuck exclaims.

His enthusiastic salutation blends in with his colleague's deeper, "Hello, Laia."

It's incredible how natural it feels to be coming into this building even though I don't work here anymore. Maybe the reason for my ease is that I've gotten into the habit of popping in on every Friday to drag my boyfriend to a proper lunch. I guess it's my way of expressing to Devon just how grateful I am that we're a couple and that he helped me land this editing assistant job in a well-reputed publishing house.

I still can't believe I'm allowed to do what I love the best—read—and get paid for it.

What's even better is I managed to negotiate a thirty-two hours per week contract with the head of my department, which grants me a day off to work on my own writing.

And have a short date with Devon.

A prickle of excitement courses through me as I think about the big news I'll share with him today.

I hurry by the reception desk and wave to Michael, who's pouring a bright-orange powder into his cup. It must be that fizzy drink Devon is running the launch campaign for.

I pat Hudson's head, a weird habit I picked up from Devon, then hurry to the elevator.

Katja jumps up from her desk as she sees me approach and closes me into an entirely awkward but all the more affectionate hug.

"So nice to see you again, Laia."

"And you too. How are your grandchildren?" I ask.

Katja launches into a detailed account of how her daughter decided to take the kiddos to Russia for a semester to pick up more of their language.

Theresa, Devon's new assistant, a redhead with countless freckles and an amiable smile, steps over just as Katja rounds up her tale.

"You better go inside, Laia. Devon has been asking whether there were any reports about subway accidents."

I roll my eyes and chuckle. "I'm only ten minutes late compared to my usual arrival time. Okay, I guess I'll be on my way before Devon can alert the firemen or something."

Devon is on the phone when I step inside his office. He stands with his face to the window, and from the warm timbre his voice is hitting, he must be speaking with Ellie. His white shirt is tucked into black jeans, while his blazer rests on his chair.

"I'm sure you'll get the break next time, sis. You're so good. Just don't lose faith in yourself," he says.

Oh, no. Ellie must have missed out on that promotion she so desired.

I pull the door shut quietly to avoid interrupting their conversation, but even the faint click alerts Devon of my presence. He whips around, and a bright smile appears on his face.

"You know who just arrived?" he tells Ellie then bobs his head. "Indeed…" He waves me closer. "Of course, I'll tell Laia. While you girls do your dinner thing, I'll catch up with Pete."

I reach Devon and plant a kiss on his neck.

As I whiff at his familiar cologne, I hear Ellie saying good-bye to her brother.

Devon says good-bye to her, too, then drops his phone on the desk. He turns back to me and snakes his arms around my waist. "You're late, love. I was beginning to worry."

"I know, Theresa told me you were making her check the local news."

A flustered glint invades Devon's eyes, and he pulls up his shoulder in a boyish what-can-I-do way. "I don't want anything bad to happen to you. I'd much rather have you drive your own car."

Devon and I have spent various weekends visiting car dealers, and I've tested many second-hand vehicles trying to find a suitable alternative to the public transportation I currently use to reach the publishing house.

But my heart is set on an Audi, and I still need to earn more before I can buy one.

"You know I promised Richard I'd buy his wagon." I grin, reminding him of the young salesman from the car show. "I can't really back out on my word, right?"

"But I want you to be safe. I'm not sure you are when

you travel with the light rail, especially when you ride it home to Laveen Village."

"That's where Chelsea and I live. I can't be going anywhere else," I huff, but I smile when I see his concern. "If you want, I can sign up for a self-defense class or something. Would that make you feel better?"

"Maybe." He gives me a mysterious glance. "But you might not need to do that."

"What do you mean?"

Devon shakes his head. "Later. First, I want to hear the big news you mentioned on the phone."

"My book is going to get published," I blurt out.

Devon has been my biggest supporter and my true inspiration for the complex, flawed, and lovable hero I wanted to write.

"That's fantastic, love. I'm so proud of you!" He lifts me from the floor and twirls me around twice before lowering me back down.

I might've wanted to create more suspense before revealing my secret, but it doesn't matter. Devon's reaction couldn't be any better if I'd made him guess what I wanted to share with him.

"Did Nora tell you this morning?" he asks, bending his forehead to mine so that our skin touches.

"Yes. They had the board meeting yesterday. And I'm one of the chosen authors."

"We'll celebrate this weekend. A special, romantic evening for the love of my life who's about to become a bestselling novelist."

"Ah, I love the sound of that," I giggle.

"And I love you," he whispers, and his mouth dives for mine.

We share a long kiss that makes me feel like I've sprouted

wings. His lips are hot, demanding, and gentle all at the same time. The perfect combination to blow my mind and make me forget where I am or what's happening around me.

He pulls back and squints. "Now, do you want to hear *my* secret?"

"Sure."

His lips curl up, and an eager light invades his irises. "Fine, then wait here but close your eyes."

I shut my eyes and stand there.

There's a shuffling noise as if Devon is moving papers on his desk. I hear a drawer open and close, and then a metallic sound like a key being dropped somewhere.

What is he doing? And why all this secrecy?

After a second, his warm fingers close on my hand and turn it upward. He smooths out my palm and places something flat and not too heavy in it.

"You can open your eyes now."

When I do, I find a lilac-colored box with a ribbon. My heart jumps to my throat.

Oh, dearest heaven. Is this happening? Is Devon…?

"Open it," he urges.

Devon has been hinting at some serious plan lately, but I didn't expect him to actually propose. Of course, I already know what my answer will be.

I loosen the ribbon and plop the box open.

But just as I want to gasp and yell an exuberant, "I do," I see a bunch of keys in the box, tied to a red key chain.

My brows drift into a confused line. "What's this?"

"What do you think it is?" Devon eyes me with a coy smirk.

I lift the keychain, and its slimy, rubbery texture almost slips from my hands. The keys start to shimmy, bouncing up and down on the string.

"Is it Ellie's self-defense toy?" I ask. This is what Devon

meant. He wants me to be safe on the subway, therefore he purchased this weird device for me.

Devon throws his head back and laughs. He draws in a few calming breaths before he speaks again. "I'm sorry, Laia. But you should've seen your face. You looked like Cat when I accidentally switched her fish pâté to a chicken one." He points at the keychain. "It's not what you expected?"

"Oh no, I didn't expect anything. This is a very… thoughtful gift. You even put some dummy keys on the chain so I can see how it works," I add, forcing my voice to not sound disappointed.

Just because I believed for a second that Devon might be asking me to tie our lives together, I shouldn't belittle his considerate gesture.

Devon runs a thumb on my jawline. "Those aren't dummy keys, my love. They're the keys to my apartment. The chain is just a bonus Ellie wanted to donate once she heard what I was planning."

My jaw drops. "Why do I need keys to your apartment? You're always there when I come over."

"You'll need them in case…"

"In case what?"

"In case you decide to accept this." Devon reaches into his back pocket and produces a small Tiffany-blue box.

Devon lowers himself to his knees. "Laia, you taught me everything worth knowing about love. I can't imagine sharing my life with anyone else but you. Will you marry me, please?"

As he opens it, the answer I knew I'd give him if he ever popped the question freezes in my throat from the sheer beauty of the ring.

Devon peers up at me, his mouth moving into a startled line. "Still not what you expected?"

His words manage to prompt my brain, and I make a little jump while squeaking, "I do, I do. Yes, I do."

His face illuminates, and he straightens. He takes the ring from the box and grabs my hand.

As he slips it on my finger, he says, "This understated and simplistic elegance reminded me of you the moment I saw it."

"It's beautiful," I sigh as I admire the gorgeous platinum eternity band, completed with tiny, baguette-cut diamonds.

"Nowhere as enchanting as you, though," he murmurs and leans into my neck. He plants countless feathery kisses leading up to my earlobe. When his hot breath reaches my ear, he says, "You're my soulmate, Laia, there is no doubt about it. Thank you for making me the happiest man alive. And…" He winks at me. "I can't wait for our wedding night."

"I was told once that I shouldn't play with a player, or else I'll get burned."

"Who told you that?"

"Katja. The night you offered to help with my book."

Devon snorts and shakes his head, but I see a flustered glint invade his eyes. Despite knowing that I love him, he still has moments where he feels guilty about his past actions.

I cup his face and raise myself on my tiptoes, pulling him closer. "But you know what, Dev? I couldn't have done better than to ignore Katja's words. Because you, Devon, are all that I never knew I needed."

Devon smiles, and his lips capture mine.

As we unite in a kiss, I realize that what I said is true. I could never have found my own fairy tale if I'd followed his secretary's wise law about love.

It doesn't have to end here…
Do you want to see more of Devon and Laia ?

Then join my Reader Club and get the Extended Epilogue of Law #2 right now. Go to: www.agnescanestri.com/lol2-bonus

Please note: if you're already a member, no need to sign-up again. You can retrieve your bonus on your VIP Reader Vault (link in the bottom of my emails)

Also, don't miss out on Ellie's (Devon's quirky sister) and Wyatt's (the hunky footballer) second chance romance …

Get Book Three in the Laws of Love series now!
Law #3: Don't Fall for the Athlete
(mybook.to/lol3-bm)

AUTHOR'S NOTE

Enjoyed this book?
You can make a big difference.

Reviews are the **most powerful tools** when it comes to getting attention to my books.
If you've enjoyed this book I'd appreciate your honest review on Amazon. *It can be as short as you like.*

Thank you very much!
You can either go to the book's Amazon page and scroll down to "*leave a review*" or click on the link **mybook.to/lol2** and scroll to "leave a review".

OTHER BOOKS BY THE AUTHOR

LAWS OF LOVE SERIES

Law #1: Never Bet on Love

A billionaire. A salsa dancer. And a bet that might mean losing their hearts..

Go to: mybook.to/lol1-bm

Law #3: Don't Fall for the Athlete

A football star. His friend's little sister.

He broke her heart years ago. Now, they need to work together to save their respective jobs. Will their collaboration lead to a second chance at love?

Go to: mybook.to/lol3-bm

GEMS OF LOVE SERIES

Loving the Boss (BOOK ONE)

It could be her fresh start. If only she can avoid falling for her boss…

Go to: mybook.to/gol1-bm

Fake-Dating the Single Dad (BOOK THREE)

It was the perfect plan. Until their feelings turned all too real….

Go to: mybook.to/gol3-bm

Saving the Brother's Best Friend (BOOK FOUR)

It was only a simple favor between friends. Until it wasn't…

Go to: mybook.to/gol4-bm

Falling for the Undercover Agent (BOOK FIVE)

She was just a job. Until she wasn't …

Go to: mybook.to/gol5-bm

Gems of Love BOXSET

All five books in one collection. The BEST DEAL on the series.

Go to: mybook.to/gol-boxset-bm

OTHER BOOKS

Saving His Heart (Jackson & Hole Firefighters)

Rule #1: Don't date a fireman.

Rule #2: Don't fall for your best friend.

Rule #3: Never forget rules one and two

Go to: mybook.to/saving-his-heart-bm

A Lesson in Love (Standalone forbidden love story)

Sometimes what's forbidden can't be ignored…

Go to: mybook.to/alessoninlove

ABOUT THE AUTHOR

Agnes Canestri writes sweet romance for all ages. Her home on the internet is https://www.agnescanestri.com. Agnes is also a psychologist and the mother of two. Agnes is passionate to understand what makes people tick especially when it comes to love. She adores capable heroes, witty heroines, and bone-tingling kisses. After living in five different countries, she is now settled in Germany with her Italian husband and her children.

You can connect with her on Facebook at www.facebook.com/agnescanestri and on Instagram at www.instagram.com/agnes.canestri using the icons below.

Whenever the mood strikes you, you should send her an email at agnes@agnescanestri.com. She loves to hear from her readers and answers all emails personally.

facebook.com/agnescanestri

instagram.com/agnes.canestri

bookbub.com/profile/agnes-canestri

COPYRIGHT

www.agnescanestri.com

Editing by Danita Mayer, Niche Editing.

Printed in Great Britain
by Amazon

64712426R00239